Festi~~ve~~

A Lucas Rathbone Mysteries Christmas Special

By Saffron Amatti

Copyright© 2020 by Saffron Amatti

All rights reserved. No part of this publication may be reproduced, stored, or transmitted in any form or by any means, electronic, mechanical, photocopying, recording, scanning, or otherwise, without written permission from the publisher. It is illegal to copy this book, post it to a website, or distribute it by any other means without permission.

This novel is entirely a work of fiction. The names, characters, and incidents portrayed in it are the work of the author's imagination. Any resemblance to actual persons, living or dead, events or localities, is entirely coincidental.

Saffron Amatti asserts the moral right to be identified as the author of this work.

Saffron Amatti has no responsibility for the persistence or accuracy of URLs for external or third-party Internet Websites referred to in this publication and does not guarantee that any content on such websites is, or will remain, accurate or appropriate.

First Edition.

For Mike

Supporter of dreams, bringer of tea,
and reader of first drafts.

'I don't see why we both need to be here,' grumbled Lucas, shoving his hands in his pockets and jigging up and down on the spot.

He looked enviously around at the plethora of snazzy cars owned by the *real* guests, wondering if he'd ever regain feeling in his feet after walking the two miles from Castlebury Magna. It was a hellishly cold day – not surprising, considering it was Christmas Eve, but unwelcome all the same.

And the snow had set in for the long run. Of course it had.

Lucas groaned inwardly and shivered. They'd be walking home again in a matter of hours. Barely enough time to thaw his frozen toes.

'Don't be miserable,' sighed Clara, tugging the door pull hanging from the shadowy sandstone portico. 'You're the official reporter, you have to be here, and I thought you'd have more fun if I came too.' She flashed him a cheeky grin. 'Besides, I know you. You wouldn't go at all if you had to go alone.'

'Not true,' complained Lucas. 'Well,' he said, catching her unimpressed expression. 'I'd go, but probably spend the evening hiding behind a curtain'

'Exactly,' said Clara triumphantly. 'Which won't help you sell any papers, will it?'

'Look, you know I love my job,' he said. 'All right, maybe *love* is a bit strong,' he amended, catching the look on her face. 'But the fact is, anything involving more than half a dozen people makes me want to run and hide.'

'I know,' said Clara, linking her arm through his. 'Which is why we're both freezing to death on the steps of Castlebury Manor.'

Lucas looked at her, from the red felt cloche atop her head, to the sapphire blue round toed shoes housing her silk stockinged feet, in between passing over the ankle-skimming grey wool coat concealing a fashionably fringed flapper dress in a similar shade of blue to the shoes.

Although knowledge of the short hemline of the frock helped warm Lucas, it left him in little wonder as to why Clara was feeling the cold.

He was much more suitably dressed in a heavy, thigh-length once-black coat over a faded pair of dark wool trousers, an almost matching blazer, and his best cream shirt, each selected by Clara and declared the least unpresentable items of clothing he owned.

A joint-aching coldness still seeped into his body, promising that the eventual return of heat would take a long time to do its job, and probably be rather uncomfortable.

It was not a happy thought.

After an age, which Clara insisted was barely a minute, a stiff-backed butler opened the imposing door of the Georgian manor house and said, 'May I help you?' with as much disdain as he could muster.

'We're here for the Christmas Ball,' said Clara, brandishing the invitation at the man before Lucas could complain at their treatment and make an excuse to leave.

'We're the reporters from The Castlebury Gazette,' she explained, as the invitation was examined with obvious displeasure.

'Her Ladyship did mention something about *newspaper people*,' said the butler, not bothering to keep the sneer out of his voice. He stood back from the door with some reluctance. 'I *suppose* you'd better come in.'

'Thank you,' said Clara, beaming at the man before shooting Lucas a warning look.

Lucas forced a grin and, against his better judgement, followed Clara into a cavernous hallway bedecked in festive winter foliage. Holly festooned the doorways leading left and right, and mistletoe berries gleamed like pearls where they were hung on a chandelier dripping shimmering crystal tears from the ceiling.

Lucas started humming *Deck The Halls With Boughs of Holly*, accompanied by the clicking of Clara's heels on the patterned marble floor and a smile from the lady herself.

But this tuneless attempt at festivities was

drowned by riotous laughter from up the sweeping staircase.

The butler summoned a housemaid to receive the snow-dusted coats of the most recent arrivals and, in equally chilly silence, led them upstairs - only to promptly abandon them at the top without quite making clear which of the many identical wood panelled doors they were supposed to be going through.

'Is he coming back, or do we just go in?' said Clara, looking up and down the hallway.

'How should I know?' replied Lucas, shivering. 'We could just leave. No-one will notice, I'll make up some nonsense about Lord So-And-So and Lady Thingmajig, and no one will be any the wiser.'

'Lady Gaylesbury will notice if you fudge the article on her Charity Christmas Ball,' said Clara, brushing her lips against his. 'And she is paying you to be here, darling. I can't imagine she'd be too impressed to learn you didn't complete the assignment.'

'I thought that rather strange, you know,' said Lucas, delaying the inevitable for as long as possible. 'Why should she be so keen to be seen doing charitable work?'

'Does it matter?' replied Clara. 'Maybe she's done some terrible deed in the past and wants the world to know how good she is now? I don't know, but I know you're better off for it.' She pinched Lucas' cheek playfully. 'Perhaps paying a poor newspaper editor like yourself is merely another act of charity.'

Lucas glared at her sullenly, but he couldn't deny it was possible. Editor of The Castlebury Gazette sounded grand enough, but Castlebury Magna was such a tiny place it hardly warranted its own paper.

But Lucas promised the previous, now very late owner, Doug Brodie, that he'd take care of it after Doug's untimely demise. Circumstances being what they were, Doug would know if Lucas welched on his promise - and then Lucas would never hear the end of it.

Some people just had trouble letting go of the past, and Doug most certainly was one of them.

He shuddered at the thought, hoping that he'd not run into any trouble of *that* sort this evening, if nothing else.

Clara looked between the doors, chose one seemingly at random, and steered Lucas toward it.

It sounded like there was a lot of people on the other side.

Far more people than Lucas could ever hope to see in his life.

'Ready?' she asked, putting her hand on a well-worn brass handle.

'No.'

'Tough.' She turned the handle and pushed the heavy oak door.

A fug of smoke, alcohol, and hot bodies assaulted Lucas' nose with some enthusiasm. Music blared from a gramophone but was barely audible over laughing and talking. A couple were Foxtrotting around the drawing room, whispering and giggling as they sidestepped furniture.

For saying there was only half a dozen people in the room, they were making a lot of noise.

'There's not many people here,' Lucas yelled in Clara's ear. 'I thought this was a ball?'

'It is, my boy,' said a woman Lucas guessed was in her mid-forties, although she wore an inappropriately short black flapper frock. The fringing swung from side to side as she sashayed towards them, albeit a little unsteadily, and the ostrich plume on her headband wobbled alarmingly with each movement. She caught up a couple of champagne flutes from a table as she passed and handed one to Clara, the other to Lucas.

There was coral lipstick on the rim of Lucas' half empty glass. He set it down on a nearby table without taking a sip.

'This isn't like any charity ball I've ever seen,' said Clara loudly, peering into her own glass. Something bobbed in the fizzy liquid.

'*This* isn't the ball, silly,' said the woman, gesturing broadly around the room. 'This is the *real* party. The ball is on the other side of the corridor. But if you're here to have a little *fun*,' she said, winking at Lucas. 'I suggest you stick with me.'

To his horror, the woman old enough to be his mother - and certainly old enough to know better - leant forward and tried to pinch his backside.

He yelped and backed into the wall with a painful thud, probably bruising something in the process. His ego was somewhat affected, if nothing else, and his cheeks flamed the colour of embarrassment.

Clara giggled with her usual amount of sympathy, and held out a hand to the woman. 'Clara Jenkins,' she said, raising her voice over the noise. 'Castlebury Gazette.'

'Ah, *you're* the newspaper people, are you?', replied the woman, taking Clara's hand and eyeing her outfit. 'I didn't expect you to be so smartly dressed, being from a local paper. No offence meant, I assure you.'

Lucas opened his mouth to defend Clara's sense of style, and received a kick to the ankle for his troubles.

There's no helping some people, he thought sullenly, rubbing the aching bone against his shin. *Not that she needs my help. Quite the opposite, but that's not the point...*

'I'm Lady Gaylesbury,' said the woman grandly, breezing straight past her offensive remarks. 'Owner of this manor, host of this party. And the dull one, of course,' she added, crinkling her nose. 'I've shown my face there, so I made my excuses and left.' She held a hand to her forehead dramatically. 'Terribly stressful, don't you know, and it gave me quite the headache.'

Clara laughed obligingly. 'I don't blame you,' she said. 'This looks like much more fun than a stuffy ball.'

'Indeed it is,' said the Lady, beaming. 'Still, one must be shown to be charitable, even if one is as a course of habit without feeling the need to shout about it.' Her mouth twisted downwards. 'Yes, you must be *seen* to be doing good, especially when -' She broke the sentence short, rearranging her expression into something jollier. 'But you young things don't want to hear the troubles of an old widow, do you?'

'Oh, I don't know -' started Lucas, but Clara interrupted him with a sharp look.

'A party isn't a place for troubles, Lady Gaylesbury,' said Clara, smiling warmly at their host.

'Quite right, my dear,' said Lady Gaylesbury brightly, lightly tapping Clara on the shoulder and saying, 'You can call me Bunty. Everyone else does - at least, all my friends do, and I have a feeling you and I will be most *marvellous* friends.'

Bunty snatched a pair of champagne flutes from the tray of a passing waiter, threw the contents of one down her throat and passed the second, thankfully clean glass to Lucas. 'And what's your name?' she purred, looking him up and down in a way that made the heat rise on the back of his neck again.

'Lucas,' he squeaked. He coughed, lowered his voice an octave or two, and tried again. 'Lucas Rathbone, also from the Castlebury Gazette.'

'Well Lucas, my darling,' said Bunty, looking him up and down, her roving eyes taking in every inch of well-mended suit. 'Once you've done your bit for that *boring* little article, I do hope you'll both come back to the *fun* side of the house.'

Somewhere in the room laughter broke out again, as though to prove the point.

Caressing the lapel on his blazer and standing far too close for Lucas' comfort, she added, 'I'm sure you can find much more interesting things in this room to write about. Then later, if you like, I'll take you upstairs and see if we can't find you a better suit.' She pouted, running her fingers across his shoulders and down his arms.

'I do *hate* to see good-looking young men badly dressed.'

Lucas wished the ground would open and swallow him whole – especially as Clara was stifling giggles beside him.

He'd never hear the end of this, and

contemplated making a run for it.

The lightness of his wallet reminded him that it might not be the best idea to offend the woman paying him to attend a party.

A party that would help him get more much-needed money in the bank over the next week or so, with the possibility of the same again next year.

He gritted his teeth and bore the unwanted attention.

Bunty leant close to his ear, breathing champagne all over him. 'You look just like my dear late husband when we first met. I expect you're just the same size as he was twenty-five years ago, too.' Her gaze wandered uncomfortably lower, lingering at a point he really, really wished it wouldn't linger at all. 'One of his old suits will fit you *perfectly*, I'm sure.'

This was too much, even at the risk of losing this evening's pay and any future work at the hall.

'Uhyesprobablyrightokaythanksbye,' gabbled Lucas, shimmying away from the predatory woman and towards the hallway.

Before he could quite escape, Bunty put a hand on his arm and murmured, 'I'll see you later, Lucas.' She turned and danced her way back to the party, pausing only to look over her shoulder and wink roguishly at the flustered young man she'd left behind.

Fighting shudders unlike any winter could bring, Lucas wrapped his arm around Clara's waist and steered her towards the door at a pace edging towards a sprint.

He didn't stop until the door swung shut behind them, with the ravenous Bunty safely on the other side.

'You could have helped, you know,' he said crossly, hoping this might alert Clara to the fact he wasn't terribly pleased at not being rescued.

She collapsed in a giggling heap against the wall.

This didn't help Lucas' sour mood one bit, so he tried again.

'Why didn't you tell the old baggage we were together?' he said, worried there was a whine in his voice. *Well, it has every right to be there if it is,* he thought sullenly. *Frightful behaviour, letting Bunty corner me like that.*

'Oh Lucas,' gasped Clara, carefully wiping tears from her eyes to avoid smudging her make-up. 'You should have seen your face.'

'I didn't need to,' he protested. 'I could tell how horrified I was by how horrified I was.'

'And of course I'm not going to tell her we're a couple, silly,' she added, bringing herself almost

back under control - but only almost. There was still a hint of amusement around her lips and a mischievous twinkle in her eye that

Lucas found terribly attractive, when it wasn't at his expense.

'Why not?' he said.

'Because not only was that *hilarious* to watch,' she replied, still fighting the urge to laugh. 'We're here to *investigate*, and we'll get more out of people if we can flirt with them a little.'

'I thought we were here to *report*,' argued Lucas. 'Look around and take notes on the, I don't know, the dancing and the dresses, that sort of thing.'

'But this is the perfect chance to get a bit of society scandal,' she replied. 'Readers love that sort of thing - and so long as it's nothing too scandalous, practically anyone is happy to see their name in print, no matter the reason. They like people talking about them, you see, and they often don't seem to care too much whether they're saying nice things or not.'

'What would you know about it?' asked Lucas. 'You work at The Illustrated Police News. I can't imagine anything that shows up *there* would be particularly welcome.'

'I know people at other papers too,' she said, pushing herself upright and taking Lucas' arm again. 'But keep mum about where I really work, darling. People might get nervy if they think I'm here investigating a crime, rather than helping out The Gazette for old time's sake. As well as keeping you company, of course.' She pouted, which Lucas suspected was rather put on. 'But if you don't want me here, I can go home again.'

Sighing, Lucas wrapped his arm around her waist and kissed her gently.

'Darling, I'm endlessly grateful for your company,' he murmured. 'You know that. And I'd hate being here without you. I'd hate it more than I currently do, anyway.'

She returned his kiss with enthusiasm, confirming his suspicions, and led him across the corridor, which was freezing in spite of the best efforts of a thick carpet and a multitude of tapestries.

The door she directed him towards leaked sedate orchestral music, well-bred chatter, and unnaturally controlled laughter.

Yes, they'd definitely found the official ball this time, unfortunately. At least if they hadn't found it, they'd have some excuse to leave without going in.

'Let's get this over with,' said Lucas with a sigh. 'We'll get our notes and sneak out as quickly as possible - preferably before that harpy tries to get her claws into me again.'

'That's the spirit,' said Clara cheerfully, pushing the door open and stepping into the room.

Lucas looked with misgiving at the whirl of satin and jewellery that cost more than his mother's house.

With a great sense of foreboding and gloom - his natural state when about to enter a party - Lucas stepped into the fray.

***

'Bunty wasn't wrong about their party being more interesting,' said Clara, leaning against the closed ballroom door with a relieved sigh. She and Lucas had snuck out of the ball after an hour or so of watching endless dances and interviewing miserably self-absorbed women in acres of expensive ballgowns and tiresomely braying men in tuxedos.

'Hmm,' replied Lucas, drifting towards the top of the stairs and pulling a slightly squashed vol-au-vent from his trouser pocket. He sniffed it suspiciously before putting it into his mouth whole.

Oh, really, thought Clara, vexed. *I haven't a pocket in this dress big enough to fit a handkerchief, and he can get food in his. How is* that *fair?*

'Still,' he said indistinctly, showering her with crumbs and not helping his case for being a civilised human being. 'We lived to tell the tale, and now we can head home for some proper food. I don't rate anything that's three to a mouthful.'

'Hold on,' said Clara, catching hold of his sleeve and dragging him back. 'Are you forgetting something?'

'Our coats,' he exclaimed, clicking his fingers. 'Well remembered, we'll flag down a servant on our way out.'

'No,' said Clara, tightening her grip on his arm to stop him from making his escape. 'We promised to go back to Bunty's side of the house, didn't we?'

Lucas grimaced, but Clara wasn't going to let him spoil her chance at getting some sort of story from the party.

Of course I'm here to keep him company and all that, she thought with a twinge of guilt. *Mostly. But I still need to make up to the boss for skipping out on my first solo assignment. It couldn't be helped, I know, and I don't really regret putting Lucas' safety ahead of my career... but nearly four months on and constant grovelling hasn't done a thing to soften the old grouch up and give me a second chance.*

However, Lucas' pleading look softened her own resolve a little.

No, she thought, sternly. *There's more to life than merely drawing the exciting stories brought to me by the "real" reporters. I want to write them myself! What a thrill to go out and investigate the news, rather than just hear about it from someone else.*

Lucas looked woefully at the door to the fun party, then back to her.

Look, the only way you're going to improve things with any speed is to present an interesting, ready to print story to the boss, she thought.

The despair on Lucas' face increased as he realised she wasn't going to be talked out of returning to Bunty's party.

True, I'll have to work hard to spin society gossip into something worthy of the Illustrated Police News, she continued to herself. *Unless something wonderfully criminal happens this evening - but I'll figure out details later. I can't let my career stagnate in 1929 the way it has this year.*

And it was Lucas' fault I messed up last time, she added, knowing this not to be entirely true and feeling like a rotter for even thinking it. *Admittedly he didn't mean to, but if blaming him helps stiffen my resolve, that's what I'll do.*

Misplaced blaming complete, Clara folded her arms across her chest, ignored the adorably sad puppy-dog look he was giving her, and tapped the toe of her shoe.

'Fine,' he said, sighing theatrically. He clearly thought he had another trick up his sleeve - but Clara was determined nothing would derail her plan, and listened impassively.

'If you're happy for me,' he continued, putting a brave, selfless note into his voice. 'Me - the love of your life, remember, the one you're supposed to support in all things and be jealous over whenever someone else starts flirting with me - if you're happy to watch me fend off that man eating Lady of the Manor for the rest of the night, then I *suppose* we can go and get your stupid society gossip story thing.'

'Excellent,' cried Clara, grabbing his arm and dragging him towards the door. 'Come on.'

'Wait, wait, wait,' said Lucas in his more familiar panicked tone as he dug his heels into the carpet. 'You're perfectly happy to sacrifice me like some virgin on a rock to that old dragon, are you?'

Clara smirked at him. 'Well, you don't really qualify for the job anymore, but… yes, I suppose I am. Off we go. Oh, don't be like that,' she groaned as he looked at her mournfully. 'It's for your own good as well, you know. I'll share the stories I get with you, and then you might actually sell a few papers this week. Won't that be nice?'

Given the mutinous expression on his face, the prospect of financial gain wasn't outweighing the prospect of Bunty.

'All right,' said Clara, thinking a little compromise might help. 'If she starts making you *really* uncomfortable, I'll drag you under the nearest piece of mistletoe and make sure she knows you're mine. Happy?'

'Not really,' said Lucas. 'Can't we just do the mistletoe bit and go home?'

'No,' said Clara, taking hand and dragging him towards the door. She spotted a sprig of green and white festive foliage hanging from the doorframe. 'Well, I suppose we can do the mistletoe bit *first* if you like,' she said, wrapping her arms around his neck and kissing him until she was sure she could get him into the party before his head stopped spinning.

'Come on,' she said once he was good and breathless. 'You never know, you might even have fun.'

'I doubt it,' he grumbled, as she opened the door and pushed him into the room.

***

Clara's idea of "fun" was clearly different from Lucas' interpretation of the word.

He was doing his best impression of a house plant whilst she was charming the entire room, making friends with all the disgustingly festive people. As the seconds dragged into minutes, Lucas stopped fooling himself that Clara would see sense and duck out of the party early.

No, that'd be too much to hope for, wouldn't it? he thought, helping himself to a glass of something sickly and an unhealthy shade of blue. He sipped it without hope of it being palatable, and was somehow disappointed even with that low expectation.

'Whatever happened to a good old glass of whiskey,' he muttered, returning it to the side table and retreating behind nearest heavy velvet curtain. So far, he'd avoided Bunty, and intended to pass the entirety of the dreadful evening doing so.

To make things worse, if that were indeed possible, Clara seemed to be having the time of her life. Lucas watched with no small amount of jealousy as she danced and flirted with the men, charmed the women, and appeared to drink anything alcoholic put in her hand, no matter how unnaturally coloured.

He grinned as he watched her surreptitiously pour the contents of the latest glass into a vase before to re-joining the fray.

'That your girl?' said a voice in his ear. 'Or do you merely wish she was?'

Lucas turned to face the speaker – a tall young man dressed in a tuxedo, the bow tie undone and draped around his neck. His dark hair was slicked back to best show off his annoyingly handsome and loathsomely friendly face. He was slim and graceful in his movements as he held out a hand towards Lucas, which he shook in mute shyness.

'Jonathon Bourbon-Busset,' said the young man. 'But please, call me Jonny. Pleased to meet you.'

'Lucas Rathbone,' Lucas answered. 'Likewise,' he added, sure it was too soon to tell whether it would be a pleasure or not.

He suspected not.

'Don't worry,' laughed Jonny, clapping Lucas on the back and knocking him forward an inch or two. 'Your secret is safe with me.'

Lucas wondered what his secret was, but decided to keep his mouth shut. Not that it mattered; Bourbon-Busset seemed quite content to do all the talking, and as Lucas was little inclined towards conversation with strangers, this suited him just fine.

As he spoke, Bourbon-Busset pulled a solid silver cigarette case from his breast pocket, and opened it with a flourish before offering it to Lucas.

Lucas, warming to the chap by the second, accepted gratefully.

'Yes,' said Bourbon-Busset with a deep sigh. 'I too know the pain of a broken heart and unrequited love.'

'Oh,' said Lucas, the penny finally dropping. 'But me and Clara are -' He stopped, remembering Clara's instructions to not let on they were there together. 'Thanks awfully,' he said, grinning weakly at his new acquaintance.

'You're very welcome, my dear fellow,' said Bourbon-Busset, applying a match to the end of his cigarette. 'But I have been fortunate to gain the affections of the girl of my dreams, so don't give up hope.'

'Uhuh,' said Lucas, looking around to see where this dream girl was.

There was a rather fine figure of a young woman tangoing with a fellow around the same age as Bourbon-Busset, who matched the chap in irritatingly good looks, and a girl who might be rather pretty if she wasn't drunkenly crying all over Clara.

There was, of course, Bunty, but Lucas hoped she wasn't the object of the fellow's affections. He looked around the same age as Lucas, and though it wasn't unheard of for a man to take up with a much older lady, the mere thought of it gave Lucas the heebie-jeebies.

'Haven't seen you around before,' said Bourbon-Busset, snapping Lucas out of his contemplations. 'What brings you here?'

'Oh, well…' said Lucas, wondering whether he should be keeping the fact he was a journalist under his hat as well. Clara hadn't mentioned that, but Lucas doubted she'd be very pleased if he let it get out without her permission.

'My guess is you're the reporter Aunt Bunty hired,' said Jonathon, blowing a stream of smoke towards the ceiling and turning a wolfish grin towards Lucas. He made a sweeping gesture towards Lucas' clothes. 'And I'd say you're feeling a little out of your depth at a shindig like this.'

Is it that obvious? thought Lucas, feeling embarrassment wash over him. *Or is it just the state of my suit? I've been meaning to get a new one for ages – well, no I haven't, but perhaps Clara has a point about the shabby state of my wardrobe after all…*

'I'd rather not be here either, old sport,'

said Bourbon-Busset, taking another drag on his cigarette. 'But when your only aunt - only living relative, for that matter - summons you for Christmas festivities, then you go. At least, you do if you want to stay in the old bird's will.' He guffawed at his own joke, which was more than Lucas did, having been distracted by a missing button on his jacket cuff.

'Besides, my Sylvia is rather keen on the whole thing,' continued Bourbon-Busset, who clearly didn't need a conversational partner. He nodded and raised his glass towards the girl dancing enthusiastically, and in Lucas' opinion rather racily, with the fellow who could have been Bourbon-Busset's brother.

Catching the surprise on Lucas' face, Bourbon-Busset said, 'Oh, but don't you worry about *that*. Sylvia is perfectly safe with Chappers – that's Gilbert Chapman, future Lord Leazes if you're making notes for your paper - and Sylvia Pettigrew. Not titled yet, no matter how much her daddy asks the right people for a knighthood. There's still some prejudice against the nouveau riche, but I suspect that'll pass with time. However, she'll be Lady Sylvia after she and I tie the knot, which will please her father no end. I might prefer Jonny, but I'm also known as Lord Cassiobury, for my many and varied sins. But only on formal occasions, and as you can see this certainly isn't one of them.' He flashed Lucas a warm smile. 'So none of that "Your

Lordship" nonsense, if you don't mind.'

'Er, are you all right with having a reporter around at such an informal gathering?', asked Lucas, trying not to sound too hopeful about getting kicked out.

The clock on the mantel chimed nine. *Lordy, have we only been in here an hour?* he thought glumly. *It feels like days.*

'Aren't you worried we – I mean, I might write something you don't like?' he added, praying Bourbon-Busset wouldn't notice the slip.

'Yes, I thought your girl might be a hack as well,' said Jonathon, completely unconcerned. 'No, we're not worried about that sort of thing, so write whatever you like, dear boy. If you must know, we rather enjoy a little scandal. For example, if you see that chap there,' he said, dropping his voice as he indicated a middle-aged man with gold wire frame specs and a pointed beard cut close to his chin.

Somehow, he was reading a book amidst the chaos.

'Yes,' said Lucas doubtfully. 'Who is he?'

'That's the famous – or rather, infamous herbalist, Dr Redmond Shank,' replied Jonathon, in a tone that suggested Lucas ought to be impressed. 'I'm sure you remember reading about his little, uh, mishaps in the paper earlier this year.'

Lucas didn't, his excuse being that he

spent too long writing newspaper articles to want to read them in his free time. Except for adventure stories written for boys, but they hardly counted, did they?

'He's the one who got into a bit of strife the other year for supplying aphrodisiacs to a number of high-profile people,' explained Bourbon-Busset.

'Oh,' said Lucas, none the wiser. 'How awful.'

'It wouldn't have been a problem if they didn't work so well,' said Jonathon, who didn't seem to have heard. 'But old Shank was named in a couple of divorce hearings. Not on his own account, I hasten to add, but some of the divorcees claimed his concoctions were so potent they simply *couldn't* control themselves.' Bourbon-Busset chuckled softly. 'Nonsense of course, but Shank got his name in the papers for it.'

'I imagine that harmed his business,' said Lucas, who felt he ought to contribute something to the conversation.

'Oh no, quite the opposite,' replied Bourbon-Busset gaily. 'Quite the opposite indeed. The Doc hasn't been busier. Bought himself a neat little house in Castlebury last month, in addition to his rather smart London flat. Belgravia, no less. No, all in all, I'd say the scandal did him the world of good. Sex sells, after all, especially when you're selling sex - or at least the means to the end, if you catch my drift.'

Lucas' ears began to burn, and not for the first time he cursed how easily he got embarrassed about such things.

'Of course,' continued Bourbon-Busset, oblivious to Lucas' discomfort. 'It was when the judge ruled it as a viable excuse for straying that old Redmond's sales really took off. You wouldn't believe the number of people who suddenly found themselves *helpless* to resist their lover, even if they'd been with them years.'

Lucas felt his mouth tighten in disapproval, which only made Bourbon-Busset laugh again.

'Of course, some people are quite happy at the idea of divorce,' he said, examining his fingernails. 'People have been known to make mistakes in their wedded bliss, only to discover there's more wedded and less bliss than they'd really like.' He gave Lucas another of his wolfish grins. 'That's the aunt's favourite form of scandal, although she'd argue she was just helping a pal out of a thoroughly awful situation.'

Lucas, to his immense shame, turned crimson at the mere mention of it. He took up the horrible blue drink again and took a gulp, hoping it might relax him a little if nothing else.

'Don't approve of divorce, old chap, or merely the methods used to get it?' asked

Bourbon-Busset, looking faintly amused. 'It's a silly old-fashioned thing this whole, "'til death do us part" nonsense, but it hardly matters. You can generally get around things like that, if you know how. Though I don't suppose that's been a problem for you so far.'

He winked at Lucas and took another pull from his glass. 'Aunt Bun being Aunt Bun didn't give two figs what anyone said about her,' he continued, apparently quite happy to air his family's dirty laundry. 'Of course, this was after Uncle Samuel bit the dust, the poor old coot. She'd have never done a thing to hurt him. Silly old thing that he was, I really believe she loved him something rotten.'

Lucas found himself wondering where all his drink had gone. Not that it mattered, because he was feeling a whole lot more relaxed already, and Jonathon Thingy-Whatsit seemed like a nice enough chap, even if he did go on a bit.

'Anyway,' said Jonathon, accosting a passing waiter and acquiring two more glasses of oddly coloured liquid. 'As you can see, we're not too worried about a little scandal here and there, so you're perfectly welcome to write whatever you see fit.' He emptied his glass in one, before adding, 'You don't mind, do you? Had to sacrifice mine to old Chappers right before I came over. Clumsy me sent his flying, and Gloria, who you can see crying all over your girl over there, had only just made it for me.

Tragic, really, but what can you do?'

'Mm, tragic, said Lucas, sipping the ruby red drink. It wasn't too bad, so he drank a little more.

'The party across the hall is full for saying there's so much salacious gossip,' said Lucas doubtfully, when he realised what had been niggling away at the back of his mind. 'I'd have thought folks would stay away from such gathering, for fear of being tainted by association.'

Jonathon Bourbon-Busset laughed again before passing Lucas another glass of something unidentifiable, which he accepted with no small degree of gratitude. After all, if one or two drinks helped a little, a third would help a little more, right?

'Perhaps the social calendar was a *little* empty for a time,' Bourbon-Busset admitted. 'But the truth is, scandal is just the thing for long-term popularity. I could tell you a hundred tales about this lot, and that's no lie.' His grey eyes twinkled mischievously. 'Would you like to hear them?'

Lucas glanced at Clara, who was still sat on the sofa, and still being cried on by Gloria whilst talking animatedly to their host. Neither seemed particularly concerned for the young lady. Lucas suspected Clara was having a similar conversation with Bunty as he was having with Bourbon-Busset.

Gossip is good for sales, he reminded himself. At this point, the man known as Chappers said something about feeling unwell and excused himself – not that it stopped him taking his half-empty glass with him. Lucas had to admit the chap was looking a little green, but no-one else seemed too worried.

'Never could hold his drink,' Jonathon laughed, watching his friend leave. 'Poor old Chappers.'

Lucas noted that the laugh didn't last long, and a moment later Jonathon's face was serious once more, his eyes drawn back to Sylvia. She watched her dance partner depart with some concern; however this didn't last long either and, after acquiring another drink, she made her way to the already crowded sofa.

Jonny's eyes tracked her around the room, but as soon as she took her seat his previous joviality returned. Lucas thought it was rather like flicking a light switch.

'Another drink, old pip?' said Jonathon, accosting another waiter. 'And more importantly, what else can I tell you that you could put in your little paper?'

***

Lucas groaned and pulled the covers further over his head. Sunlight pierced the darkness through a crack in the curtains and burned through the sheets, filling his eyes with painful light despite the lids being squeezed tightly shut.

What the hell happened last night?
Memories flitted back in patches.
Talking, laughing, drinking – lots of drinking.
He groaned again.
Dancing.
No.
Surely not.
Good Lord, Clara let me dance?
He winced.

He remembered Clara dancing on a table, and groaned a third time.

She probably didn't just let *me dance but actively encouraged it.*

Lucas was glad he'd never have to see anyone from the party again.

What else, what else...
There was a man.
A man with a silly name and snooty manner.
A silly name, snooty manner, and a fondness for talking.

No, not just talking. Gossiping. *He said things my mum would be ashamed of, and I didn't think that was possible.*

Lucas scrunched his eyes up as he concentrated on reassembling the jigsaw of the previous night.

Words, he thought. *Lots of words, most of them quite salacious.*

Salacious? Did my brain really just come up with that word?

Urgh, he thought, realising his mouth felt furry and tasted worse.

Water. Water would be good.

He stretched tentatively, hoping the top of his head wouldn't fall off. He was faintly aware that something wasn't right, however his fuddled brain wasn't quite letting him see what. His aching bones told him he wasn't in his own bed, but that still left rather a lot of options. He was just wondering which of the options felt like floorboards when his fingers brushed against a warm body next to him.

He sat bolt upright, hangover forgotten, cold air assaulting his skin.

He froze as all manner of awful scenarios flashed through his mind. He was fairly certain he'd not do anything like that, not even whilst drunk...

But people did all manner of things they didn't mean to when under the influence.

Swearing never to drink again, he peeked under the covers. A chilly mistake, considering how little he appeared to be wearing, but one he was more than happy to make considering what - or rather, *who* else it revealed.

A familiar, wonderful snore next to him confirmed it was Clara - sweet, beautiful, adorable Clara - and Lucas laughed at himself.

Of course he'd not do anything so silly –

and besides, Clara had promised not to let Bunty get her talons into him.

He lay back down and traced his fingers across Clara's sleeping form, eliciting a sleepy jumble of words muttered in response.

He smiled as he glanced around the bedroom, rather confused as to why it was his office at the Castlebury Gazette.

Of course, now he remembered. He'd brought bedding to the office so he wouldn't disturb his mother when he returned from that damned party.

An excellent idea, all things considered. He really didn't fancy facing his mother like this. Not that she'd disapprove, oh no, but because she'd tease him relentlessly for the next ten years. At least.

Not to mention that it was rather nice to have a little privacy with Clara.

Very nice, in fact.

Yes, he could get used to that.

He twitched the covers away from her head, which was greeted with some complaints.

'Wakey, wakey,' he murmured, kissing the soft skin on the nape of her neck. He decided another peek under the covers was in order, especially as Lucas wasn't alone in wearing far fewer clothes to bed than usual. He smiled as vague but delightful recollections came back to him, and ran his hand over her curves.

She muttered something unintelligible

but unmistakably cross, and yanked the sheets over her head again. Lucas smiled and stuck a foot out from under the covers, only to pull it back a second later as the air stabbed his skin with frosty needles.

He shivered for a minute, then decided Clara would be fine without the top sheet for a few minutes – better than he'd be without it, anyway – and wrapped it around himself, for what little warmth it gave.

He managed to stand on the third try, his head nearly splitting in two with the effort, and performed all kinds of unnatural gymnastics to retrieve his clothes from wherever they'd landed on the floor last night, whilst exposing as little of his naked flesh to the air and avoiding moving too much. There was still the risk of his head falling off, after all.

Slightly better protected against the elements, he draped the sheet back over Clara and slowly made his way first to his desk drawer to find two doses of aspirin, then to the office kitchenette.

Trying to make as little noise as possible, he gathered things for tea and breakfast – plain toast unevenly cut and singed on the gas ring, and an egg boiled in a tin mug for dipping – and ate his share whilst preparing Clara's meal. He inexpertly arranged everything on a chipped plate before refilling the mug with cold water, and returned to their makeshift bedroom.

'Good morning, sweetheart,' he said, plonking himself back on the floorboards and bending over to kiss the top of her head. The aspirin was working, improving his mood by the second.

Clara buried herself further under the sheets, groaning complaints.

'Come, come,' he said sympathetically, finding a small gap in the blankets and peeking through at her. 'I made breakfast. And got you aspirin,' he added in response to muffled denials of hunger. 'You'll feel better once you eat something, and maybe it'll teach you not to drink so much.'

'You're a fine one to talk, Lucas Rathbone,' she grumbled, pushing herself upright at last and clutching her head. 'You were absolutely gone, don't try to deny it.'

'Wouldn't try,' he said brightly, his headache easing rapidly with the addition of fluids, food, and painkillers. 'But it's hardly *my* fault if I'm feeling bright and breezy this morning and you're not, is it?'

Clara glared at him and knocked back the water and aspirin before leaning against the wall with the covers pulled around her neck.

'Well, hopefully it's worth it,' she said, risking a nibble of toast and deciding against that course of action. 'Bunty is a chatty thing when she gets going, especially with a little social lubrication.'

'Family trait, I think,' replied Lucas, taking the top off Clara's egg for her and stealing a piece of toast for himself. He dunked it in the runny yolk and took a large bite, causing Clara to blanch. 'Her nephew is quite talkative as well. I hope I remembered to make notes.'

'Find your notebook and see,' said Clara, trying the toast again.

This took a little time, as the notebook wasn't in his trouser pocket, nor his blazer, nor his outdoor coat. It was eventually discovered dropped behind the chair he'd tossed his coat onto as Clara helped him undress on their late-night return to the office.

'Got it,' he said, holding it aloft.

'Urgh, *must* you be so loud?' said Clara, trying the toast for the umpteenth time and deciding tea might be a safer option. 'When you've finished crowing, sit down and let me look.'

Lucas plonked himself on the cold floorboards next to her and handed over the notebook, before stealing the rejected toast and egg. Clara hardly complained, which Lucas took as a sign that she really was feeling rough.

Oh well, he thought, munching away happily. *More brekkie for me. No point wasting good food.*

'Very interesting,' said Clara thoughtfully as the finished the last page. 'Very interesting indeed.'

Lucas was glad to see she was sipping her tea with a little more enthusiasm, and guiltily wondered if he shouldn't have eaten all the toast after all.

'Bunty didn't mention her own indiscretions,' said Clara, reviewing the notes again. 'Though I suppose that's no surprise. She also failed to mention anything about this Shank chap, which is more interesting - but perhaps it just slipped her mind.' Satisfied, she closed the notebook and handed it back to Lucas. 'This Bourbon-Busset chap was thorough, I'll give him that. In all but one thing.'

'Oh?' said Lucas, stealing her tea. 'What was that?

'He didn't tell you how awfully he treated poor Gloria.'

Gloria, Gloria... Had he met a Gloria?

'Young woman, about my age,' said Clara, obviously realising Lucas had no hope of matching the name with a face, 'Gets weepy when drunk.'

'Oh, *her*,' said Lucas, light dawning as he sprawled across the floor next to Clara. 'What about her?'

'Well, as far as I could tell through floods of tears and insistences that I was her best friend, Gloria used to be your new pal's girl - until he replaced her with a better prospect.'

'That'd be... Sylvia, right?' said Lucas, racking his brains. He pictured the woman who'd been fawning all over the brash and hard-drinking Chappers.

Not hard drinking, he reminded himself. *Just a lightweight, according to Jonathon. Certainly acting drunk enough for four, though. Worse than me for holding his drink.*

'That's right,' replied Clara, nodding. 'All was set for Gloria and "dear, dear Jono's" nuptials when in swans "that damned woman" – Glo's words, not mine, though frankly I'm inclined to agree – and steals the rotter from under her nose. She took it pretty hard, poor thing, as I'm sure you can imagine.' Clara sniffed. 'She's better off without him, if you ask me.'

'Hmm,' said Lucas, investigating the teapot and finding it disappointingly empty. 'Well, from the way Sylvia was behaving with Chappers – Gilbert Chapman, I should say – I reckon "dear Jono" is looking at a similar comeuppance if he's not careful.'

'Oh, I shouldn't think so,' said Clara airily. 'Chapman is a flirt, as I'm sure you could tell, but by all accounts, Sylvia is devoted to Bourbon-Busset. Besides, Sylvia has a dark secret of her own.'

'Really?' said Lucas, feeling rather hollow still and debating another raid on the cupboards. 'Do tell, darling.'

'Well, I *say* secret, but apparently she's rather proud of it.' Clara leaned forward and whispered, entirely unnecessarily considering they were alone. 'She's a mystic.'

'Oh, give over,' said Lucas incredulously.

'That's what they say,' said Clara, leaning back against the pillows again. 'Well, that's what *she* said, actually. Went to one of those fashionable séances apparently, and the psychic told her she'd got latent powers.'

'Bah, *psychics*,' said Lucas, scowling. 'What do they know about anything?'

'Well, *you* seem to know a fair amount,' retorted Clara.

'Yes, but I really *can* talk to the dead,' argued Lucas. 'Not that I bloody well want to, mind you.'

'I'm quite aware of that, dear,' said his long-suffering beloved, patting his hand. 'But did it never occur to you that *other* people might be the genuine article as well?'

'It's not *im*possible, I suppose,' said Lucas. 'I'm yet to find anyone, though.'

'Try being a little more open-minded, dear,' replied Clara. 'But more importantly, you should let me get on with what I was saying.'

She paused, frowning.

'Which was?' prompted Lucas.

'Well, I don't know now, do I?' she said crossly. 'You interrupted me and threw off my train of thought.' She shook her head irritably.

'About some psychic or witch or something,' suggested Lucas.

'Oh yes, that was it,' said Clara, expression clearing. 'Sylvia went off the deep end a few months ago and started getting into spells and seances and all that. Even claims her family has ties to the ancient Druids, though how she figured that one out is anyone's guess.'

'I thought we were sharing scandalous secrets,' said Lucas. 'If this nutjob is proud of all this, it's not much of a secret, is it?'

'Her dear old daddy isn't keen on having a "mystic" in the family,' explained Clara. 'Thinks it might harm his ambitious social climbing campaign, and I must say I think he's got a point. Anyway, he's threatened to cut her out of his will if she doesn't drop it, and cut her allowance to boot. So officially she's renounced all that, but…'

'But in private she's still doing the spells et cetera,' finished Lucas. 'Yes, I see. Worth a bob or two is he, her old man?'

'I should say!' exclaimed Clara, before wincing. Seemingly her aspirin hadn't quite done the trick yet. 'Her grandad made a stack on the railways back in the day,' continued Clara in a more subdued voice. 'And her dad took his inheritance and went into luxury imports. In short, the Pettigrews are rolling in it.'

'So it's in her interests to keep her stupid hobby quiet,' mused Lucas. 'Funny, her boyfriend didn't mention that, either.'

'Fiancé,' corrected Clara. 'The wedding is

planned for April.' She leant close again. 'They'd not been together a fortnight before he'd stuck a ring on her finger. Did you see the size of that emerald? Like a baby's fist.'

Lucas looked guiltily at the miniscule ruby and microscopic diamonds in Clara's engagement ring.

She followed his gaze and smiled affectionately. 'I much prefer mine,' she said, kissing his cheek.

'That's a relief,' he replied, the guilt not quite vanishing. 'Because I can't afford anything the size of a baby's fist.'

'Neither can Jono,' replied Clara. 'It's a family heirloom, and lucky for Jono he's got heirlooms like that to give. Bunty mentioned her nephew's profligate spending...'

'You spent altogether too much time talking to that old bat,' said Lucas.

'All in a good cause, my love,' replied Clara lightly. 'Not only was I getting plenty of information for the papers, but I was also keeping her away from you.' She grinned and took Lucas' hand, pulling him gently towards her. 'I'm the only woman allowed to get my paws on you, you know that.'

'Thank God for that,' said Lucas with feeling, pressing his lips against hers and ignoring the stale alcohol on her breath as best he could.

'Indeed,' she replied, slightly breathlessly,

caressing his face. 'Do you think we've got time…?'

Lucas checked his watch and groaned. 'I wish,' he said. 'I really do. But we're supposed to be at church for ten for Christmas service, and it's quarter to now.' He rubbed his eyes. 'Urgh, why are we doing that?'

'Because it's traditional,' said Clara, making no effort to move. 'And it's the only time of year we show our faces at St Crispin's, and we're going to my brother's for Christmas dinner straight afterwards.'

Lucas winced. As much as he loved their big family Christmases, he'd had enough of people last night.

'It's baby Ezra's first Christmas,' said Clara firmly. 'We can't miss it. Henry has been looking forward to a big family celebration for months.'

Clara wrapped a bedsheet around herself and finally staggered upright, tugging a cardigan onto her shoulders as quickly as possible. She stood for a moment, chafing her arms to get some heat into her skin. 'But apparently we forgot what hangovers are like,' she added, looking peaky again. 'Ye gods, Lucas, I feel dead.'

'Serves you right for getting drunk and gossiping,' he said, standing and wrapping his arms around her to lend her some heat. He kissed the top of her head lightly. 'Come on, let's get church over with so we can start enjoying ourselves.'

Clara shoved his shoulder playfully. 'Heathen,' she said. 'Make yourself useful and pass me my clothes so I don't have to move.'

***

After the mercifully short service - Lucas never saw the point of a Christmas service, seeing as there hadn't been anything new to say about it in approximately one thousand, nine hundred and twenty-eight years - he and Clara took the long way from St Crispin's to the Jenkins' house. It allowed them a few extra minutes alone, although nowhere in Castlebury Magna was really far enough from anywhere else to have a "long" journey.

Still, it meant they were amongst the last to arrive, and the house was already full of happy, noisy guests when Henry's wife, Debra, answered the door and welcomed the new arrivals.

Lucas stepped through the door with joyful anticipation as Debra hugged her sister-in-law and they dissolved into meaningless chatter.

To his surprise, he was rather looking forward to Christmas with his extended family, despite his usual dislike of anything vaguely resembling a party. True, there'd be a lot of people there, and at some point *someone* would suggest a jolly game of Charades or Sardines or Hunt The Slipper or something equally frightful, but there was something rather lovely about spending the dark, cold end of the year with friends and family he barely saw the rest of the time.

Perhaps that's the appeal? he mused, unbuttoning his coat. *Knowing that after a few days it'd be a full twelve months before having to see any of them again.*

Lucas' attention was caught by a piece of very unwelcome news.

'Henry's been called in to work,' said Debra, hanging Clara's coat on the already overflowing hall stand and holding out her hand for Lucas' snow-dusted overcoat.

'But it's Christmas Day,' protested Clara, unwinding the hand-knitted muffler from her throat. 'What could possibly be so important? Can't Jonesy handle it? He's the boss after all, it's his responsibility to handle emergencies.'

'Unfortunately, trouble at the Castlebury Manor apparently calls for all hands on deck,' said Debra, shaking her head sadly. 'Jones cornered Henry outside church as we were leaving.'

'I don't care what happened, or where,' started Lucas, righteous indignation rising at the thought of his best friend having to miss out on the festive fun he'd been looking forward to for weeks. 'It's not fair to -'

'Murder's murder, even at Christmas,' interrupted Debra.

'Murder!' exclaimed Clara. 'Who...?'

'Couldn't say,' said Debra. 'Henry didn't know, Jones was going to give him the details on the way.'

Lucas looked at Clara, desperately trying to silently impress on her that they should leave well enough alone.

It's Christmas, he pleaded silently. *We'll only get in the way. Not to mention the smell of cooked goose is making my stomach rumble.*

She returned his silent pleas with a look saying they were going to find out what was going on, and that was that.

'I suppose you two will be wanting to get the story for your papers?' suggested Debra, observing the silent conversation and evidently coming down on the side of her sister-in-law. 'Lucas, dear, you know there's nothing people like better than the misfortune of their neighbours, and I'm sure the Illustrated Police News would be interested in a Christmas murder.'

'Clara,' begged Lucas as his belly growled again, but she waved a hand at him impatiently.

'You're quite right,' said Clara, hugging Debra. 'This could be just the thing I need to make up for skipping out on that story the other month.'

Lucas whimpered involuntarily. Another

delicious scent had wound its way through the house from the kitchen and into his nostrils, which apparently were connected directly with his stomach, reminding him how little he'd eaten.

'I know,' said Debra, smiling warmly at Clara. 'And I know how disappointed you were that it didn't go as planned.'

'What's the rush?' said Lucas, edging his way towards the front room. The cosy front room was filled with festive cheer, food, fun, and completely devoid of ghosts. It was perfect. 'Whoever bit the dust isn't going to get any deader if we at least thaw out and eat something, are they?'

'We'll say hello to everyone,' said Clara, rolling her eyes at him. 'Then we'll make our excuses and get up there as quickly as possible.' She picked her coat up again and passed Lucas his.

'We'll be back for lunch, though,' said Lucas, hoping this to be true.

'I promise to save you some dinner,' said Debra, laughing as they made their way down the narrow hallway. 'But perhaps you'd like a sandwich to keep you going until then?'

'Please,' said Lucas gratefully.

He always knew Henry married a good woman, but Lucas hadn't realised just what a saint Debra was until that moment.

***

'Who do you think it is?' asked Clara as they trudged up the snow-blanketed slope to Castlebury Manor an all-too-short time later.

'How should I know?' replied Lucas, who had been thinking more about not falling flat on his face than worrying at all about who got themselves murdered at such an inconvenient time of year. 'Could be anyone. There were enough people there last night, after all.'

'I bet it was someone from our side of the house,' speculated Clara, slipping and steadying herself against Lucas, which didn't really help either of them much. 'No one from the official ball would do anything nearly so interesting as get themselves bumped off.'

'I don't know about that,' said Lucas, regaining his balance. 'You don't know what people get up to behind closed doors, and you don't know that people from "our side of the house" are any worse than those at the "official" party.'

'You don't read gossip columns, do you?' she said, straightening her coat. 'Because if you did, you'd know that our party was filled with the most dreadful rogues and scoundrels.'

'Give over, it was not,' said Lucas, catching Clara as her feet slid from under her once more.

He thought for a second and decided he

ought to amend that.

'Probably not,' he corrected. 'Although how can you say that when you know full well that people everywhere do simply awful things to each other all the time.

'Of course I know that,' said Clara. 'I wouldn't have a job if they didn't, and believe me I know how thoroughly nasty people can be.'

'Well there you go,' said Lucas. 'So there's nothing special about this one and we can just go home again.'

He turned to do just that and Clara spun him back round again, taking his arm to prevent any further attempt at escape.

'The special thing about this one,' she said, half leading, half dragging him up the hill. 'Is that it happened to those who just so happen to have been born into wealth and privilege and all that. Which means the likes of you and I - the plebs, if you will -'

'Oi, who are you calling a pleb?'

'Both of us, darling,' she said, melting some of his annoyance with her warm, soft lips against his cheek. 'But you know how much people like knowing that our "social superiors" are just as thoroughly rotten as the rest of us, and that, my darling, will be the saviour of both of our careers in journalism.'

'Speak for yourself,' said Lucas. 'I own a newspaper.'

She didn't reply with words, but the look

he received in return spoke volumes.

'Oh all right,' he grumbled. 'Who do you think bought it? My money is on Shank.'

'Why Shank?' said Clara, a bounce returning to her step now she'd won the battle.

'I don't know,' said Lucas. 'He's an interloper, isn't he? He wasn't born into wealth, so he probably did something untoward to make his money, and that got him into trouble with the old money.'

'You're just jealous because you haven't made your fortune yet,' said Clara. 'Just because someone has a lot of money doesn't mean they did anything bad to get it.'

'Perhaps not,' said Lucas, thankful that Castlebury Manor was in sight at last. 'But a lot of people do.'

'Well, maybe,' conceded Clara. 'But you can't assume these things.'

'I jolly well can,' said Lucas, nearly losing his footing again.

'All right, you shouldn't, then.' said Clara, before lapsing into thoughtful silence. 'Perhaps it's best not to speculate after all,' she said. 'There's no real way of knowing until we get there.'

'Whoever the chap is,' said Lucas, slightly miffed as he was starting to enjoy the speculation. 'I'm sure he deserved it.'

'It mightn't be a chap at all,' said Clara. 'It could just as easily be one of the girls.' She surveyed the landscape with a sigh. 'I can think of much nicer things to be thinking about today than writing up a report on a murder.'

'Yes, like eating your sister-in-law's goose dinner,' said Lucas. The kindly packed cheese sandwich hadn't lasted very long at all, and his belly grumbled again at the thought of the culinary delights they were missing.

'I was thinking of tobogganing down this hill, but yes, that too,' she said, looking wistfully at the smooth white slope before turning to the large Georgian mansion behind them. 'Maybe it'll be nice and quick, and we can get back to having fun?'

'Maybe,' said Lucas doubtfully, past experience telling him this was unlikely. 'Let's just get it over with, shall we?'

**

This time, ringing the front doorbell produced Henry Jenkins, togged up in his official navy-blue woollen policeman's uniform rather than the comfortable tweeds and woolly jumper he should have been wearing at lunchtime on Christmas Day.

He glanced over his shoulder, loudly announced that visitors to the manor were not permitted today, then stepped outside before half pulling the door behind him.

'What are you doing here?' he hissed,

glaring at his little sister and his best friend in turn. 'You should be at home eating yourselves stupid at my expense, not tramping through the snow.'

'You shouldn't be doing more interesting things than we are then, should you,' replied Clara, trying to peer over his shoulder through the two-inch crack he'd left between the door and frame. 'We heard someone's been bumped off, that's far more exciting than making nicey-nicey with relatives we've hardly seen for twelve months.'

'Oh shush,' scolded Henry. 'There's no one there you don't like. You just wanted to be nosy parkers, that's all.' He glared at Lucas. 'Was this your idea?'

'Certainly not!' he replied, affronted. 'I'd much rather be scoffing roast spuds and dozing in front of the fire. Definitely Clara's idea.'

'Yes, that sounds about right' replied Henry grimly. 'But you know I can't tell you anything, so I'm afraid you've had a wasted journey.' To make his point, he retreated back a step, pushing the door to the cavernous and freezing hallway open again.

'Oh come on, Henry,' begged Clara. 'We were here last night. We could be witnesses. We - we want to help. That's why we're here, isn't it Lucas? Lucas.'

'Ow,' yelped Lucas, rubbing ribs freshly jabbed by her elbow. 'I mean, yes, of course we want to help.'

He briefly wondered whether lying was a worse sin on Christmas Day than on any other day of the year, before deciding God would likely deal with him later, whereas Clara would most certainly deal with him now.

He was sure God would understand, given the circumstances.

Henry rubbed the back of his neck irritably. 'Lord above, you were here, weren't you? I forgot – and nobody else mentioned it, either.' He sighed and pushed the door fully open again. 'I suppose you'd better come in. Better than us all out here catching our deaths of cold, at any rate.'

However, the stone-flagged entrance hall was somehow colder inside than it was out, and Lucas shivered as the chilly but fresh caress of the white world outside changed to the cold of an unloved but grand space.

These rooms designed to impress do the job, though Lucas, reluctantly shedding his coat and hat. *But they're not what you'd call welcoming. Says something about the people that have them, doesn't it...?*

Fortunately, this wasn't a problem for long as Lucas and Clara were swiftly led through to a cosy parlour room, decked out in a style fashionable fifty years previously.

Bottle green wallpaper adorned the walls not shrouded by mahogany and brass bookshelves, each lined with leather-bound tomes of a likely serious and cerebral nature. Just looking at them made Lucas feel slow-witted, so he swiftly turned his attention to the welcoming fire crackling in a mantlepiece carved from stone speckled with fossils. An assortment of overstuffed chairs and sofas dotted the room, and were filled with, as Clara predicted, the other members of the previous night's "fun" party.

As they entered, sombre faces of Lucas and Clara's new acquaintances turned with dull interest towards the newcomers.

Bunty sported a large pair of sunglasses and sprawled on a chaise-longue, gently rubbing her temples. Even hungover and with the shadow of death hanging over the house, she was glamorously attired in an olive-green tweed trouser suit, pearls, and, rather incongruously, house slippers with a band of black swansdown arching over the top of each foot. A glass of water on the occasional table at her elbow fizzed slightly and a medicinal-looking white substance languished at the bottom.

The herbalist, Dr Shank, fared somewhat better. In fact, to Lucas' mind, he was almost suspiciously calm and collected, seated in a wingback chair with his gold rimmed glassed balancing on the tip of his nose, threatening to tumble onto the open book balanced on his knee. He appeared unaffected by last night's revelries, and equally unaffected by this morning's tragic revelations.

Not so Sylvia, who wept noisily on the shoulder of her fiancé. Jonathon was doing his best to comfort her and failing, but he himself seemed quite well composed, if a little tired and wan. He seemed a tad red and puffy around the eyes, though whether this was due to crying or an abundance of cocktails it was impossible to say.

As Lucas and Clara entered the room, Bourbon-Busset nodded a greeting.

'Terrible business, old chum,' he said quietly, trying not to disturb Sylvia, who subsided into gentler sobs in front of the newcomers. He glanced at her cautiously, looked on the verge of saying something, but held his tongue instead.

Curious, but Lucas squashed that curiosity almost as quickly as it arrived.

We're not getting involved in this mess, he thought sternly, hoping Clara might let him carry this intention through. *As far as I'm concerned, we're here to get the story and get out again – preferably before the flock of relatives devours all the roast potatoes. I really don't fancy a miserable dinner of Brussel sprouts and cold, lumpy gravy.*

Lucas' eyes drifted around the group, trying to remember who was there the previous night.

As far as he could tell, two faces were

missing from the group: the loudmouth Chapman, and the weepy Gloria.

He frowned. He hoped it wasn't the girl. Though they'd barely said two words to each other, he felt no one should spend their last night on earth crying their heart out on the shoulder of a stranger - even if that stranger was as lovely as Clara.

'What are they doing here?' growled D.I. Wilberforce Jones, storming across the room.

An all too familiar knot of anxiety tightened in Lucas' stomach. What with one thing and another, he'd had a few, mostly unpleasant encounters with Jones over the years, and seeing that the older copper was even more irascible than usual didn't bode well.

'Potential witnesses, sir,' said Henry smartly, long immune to his boss' foul temper. 'They were at the party last night and came to offer their help as soon as they heard there was a problem, sir.'

'*You* were here last night?' said Jones, raising a bushy eyebrow incredulously. 'Didn't realise this was... *your* sort of crowd.'

'We were asked to report on the ball,' Clara explained briefly before Lucas could get them into hot water with a sarcastic comment.

'Then you can scram,' said Jones, turning his back on them. 'You won't have had any business with these people who, by their own admission didn't go near the,' he checked his notes, '"stuffy, jumped-up, socially septic" group of people in the official gathering.'

'Oh, do be quiet,' groaned Bunty, fingers pressed against her forehead. 'I asked them if they wanted to come to a *real* party. They had every right to be with us.' She looked at Jones over the top of her sunglasses, eyes bloodshot and surrounded by dark circles. She looked much older than she had just a few hours previously, but she still spoke with the authority her rank gave her. 'They were my *guests*,' she said, in a tone that allowed no argument from a mere detective of the local police force.

Lucas was rather pleased to see a faint blush appear on the man's cheeks.

Perhaps having friends in high places mightn't be so bad after all?

'Now you're here,' said Jones in a slightly huffy voice, turning back to Lucas and Clara. 'I may as well ask you a few questions. Or rather, Constable Jenkins can do the honours, seeing as I'm busy with actual witnesses. I doubt you'd be half so chatty with me as you would be with him, anyway.'

Too bloody right, thought Lucas as Henry hurried them out of the room. *And we'll get a better idea of what's going on, too. We have reports to write, after all.*

Henry led them to the cavernous ballroom, chilly now it was empty of dancers. The gleaming parquet floor made every step echo, the long buffet table empty and waiting to be returned to storage. Cold winter sun streamed through the large windows, sending oddly flat light bouncing off the cream wallpaper and glittering from gilded mirror frames and the pinchbeck candelabras jutting from the walls.

The trio dragged highly decorative, highly uncomfortable chairs into a huddle, and Henry pulled his notebook from a pocket on his jacket.

'All right,' he said, licking the tip of his pencil. 'What - if anything - can you tell me about the party last night?'

'Quite a bit, as it happens,' said Clara. 'Lucas, give him your notebook.'

'You took *notes*?' said Henry, turning to his best friend, aghast. 'At a *party*? Really Lucas, you're no fun anymore. I've been saying it for years, but this just proves it.'

'Do you want the notebook or not?' replied Lucas, holding it out of reach of Henry's grasping fingertips. 'You know we were here to write an article or two, what did you think I'd be doing?'

'Fine, I'm sorry,' said Henry, leaning forward and lifting the notebook from Lucas' unresisting grasp. 'Working man and all that.' Clara coughed. 'And working woman too, of course, though what the Illustrated Police News could find interesting about a ball is beyond me.'

'There's been a murder,' protested Clara. 'They might be interested in *that*.'

'Yes, but you didn't know that'd happen, did you? Unless…' Henry fixed his sister with a disapproving look. 'Did you have any quarrels with the victim, miss?'

'Henry, don't be a bore. We don't even know who the victim is yet.'

The policeman blinked. 'You don't? Oh no, I suppose you wouldn't. The body wasn't discovered until seven-thirty this morning, though we're having trouble getting the coroner and doctors down here to take a look. Dr Ibbotson is spending Christmas at his sister's in Cornwall, and the county coroner is claiming he's snowed in, though seeing as no one else is, I suspect he just didn't want to turn out in the cold.'

'Can't say I blame him,' said Lucas, who was swiftly shushed by Clara.

'Jones has already vowed to get him out here, even if he's got to dig the fellow out himself,' continued Henry with a grim smile. 'But at this rate we'll have to call in old June Westerly to take a look at the body.' He shook his head disapprovingly. 'I know Ibbotson rates her "healing" skills for keeping the villagers in one piece whilst he's out of town, but *really*, we can't have the local witch in charge of a murder victim.'

'You're positively medieval at times, you

know that don't you?' scolded Clara. 'Mrs Westerly isn't a *witch* just because she knows how to heal people with herbs. You may as well say the same of Dr Shank if that's the attitude you're taking.'

'Yes, well I don't like him much either,' said Henry, glancing over his shoulder in case he was somehow overheard. Seeing he wasn't, he added. 'Gives me the creeps, if you must know.'

'Yes,' said Lucas, relieved to hear someone else say what he was thinking. 'There's something a bit off about him, isn't there?'

'That's just because you don't like people who know more words than you do,' said Clara before Henry could agree.

Lucas was about to argue his case when a familiar figure drifted through the doors and into the ballroom.

Familiar, morose, and ever so slightly transparent.

'So,' said Lucas, turning his attention back to Henry, feeling rather happy at being able to get one up on his friend for once. 'How did Mr Gilbert Chapman, meet his maker?'

At the sound of his name, Chapman - or rather, what was left of him - jerked his head and stared across the room. The dead man peered at Lucas, tilting his head this way and that, trying to figure out whether Lucas could see him or not.

Lucas put the spirit out of his misery –

well, that misery, at least - and waved at him.

Chapman let out a delighted cry and strode across the room, talking incessantly.

Damn, thought Lucas, already regretting his decision. *I hate it when they won't shut up. Still, at least he'll be able to tell us what happened. When he stops going on about how simply marvellous it is that I can see him, anyway.*

Henry turned around and followed Lucas' eye. 'I should have known,' he grumbled. 'He's here, isn't he?'

Lucas' head thudded dully again, though this time it was because of a tide of words bypassing his ears and appearing unbidden in his head.

Then again, maybe the aspirin had just worn off.

He was going to blame the ghost, though. If in doubt, blame it on a ghost.

'Uhuh,' he confirmed, trying to push the ghostly chatter to the back of his mind. 'He certainly has a lot to say for himself.'

'Well, of course I do!' cried Chapman. 'You would too, in my position. Think it's fun, do you, having a good time and then dropping dead in a water closet? Most undignified. Of course,' he added, a wry smile creeping across his handsome face. 'I've been found in more compromising situations, but usually I can talk my way out of them. No such luck this time though.'

'Excellent!' cried Henry, leaning forward eagerly, pencil poised for notetaking. 'Ask him who did it, and we might get home for Christmas dinner yet.'

Lucas looked at Chapman expectantly, who jabbed himself in the chest with a look of surprise on his face.

'Who, me?' he cried. 'How should I know?'

'You were there,' said Lucas aloud, thankful for not having to conduct his ghostly enquiries quietly for once. 'And you were, well, you. Who better to have an inkling of such a thing?'

'I jolly well don't, I'm afraid,' said Chapman, quite annoyingly cheerful about it. 'But I'm sure you clever chaps will work it all out toot sweet, what?'

Lucas groaned and put his head in his hands. Dreams of roast potatoes drenched in gravy faded before his mind's eye.

'He doesn't know?' said Clara, guessing what was wrong. 'How can he not know?'

'That's what I'm trying to find out, darling,' muttered Lucas, sitting up again as he massaged his temples. She rubbed his back sympathetically, which helped a little, and kissed his cheek, which helped rather more. He smiled at her gratefully.

The ghost pointed between them in amazement. 'You're a couple?' he exclaimed.

'Well, I suppose that explains a few things, like why I wasn't getting anywhere with my trademark charm and wit.' He ran a critical eye over Clara. 'Though I must say she looked a darned sight better in that frock of hers last night. Winter clothes are so unflattering, don't you think?'

'Just answer the question,' said Lucas wearily. It was bad enough being dragged away from the festivities, and most importantly, dinner, without having to listen to Clara's sensibly warm clothing being criticised.

'I told you, I don't know,' said the ghost irritably. 'There I was, having a jolly time of it, dancing with that saucy young Sylvia, and I get the most awful stomach cramps. Thought I was going to decorate the room, if you catch my drift, so I excused myself in search of a more private place to lose my lunch. Stumbled into a bathroom, collapsed on the floor and then it all went a bit wrong. More wrong, anyway.' Chappers ran a hand through his hair. 'Look, I'd rather not relive the experience, if you don't mind. Once was more than enough. Let's just say it wasn't pretty, and then I died.'

'Suits me,' said Lucas, who didn't want to hear the details anyway. Turning to Henry, he said, 'Chapman felt sick, went to find somewhere quieter to do so, collapsed and died. But I suspect you already knew that.'

'Yes, that was pretty obvious,' said Henry, disappointed. 'We're fairly sure it was poison, though we won't know for sure until the coroner has cut him up.'

'I say, steady on,' protested the late Chapman, looking more than a little queasy. However, seeing as Lucas was the only one who heard the complaint, and he wasn't going to let anything slow his return to lunch, it didn't earn the ghost any apology.

'Thankfully the servants were given strict instructions not to disturb the *other* party until they were called for,' said Henry, oblivious to the interruption. 'So we've collected all the food and drink, as that's the most obvious place to start looking, and we should discover what it was fairly quickly. Although I doubt we'll need to look much further than the glass by the body. If we're really lucky, there might even be some unexplained finger marks, which will make our lives easier.'

'Jolly good show,' exclaimed Chapman, clapping Henry on the back or thereabouts, his uneasiness at the future of his mortal remains forgotten. 'I always said the rozzers were a good lot. I mostly said that, anyway. I must have said it once, even if just by accident. Anyway, it doesn't look like it matters too much that I'm at a total loss as to who'd want poor old Chappers dead.'

'Yes, but you can still help us work it out,'

said Lucas, turning back to his latest headache. 'Even if you don't know who actually did it, you must have your suspicions.'

The ghost spread his hands wide. 'Haven't the foggiest, dear chap. Loved by all, and loving all, that's me. Or it was, I suppose.' He sighed. 'I suppose I'll have to get used to the past tense, won't I?'

'Yes, you will,' said Lucas unsympathetically.

Loved by all, my foot, he thought. *You don't get yourself bumped off for no good reason – unless...*

'Maybe it was an accident?' asked Lucas aloud, ignoring Henry's frown and Clara's thrilled gasp. 'It wasn't exactly a sit-down affair; it would have been easy enough to muddle the glasses up. Did you pick up someone else's glass by mistake?'

'Quite possibly, my good man, quite possibly,' said Chapman thoughtfully. 'And as I say, I really don't think anyone would have cause to bump off poor Chappers. We're a pretty happy lot all round, so I can't think who'd want to kill anyone else either, if I'm honest.'

'He's claiming no one would want to kill him or anyone else at last night's party,' said Lucas to the room at large. 'Do we believe that?'

'Not for a second,' said Clara, shaking her head. 'Certainly not considering what I was hearing last night.'

'Oh, *gossip*,' said Chapman, waving his

hand dismissively. 'Don't pay any heed to *that*.'

'What gossip?' said Lucas, turning to Clara. 'Worse than what you told me earlier?'

'Already been talking about me, eh?' said Chapman with evident pleasure. Lucas thought the deceased man sounded a little anxious, which was curious for a man claiming to be so loved by his friends.

'Well, you remember Gloria and Jonny were engaged before he ditched her for rich little Sylvia Pettigrew?' said Clara. Henry scribbled furiously in his notebook; morning soberness had presumably tightened locks on lips loosened by alcohol the previous evening. 'I'd say that's a motive, wouldn't you?'

'Yes, but to kill *Jonny*, not me,' argued Chapman. 'I never did a thing to hurt Glo.'

'But if you picked up his glass by mistake, you have bought it instead,' said Lucas. He looked at his living companions and was about to offer an explanation, but the look on their faces told him there was no need. The Jenkins' siblings were quite used to filling in the gaps of conversation between Lucas and the other side, which made his life easier.

'Or vice versa,' said Henry, pointing his pencil at Clara. 'What if Gloria knew something about Bourbon-Busset and he decided to shut her up?'

'Oh, Jono's as honest as the day is long,' said Chapman. 'Hasn't got it in him to kill anyone, let alone *her*, for all his ditching her for a better prospect. No,' he said firmly. 'You're looking for someone else.'

'Apparently Bourbon-Busset is "as honest as the day is long,"' said Lucas. 'But seeing as the days are pretty short this time of year, perhaps that's not much of a recommendation.'

'If you're not going to listen, I can just go,' snapped Chapman, stalking towards the double doors at the end of the room.

'Leave if you like,' Lucas called after him with a shrug. 'No skin off my nose if they don't catch your killer. But I suspect you won't be going anywhere until you know who did the deed, so you might as well help.'

The ghost sighed and sloped back to the group. 'All right, I see your point,' he grumbled. 'But you're wasting your time. It must have been an accident. No one in our little group had any *real* grievances against each other.'

'Gloria can't have liked Sylvia too much for running off with her fellow,' mused Clara. 'I'd certainly not be too chuffed in her position.'

Chapman snorted. 'Well, she leapt straight into my bed, so she wasn't too cut up about it.'

Not so much as a hint of shame, thought Lucas as heat crawled above his collar, despite the room being so cold their breath formed clouds around them. *And I thought he and Bourbon-Busset were friends.*

'What is it?' said Henry, with a smirk. 'Has the ghost said something rude?' He turned to his sister with a mischievous twinkle in his eye. 'I can always tell, you know.'

Clara looked at Lucas' now flaming cheeks and snickered. 'Me too,' she said gleefully. 'Come on Lucas, out with it.'

'Yes, tell them, man,' said Chapman crossly. 'Now you know, you may as well let the cat out of the bag. It's not like I'm ashamed of it anyway. But I'm amazed your girl hasn't heard already. Generally speaking we're not the most discreet of groups, as you might have noticed.'

'Er, apparently Gloria took comfort in Chapman's arms,' mumbled Lucas, trying to ignore the intense scrutiny he was under, which only stoked his embarrassment further.

Clara sniggered. 'Oh yes, she told me,' she said. 'Only it was more like in his bed, and once against a wardrobe.'

'Oh yes,' said the ghost, sighing wistfully at the recollection. 'Quite the little firecracker once she got going, you know.'

'Clara,' scolded her brother. 'Is that any way for a nice young lady to speak?'

'No, but Gloria told me anyway,' replied Clara, deliberately misinterpreting him. 'But that would give Bourbon-Busset motive, wouldn't it? His ex-fiancée taking up with his best friend straight after they broke up.'

'Jonny didn't care about that,' said

Chapman. 'Besides, he did the same to me, more or less. Syl and I were getting married until Jonny stole her from me.' He smirked. 'Glo wasn't the only one enjoying a little revenge that weekend. And a most enjoyable way to get revenge, might I add.'

Lucas groaned and sunk his head into his hands. 'Sylvia and Chapman were supposed to be married before Jonny took up with her –'

'Stole her,' corrected the ghost.

'All right, *stole her*,' said Lucas. 'So they're all as bad as each other really.'

'He started it,' said Chapman grumpily. 'Once we'd cleared the air, we were all friends again. Even asked me to be his best man.'

'But apparently they made up, so perhaps we're barking up the wrong tree there,' said Lucas for the sake of the non-psychically inclined.

Henry sighed. 'Damn. I was rather hoping we could tie this up quickly and get back in time for lighting the pudding.'

'Me too,' said Lucas, wondering if any festive treats would be left by the time they got back. Despite Debbie's promise that she'd save them some, a number of elderly aunts had been invited for the day. Lucas knew from bitter experience that they did exactly as they pleased and had insatiable appetites.

'Who else could have done it?' said Clara. 'We've not looked at Bunty or Dr Shank yet.'

'Well, I shouldn't think it was either of them either,' said Chapman, warming to the task at last.

'Someone tried to kill someone,' said Lucas, turning around to face the ghost. 'You can't all have been so well liked that no one wanted to kill any of you, otherwise you wouldn't be dead, would you?'

The ghost grumbled, but much to Lucas' surprise seemed to have no real argument to this logic.

'All right then,' said Lucas, feeling encouraged. 'Who would want whom dead?'

'How should I know?' replied the ghost sulkily.

'They're your friends!' cried Lucas, feeling the briefly gained upper ground slide away from underneath his feet. 'I thought you knew all their dirty little secrets?'

'They wouldn't be secrets if I knew them, would they?'

'Are you so incapable of keeping anything to yourself?'

'In a word, yes. I'm no good at keeping this kind of thing to myself, especially not when the drink is flowing – which it generally does.'

'Hang on,' said Henry, interrupting the half of the conversation he could hear. 'What if this Chapman chap told someone's secret, and that someone killed him from revenge - or perhaps Chapman knew something he shouldn't have and they decided to keep him quiet?'

Three sets of eyes turned towards the ghost – well, one set of eyes and two others looked vaguely in the right direction.

Regardless, the ghost squirmed under the perceived scrutiny.

'Look, I really shouldn't say,' he said, examining his shirt cuff with unusual interest.

'It's a little late for that,' said Lucas. 'The worst has already happened to you, so you haven't much to lose by coming clean.'

'Urgh, fine,' said Chapman, eyes darting around anywhere but at Lucas. He blew his cheeks out, looked around the room, and leaned in needlessly close. 'One of the few secrets I did manage to keep is that – well, the fact of the matter is…'

'Spit it out, man,' said Lucas, shivering. Sitting still for so long had allowed the cold to creep though his clothing, and he was worried his teeth were about to start chattering.

'Bun and I got tipsy and one thing led to another, you know,' said Chapman in a rush, as though saying the words faster would make them easier to say. 'One-time thing, swore each other to secrecy, et cetera, but we didn't exactly want that to be public knowledge. Not that it entirely stayed secret for long, but mostly - mostly no one knows.'

'Why not?' said Lucas, feeling hot and embarrassed again, which at least solved the problem of feeling cold. He could understand the young man not wanting to admit to a fling like that, but surely Bunty wouldn't care…

'Come on, man,' cried the ghost, standing up straight. 'Would you want the world knowing you're had a bit of how's-your-father with your best pal's aunt? It's shameful!'

'Agreed, but why would Bunty agree to keep it quiet?'

'Look, I shouldn't be telling you this,' said Chapman, leaning even closer this time and almost whispering by this point. 'But she'd got plans to get her mitts on the good doctor.'

'Shank?' cried Lucas, causing raised eyebrows from the less "gifted" in the room.

'Shh,' said Chapman, looking around in alarm. 'Yes, of course Shank, who else? Yes,' he said, composing himself again. 'Bunty had her sights set on Shank – or his newfound fortune, anyway – and he had his sights set on being Lord of the Manor. All in, it would have suited them down to the ground.'

Lucas waited expectantly. 'I sense the word "but" hovering on the tip of your tongue,' he prompted.

'But,' said Chapman obligingly. 'That would've gone to pot had he found out about me and Bun doing the horizontal tango, wouldn't it?'

Lucas rubbed his eyes. 'Right, so let me get this straight,' he said, wishing his head would stop aching. 'You slept with Bunty –'

'Hang on, old thing,' cried the ghost. 'I told you that in confidence!'

'It's a murder investigation,' said Lucas, acutely aware of the pencil dancing on Henry's notepad and Clara's widening smirk. 'How much of your private life do you think will remain private over the next few days, hmm? So you might as well spill the beans now and save it being dragged out.'

'Oh, fine,' grumbled Chapman. 'Tell the copper if you must - I suppose it's too late now anyway. But it's unrelated, I assure you.'

'We'll see about that,' said Lucas. He cleared his throat. 'As I was saying,' he continued, 'You had a night of passion with Bunty –'

'Alcohol induced,' interjected the ghost.

'All right, alcohol induced passion, if it makes you feel better,' said Lucas. 'But you swore each other to secrecy because you were ashamed of your actions – quite rightly so, I might add – and because Bunty was trying to hook herself a wealthy husband…'

'Who?' asked Clara, astounded.

'Shank,' replied Lucas. 'He made a stack with his supposedly marvellous aphrodisiac. Would have worked out well for both of them, as apparently he fancies being lord of the manor.'

'Is that how that works?' mused Clara.

'Just marry into it?'

'I suppose so,' said Lucas, who had no idea and couldn't care less anyway. 'Either way, he'd get to swan around the big house and play at it, and do all those things posh folks do, like go to parties and rub shoulders with other posh folks, so even if he wasn't a *Lord* as such, it'd probably do his business the world of good.'

'That's a bit uncharitable,' said Chapman. 'As far as I can tell, they'd be a rather good match.'

'Yes, that sounds about right,' said Clara. 'Excellent business move, making connections with rich people.' She nudged Lucas' knee with hers. 'Perhaps you should try it sometime?'

'Look,' said Lucas, keen to avoid talking about his dire personal finances. 'All I know is that neither of them wanted to admit the affair, and who can blame them?'

'I can understand Chapman not wanting to own up to it,' said Clara, thankfully taking the diversion. 'But Bunty was eyeing you up all night, wasn't she? I doubt she'd object to an affair with a man young enough to be her son becoming public knowledge.'

Lucas groaned; he'd hoped they could get through this without revealing that little bit of information to Henry, who was always ready to tease Lucas about his painful shyness with the opposite sex.

'You didn't tell me that,' said Henry, not

bothering to hide his glee.

'Maybe she was trying to make him jealous,' said Lucas, ignoring Henry.

'How could we?' said Clara to her brother. 'We've barely seen you since.'

'That would make sense,' said Chapman. 'The jealous thing, not telling your policeman pal about Bunty's roving eye.'

'It wasn't her eyes I was worried about,' muttered Lucas sullenly.

'But still,' said Henry, still addressing Clara. 'You could have told me sooner.'

'Yes, quite,' said Chapman, with a small cough. 'But my point is, it's absolutely the kind of trick Bunty might try. Especially as Shank had been cool towards her lately.'

'I've told you now, haven't I?' said Clara crossly.

Lucas decided to tune the squabbling siblings out - something he was well practiced at - as this felt like a lead. An important lead, at that.

'Oh?' he said, trying not to sound too excited by the prospect of a speedy solution. 'Any idea why Shank had gone off Bunty?'

'What am I, omniscient?' said Chapman with a shrug. 'How should I know why the silly old fool has gone off the woman? Perhaps he tired of her, or found someone else, or found out about one of her, er, indiscretions.' He scratched the back of his head in embarrassment. 'For all his touting love potions, he's a bit of a stick in the mud when it comes to that sort of thing.'

'Maybe he did you in because he was jealous?' suggested Lucas. 'Even if his initial passion for her had cooled, he still might not have liked someone else making a move on her.'

'I suppose so,' said the ghost, though he sounded uncertain. 'Anything's possible. But he's really not the type, and it was months ago anyway. If he was going to kill off old Chappers why wait until Christmas?'

'Good question,' said Lucas. 'Maybe he'd finally worked himself up to it? Or taken his time planning it? Or maybe there was another factor to the murder - after all, anyone's the type to commit murder in the right circumstances.'

'I never would,' declared the ghost.

'What, even you?' said Clara incredulously, the dramatic statement drawing her out of the dwindling argument with Henry.

'I expect so,' he replied, squeezing her hand. 'I'm just trying to make a point really, but if anyone tried to hurt you, I very well might kill them.'

She beamed at him. 'You're sweet,' she said, kissing his cheek. 'I'd do the same for you, of course.'

'I'll pretend I didn't hear either of you say that,' said Henry, looking at the couple with heaps of disapproval.

'What would you do if someone tried to

hurt your Debbie?' said Lucas, feeling his gallantry ought to be praised, not quashed. 'Or Ezra? You're telling me that if someone hurt your family, you'd not kill them?'

Henry thought about this. 'Everyone has a tipping point,' he conceded in hushed tones, looking over his shoulder. 'Though I'd not admit as much in front of the boss. He doesn't have much of a sense of humour about these things.'

'Or anything else, as far as I can tell,' added Lucas.

'Yes,' said Henry gloomily. 'Do you know how depressing that is at times?'

'Nothing would ever make me kill someone,' insisted Chapman. 'I just don't have it in me.'

'Oh, that's not true,' said Lucas, turning back to him. 'Well, obviously now it is, but in life I'm sure there were dozens, maybe hundreds of times you could have killed someone. It could have been revenge, or jealousy, or because you were frightened of that person, or the consequences of them doing or saying something, or to protect someone else, or greed, or because they were blackmailing you, or –'

'Yes, yes, I get the idea,' said the ghost, waving a hand. 'But I never reached that point, all right?'

'That's not really the issue, is it?' said Lucas.' 'Someone else *did* reach that point, and whether you deserved it or not -'

'Which I didn't,' interjected Chapman.

'We need to figure out who, and why,' concluded Lucas, who was getting rather good at ignoring ghostly interruptions.

'And who they actually wanted to kill in the first place,' insisted the ghost. 'I still can't imagine any one of them would want to kill me.'

'I can see plenty of reasons why someone might want you dead,' said Lucas, fixing the spirit with a disparaging look. 'But, if you insist, we'll look at the "accident" option too.'

'Thank you,' said Chapman. 'I'm sure that's the solution to this conundrum.'

'All right,' said Lucas, deciding to let this point drop in the interests of getting home before the collected aunts polished off every scrap of food in Henry's house. 'I've got to tell Clara and Henry everything you've just told me.'

'I'm sure they got the general gist,' said Chapman uncomfortably. 'Do you really need to tell them *everything*?'

'Yes,' said Lucas. 'And it'll be a lot easier if you don't interrupt me.'

Chapman nibbled his bottom lip anxiously, shrugged, and said, 'Fine by me. I didn't tell you anything you wouldn't have found out anyway.'

'Er, good,' said Lucas, wondering what it was he apparently wouldn't find out anyway. 'Now, if you don't mind...'

'Say,' said the ghost. 'I could use a drink. Do they have cocktails in the ghostly world, or realm, or whatever this is? I'm positively dying for a snifter - so to speak.' He chortled at his own joke, and repeated it a couple of times, just to make sure the unlaughing Lucas had heard correctly.

'Could do,' said Lucas, feeling a little more cheerful himself at the prospect of getting some much-needed peace from the paranormal. 'Why not have a look?'

'Good idea,' said Chappers, slapping Lucas approximately on the back, making his already chilly skin tingle in a different, much more unpleasant way. 'See you later.'

Lucas felt the tension leave his shoulders as the dearly departed Chapman departed once more through the double doors at the end of the ballroom, taking at least half Lucas' headache with him.

'Now,' said Lucas, turning to Henry. 'Did you get all that?'

***

'Who knew the upper crust were as depraved as the rest of us, eh?' said Henry as Lucas concluded his recounting of what the late Mr Chapman had told him.

'Speak for yourself,' protested Clara. '*I'm* not depraved.'

'But you're not sweetness and light either,' Henry retorted. 'I've heard what you get up to, picking locks and snooping on people and all that.'

Clara waved his reproof away carelessly. 'That's not the same. I don't do that for revenge or greed or to get a leg up on someone who is supposed to be my friend. No, it's professional curiosity or to help someone out of a sticky patch.'

'Hmm,' replied Henry disapprovingly, despite occasionally being helped by his little sister's less than legal skills. He looked at the scrawl of shorthand tangled across his notebook and sighed. 'As much as I'd love to, I can't go chasing after these leads - at least not straight away.'

'Why not?' said Clara. 'It'll give you a good start.'

'But I can't tell Jones a ghost told my friend all this stuff, can I?' protested Henry, scratching his head. 'What am I meant to do about that?'

'Not my problem,' said Lucas, leaning back in his chair and stretching, thinking for the umpteenth time that he was glad he didn't follow in his friend's footsteps. 'Do you think the kitchen staff would be friendly to a stray newspaper reporter far from home on a cold Christmas day?'

'Maybe,' said Clara. 'Except you're not a

stray, nor far from home.'

'But it is cold,' argued Lucas. 'And Christmas Day, and well past lunchtime. I'll gnaw my own leg off if I don't eat something soon.'

'Lucas Rathbone, you had an enormous sandwich on the way here,' cried Clara.

'And it vanished long ago,' said Lucas, his stomach growling in conformation. 'And I've been helping with a police investigation, that should gain me some sympathy, shouldn't it?'

'Yes, you've been very helpful,' said Henry with a deep sigh, still frowning at the page of notes.

'See,' said Lucas, sticking his tongue out at Clara. 'That's got to be worth a biscuit, at least. Maybe even a slice of Christmas cake.'

'And I know you've got enough problems dealing with them in the first place,' said Henry, who wasn't listening and had upgraded his frown into a full scowl. 'It's just rather awkward trying to explain to Jones how I "instinctively" know these things.'

'You should think of an explanation quickly, then,' advised Clara. 'We've been here ages. Jonesy will be wondering where you've got to.'

Henry groaned, apparently sinking to new depths of work-based despair. 'He's bad enough at the best of times, but when he'd rather be face down in a pile of turkey, he's unbearable.' He turned back to his notes, as though looking again would solve all his problems. 'I wouldn't be surprised if he just put it down to natural causes and that was that.'

'If it were natural, Chapman wouldn't still be here,' said Lucas.

'I know,' said Henry. 'But what can I do if Jones takes it into his head that's what it is, eh? It's a far easier solution, after all.'

'Well, I guess we could just leave Chapman to haunt this place,' replied Lucas, stretching his limbs stiffened from sitting so long. 'It's not like he knows where I live, unlike some. I can just leave and never come back.'

'Don't be rotten,' said Clara. 'How would you like it if you were just left hanging around a place forever, seeing those you know and love grow old and die?'

'It's hardly my fault if he did something to get himself bumped off, is it?' argued Lucas, his colour rising and bringing a little warmth to his frozen body. 'If people didn't deserve it, they wouldn't get murdered. It's as simple as that.'

'That's not true,' said Henry. 'People get killed for all sorts of reasons that weren't their fault. Having lots of money and greedy relatives, for example, or because they married someone that someone else took a shine to. You could be leaving an innocent spirit lingering for no reason.'

'Listen,' said Lucas, his hunger-shortened

temper not appreciating the lecture. 'The man slept with his best friend's ex-fiancée, and the same friend's aunt, damaging her fledgeling romance in the process, and I have no doubt he's done dozens of other reprehensible things that we don't know even about yet.'

'Most likely, yes,' said Henry with irritating calmness. 'But -'

'And even if it turns out he didn't do anything to get *himself* murdered,' continued Lucas. 'He's not some sweet innocent fellow who never did anything wrong in their life, is he?'

'That's no reason to abandon him to haunt a place forever, is it?' said Clara, echoing her brother's annoyingly reasonable tone. 'How would you like it if you knew someone could have helped you, but chose not to?'

Lucas suppressed a groan. He hated it when they were right, especially when he was so very wrong.

Besides, if the ghostly Mrs Bird ever discovered Lucas had welched on his so-called duty to help the dead but not quite gone, he'd never hear the end of it.

'*Fine*,' he said grumpily, unwilling to concede defeat without at least some protest. 'But can we go home and eat first? I'm half starved, and we can't do any more until the doctor has looked at the body.'

At that moment, a tinkly bell chimed two

o'clock somewhere in the room, confirming Lucas' unhappy theory that they'd likely missed the best part of the dinner, and leftovers were less likely by the minute.

'I don't see why not,' said Clara, taking his hand in her own chilly fingers.

'Though some of us still have work to do,' said Henry, looking as sorrowful as he could manage. 'At Christmas, when they should be home with their wife and baby son.'

'There's a reason I didn't follow you into the force,' said Lucas, ignoring Clara's pleading eyes, her soft heart clearly wounded by her brother's speech.

'Yes, you'd have to answer awkward questions about how you knew who the killer was,' said Clara, arching an eyebrow at him.

'That was a consideration too,' said Lucas, though it had admittedly been the main consideration. 'But that's Henry's problem now, not mine.' He leant over to Clara and whispered, 'Roast potatoes. Yorkshire puddings. Gravy.'

As her resolve visibly wavered, he added, 'And your Aunt Joan can eat for England.'

'We'll go home and make sure you have a plate saved,' said Clara quickly. Her stomach growled. 'Er, we're doing it for you, Henry, I swear.'

That was easier than expected, thought Lucas, fighting a grin. *Then again, the unpredictable Clara Jenkins is occasionally very predictable indeed.*

'Oh come on, don't leave me on my own,' whined Henry.

'You're not on your own, you've got Jones and all the posh folks to play with,' said Lucas, wrapping Clara's icy fingers in his hands to get some warmth back into them. She smiled at him gratefully. 'And Clara is positively frozen,' he added, appealing to Henry's protective nature.

'Then come through to the front room where the fire is,' said Henry. 'Along with the other suspects.'

'*Other* suspects?' said Clara, aghast. 'But you know we didn't do it.'

'Well, I must admit it seems unlikely,' said Henry, scratching his head with his pencil. 'But could I *say* you're still suspects so you have to stay,' replied her brother with a mischievous twinkle in his eye. He let out a dramatic sigh. 'But I can't think of any reason why either of you would want Chapman dead…'

'Quite right too,' said Clara huffily.

'… so I *suppose* it's all right for you to leave,' concluded Henry. 'For now. Don't leave town, and all that. And make sure you save me the crispiest roast spuds, all right? They're my favourite.'

Clara bobbed up on to the balls of her feet and planted a kiss on Henry's cheek. 'We will, darling, don't you worry.'

***

'You know, I feel pretty rotten about leaving Henry there like that,' said Clara, shovelling another forkful of goose, batter pudding, and roast potatoes into her mouth.

They were eating at the scrubbed pine table in the kitchen, a pristine white tablecloth spread over it at Debra's insistence, because it *was* Christmas after all. The dining table in the living room had been folded away hours ago to allow for party games and dancing.

Through the ajar door, Lucas could hear Tommy - Clara's friend and co-worker, Lucas' allegedly former love rival, and the latest of Mrs Jenkin's ever-increasing adopted family - playing Charades with enthusiasm and thoroughly charming the guests who'd piled into Henry and Debra's small house.

Despite their fraught history, and not entirely comfortable present, Lucas couldn't begrudge Tommy for enjoying Christmas with a loving family around him for the first time since he was a small child.

But still, he thought, as another burst of cheer erupted from the other room, Tommy's laughter the loudest and most irritating to Lucas' ears. *He could at least keep it down a bit. Doesn't he know we're trying to have a perfectly civil conversation about murder?*

'I see you're thoroughly devastated at

having abandoned your brother,' said Lucas, turning back to more important matters, like spearing a small, perfectly crisp roast potato with his fork and using it to mop up gravy. 'Can't say I am, though. No one made him become a police officer.'

'Only his sense of civic duty and wanting to serve the community he loves, and all that,' said Clara, eyeing Lucas' table manners with despair. 'He's proud to help keep people safe.'

'That's all very noble, of course,' replied Lucas, ignoring another cheer from the living room. 'But he knew what the job involved when he signed up for it.'

'He never expected a murder on Christmas Day though.'

'Murderers don't take a break for Christmas, do they?'

'Well they should,' said Clara decisively, stealing Lucas' tankard and taking a sip of Henry's home-brewed ale. 'Don't they know people have a family and a home?'

'Probably,' said Lucas, debating whether he wanted that last Brussel sprout or not. 'Maybe they thought it's a good time of year for killing someone, because the cops won't want to spend Christmas Day investigating a murder when there's other things they'd rather be doing.'

Clara's fork slipped from her fingers, landing on her plate with a clatter and splashing gravy on the tablecloth.

'Do you suppose that's what happened?' she said, dabbing the spillage with the side of her hand. 'Do you think Debbie will notice?' she added, looking through the living room door guiltily.

'I don't know,' said Lucas, frowning at her. 'Not about Debbie, I meant about the murderer choosing Christmas to do the deed. No, Debbie will definitely notice that.'

Clara groaned and scrubbed a little harder at the cloth.

Lucas ran his thumb over a stray drip of gravy on the rim of his plate and licked it thoughtfully. The suggestion hadn't been entirely serious, but now he thought about it, why not? Why not choose Christmas for murder?

'It could just be that Chapman got under someone's skin and did something to tip them over the edge, though,' he said aloud, not wanting to fuel Clara's overactive imagination. 'He sounds like a pretty unsavoury character, you must admit.'

'Well yes,' said Clara, an attractive rose-pink hue appearing on her cheeks. 'He was flirting shamelessly with all the girls the whole night.'

'Was he?' asked Lucas indistinctly, having just pulled another lump of perfectly cooked goose off the remains of the bird. 'Even you?'

'Yes, *even me*,' said Clara indignantly, turning a far less charming shade of angry red. 'Why not me? Is it so surprising? Why *shouldn't* he flirt with me? Am I so, so *un-flirtable* with?'

Lucas swallowed hastily, coughing a little as he did so. 'I didn't mean it like that, darling,' he said, reaching across the table for her hand, which was pulled away. 'I'm sorry. You're very, uh, flirtable with, really you are. I just hadn't noticed Chapman flirting with you, that's all.'

Tommy, however... he added silently, but chose not to prod that particular wasp's nest again. Not today. It really wasn't worth the hassle.

'Well, you weren't noticing much of anything by your third drink,' replied Clara grumpily, though she placed her hand in his so Lucas supposed he hadn't upset her too much. 'Very unprofessional, considering we were supposed to be working.'

'Er, quite,' said Lucas, wondering what else he'd missed in the blur of the previous evening. 'I just meant I thought he'd, um, have his sights set on a bird with money, that's all. It wasn't anything against you, I swear. Chapman just seems the type to chase a bank balance over personality.'

Not that Lucas had a clue about that, or anything else for that matter, but it might just get him off the hook.

'He did rather, didn't he?', said Clara, settling back to her meal again as another burst of laughter drifted through from the next room. 'Perhaps that's what got him bumped off? Perhaps he'd been running some scheme or other.'

'That's assuming he was the intended victim,' said Lucas. 'He could have picked up someone's glass and drank the poison accidentally.'

'Urgh, what a horrible thought,' said Clara, shuddering and laying her cutlery down again. 'It could have been any of us who could have died.' She shuddered and rubbed her arms. 'I'd much rather Chapman was the target - though of course, I wouldn't wish anyone dead.'

'We'll have to see what Henry says when he gets here,' said Lucas, picking up his tankard of ale, sure it was much heavier the last time he'd held it. 'How much of this did you have?'

'Henry won't mind you having a second.'

'Or a first,' grumbled Lucas.

As though mention of his name summoned him, Henry arrived at that very moment, knocking the snow off his boots with enough vigour that even Lucas and Clara on the other side of the house could hear it. They got to the kitchen door in time to see the host of the party welcomed home with cheers and festive greetings, which were returned happily enough, although Henry looked more tired than usual.

He swept his young son into his arms to give him a big squeeze, before handing the child to Debra and kissing her hello.

'Merry Christmas, everyone,' said Henry cheerfully, stripping off his overcoat and hanging it on a peg in the hallway. 'I'll change into something less formal and join you in a minute.

'Excellent,' said Clara to Lucas as they sat back down to finish their dinner. 'We can question him all about what's been going on when he gets back.'

'Let the man have a *little* fun,' said Lucas. 'I think he's earned it, don't you?'

'Oh, all right,' sighed Clara. 'We'll question him later.' She brightened. 'In fact, that's even better. When he's had a couple of drinks, he'll be all the more likely to tell us everything. I'll keep his glass topped up.'

'Yes dear,' said Lucas with a smile, knowing Henry would tell them everything even without a drop of alcohol. 'I'm sure you're right.'

***

After gifts had been exchanged and the house emptied of guests, with most of them returning to Mrs Jenkins' tiny terrace where they would be scattered throughout the house to sleep on an assortment of makeshift beds, Clara sat in Lucas' lap as they chatted with Henry in front of the fire. Debra was putting baby Ezra to bed, and was under strict instructions from her husband to have a lie down herself after putting on a magnificent show for Christmas Day.

After all, unbeknownst to his two remaining guests – although they hardly counted as such – he'd volunteered the three of them for cleaning up duties.

'So,' said Clara, arms draped around Lucas' neck, his wrapped around her waist. 'What happened up at the big house?'

Henry put on his best stern-older-brother face, though this was rather compromised by the sherry whizzing around his bloodstream. He'd noticed Clara surreptitiously keeping his glass topped up all evening, of course. She'd never been any good at getting things past him, but it was rather adorable that she tried - and it saved Henry the task of refilling his glass himself. He guessed she wanted to quiz him on the day's events, and it was rather sweet that she thought his tongue could be loosened by drink.

He'd intended to share the news anyway, but he wouldn't spoil her fun by saying so.

No, it wasn't often his path took him to somewhere as fancy as Castlebury Manor, and it was rather heartening to learn that it wasn't just the common man in the street capable of wickedness.

And the denizens of Castlebury Magna didn't stop to murder too often, so a murder at the manor was doubly interesting for everyone.

'Well,' he said, kicking his feet up on to a footstool and examining the sweet, honey-coloured liquid in his glass. 'As you might expect, none of the other guests were keen on opening up. Not surprising, they must realise one of them did it. However, no one wanted to say anything bad about Chapman, just in case doing so moved them to the top of a very short list.' His eyes twinkled, delighting in hooking his audience with the tale. 'But of course, it didn't take long to scratch the surface and reveal the wickedness beneath.'

Clara gasped with gleeful anticipation, but Lucas laid his head against the side of the threadbare and exceedingly comfortable wingback chair.

'Oi, Rathbone,' called Henry, lobbing a stray piece of popcorn at him. 'Wakey, wakey. I'm telling you something vitally important about your latest dead chum.'

'Huh,' replied Lucas blearily, twitching awake. He rubbed his eyes and groaned. 'Cut a chap a little slack, won't you?'

'No,' replied Henry. 'You want to interfere in the case -'

'I do not,' protested Lucas. 'That's your sister's idea.'

'It doesn't matter whose idea it was, you both went along with it,' said Henry, arching a disapproving eyebrow. 'Anyway, *as* I was saying,' he continued, ignoring the grumbling from Lucas. 'You want to know what was going on, so I'm telling you.'

Clara snuggled up to Lucas a little more and waited eagerly, as Lucas rested his head on her shoulder and battled drowsiness.

Henry frowned. Even months after discovering his little sister had fallen head over heels for the one chap Henry trusted her with, and apparently the feeling was mutual, it still seemed odd to see them together like that.

'You know everything you told me?' said Henry, deciding to put the thought out of his head for now. 'As far as I can tell, it was pretty accurate - though of course no one wanted to admit Chapman was an all-round rotter. Then again, everyone at that party has their own secrets.'

'We were there too,' Clara reminded him. '*We* don't have any secrets.'

'And if we did, we wouldn't be sharing them with you,' murmured Lucas.

'Hmm,' said Henry, not liking the sound of that. 'The point is, I think I can add to Chapman's knowledge. For a start, I discovered why this Shank chap had cooled off on Her Ladyship.'

He paused for dramatic effect, though this was lost on Lucas who began to snore gently.

Clara nudged him with her elbow and he regained what was likely a temporary consciousness.

'Well?' said Clara excitedly. 'Tell us, already!'

'Let a chap have his moment in the sun, won't you?' said Henry peevishly. 'Shank is stony broke and up to his eyeballs in debt. That's why he's been avoiding Lady Gaylesbury. He's frightfully ashamed to admit it.'

'But I thought he made a packet with his quack remedies,' said Lucas, rubbing his eyes and yawning.

'Not quack, according to the man himself – than again, he would say that, wouldn't he? – but he lost it all and then some on the gee gees,' said Henry. 'Doesn't want Her Ladyship to know, so he's been avoiding her. Worried she'll ditch him as soon as she finds out, and he does *so* like the idea of living in the big house.' Henry chuckled. 'Just goes to show you can have all the outer trappings of wealth, but it can be all owed to someone else.'

'Shank has gambling debts,' mused Clara. 'I wonder who he owed money to?'

'Take a guess,' said Henry.

'Chapman?'

Henry tapped the side of his nose and nodded. 'Got it in one.'

'But Chapman didn't mention that,' protested Lucas. 'I'd have told you if he did.'

'Maybe he didn't think of it,' said Henry with a shrug. 'He doesn't sound like the most straightforward-thinking man on the planet.'

'True,' agreed Lucas, yawning.

'All right, so Shank owed Chapman money,' said Clara. 'And presumably he was worried Chapman would tell Bunty. That's a motive right there. Not to mention Chapman slept with Bunty, so if Shank found out he could have killed Chapman for revenge.' She beamed proudly. 'Therefore, I assume the doctor is top of your list of suspects?'

'Top, but sharing the honour with a few others,' said Henry, shaking his head. 'Chapman isn't as squeaky clean as he'd like to make out.'

'People don't get more truthful just because they've died, you know,' said Lucas moodily, obviously taking this observation as a slight on his honesty or usefulness or some such nonsense. 'I can only tell you what they've told me, you know.'

'I know, and I'm grateful for what you do tell me,' said Henry soothingly. 'Do you know how much easier it makes my life? Well, apart from the difficult questions about how I came by the information, but I just tell Jones it's a policeman's hunch and leave it at that.'

'Why didn't you think of that?' said Clara, turning to Lucas. 'See, you could have joined Henry in the force after all.'

'Unfortunately, Jones reckons I'm after his job,' said Henry, defending his friend's career choice, if indeed it could be called a career. Or a choice, for that matter. 'But being a Detective Inspector isn't for me. I like the quiet life of a country copper. I'd absolutely loathe all the paperwork and meetings the poor chap has to deal with. And he's just an old D.I. put out to pasture in the quietest station they could find.' Henry gave a wry smile. 'Though I must say, murder isn't very quiet at all.'

'That's all well and good,' put in Clara, losing patience with this detour at last. 'But who else is on your list?'

'Lady Gaylesbury, of course,' said Henry, returning to the task at hand. 'If her affair with the Chapman was public knowledge, her reputation would be ruined.'

'I doubt she'd care,' said Lucas, shifting uncomfortably. 'It was pretty clear they were the kind of people who relished a little scandal.'

'Not to mention she tried to take you upstairs,' said Clara cheerfully, pecking Lucas on his rapidly blushing cheek. 'Don't worry, old thing, I'd have kept you safe from her.'

'I should think you would,' said Henry with a chuckle, imagining his sister in an all-out battle with the formidable Lady Gaylesbury over Lucas. Henry knew where he'd be putting his money. 'Nonetheless, it's worth considering when thinking about suspects – not to mention her supposed flirtation with the doctor.' Henry shook his head. 'How he deserves the title is beyond me, messing about with herbs and plants...'

'*Supposed* flirtation?' asked Lucas. 'I thought it was known fact?'

'I couldn't ask outright,' said Henry. 'But nothing was mentioned by any of the guests. Either it fizzled out or it never happened in the first place.'

'Interesting, said Lucas thoughtfully. 'Perhaps I need to talk to Chapman again. He seemed to know about it, after all.'

'So you've only got two suspects?' said Clara.

'Give me a chance, girl,' said Henry. 'Gloria Hawkes is a suspect for much the same reason as Bunty – that is, she was clearly hoping to regain Lord Cassiobury's affections and was scared stiff about him finding out about her fling with Chapman. Again, I couldn't ask outright – having more information than you're supposed to is jolly hard work – but when I asked about her relationship with the deceased, she got frightfully shifty. Pale and pink by turns and didn't quite meet my eye, you know how it goes.' Henry grinned and finished his latest sherry. 'Of course, I played the dumb copper card and pretended not to notice the signs, but nothing gets past Henry Jenkins.'

Clara muttered something that sounded like *"I don't know about that."* Lucas turned scarlet and shushed her, worried eyes darting to Henry and then away again.

Henry decided not to ask questions in case he didn't like the answers.

No, he'd *certainly* not like the answers.

'Then there's Sylvia Pettigrew,' continued Henry, a little more loudly than strictly necessary.

'Why would Sylvia have it in for Chapman?' asked Clara, straightening her face.

No, Henry definitely didn't want to know what *that* was about. Ignorance was bliss, and about Clara's relationship with Lucas, Henry long ago chose the blissful path for all their sakes.

'She was Chapman's girl before she took up with Lord Cassiobury,' replied Henry. 'What if Chapman knew something about her that he was threatening to make public if she didn't go back to him?'

'He didn't mention anything,' said Lucas, a little peevishly. 'I'd have told you if he did.'

Ah, Lucas, thought Henry, smiling to himself. *You don't want to help, but you can't stand not being helpful either. No wonder you get headaches with thinking as scrambled as that.*

'He wouldn't have done, would he darling? said Clara soothingly, toying with Lucas' hair. 'He'd hardly admit to a blackmail scheme when he's trying to convince you to help him, is he?'

'But the way she treated him it wouldn't surprise me if he'd raked up something unsavoury from her past to spite her,' said Henry. 'Whether he mentioned it to you or not.'

'I thought that's what his fling with Glo was about,' said Clara, turning back to her brother. 'Poor Glo isn't exactly pleased with herself though, which I suppose also gives her motive to kill off Chappers.'

'True,' said Henry. 'Perhaps she had hopes of replacing her lost love with a new one quite swiftly, and Chapman turned her down.'

'I don't think so,' said Clara. 'The silly girl rather hopes "dear Jono" will ditch Syl and take her back. Personally, I'd not *want* him back after that, not even if he promised me every star in heaven by way of apology - but each to their own, I suppose.'

'Speaking of Lord Cassiobury,' said Henry. 'He's got ample motive, given all the partner swapping and the fact Chapman had a drunken fling with Lord Cassiobury's aunt. Who's to say that Chapman wasn't trying to work his way into her affection and be her next husband? That's put the brakes on any inheritance that might be due to the nephew.'

'Oh Henry, do *try* to be sensible,' said Clara. 'Bunty wouldn't take up with someone so much younger than she is.'

'She might,' said Lucas darkly. 'She tried with me, didn't she?'

'Well yes, but that was just a bit of fun on her part,' replied Clara, apparently unconcerned by Lucas' attractiveness to much older women. 'That's different to getting married, isn't it?'

Lucas lapsed into discontented grumbling, and Clara added, 'Besides, she couldn't very well marry Chappers without his consent, could she? And I can't imagine *him* enjoying being married to someone almost twice his age.'

'That just means they might not be married for very long,' argued Lucas. 'Marriage is only "'til death," after all, and she's not getting any younger.'

'None of us are, my love,' said Clara. 'And why would Chapman want to marry her, anyway? He's a good-looking enough chap to take his pick of girls. Well, he was, anyway.'

'I might know the answer to that,' said Henry. 'The late Sir Samuel made sure his wife was very well provided for. *Very* well provided for. No children from the marriage to contest her will either, so any new husband of hers would be in line for quite the windfall on her inevitable, and hopefully unhastened, demise.'

'Really Henry, that's too much of a stretch,' said Clara.

'I don't think so, sister dear,' said Henry, steepling his fingers and peering over the top. 'In fact, it rather gives motives to both Her Ladyship and your friend Miss Hawkes. Lady Gaylesbury may have discovered Chapman's ploy and decided she couldn't bare the shame of it being discovered, and I can't imagine Miss Hawkes being too pleased about being rejected a second time.'

Clara bit her lip sullenly, a tell-tale sign Henry rarely saw, as it meant he'd won the argument.

'Of course,' he said, deciding to drive the point home just a little further, for novelty's sake if nothing else. 'That's just the dirty laundry we know about. A history like theirs? I'd be very surprised if there weren't more skeletons in their closets.'

'So what you're saying,' said Clara. 'Is that of all the people at the party last night, Lucas and I are the only two without a motive?'

'Well, I'm sure I could think of some for you two as well,' said Henry, stretching. He gave her a mischievous smile, enjoying having the upper hand. 'Unwelcome attentions for you, and jealousy for Lucas. But,' he said, raising a hand against their objections. 'But I know you both well enough to know you'd never be daft enough to do something like that.'

'I should think so too,' said Clara, snuggling up to Lucas. 'Besides, we were home by one. Bunty said we could stay if we wanted, but seeing as we'd got a rather jolly family Christmas planned, she very kindly sent us home in the Rolls Royce.'

'Did she?' said Lucas. 'I don't remember that.'

'Yes dear, but you don't remember much about last night,' said Clara, patting his cheek affectionately. 'My point is, Chapman died after that, didn't he? So we couldn't have done it.'

'I'm afraid that wouldn't get you off the hook either,' said Henry. 'Looks like poison – they're still trying to determine the exact one, the symptoms could apply to a few – and if it's something slow acting it could have been administered hours before death.'

Clara shuddered and folded herself more into Lucas' arms, and he pulled her in tight.

For all he'd disapproved Lucas taking up with Clara – at least to start with - Henry knew he'd never let anything bad happen to her. If he had to trust his little sister to anyone, and he supposed it was inevitable at some point, she could have picked a lot worse than Lucas.

Like that cad Tommy, for instance. Horrible little man, thinks he can charm his way through life. Even worse, he appeared to be right.

No, Lucas wasn't *so* bad, really. Not considering the alternatives.

Not that Henry would ever admit as much to either Clara or Lucas, as that'd mean he'd lose his disapproving older brother rights, but it put Henry's mind at ease a little.

'Let's stop talking shop now,' said Henry as footsteps descended the stairs. 'Our Debbie is coming back, and I don't want to upset her by talking about death and all that.'

***

As Henry and Debra disappeared into the kitchen, Lucas settled back in his chair and closed his eyes. He was cosy in front of the fire, full of delicious food, and snuggled up with the woman he loved.

All in all, he couldn't ask for anything more.

Well, perhaps for some old and wealthy distant relative to die and leave him a fortune, but he hadn't got any of those, so he'd have to be content with the intangible riches of life for a little while longer.

Yes, when it comes to intangible riches, I'm a very well-off fellow indeed, thought Lucas happily. *Some tangible riches would be nice too, of course, but things could be a lot worse.*

But of course, his contented contemplation couldn't last long.

'Now Henry's gone,' said Clara, looking over her shoulder to make sure that really was the case. 'Who do you think did it?'

'I agree with Henry,' said Lucas, without opening his eyes. 'Let's put the grim realities of life and death out of our minds and enjoy the last few hours of Christmas.'

'Who's not enjoying themselves?' retorted Clara, prodding him gently until he opened a sleepy eye. 'I always enjoy a good mystery, and this one is quite mysterious.'

'Yes, but you're morbid,' said Lucas. She was terribly pretty when something sparked her interest – which was often – and he couldn't resist stealing a kiss from her scarlet-stained lips whilst they were alone for the first time in hours. 'Some of us like our Christmas *without* any murder, thank you very much.'

'Oh, all right,' grumbled Clara, kissing him again. 'But we should go back to the manor in the morning and have another snoop.'

'Why?' asked Lucas, seeing the prospect of a delightfully languid Boxing Day fade before his eyes. 'Unless Henry thinks we were involved somehow, which obviously he doesn't because we weren't, we're well out of it.' Lucas closed his eyes again, determined not to be railroaded into once again sticking their noses where they didn't belong. 'He'll figure out whodunnit - without our help, I might add - and we can carry on as normal.'

Checking to ensure Henry was still out of earshot, Clara whispered, 'Look, not wanting to cast doubt on Henry's ability at digging the dirt, but folks don't talk to coppers like they do normal people, do they? Especially not people like that. They only really talk to their own kind.'

'But we're not people "their kind",' argued Lucas, giving up on the prospect of a doze. 'We're commoners, and lowly newspaper reporters to boot. Why would they talk to us?'

'We knew the victim,' said Clara. 'Albeit briefly. Very briefly, I suppose. We met him, at least, and we were at the party. Plus we were all getting on awfully well. I must say I rather like Glo, for all her snivelling over that pretty boy Jonny. He sounds like a complete waste of space to me - but what do I know? Maybe he's loaded, despite Bunty claiming he spends money like water.'

'No, I got the impression he was rather hard up,' said Lucas. 'Kept mentioning how he was at his aunt's beck and call but he'd rather be in London, that sort of thing. And I noticed a stain on his shirt sleeve.'

Clara pointed to a glob of gravy marring Lucas' own shirt cuff.

'I meant an *old* stain on his shirt sleeve,' said Lucas, rubbing the gravy mark on his trouser leg. 'No one with any amount of money would wear an old, stained shirt to a Christmas shindig, would they?'

'I suppose not,' said Clara, though she didn't seem convinced with Lucas' expert logic, which was rather vexing. 'Anyway, I think the crux of this matter lies in this business with Jonny and Sylvia, and Chappers and Gloria. Have you ever heard of such a thing?'

'No,' said Lucas. 'And I wish that were still the case.'

'Well it's perfectly scandalous, if you ask

me,' said Clara, clearly enjoying the misfortune of others. 'And it wouldn't surprise me at all if it wasn't one of the other three who did the poor chap in.'

'Whatever happened, Henry will figure it out,' said Lucas firmly, not keen on getting ravelled up in an investigation. Especially not at Christmas, but he wasn't exactly keen any other day of the year either.

'Aren't you even a little bit curious?' said Clara. 'After all, we were there when the deed was done. Doesn't that make it more interesting?'

'No,' replied Lucas. 'Quite the opposite, in fact. And if, by some miracle, Chapman is right and he wasn't the intended victim, anyone could have drunk the poisoned cup, or ate the poisoned vol-au-vent, or whatever it was.'

Clara shuddered. 'Don't remind me,' she said. 'Urgh, what a truly horrible thought.'

As she snuggled up to him again, Lucas felt rather pleased with himself. He'd expected her to insist on finding out what happened, and so was pleased that his cunning ploy had worked.

He settled back in the chair, glad of this Christmas miracle.

'Well, I'm going back up to the manor, even if you're not,' declared Clara after a moment's thought, starting to stand up.

'But there's a murderer in that house,'

exclaimed Lucas, his eyes snapping open. He pulled her back into his lap and tried not to give in to the despair settling on him like falling snow.

I should have known better, he thought glumly. *Christmas miracles stand no chance against Miss Clara Jenkins when she can smell adventure.*

'There was a murderer in the house last night as well,' she replied. 'We didn't die then.'

'Yes, but now we *know* there's a murderer there, and *they* know we know there's a murderer there,' reasoned Lucas, wrapping his arms around her in a loving embrace that definitely wasn't designed to stop her from rushing directly into danger. 'What if they realise we're there to snoop, or we discover something incriminating, and they decide to get rid of us as well?'

'That's a risk we'll have to take,' said Clara.

'But what about the whole, "We could have been accidentally poisoned" thing?' protested Lucas. 'I'd have thought you wouldn't have wanted to go back after that.'

'Oh Lucas, don't you know me at all?' she said teasingly, kissing his forehead. 'It just makes me more determined to find out what did it.'

Lucas groaned. *It wouldn't, wouldn't it?* he thought. *I should have realised.*

'Besides,' continued Clara, rubbing the lip

print off his skin. 'Bunty invited you to the party because you work at the Gazette. She knows where you work and how to find you.'

Lucas thought a string of words that'd earn him a clip round the ear if his mother discovered he knew them.

'And I'm sure she wouldn't think twice about telling anyone who asked which paper you were from, if they asked,' said Clara. 'Assuming everyone doesn't know already, of course.'

Lucas closed his eyes again, but this time in despair.

'And if they decided to bump you off as well,' said Clara, sounding a little too triumphant for Lucas' liking. 'That's where they'd go, right? So we may as well help Henry discover who did for poor Chappers as quickly as possible, so they can get the rogue locked up and we can stop looking over our shoulders.'

As much as he hated the idea, there was a certain logic in her words.

A bit twisted, perhaps, but logic nonetheless.

Besides, she'd not stop going on about it until she got what she wanted.

'I suppose you're right,' he said with a resigned sigh.

'Naturally,' she said, dropping a light kiss on to the end of his nose and making it tingle. She went to stand up again and he pulled her back down.

'But we can't do anything about it now,' he said firmly, giving her a stern look. Judging by her smirk it wasn't working, but he ploughed on regardless. 'It's far too late to go gallivanting about the countryside. It's pitch black out there, and the snow must be up to our knees by now. I am not trudging back up to the manor at –' he craned his neck to look at his watch – 'twenty past nine at night. On any day, let alone Christmas Day.'

'Of course not,' she said, triumph dancing in her eyes. 'But first thing in the morning we'll get our walking boots on and head up there, all right?'

'All right,' said Lucas, somewhat grudgingly. The heat from the fire was making him sleepy again, though it could also have had something to do with the food and alcohol. He wasn't in any mood to argue. Clara could have demanded a million and one things from him at that point, and he'd likely agree to them all.

'Excellent,' declared Clara, wiggling off his lap. 'Now, I don't know about you, but I'm hungry. Fancy some more Christmas pud?'

***

Lucas woke up, though he quickly decided he shouldn't have bothered.

Every muscle ached and every joint

creaked. His neck was agony and crunched unpleasantly with each tiny movement. He blearily looked around in the darkness, trying to work out where exactly he was.

At least he wasn't at the office this time, and Henry's wing-backed chair was more comfortable than floorboards - though not after sleeping in it for hours on end. The fire smouldered in the grate, giving a little light to see by. Someone had pulled a heavy woollen blanket over him, which spilled to the floor as he sat up and looked around as his eyes adapted to the gloom.

Clara snored gently on the sofa, tucked under another blanket and looking so adorably peaceful that Lucas couldn't help but smile. He rubbed his eyes and groped around in the near darkness until he found the stub of candle in a stick on the mantlepiece. He lit the wick with the dying embers, lifted the light to the old clock on the mantlepiece, and groaned quietly.

Five twenty-five. Far too early for a body to be awake - but as he only had the chair to return to, going back to sleep wasn't an option he really wanted to take.

Tying the blanket around his shoulders, he shuffled to the kitchen in search of a cup of tea. Lord knew he needed something to kick start his brain, but after a little deliberation decided it'd be a waste to steal his host's coal for a lonely pot of tea, and settled on a tooth-achingly cold glass of water instead.

He drained it dry, which was fortunate as seconds later a voice with an oddly echoey quality spoke to him from the shadows.

'Oh good,' it said. 'You're finally awake.'

Lucas caught the glass before it shattered on the terracotta tiles.

'Bloody hell, man,' he exclaimed in a hoarse whisper, his heart thudding uncomfortably as he turned to face the ghost of Chapman. He put the miraculously unbroken glass on the table with a shaking hand. 'Are you trying to give me a heart attack?'

'No,' replied Chapman, peering around the humble kitchen with interest. 'I was bored after that policeman chappie had finished interviewing everyone yesterday, so I thought I'd follow him home. It was far too gloomy watching everyone having fun here, so I headed back to the big house. They were sombre, poor things, but still trying to make the best of it. It was rather heartening watching them sit at the table and tell those feeble cracker jokes.' The ghost smiled wistfully at the recollection. 'They did their best to be cheerful, and I'm glad. I wouldn't want them to lose heart simply because mine stopped beating.'

'But why are you here now?' pressed Lucas, his own heart almost back to its normal rate.

'I wanted to talk to you again, of course,'

said Chapman, snapping out of his dreamy reminiscences. 'Didn't know you'd still be here, I just figured you were friends with Constable Jenkins and he'd eventually lead me to you. What a stroke of luck finding you in his house! Of course,' he said, adopting a humble attitude. 'I figured you'd not thank me for interrupting your festivities a second time, so just thought I'd, you know, stick around a bit and talk to you tomorrow. Today, rather.'

'Hmm,' said Lucas, eyeing the spirit with suspicion. 'What do you want to talk about?'

'Oh, I don't know,' said the ghost. 'Anything, really. It's frightfully dull being dead, you know.'

'So I'm told,' said Lucas. 'But aren't there other ghosts at the manor you can talk to? I can't imagine an old place like that not having any other spirits lingering about the place.'

'Of course there are,' said Chapman. 'But they're all rather gloomy. I'm in the mood for cheering up, not dealing with screaming parlour maids or Civil War soldiers groaning in agony, and all that business. Urgh. I must say the murdered Tudor gent was good company for a while, despite the distressing stain on his whatsit, thingy, you know…'

Lucas hadn't a clue, and pulled the blanket a little tighter around his shoulders.

Perhaps if I don't answer, he'll forget what he's saying and drift off somewhere, thought Lucas, struggling to focus. *Not that it's likely, but it'd be nice. A sort of extra Christmas gift, perhaps.*

Chapman clicked his translucent fingers. 'Doublet, that's what it's called. Big bloodstain on his doublet, right where his heart was, poor chappie. Never did work out what happened there, all that old-timey speech made my head ache something rotten.'

I know the feeling, thought Lucas uncharitably, wishing he'd remembered to put slippers on. *Not that I planned on being in the kitchen more than a few minutes,* he thought. *That'll teach me. Always be prepared for ghosts, because the buggers will show up whenever they damn well feel like it.*

'And the chappie who ended up in the priest hole a bit too long went on and on with his moralizing,' continued Chapman, who apparently was another fellow who didn't need two people to have a conversation. 'I don't want to hear that sort of thing,' he said. 'Dashed lot I can do about it now, even if I did. And, thinks I, if he's as saintly as he claims, what's he still doing here? That's what I want to know.'

Urgh, has he stopped talking yet? thought Lucas, his head starting its familiar ache. *I thought he was here for a reason.*

The ghost settled himself on, and slightly through, the kitchen table. 'Dull, dull, dull, the whole bally lot of them. Can't blame a chap for wanting to get out of there, can you?'

Lucas groaned and rubbed his eyes, wondering where all the fur on his tongue had come from. It was far, *far* too early in the morning for this, and was just about to tell the dead but sadly not quite departed Chapman to scram, when the ghost said, 'Of course, I know who did it.'

'What?' cried Lucas, a little too loudly. Lowering his voice, he asked, 'Who? How? Why?'

'Well, it was that rotter Shank, of course,' declared the ghost. 'I expect he found out about me and Bun – it was just a one-time thing, and though I know *you* understand, not everyone does – and that was the final straw for the chap.' Chapman gave Lucas a knowing look. 'Never been totally stable that one, if you want my opinion.'

'But how do you know it was him?' pressed Lucas, who couldn't care less what Chapman thought about anything, unless it'd get rid of the blighter a bit sooner.

'I was poisoned with mistletoe,' said the ghost matter-of-factly. 'I heard the whatsit, coroner bloke telling your pal's boss. That D.I. Jones is a top bloke, you know, very fast moving, especially as it was Christmas day.'

'Uh, sure,' said Lucas, who was still stunned at this assessment of D.I. Jones, who had been born intolerable and grouchy, as far as Lucas could tell.

'What rotten luck,' sighed the ghost. 'Getting murdered at Christmas. And with something that's usually so festive.'

'Are they sure it's mistletoe?' said Lucas, getting back to the problem in hand - although Chapman was technically sat in the table.

'Oh yes, quite sure,' said Chapman with a careless wave of his transparent hand. 'They checked my glass and everything. The one next to my body, I must have had it in my hand when... Anyway, he said something about extra tests and all that, but this coroner chappie sounded fairly sure. He took his time getting to the manor, and wasn't very happy to be there - but then again, neither was I.'

Chapman laughed at his own joke, even if Lucas didn't.

'But my point is,' said the ghost. 'Who do we know that has an idea or two about plants?'

'Shank,' said Lucas, feeling this was a little too easy. Then again, he was overdue a Christmas miracle since Clara dashed his earlier hopes, so who knew? 'But surely anyone could find out about that?' he added, looking for the fly in the ointment.

'Probably,' said Chapman with a flippant wave of the hand. 'I dare say anyone could find out *anything*, if they really wanted to.'

There we go, thought Lucas with a gloomy sort of smugness. *I knew there'd be a problem somewhere.*

'But most folks wouldn't use something like that to do a chap in, would they?' continued Chapman. 'No, they'd stab him or bash him on the coconut or drop a spoon of rat poison in his whiskey or something. Nothing half so clever as using *mistletoe*.' He gave a half-shrug. 'I'd admire his ingenuity, if it hadn't resulted in such a horrible outcome for myself.'

'Well, at least that's the mystery solved nice and fast,' said Lucas, deciding not to query such an odd admiration.

'True, but I guess that means I'm here until justice is done,' said Chapman, a note of despondency creeping into his voice. 'At least, I've worked it out and I thought I'd, I don't know, fade away or something once I knew the truth.'

'Every ghost is different,' said Lucas, not really wanting to get into details at – good Lord, twenty to six in the morning. Was that all? 'You'll go when you go. Sorry I can't be more help.'

'Oh no, don't worry about that,' said Chapman. 'Bally good show you talking to me like this at all. I can't imagine everyone would want to have a nice little chat with a spooky old ghostie, what? And it'll be rather fun to see how all the detective stuff works in real life. I can't imagine it's a thing like it is in those murder mystery books. Do you read them?'

'Not if there's another option,' said Lucas.

'You should, they're frightfully good fun,' said the ghost. 'Try Agatha Christie, she writes the most wonderfully tricksy mysteries. I can never guess who the killer is - thankfully I seem to be better at it in real life. Or afterlife, I suppose.'

'I'll pass all the same, if you don't mind,' replied Lucas, who already had more "tricksy" mysteries to deal with than he ever wanted. 'Well, I suppose I'd better tell Henry you've got it all tied up in a bow. I'll do that after breakfast, though. He's like a bear with a sore head in the morning - at least until he's eaten something, so I'm certainly not disturbing him at,' – he checked the time again – 'quarter to six in the morning. It's far too early to think about mysteries and murder,' he added pointedly.

'I don't blame you, old chap,' said Chapman, missing the rebuke. 'And it's not like I'll get any more dead if you hold off for another few hours, is it?'

The spirit, still sat on the table, swung his legs and looked around the small kitchen as though he hadn't a care in the world. Lucas thought he'd had adapted to being a ghost rather well, all things considered.

Lucas and Chapman looked expectantly at each other for a few moments.

'Well?' said Lucas at last.

'Well what?'

'*Well*, are you just going to sit there all

day?'

'Oh.' The ghost looked somewhat flummoxed. 'I hadn't really thought about it. I can if you want, I suppose. It's not like I'm needed anywhere else.'

'No, that's all right,' said Lucas hurriedly. 'Why don't you, er, go back up to the hall and, um, see if you can find out any more evidence about how Shank is the murderer. Yes, that's the thing. Like someone in one of those detective novels.'

'Good thinking that man, good thinking,' said Chappers, nodding agreeably. 'I'll hop to it right away. Always fancied doing a bit of sleuthing.' He gave a mock salute, and stepped through the bolted kitchen door.

Lucas breathed a sigh of relief and looked at the stove.

'Oh, hang it all, I deserve a cup of tea after all that,' he said, and started building the fire up.

***

Henry thanked Lucas for the information from Chapman, but announced there was no way he was missing another moment of festive time with his family, thank you very much. He had no intention of doing any form of work unless specifically called on by Jones, and planned on putting the whole sorry business out of his mind until it became unavoidable.

Words like "busman's holiday" and "leave well enough alone, can't you?" may also have passed his lips.

Lucas thought this was fair enough - a jolly good idea in fact - and suggested he and Clara do likewise. After all, what was one more day? Chapman wouldn't get any more dead, would he?

Clara didn't agree at all, and, after a short discussion, which Lucas inevitably lost, they were now within sight of Castlebury Manor with rosy, frost-stung cheeks and aching feet.

At least, Lucas' feet were aching. Clara and Tommy were bounding through the snow like it was nothing.

Tommy.

Another irritation Lucas could do without.

The permanently cheerful fellow had all but invited himself along when he heard how Clara and Lucas were planning on spending their day, which happened when Clara dropped in at her mother's house for a change of clothes. A simple task of a few minutes had turned into a morning's worth of unpleasantness for Lucas, who had been looking forward to a little time alone with Clara.

Oh, he understood Clara was terribly fond of the chap, and Lucas felt sorry for him because really, who deserved a childhood like that?

But sympathy and wanting to spend any time with him were very different things.

True, Tommy didn't ask outright to join them, instead saying he'd barely been to the country, and what a wonderful thing it must be to go for a walk over the hills in the pristine snow - not like that grubby London snow that fell through smog-filled air and was never truly white, not for a second - and generally made himself look as sad and helpless as possible, until Clara took pity and invited him to join them.

In the moment, Lucas hadn't minded too much.

But it wasn't the moment anymore, and Tommy's irrepressible joy at simple things like fox tracks in the snow was wearing Lucas' patience thin to the point of transparency.

Not to mention that it made talking to Clara about things of a ghostly nature more difficult. Although Tommy knew about Lucas' "gift" and had seen it in action once or twice, he made it all too clear he didn't think it was either real, or something to be proud of if, against all logic, Lucas really *could* speak to the dead.

On top of everything else he'd have to put up with today, Lucas couldn't stand Tommy sneering at something he hated so much about himself.

But thankfully, Tommy was easily distracted by the novelty of a snowy landscape and scampered off like an overgrown puppy, leaving Lucas and Clara with a little privacy to discuss the matter of the late Chapman.

'But why mistletoe?' said Clara, snow crunching underfoot as they trudged back up to the hall. 'A very festive way of killing someone, I'm sure, but not a terribly efficient poison, is it?'

'No idea,' said Lucas, huffing as he struggled to keep up with Clara. She bounded across snowdrifts as sure-footed as a mountain goat. Most irritating, particularly as the horrible damp patch on his knees bore testament to a tumble he'd taken earlier. 'But whatever makes mistletoe berries deadly was apparently in his cocktail glass, so what else could it be?'

'But isn't it rather difficult to kill someone with mistletoe?' said Clara, pausing to wait for Lucas. 'No end of children eat a berry or two every year. They're a bit poorly but it's not often they die.'

'Look, what do you want?' said Lucas grumpily, as his feet slid again. Clara caught his hand and prevented him from taking another fall. Making sure Tommy was out of earshot, he added, 'I'm only telling you what the ghost said, and they rarely get anything right. I don't know any more than that, which is why we're out here freezing to death.'

'I'm not debating that, darling, I'm just saying it's a strange choice for killing someone,' she said, sneaking a kiss and bringing a smile to

Lucas' chilly lips. 'There must be easier ways of doing a chap in, that's all.'

'You have a point,' said Lucas, taking her mittened hand in his and continuing the trudge up the hill.

Tommy was quite far ahead of them by now, in his element having never spent a winter outside of London. Over his annoyingly golden curls he wore a scarlet hand-knitted hat with a blue pompom sat atop in a sprightly manner – a Christmas gift from Clara's mother - which made him visible from quite a distance. Despite being a couple of years older than Lucas, and several older than Clara, Tommy frolicked in the white drifts like a child, making detours to mark unspoilt snow or to examine the ever fascinating animal tracks, and marvelling at the pristine beauty of the scene.

If the chap hadn't tried to weasel his way into Clara's affections on several occasions, declared himself hopelessly in love with her at every opportunity, and generally been a scoundrel and a cad, the sight of such innocent, boundless joy would have warmed Lucas' heart.

But as it was, Lucas rather wished they'd left him back at Mrs Jenkins' house with the rest of the seasonal interlopers.

He could almost sympathise with people who killed at Christmas.

'Perhaps it wasn't planned,' he said as the idea struck him. 'And Shank just used something to hand that he knew would work? There was plenty of the stuff hanging all over the place, it wouldn't have been difficult to sneak some into Chapman's glass.'

'Maybe,' said Clara, grinning at Tommy making snow angels near the crest of the hill. 'In which case, something must have tipped him over the edge to act so quickly. I wonder what it was?'

'We can't find anything out from here,' said Lucas, wondering how many of his toes were still attached to his feet. He guessed maybe three. 'So let's hurry up and get inside. With a bit of luck they'll have a roaring fire going and I can thaw out a bit.'

'That's supposing it was Shank at all, of course,' said Clara thoughtfully. 'We can't rule anyone out at this stage.'

Lucas didn't like that. It sounded like this thing could go on for far longer than he'd hoped - although that happened quite a long time ago, so he supposed it was too late really.

Just in case the day could yet be salvaged, he asked, 'But how many people know mistletoe is poisonous?'

He hoped it mightn't be many people at all.

'Pretty much everyone, I expect,' said Clara, dashing Lucas' misplaced hopes into tiny pieces.

He groaned. 'I suppose you're right,' he

said, wishing she wasn't. 'Although I'd like to point out that I didn't know.'

'That's because you don't take an interest in the world around you.'

'But really,' said Lucas, ignoring this. 'Shouldn't we just leave it to the police? It is their job after all.'

'How much attention will Jones be paying?' said Clara. 'And what happens if someone else gets murdered in the meantime?'

'So what if they do?' said Lucas, with a charity as cold as the weather. 'We don't know them, nor are we ever likely to. I don't see what business it is of ours if someone decided to bump off the lot of them.'

'That's not the attitude, is it?' said Clara, puffing slightly as they struggled up the last stretch of slope leading to the hall.

Unfortunately for Lucas' mood, he could see Tommy already at the door. Lucas privately hoped he'd have got lost somewhere, or fallen into a ditch or something - but no such luck. Instead, the dratted man was jigging up and down on the spot as he waited for his companions, hands thrust deeply in his pockets. He was shrouded in a cloud of steam and snow clung to the back of his coat and trousers.

With a grim smile, Lucas wondered what sort of reception that would get Tommy - then remembered Tommy's angelically handsome face and easy charms made him welcome almost anywhere.

He suspected this would be doubly true for Bunty.

'And as for never knowing them,' continued Clara, cutting through Lucas' envious musings. 'Glo invited me to tea at the Ritz next time she's in London - though whether she remembers or not remains to be seen, she was a bit of a mess last night - and Sylvia asked us to dinner with her and Jonny some time. I was thinking some time in February, if that suits your hectic schedule.'

'You didn't tell me that,' said Lucas, aghast. 'You weren't making *friends* with them, were you? Don't do that, Clara, please. These people are way out of our circle.'

'Don't be ridiculous, darling,' she said cheerfully. 'No one bothers with the whole upper class, lower class nonsense since the War put all the nice young gentleman and riff-raff like us through the same mud-soaked hell. If you like someone you can be friends with them even if you're from different worlds, and that's that.'

Lucas lapsed into discontented grumbling for the rest of their trek, which was mercifully short. As he stood on the doorstep of Castlebury Manor for the third time in as many days, Lucas reflected on how on each occasion it was under severe duress.

The fact Tommy was like an excited puppy and, to be perfectly honest, there at all, merely soured Lucas' mood further.

The butler opened the door to the snow-dusted trio.

'Her Ladyship is not at home to visitors,' he said solemnly, looking down his beaky nose at them. Quite a trick, considering he was a several inches shorter than Lucas and Tommy, and barely taller than Clara.

It was quite impressive, in a way.

Annoying, offensive, and downright rude, but impressive, nonetheless.

'Bosh!' cried her ladyship from the top of the stairs, which she descended at an alarming rate. She pushed past the hateful butler and threw her arms around Clara.

'Oh Clara, sweetie, it's just all too, too terrible,' she cried, a noticeably more enthusiastic welcome than yesterday's hungover misery. 'And how good of you both to come and check on dear old Bunty.'

She released Clara, kissed the air next to her cheeks twice in the French fashion, and patted Lucas on the cheek in a disconcertingly motherly fashion. Tommy was introduced, whereupon he kissed Bunty's hand ingratiatingly and murmured sweet nothings about her beauty and charm, making the older lady blush. Tommy twinkled his ice blue eyes at her, and gave Lucas a wink when Her Ladyship wasn't looking.

'Easy,' he mouthed at Lucas, who

scowled at Tommy's back as he and Clara followed Bunty and her new favourite into the manor.

'Lewis, take their coats then fetch us some tea,' she commanded, releasing Tommy's arm at last.

The butler's expression was frostier than anything outside, but he stiffly bowed his head and dutifully held out his arm for their outer clothes.

'Darlings, you simply *must* come through to the Blue Drawing Room and let me tell you all about this *beastly* business,' cried Bunty, her voice edging on the hysterical, though Lucas suspected it was put on for effect. 'Really, it's just all too, *too* much.'

Lewis took the last of their coats and hats, holding them as though he expected to catch something from the slightly worn fabric, then pointedly looked at the cuffs of the interloper's trousers, which dripped melting snow on the pristine marble floor. He sniffed, before whisking their outdoor things away.

'Oh dear,' said Clara guiltily, looking at the water pooling around her boots. 'I hope it won't cause any damage.'

'It's stone, darling, it'll be fine,' said Bunty, pulling Clara's hand through the crook of her left arm, Tommy's through her right, and leading them towards a dimly lit corridor.

As he followed, Lucas debated what effect

the smattering of moth-eaten tapestries were having to prevent the chill infiltrating the room, and decided it was probably none whatsoever. Festive greenery decorated the tops of doorways and picture frames, delicate pearly mistletoe berries complementing the red fruit of the holly, both nestling in an abundance of waxy evergreen leaves.

It's hard to think something so pretty could be deadly, he thought. *I wonder how many of the things it'd take to do the deed. One? Three? A hundred?*

He followed them into the appropriately named Blue Drawing Room just in time to hear Bunty playfully scolding Clara.

'Now, you mustn't call me "Your Ladyship," you naughty thing,' she said, tapping Clara lightly on the wrist. 'It's Bunty to my friends, and I *do* hope we're friends.'

She took Clara by the hand and gave her a tired smile. 'It's so nice to have young people around the place, especially with no children of my own. Sam didn't have any children with his first wife either, and he was rather older than I when we married - over twenty years older in fact, and I was no spring chicken myself at that point,' she explained, steering Clara onto a large Georgian sofa. 'So sadly, the blessing of motherhood passed me by. But,' she added, beaming at her trio of guests. 'With so many young people like yourselves taking time to be kind to a silly old lady like myself, I hardly feel like I'm missing out. Come on, my dears, make yourselves comfortable.'

Lucas took a seat next to Clara as Tommy settled into the seat next to Bunty.

As Bunty chatted at her guests about the allegedly fascinating history of the Manor, they waited for what, to Lucas' mind, was the far more interesting topic of tea and cake.

He found his attention drifting to the magnificent surroundings. The Blue Drawing Room was large and filled with ornate Rococo furniture, exquisite paintings in the style of Stubbs and Gainsborough adorned every wall, and gilded sconces and mirror frames glittered in the winter sunlight streaming through double height windows and shimmering on the pale blue silk damask adorning the walls.

However, the wonders of the room were mere trifles compared to the magnificent view overlooking the slope leading up to the house, even if the persistent snowfall gave everything an unnatural yellowy off-white tone and shortened the view of the surrounding countryside.

Lucas noted glumly that the uneven scars of their approach were already softening thanks to the rapid snowfall, and a brisk wind was also taking the edge off the scuffed tracks with some enthusiasm. And there he was, thawing out nicely at last...

'But I'm sure you didn't walk all this way

for a lecture on Castlebury Manor,' said Bunty, reaching for the teapot, which must have arrived at some point whilst Lucas wasn't paying attention. 'I suppose you *really* want to hear about what the police have to say about dear Bertie's death. Gilbert Chapman, if you prefer,' she added, seeing the confusion on her guest's faces. 'We're a very informal bunch, really.'

'Oh yes, Clara had mentioned something about a little, uh, accident the other day,' said Tommy, receiving a teacup gratefully and dropping one, two – no, good grief, *three* cubes of sugar into the steaming liquid.

'It was no accident, my dear boy,' said Bunty, her voice wobbling as she handed tea to her other two guests. 'It was murder, plain and simple.'

'How awful,' murmured Tommy.

'Quite,' replied Bunty primly. 'And as much as I was fond of dear Bertie – I've known him since he was a mere babe in arms, you see, and we were terribly, *terribly* attached to each other –'

Lucas choked on his tea.

'I still use his childhood nickname from time to time,' continued Bunty, narrowing her eyes at Lucas. 'Some habits are hard to break, and he was as dear to me as Jonathon is.'

'I'm sure you'll miss him terribly,' said Clara, slapping Lucas on the back with more force than he considered necessary.

Bunty's eyes welled with tears. 'I shall,' she said, voice trembling dramatically. 'What a terrible tragedy. And in my own house, as well!'

Tommy leant across to pat her hand sympathetically, and she clung to him gratefully. 'You know, you look a lot like him,' she told the handsome young man.

Lucas almost managed to hide a snort of laughter, and blamed it on the previous tea-based incident.

'How did you know Chappers?' asked Clara, pressing the heel of her shoe surreptitiously on Lucas' toes, adding to the agony of thawing flesh.

'Well, as I'm sure you know,' said Bunty, filling her cup with a second round of steaming tea. 'Jonny – that is, Jonathon Bourbon-Busset, Lord Cassiobury of Fanshawegate Hall – is my nephew. The only one I had left after that frightful War.' She sighed heavily, looking much older than the moment before. 'My sister Octavia, God rest her, lost four of her five sons in the trenches. Four! They say it was the influenza that took her in the end, but I say it was a broken heart.'

Bunty turned to the occasional table at her elbow and picked up at a tortoiseshell framed photograph nestling amongst silver-framed depictions of herself in numerous theatrical costumes, with varying degrees of ridiculousness as these things often are.

'Jonny was the youngest, too young to enlist, thank God,' she explained, passing the photograph to Clara. 'That's him with his brothers when he was about three, I think. As you can see, there was quite a gap in ages - almost eight years between him and Paul, the next youngest. It was somewhat difficult for poor Octavia at the time, as I'm sure you can imagine, but at least it spared her from losing all her children in one fell swoop.'

'How terrible,' said Clara, with a little sniff. Lucas took her hand and she squeezed his fingers gratefully. 'Neither my nor Lucas' dads ever came back from the trenches either,' she continued, her voice thick with emotion. 'I can only imagine how awful it must have been to lose so many people she loved all at once.'

'It was terrible,' said Bunty, giving them both a sympathetic look. She turned to Tommy and said, 'I suppose you lost people in the War too? We all did.'

'Not me,' said Tommy with forced cheerfulness. 'But only because I had no one to lose. Poor little orphan boy, me. Went into a home when I was three years old.'

Bunty let out a small cry and pressed the back of her hand to her mouth. Tommy took her sympathies with overdone gratitude, and half winked at Lucas to show he knew exactly what he was doing.

Lucas could spot it a mile off too, but

Bunty didn't, and Clara was either equally oblivious or sitting by and letting it happen.

Oh well, thought Lucas. *Who am I to argue? I suppose I'll stop it if he gets out of hand. Bunty might be a murderer, but she doesn't deserve the full Tommy treatment.*

'My poor Jonathon is an orphan too,' said Bunty, who seemed to have a knack for turning the conversation back to herself. 'Of course, Jonny was nineteen or twenty when his father popped his clogs, although as it was drink that did for him in the end, perhaps I'm less sympathetic than I ought to be. Jonny spent a lot of time here with me and Sam after that, but Sir Samuel's heart finally gave out around three years ago – awful high blood pressure, suffered for simply ages with it - so now it's just me and dear Jonathon.'

'That's very sad,' said Tommy with sympathy Lucas didn't think was genuine.

'But have you never thought of remarrying?' said Clara, which Lucas thought would just give Tommy ideas. 'You're plenty young enough, and I dare say it must be lonely rattling around this old place on your own.'

Bunty smiled sadly. 'I've thought about it,' she said, shaking her head. 'But I've not found anyone suitable. A few who are a lot of fun, but no-one who's a patch on my Sam.'

'What about Dr Shank?' said Lucas, deciding he'd had enough of sitting to the side and letting everyone else do the questioning. Clara coughed loudly and gave him a Look, but he wouldn't be deterred that easily. 'He seems like a nice enough chap,' he added, shuffling his feet away from Clara in case she trod on his toes again.

Bunty's cheeks coloured a little, but she replied quite calmly. 'We had a – brief liaison,' she said. 'Redmond is a charming man – very charming indeed – but charm isn't enough nowadays.'

No, but I bet his money would have been, added Lucas silently. *Can't be cheap running a place like this.*

'Lucas, don't be nosy,' scolded Clara, although he knew full well that if he hadn't asked the question, it wouldn't have been long before she did.

Bunty laughed. 'No, no, my dear,' she said, waving a hand. 'It's quite all right. I suppose you've heard the rumours about us?' She flashed Lucas an interrogating look. 'I saw you talking to Jonny, and as much as I love that boy, he does have trouble keeping his lip buttoned, especially when it comes to other people's business.'

Lucas felt his cheeks colour, making him suddenly far too warm. *That's hardly my fault, is it?* he thought defiantly. *I never asked to be told all those things. All right, I took notes, but how else would I remember?*

'Yes, I thought so,' said Bunty with a wry smile. 'Still, as I'm sure you know, nothing in a murder investigation stays private for very long, so it'll come out eventually – though I'd rather you didn't put it in your little paper, if you don't mind.'

Lucas was just about to agree - after all, she'd asked nicely, and welcomed them into her home and given them tea and biscuits - when Bunty said:

'In fact, I'd be very grateful – very grateful indeed – if this entire, uh, *incident* didn't get into the papers at all.' Her eyes darted between her guests, looking rather worried. 'It wouldn't do to have a, a *murder* in one's house to be common knowledge, especially not after…'

'Yes?' prompted Tommy softly, her hand still in his.

'Well, after dear Sam's death,' said Bunty, turning to him after a pause. 'Some of the papers made... insinuations that I'd had a hand in it. Pure nonsense, of course -'

Not my fault, thought Lucas guiltily, remembering the article about the demise of Sir Samuel of Castlebury Manor he'd written on the instructions of his now equally late editor. *I only wrote what Doug told me to. How could I know it wasn't as true as it might be...?*

'- but a second death in the house would look bad,' concluded Bunty, thankfully not noticing Lucas' blushes. 'I simply don't have the energy for yet another scandal.'

'*Yet* another scandal?' enquired Tommy with an innocent tone that made Lucas' hackles rise. 'Surely someone as delightful as you can't have any skeletons in the closet.' Tommy sipped his overly sweetened tea and added, 'I simply can't believe you're capable of anything remotely scandalous.'

Bunty pursed her lips and gave Tommy an odd look, which she then turned on Clara, and finally Lucas, who risked a glance at the other two. They appeared equally mystified, though infinitely more curious, as to what Bunty was thinking.

'I see,' she said quietly. 'So you know, do you?'

'Bunty,' said Clara, sounding a little anxious. 'I assure you we don't know a thing -'

'No, no,' said Bunty, holding up her hand towards Clara and turning her head away. 'I'm not a fool. I should have realised why you were here.'

'Realised what?' said Clara, definitely worried now. She looked to Lucas for support.

'Oh, yes,' he said, eventually, when he realised what Clara wanted. 'No, we don't know anything, honest.'

Bunty looked at them all again, still sceptical. Tommy saluted her with a half-eaten shortbread biscuit, and confirmed that he didn't know anything either.

'Hmm,' said Bunty, clearly unconvinced. 'I suppose you'd be too young to remember anyway, but... no doubt you'll hear the rumours eventually.'

'We can't help what we hear,' said Lucas, earning him a glare from Clara. 'Well we can't,' he whispered in his defence.

Bunty swallowed hard and passed a hand across her face, then gave her guests a feeble smile.

'Well,' she said, standing elegantly and walking across the room to a small escritoire. 'When you *do* hear, I hope you'll remember old Bunty's kindness and keep the details out of your newspaper.' She retrieved a chequebook and gold fountain pen from a drawer and returned to her seat.

'Bunty,' started Clara, but she was interrupted.

'Two hundred each,' said Bunty, uncapping the pen. 'Is that enough?'

Tommy nearly inhaled his latest biscuit and started chewing faster, clearly eager to claim his share of the hush-money.

'That'll be marv-' began Lucas.

'Quite unnecessary,' interrupted Clara loudly. 'You have our word that nothing relating to you will ever be printed in our paper.'

Tommy made an odd, strangled noise, then coughed on a stray crumb.

'Might I have a word in your shell-like

ear, oh love of my life?' murmured Lucas, leaning in towards Clara.

Four hundred pounds would set them up very nicely…

The look she gave him said no, he may not have a word in her ear, regardless of its shape.

Bunty closed her eyes and let her head fall backwards, her shoulders unhunching. 'I knew you were good people the second I laid eyes on you. Now,' she said, recapping the pen. 'Let's stop talking about all this nastiness. It's really quite frightful. I'll ring for more tea and see if Cook has some cake baked yet. Do you like Victoria sponge, my dears?'

***

'Four hundred pounds,' cried Lucas as the heavy wooden door shut behind them. 'Four hundred! And you turned it down, just like that.'

'How dare she!' fumed Clara, stomping down the drive. 'Does she think she can buy us off like that?'

'She could have bought *me* off,' interjected Tommy, tugging his bobble hat over his ears again as he hurried to catch her up. 'London isn't cheap to live in, you know.'

'I know,' snapped Clara. 'I live there too, remember? And you get paid more than I do, so don't go pleading poverty with me, Thomas

Kilbourne.'

'Do not,' protested Tommy. 'Do I? That hardly seems fair.'

'It's not fair,' said Clara. 'But that's the way it is. And if *I'm* not taking the money, neither are you.'

'That's all right for you two,' said Lucas. 'You both have regular pay packets. Some of us are barely keeping our heads above water.'

'Then join us at the Illustrated Police News if you want a steady wage,' cried Clara. 'You have yourself to blame.'

'You know why -' started Lucas, but Clara interrupted.

'If you two want to get paid to keep her grubby secrets for her, that's up to you,' said Clara. 'Because that's what she was doing.'

'Yes, with four hundred quid,' returned Lucas. 'Do you know what that would do for us?'

'Of course I do, Lucas,' she said with a sigh, catching hold of Tommy's sleeve as he started to go back towards the house. 'I'm well aware. It's enough for a house, and then some, and in different circumstances I'd gladly take such a gift. But it's more than just morals at stake here.'

'It's the four hundred pounds that I'm interested in,' cried Lucas. 'Morals! We can't live in *morals*, Clara.'

'And my two hundred,' added Tommy,

trying to pull his sleeve free. 'Don't forget that.'

'If Bunty *is* the murderer,' continued Clara patiently, ignoring the complaining men. 'And for all we know she very well could be, what do you think will happen if anything *does* get out and she thinks it's us that spilled the beans, hmm? Do you fancy a mistletoe cocktail as well? Because I don't.'

This rather sobered Lucas and Tommy, who shared a sheepish look.

'Fair point,' said Tommy, rubbing the back of his neck and grinning awkwardly.

'I never thought of that', said Lucas, wrapping his arms around her shoulders and giving her a grateful squeeze. He ignored the look of envy from Tommy that gave Lucas a shameful flicker of satisfaction. 'Thank you for saving me from a probably fatal error.'

'Yes, well someone's got to be the brains in this outfit,' she said, snuggling up to him. 'But it's frightfully suspicious, don't you think?'

'I do,' said Lucas, taking her hand as the trio started making their way home again. 'Should we tell Henry?'

'I suppose so,' said Clara reluctantly. 'Urgh, he's going to be furious we've been having tea with a murder suspect.'

'What do you think Bunty's big secret is?' asked Tommy, his eyes delightedly tracking a passing wood pigeon. 'It must be something pretty bad if she's *that* terrified of it being remembered.'

'I haven't a clue,' said Clara, following his eyeline with some amusement. 'But someone must know. Any ideas who, Lucas?'

'Not really,' replied Lucas, pulling her arm through his and earning a glare from Tommy. 'I suppose it rather depends on when this huge scandal took place, and how well known it was anyway.'

'She said we were too young to remember,' mused Clara. 'So it must be at least twenty, twenty-five years ago.'

'It must be something pretty bad,' said Tommy, who was cheerful again even if it felt a little forced. 'Considering everything you've told me about her and her crowd. They aren't ashamed of anything, and some of that happened quite recently.'

'I agree,' said Clara. 'Doesn't it make you want to find out all the more?'

'No,' said Lucas 'I'd rather not know, that way I can't accidentally tell anyone.'

'Hear, hear,' said Tommy, for once in agreement with Lucas. 'As fascinating as this little mystery is, I don't fancy getting bumped off during the first Christmas I've actually enjoyed.' He pulled a face. 'Might put a bit of a damper on the whole thing.'

'Well, you're right about that,' said Clara. 'But *when* we find out, we'll just have to be extra careful about not telling anyone what it is, won't we?'

'Hmm,' said Lucas, not sure he liked the sound of that. 'However, it does make Bunty look like she could have done it, or maybe knows who did and is trying to cover for them.'

'Perhaps,' said Clara. 'I hope it's not her, though. I quite like the old bird.'

'So do I,' said Lucas.

'You didn't at the party,' said Clara teasingly. 'At least, not whilst she was trying to seduce you.'

Lucas felt his ears burn. 'No, I didn't like that so much,' he admitted quietly, praying this revelation had somehow gone unnoticed by his least favourite member of the party.

Which of course, it hadn't.

'Excuse me?' exclaimed Tommy, prancing around gleefully. 'You didn't tell me *that*.' He winked roguishly over the top of Clara's head. 'Didn't think you had it in you, old boy. Do tell all - though I understand if you want to wait until, you know,' he nodded at Clara and pulled all sorts of faces behind her back. 'Wouldn't want to get you in trouble with the Mrs.'

Lucas felt his cheeks glow again, and tried to convince himself it was just because of the physical excursion of trekking through the increasingly deep snow.

'Oh, that was just a bit of sport on her part,' said Clara, waving away Tommy's accusations. 'She packed it in as soon as I told her we were a couple.'

'I thought we weren't telling anyone?' asked Lucas, faintly annoyed. 'Sleuthing and all that?'

'Yes, well I didn't want her making another play for you, did I?' replied Clara, fidgeting with the brim of her hat and avoiding his eye. 'Especially not when you were utterly zozzled.'

Tommy squeaked at this revelation, and pressed his mittened hand to his mouth. 'You – you didn't get *drunk*, did you?' he whispered with mock horror. 'The saintly Rathbone? Surely not. Say it ain't so!'

'You may have a point,' admitted Lucas, choosing not to rise to the bait. 'I can't say I remember much about that night at all.'

'I'll teach you how to pretend to drink sometime,' said Clara, smirking. 'It's a very useful skill to have.'

'Yes, I spotted you tipping cocktails into vases,' said Lucas. 'Then pretending it'd gone straight to your head.'

'Better to just learn how to handle your drink,' muttered Tommy, smirking.

'You have a lot of "useful" skills,' said Lucas, employing his own useful and increasingly well-practiced skill of ignoring Tommy. 'It's rather worrying, mostly because we find them useful.'

'They're only useful because our life is

interesting,' she replied, twinkling her eyes at him. 'Better than being stuck in a stuffy office tapping out drab articles about cake competitions and all that.'

'They sell papers,' said Lucas reproachfully. 'Everyone likes to see their name in print, after all.'

'Unless they've done something really bad,' interjected Tommy. 'Bunty didn't seem keen on the idea.'

'What do you think the chances of Bunty's terrible secret made it to the papers?' said Clara thoughtfully.

'Almost certain, if it was bad enough,' said Lucas, heart sinking at the thought of wading through stacks of newspapers in search of goodness knows what. 'But we should narrow it down first, otherwise it'll take us years.'

'You're right,' said Clara. 'What do you suggest?'

'We could quiz the servants,' suggested Tommy. 'I like quizzing servants.'

'You would,' muttered Lucas under his breath.

'Especially the female ones,' said Tommy, grinning broadly. 'Clara, you could charm the men, and we'll be done in half the time.'

'It's a good idea,' she said, going completely against Lucas' feelings on the subject. 'Except for one thing.'

'Oh, I'm sure we can work something

out,' said Tommy, waving away her pessimism. 'But go on, let's hear it.'

'One of the girls in the village once told me Bunty and the late Sir Samuel were somewhat difficult to work for,' said Clara. 'No one ever stayed long if they could help it.'

'Someone must still be there from the old days,' argued Tommy. 'Even if it's that stuffed shirt of a butler.'

'He won't talk to us,' said Lucas, looking glumly a long way back up the snow-blanketed hill the manor stood on. 'He couldn't wait to get us out of there.'

'Tommy makes a good point though,' said Clara thoughtfully. 'You do too, darling, of course,' she added, catching the offence on Lucas' face. 'But we've got to start somewhere, and you know what servants are like for rumours. Someone must know something about what happened, even if it's just rumours of rumours.'

'We just need a place to start,' said Tommy, keen to start his "quizzing."

'We should start by letting Henry do his job,' said Lucas, keen to get home.

'Good idea,' replied Clara, taking his hand and walking with a little more purpose back towards Castlebury Magna. 'Then we can make him tell us everything he knows and save ourselves a lot of time and effort.'

'That's not what I meant,' complained

Lucas. 'But it's no day to be trudging about when there's a warm fire and cocoa at home, and if this gets us home quicker than traipsing back up to the manor, I'm all for it.'

'Exactly, darling,' said Clara, stretching up to kiss his cheek. 'Not to mention I'm going to lose a toe if I spend a minute longer outside today than I have to.'

Tommy made a disgruntled noise, clearly feeling cheated of his favourite sport, but didn't argue too hard. Mrs Jenkins' cocoa was a rare treat, particularly after a cold walk, whereas Tommy never struggled for female attention.

As they walked, the conversation drifted to more mundane topics, and Tommy drifted off to explore the pristine white countryside again. Hardly surprising, given that there was so much grime in the London air that Clara swore the snow there fell grey. Lucas had put this claim down to her overactive imagination, but seeing a city mouse's wonder at the dazzling landscape, he was less sure by the second.

'Can't you ask Chappers if he knows Bunty's secret?' asked Clara, when Tommy was out of earshot and trying to befriend a horse.

'I would if I knew where he was,' replied Lucas, slowing his pace to give them more time to talk. 'I doubt he'd tell me, mind you. But he wasn't at the manor as far as I could see - goodness only knows where he's ended up, but I wasn't complaining. It gives me a headache when I have to concentrate on two conversations at once.'

'I know darling,' she said, tilting her head up and kissing his cheek softly. 'Hopefully he's been getting some information for us.'

'I certainly hope so,' said Lucas. 'Then we can stop sticking our noses where they don't belong.'

'Where could he have got to?' mused Clara. 'Where do spirits go where they're not bothering you?'

'With a bit of luck he'll be back at Henry's house,' replied Lucas, who never wondered silly things like that in case it somehow jinxed the peace he got between ghostly harassment. 'He seems to think that's where he can find me, which is fine by me. The last thing I need is ghosts showing up in my house.'

'Your mum's house,' corrected Clara teasingly.

'Ghosts forget that the living need unimportant things like sleep,' said Lucas, ignoring this comment on his living arrangements. 'They have no problem waking a fellow up because they've had some dazzling idea at three in the morning.'

'I've heard you talking in your sleep to them,' said Clara, giving his arm a sympathetic squeeze. 'It must be frightfully irritating.'

'It is,' agreed Lucas, though he didn't know he talked in his sleep at all. He nearly asked what he said, then decided he'd rather not know.

'But it must feel good to help them,' said Clara.

Lucas thought about this. Mainly he was motivated to help by a desire for a peaceful life, but he couldn't deny knowing there were fewer lost souls in the world was a good feeling.

Entirely for their sake, of course, and not because it meant he was less likely to run into them again unexpectedly and start the whole rigmarole over.

Mostly for their sake, at least.

Not his own at all.

'Yes, I suppose you're right,' he said. 'And I'd want someone to do the same for me if I were in their position, after all.'

'Exactly,' said Clara. 'Do unto others, and all that.'

'Indeed,' said Lucas, wrapping his arm around her shoulder and pulling her into a kiss. 'Like that, you mean?'

'If you insist,' she said, kissing him back with feeling. 'Come on, we'd better get a wiggle on or Tommy will have drunk all the cocoa by the time we get home.'

'I know a better way of warming you up,' said Lucas in between kisses.

'I'm sure you do,' replied Clara, slightly breathlessly. 'But it'll have to wait.'

'You're right, it's far too cold out here.'

'I actually meant we have a murder to solve,' said Clara, grinning at him beautifully. 'But maybe later.'

***

Having satisfactorily thawed out, Clara and Lucas wrapped against the biting chill once more and made their way to Henry's house.

As Henry cared for Tommy even less than Lucas did, and Mrs Jenkins was mothering him in a way he rather enjoyed, Tommy elected to stay in his temporary lodgings and play Whist and Gin Rummy with the assortment of relatives who had descended on Mrs J over the Christmas period.

Which was fine by Clara. As fond as she was of the chap, Tommy's mostly gentle, mostly good-natured teasing of Lucas, and Lucas' complete lack of understanding that it was done with a twisted sort of affection, was entertaining for a time. But it was wearing after a while, and it was nice to not have to deal with the backlash when Tommy inevitably took it a little too far.

Besides, it was nice to have Lucas all to herself for a while. As lovely as festive gatherings were, there was nothing like time to themselves to really warm Clara's heart.

His arm was cosy around her shoulder and she snuggled against him they walked down the street. Snow drifted down around them, remnants of an earlier blizzard that hadn't heard the storm was over, and the sun was already sinking towards the horizon. Their shadows stretched long behind them, though no one saw as Castlebury Magna was deserted, the villagers cocooned indoors, presumably finishing off the last of the Christmas feast and dozing by the fire.

It was still and perfect, and too soon they found themselves at Henry's house, where they were welcomed with enthusiasm and love.

They settled in the front room, baby Ezra crawling into his aunt's lap and gurgling contentedly as soon as she sat down.

Being an auntie is jolly good fun, she thought, pulling faces at her nephew. *Even better because I can hand him back when he gets grizzly.*

As Henry made a pot of tea, they caught each other up on progress.

'She tried to bribe you?' said Henry incredulously, putting a steaming cup of tea on the table next to her. 'That's suspicious.'

'We thought so,' said Clara, thanking him before resuming the far more important task of entertaining Ezra. 'Any idea what that's about?'

'None whatsoever,' said Henry. 'But I'll find out.'

'Yes, but make sure you don't ask anyone directly about it,' said Lucas. 'Otherwise she'll know we tipped off the cops and if Bunty's the killer... Well, I'd rather not find a handful of mistletoe berries in my dinner, if you see what I mean.'

Clara smiled. It was nice when he listened to her. Rare, but nice when it happened.

'Say no more,' replied Henry with a wave of the hand. 'She'll never know it was you, I promise.'

'Thanks,' said Lucas, relieved. 'And with a bit of luck, she'll still offer us a little incentive to keep it out of the papers.' He rubbed his thumb and forefingers together in an unmistakably moneygrubbing way.

So much for him listening to her...

'Lucas Rathbone,' scolded Clara, keeping her voice low so as not to disturb the baby, who was getting sleepy. 'Don't be so, so...'

'What?' he asked, affronted. 'I don't see why our discretion shouldn't be rewarded.'

'But what if she's the murderer?'

'All right, why don't we accept anything she offers if she's *not* the murderer?' countered Lucas. 'There's nothing wrong with *that*, is there?'

Clara pretended she didn't see Henry smirking into his teacup.

Unfortunately, Clara couldn't think of an argument against this suggestion, and clearly waited too long because Lucas followed up with:

'Good,' in a self-satisfied voice that grated the nerves. 'But I don't think it was her at all.'

'You're just saying that because you want

her money,' said Clara crossly.

'... No,' said Lucas, though Clara knew one of his lies when she saw one. He was the most useless liar she'd ever come across.

'No?' she queried. 'Then what exactly *is* convincing you of her innocence?'

'I think she's a jolly nice person,' declared Lucas. 'One incapable of hurting another living soul. Don't pretend you think otherwise, because I know you don't think she did it either. Not really.'

'She still might have done it,' grumbled Clara, but she couldn't deny he was right. She hadn't the least doubt of Bunty's innocence, which naturally annoyed her all the more. 'You said it yourself, anyone could be a killer given the right circumstances.'

'Yes, but I don't think a failed love affair and an indiscreet dalliance would be enough to tip her over the edge,' said Lucas.

'Why not?' asked Henry, frowning. 'It'd tip most people over the edge.'

'And for all we know, Chapman could have been murdered because of this terrible secret of hers,' said Clara.

'She's got means, motive and opportunity,' continued Henry. 'The Holy Trinity of murder. Mistletoe was everywhere that night, Shank could have told her about its toxic properties, trying to impress her perhaps, and it would have been simple enough to slip some berries into the victim's food or squeeze the juice into the deadly cocktail.' He leant back in his chair and placed his hands behind his head. 'Given the evidence, I'd say it very well could be Her Ladyship.'

'But if she's willing to pay us off to avoid revising a past scandal,' said Lucas, clearly still obsessing over the bribe money. 'Would she really *kill* someone? At her own party, no less? And with half a dozen witnesses? Murder is about as scandalous as you can get.'

'What if Chapman forced her hand?' said Henry, clearly enjoying this battle of wits. 'What if he was going to tell everyone that very evening about this big secret, and she just couldn't let that happen?'

'She'd have paid him off,' said Lucas. 'That's what she did with us. She just reached straight for her chequebook without a second thought. She even offered Tommy money, and she'd only just met him. No threats of any kind, just bribery, pure and simple.'

'You may have a point,' said Henry. 'But what if Chapman refused her money for some reason?'

'Who refuses money?' said Lucas, glaring ineffectually at Clara. 'And she's probably got pots of the stuff, she'd have offered more and more until he took it.'

'Perhaps,' said Henry. 'But let's not remove Lady Gaylesbury from the list just yet.

Not until we find out what this secret of hers is, and whether it's relevant at all.'

'Fair enough,' said Clara, before Lucas could argue any further. 'Bunty is still a suspect for now, but what about the others? What have your enquiries told you so far?'

'Practically nothing, seeing as it's Boxing Day and I haven't been making any,' said Henry, raising an unimpressed eyebrow. 'But as it happens, Jones dropped round to pick my brains over a couple of things earlier.'

Clara's ears pricked up.

'That and I think Mrs Jones was fed up with him moping around the house complaining about having to work,' continued Henry, rather smugly. 'Hah, and he wonders why I don't fancy a promotion! But it won't do any harm to tell you, especially as you're insisting on involving yourselves anyway.'

'Not willingly,' said Lucas darkly.

'Even though Jones insists you could still be suspects,' added Henry.

'Oh, don't be tiresome,' said Clara wearily. An infant complaint told her she'd been too loud, and she jiggled Ezra gently until he settled again.

'I was just teasing, you silly thing,' replied her brother with a smirk, leaning across the tiny sitting room to pinch her cheek playfully. 'No harm in that, is there?'

'Humph,' said Clara, batting his hand

away. 'So, what did Jonesy have to say that was urgent enough to disturb your day off?'

'Well,' said Henry, sitting back in his chair. 'It's only a first report from the coroner, you understand, but it seems the poor chap was done in with mistletoe.'

'We know that,' said Lucas. 'You knew too, I told you this morning.'

'Yes, but I couldn't tell Jones that, could I?' said Henry, peeved at the interruption. 'Reckons it was in the fellow's cocktail, or someone rubbed a berry around the rim of the glass, something like that. You know, how they do when they're putting sugar around a glass? Except with something rather more horrible than lemon juice.'

'Is that enough to kill a man?' said Clara, who still wasn't convinced of mistletoe as a murder weapon, no matter how seasonally appropriate it might be. 'I always thought mistletoe wasn't as dangerous as folks always made out.'

'Not for me to say,' replied Henry with a shrug. 'I'm just telling you what Jones told me. Perhaps he had an allergic reaction or something? Can you be allergic to mistletoe?'

'All the same,' said Clara, who didn't know and hated admitting ignorance. 'It's an uncertain way to kill a chap, isn't it? Drain cleaner or rat poison or something would seem more practical.'

'Maybe it was an impromptu thing,' said Henry. 'And he - or she, or course - just used the closest toxic thing to hand.'

'You think it was a man?' said Lucas, giving a sly look to Clara. 'Not Bunty, then?'

Clara stuck her tongue out at him. He was really most annoying at times, mainly when he was right. Of course, she was *glad* it probably wasn't Bunty, but Lucas would likely make a play for that bribe money and Clara didn't feel right about taking it, not having given her word not to print anything bad about Bunty.

'I bet I can guess who,' continued Lucas with a smugness that didn't become him.

'Well, it's hardly difficult, is it,' said Clara sharply. He grinned, which only made him adorable and annoying. 'There were four chaps at the party. One of them was you, and you don't count –'

'Quite right too,' said Lucas, scowling at Henry.

'One is dead,' continued Clara. 'And he didn't kill himself or he'd have told us so –'

'Not necessarily,' interjected Lucas. 'Remember Frankie? He swore 'til he was blue in the face that someone else killed him, and how did that work out, hmm?'

'All right, you have a point there,' conceded Clara. 'But Chapman didn't seem the type, you know? Or if he *was*, why would he choose that way? In that place? And at a party?'

'Maybe he just wanted to go out in a good mood,' said Lucas. 'Where happier than at a party?'

'But with mistletoe?' insisted Clara. 'Isn't it a rather horrible way to go?'

'The coroner seemed to think so,' said Henry. 'Stomach cramps, vomiting, diarrhoea...'

'Yes, all right, I get the idea,' said Lucas, looking queasy. He lapsed into discontented grumbling, which probably meant the Jenkins siblings won this argument.

'Anyway, don't interrupt me when I'm thinking,' said Clara, pulling faces at him until his smile came back. It suited him much better than a scowl, and she grinned when he playfully crossed his eyes at her in return.

'As I was saying,' she continued, turning her attentions back to her brother. 'There's only two men who could have done it.'

'And four women,' said Henry. 'Three if we exclude you, of course.'

'Yes, yes, I'll get to them in a minute,' said Clara, waving her non-nephew-cuddling hand irritably. 'Even though I'm sure it wasn't any of them.'

'I told you, we can't rule anyone out yet,' said Henry, shifting uncomfortably in his seat. 'I'm just making sure you don't either.'

'But you've ruled *us* out,' said Lucas pointedly. 'You were only joking about us still being suspects. Weren't you?'

There was an unpleasant pause.

'*I* don't think you did it,' said Henry eventually, examining his nails as he spoke. 'In fact, know neither of you would do a thing like that. But Jones... Well, Jones isn't so sure'

'You can't be serious,' exclaimed Clara, dropping her voice again as the baby stirred. 'Why would we do that?'

'The gentleman in question was seen *flirting* with you, sister dear,' said Henry with undisguised disapproval. 'Unwanted attention and all that. Or perhaps the protective boyfriend –'

'Fiancé,' corrected Lucas indignantly. 'You can't still be put out that I didn't ask your permission before proposing.'

'I jolly well can,' said Henry, though the twitch at the corner of his mouth suggested he wasn't wholly serious.

Lucas was about to argue the point - really, would the boy ever learn when people were teasing him? - when Henry continued with the much more important matter at hand.

'Jones won't rule you out yet,' he said, which halted Lucas' complaints. 'And frankly if I were in his position I wouldn't either. These toffs press their suit a little too much at times, and it wouldn't be the first time someone took drastic measures to stop them.'

'Don't be *absurd*,' said Clara. 'I'd never do a thing like that.'

'Me either,' said Lucas.

'I've been dealing with unwanted attention for years,' said Clara.

'Me too,' said Lucas, although this was a lie.

'I can get rid of men I don't like without ending up with a body on my hands,' said Clara, fighting a smile at the thought of Lucas fending off hordes of women.

'Same here,' added Lucas. 'Well, women in my case, obviously.'

'I'd be up to my ears in corpses otherwise,' continued Clara, ignoring him. 'And Lucas hasn't got it in him to kill someone.'

'Hang on,' complained Lucas. 'I might.'

'Exactly,' said Henry. 'He's already admitted he'd take drastic action if you were in danger.'

'Wait,' said Lucas, alarmed. 'I was just making a point to the ghost, I'd never -'

'I know, don't get bent out of shape,' said Henry, rolling his eyes. 'But Jones doesn't know you like I do, does he?'

'Thank goodness,' said Lucas. 'I don't fancy having someone like him as a pal.'

'I don't think many people do,' said Henry.

'You didn't *tell* Jones what we said about exceptional circumstances, did you?' said Clara, keen to clarify the point. 'Henry, tell me you didn't.'

'But the fact remains,' said Henry, suspiciously not answering the question. 'That you were there and saw Chapman flirting with your girlfriend – sorry, *fiancée*.'

'But –'

'I'm sorry,' said Henry with a sigh. 'But officially you're both still suspects, even though I know you're innocent.'

'But Jones…?' said Clara, aghast. 'How could he think such a thing?'

'I don't think he's serious,' said Henry, sounding worryingly uncertain. 'But you know what he's like. When he gets an idea into his head, it can take some shifting.'

'It's a miracle he managed to fit one whole idea into that fat head of his,' grumbled Lucas.

'It's just a shame it's that one,' added Clara.

'I don't like it either,' said Henry. 'But I can't change it and that's that. I shouldn't even be talking to you, but what Jones doesn't know won't hurt him. Or me, more importantly, so keep this under your hats, all right?'

'Oh, all right,' said Clara irritably. 'But you've got a lot of apologising to do when this is all over.'

'You can get yourselves off the suspects list as soon as possible by bringing me any information you come across, though,' said Henry. 'You're getting on rather well with Lady

Gaylesbury and her set. Lord knows they clam up as soon as we start asking awkward questions.'

'You want us to spy for you?' said Clara, brightening at the prospect of brotherly sanctioned mischief.

'No,' said Lucas, wagging a disapproving finger at her. 'No spying.'

'Not spy so much, but… well, yes, I suppose so,' admitted Henry sheepishly.

'Wonderful,' cried Clara, cutting off whatever Lucas was about to say. 'We'll be delighted to help, won't we darling?'

'Actually…'

'That's settled then,' said Clara, bundling baby Ezra into his father's arms and dragging Lucas to his feet. 'We'll start snooping right away. We'll be like Sherlock and Watson. I'm Sherlock, obviously.'

'Why am I not Sherlock?' complained Lucas, apparently forgetting he was opposed to the scheme. 'I'd be a good Sherlock.'

'You're not really cut out for detective work, are you darling?' she said, bobbing onto the balls of her feet and pecking his cheek.

'Doesn't mean I couldn't if I didn't want to,' argued Lucas. 'I solve all sorts of mysteries.'

'But you never *want* to help, darling, and that's the difference,' said Clara, taking his hand and dragging him and his complaints towards the door. 'No time like the present,' she said, eager to start snooping before Henry changed his mind. 'So we'll be off then.'

'Cheery-bye,' called Henry, cooing over his baby son. 'Report back as soon as you can, all right?'

'Will do,' replied Clara, shrugging her coat onto her shoulders and thrusting Lucas' worn felt overcoat into his hand. 'We'll start by finding out Bunty's secret.' She bundled Lucas towards the door, ignoring his protests that he should be properly attired before stepping out into a blizzard. 'Toodle pip, Henry. See you soon.'

When he'd finally got his coat and hat on, Lucas said, 'Where do you propose we start?' He made a great show of turning up his coat collar against the chill. 'We don't even know when this scandal happened.'

'This is why I'm Sherlock and you're Watson,' she said, linking her arm through his. 'We'll ask our mothers, of course. They know everything about everything in this place. And if they *don't* know, it can't have happened in the past thirty years.'

'What will we do if they don't know anything?'

Clara paused, knowing Lucas wouldn't like the answer.

'You could ask Mrs Bird,' she suggested, avoiding his eye.

'Mrs B is a dear, of course,' he said,

looking around cautiously, presumably to make sure she wasn't eavesdropping. The coast must have been clear, because he continued by saying, 'But you know I hate asking ghosts for help. Even Mrs B. I don't like it when they do it to me, I don't see why I should do the same to them.'

'That's not the reason, is it?'

'Well, all right,' he conceded. 'I hate asking for their help because they get so involved I can't get rid of them afterwards.'

'And who could blame them?' said Clara. 'It must be frightfully dull, being dead and all that.'

'Probably,' said Lucas. 'But I end up owing them a favour, and I can't very well tell them to buzz off then, can I?'

'You said Mrs Bird never listens anyway,' replied Clara. 'So I don't think you've got anything to lose by asking her.'

'That's true,' said Lucas with a sigh. 'Not that I want to get rid of her, of course. Not permanently anyway, but she has got a knack for appearing at the most inconvenient times.'

He looked around to make sure this wasn't one of them before continuing.

'She's been a fixture in my life for as long as I can remember,' he said. And she's a dear old thing really...'

'But you'd rather not owe her a favour if you don't have to,' guessed Clara.

'Exactly.'

Clara decided a little sympathy might be in order, which had the added bonus of getting Lucas to come around to her point of view.

'If we run out of options,' said Lucas, after a few calming words had soothed him. 'I'll ask her. But only if there's no other option, okay?'

'Cross my heart and hope to die,' chanted Clara happily, kissing his freezing cheek again.

'Is that really appropriate, considering we're investigating a murder?'

'Probably not,' said Clara cheerfully. 'But it's only you hearing it, so I don't suppose it matters.' The daylight had faded to blackest night, sinking the temperature even lower, so before Lucas could criticise her rather tasteless choice of words again she added, 'Let's find our mothers, before the snow starts.'

'All right,' he said, blowing a cloud of steam from his mouth to emphasise the chill. 'Where do you think they'll be?'

'It's Boxing Day at five-thirty in the evening,' replied Clara. 'So they'll be… At your house. Your mum's house, anyway,' she added cheekily. 'You only live there.'

'They could be at *your* mum's,' said Lucas, determined not to be Watson despite the evidence to the contrary. 'What makes you so sure they'll be at my house?'

'Well,' said Clara confidently. '*My* mum was helping Debbie with the cooking yesterday, so she'll have been on her feet all day.'

'My mum was helping too,' argued Lucas.

'And she's a love for doing it,' said Clara. 'She always does.'

'Yes,' said Lucas, appeased. 'And it was always good of your family to let us join your celebrations.'

'It would have been miserable with just the two of you,' said Clara. 'We couldn't have you spending Christmas like that when we'd got plenty to spare.'

'You never had plenty to spare,' said Lucas, hugging her tightly. 'None of us did.'

'Enough to share, if not to spare,' said Clara, smiling.

'All right,' said Lucas, after kissing her rather sweetly. 'So we've established your mum – and mine - helped Debbie yesterday. That doesn't explain why you think they're at *my* mum's house, does it? They could just as easily be at your mum's house.'

'I can't tell you, can I?' said Clara. 'You keep interrupting.'

'Go on, then. Astound me.'

'They'll be at your house,' said Clara. 'Because my mum was cooking and looking after Ezra, and Aunt Vi is staying with her, and so is Uncle Freddie. Those two will be having a right tiff by now. That, or they'll will be talking about Ancient Greeks or Celtic farming methods some other frightful topic. You know what they're like when they get going.'

'Oh yes,' said Lucas, with a shudder of grim recollection. 'Freddie cornered me one year and subjected me to a lecture on the battles of the Visigoths.'

'It's not his fault, poor old thing,' said Clara charitably. 'But he does get interested in the most awful things.'

'Agreed,' said Lucas, less charitably.

'Still, Aunt Vi humours him, for the most part,' continued Clara. 'She even finds some of it interesting, apparently.'

'All right then,' said Lucas, taking her arm and starting walking again. 'So things will be dire in terms of conversation. There's lots of other people there she could talk to.'

'True, but Mum will be tired after cooking and cleaning for all her guests. There's six this year, since she's adopted Tommy as one of her own,' said Clara, with an affectionate smile. 'By now, having a house full of people will be driving her crazy, so she'll have invented some excuse to visit your mum instead.' Clara walked with a new bounce in her step. 'Really rather simple, when you think about it.'

'Hmm,' said Lucas, unconvinced by this magnificent piece of logic. 'We're nearly home now, so we'll find out soon enough.'

Much to Clara's delight, and Lucas' undisguised annoyance, light glowed behind the drawn curtains of his mother's front room window. Two familiar shadows were moving around inside.

'Told you,' she crowed, practically dancing up the path. 'I'm Sherlock, you're Watson.'

'Oh, all right,' grumbled Lucas, though this arrangement was inevitable wherever their mothers were spending the evening. 'You can have this one. If nothing else, it'll make it easier for us to ask questions about Bunty's family.'

'Exactly,' said Clara, standing on the doorstep and turning back to beam at him. She kissed the tip of his nose, which was level with her own for a change.

'Snowflake,' she said, as if an explanation was needed.

Lucas kissed her softly on the lips, again and again, making the most of the last few moments of privacy before they were subjected to an evening of maternal scrutiny and inevitable teasing.

Oh, how they liked to tease him. Not that it bothered Clara, of course, and she didn't resent their good-natured humour in the slightest - even though it was at her expense as well.

After all, it was such fun to tease Lucas. He blushed so easily. Rather adorable, really.

But Clara sympathised, even if she did contribute to his blushes as frequently as possible, so she lingered on the doorstep with him far longer than the icy temperature suggested was wise.

Funnily enough, she barely felt the chill.

'Come on, darling, let's get inside where it's warm,' she said eventually, slightly breathless after their stolen romantic moment. She kissed him again, brushing her lips against his for just a moment, before taking the key from his breast pocket and letting herself in.

***

His lips tingling, though not from the cold, Lucas followed Clara into his house – his house, not just his mother's - and allowed the familiar scents of home to wrap him in their comforting, familiar embrace.

Laughter from the front room masked their entrance to the house, and he and Clara removed their snow-sodden coats and hats in peace, with a few more delightful moments helping warm them, and changed wet boots for comfortable and cosy house slippers.

He gave Clara one last kiss before steeling himself for the onslaught of maternal torment. He knew it was done with love, really he did, but he frequently found himself wishing to be anywhere else when they got started.

There was another shriek of laughter from the living room, and Lucas started wishing before even opening the door.

He took a deep breath, and pushed the door open.

'Hullo, mum,' said Lucas with a forced grin, sticking his head around the door. Clara pushed him into the room and made a much more enthusiastic greeting, immediately plumping herself down on the sofa between the two older women and being enveloped in hugs, kisses, and yet more giggling.

Lucas smiled at three of the people he loved most in the world as he settled into the threadbare comfort of the fifth-hand armchair opposite the almost matching sofa that sagged in the middle – especially with three fully grown women sat on it. He kicked his feet onto a low footstool and warmed his toes by the small but cheerful fire in the grate.

I don't know why I argued, he thought, growing drowsier by the second. *They always get fed up with the people they were delighted to see three days before, and slope off somewhere to cheer themselves up. Usually with* – he sniffed the air – *yes, sherry. Urgh. Always sherry.*

He looked with deep affection, and some trepidation, at the flushed faces of his mother and her best friend.

Mrs Rathbone, much to her son's despair, wore a daffodil yellow paper crown from a cracker. It had slipped rakishly over one eye, creating some sort of effect, although Lucas wouldn't want to comment what that was.

At least, not out loud.

Certainly not if he wanted his dinner for the rest of the week.

Mrs Jenkins wore a similar article in holly leaf green, although hers still sat atop her salt and pepper curls. Her flushed cheeks and slightly lopsided smile told Lucas this might be the only illusion of civility the evening might hold.

'Hullo, son,' said Mrs Rathbone, pushing herself awkwardly to her feet to go and greet him properly, before collapsing back in a fit of giggles. 'Whoops,' she said, tittering. She beckoned to him. 'Come give your old mum a proper hug.'

Ignoring his feet, which protested against too much use and too little rest over the last few days, Lucas hauled himself upright and leant forward to kiss his mother's cheek, then Mrs Jenkins', and finally pressing his lips chastely against Clara's forehead so she wouldn't feel left out.

This caused much hilarity amongst the older women, who made several embarrassing comments about their own youthful, apparently far more adventurous, love affairs.

Lucas pretended he hadn't heard, for the sake of his own sanity.

Mrs Rathbone said something about Lucas needing to loosen up a little, and there was just the ticket in the drinks cabinet.

However, her balance still proved elusive, which naturally resulted in much more laughter.

This was going to be a very, *very* long evening.

'You stay there, Mrs R,' said Clara, holding her hands out to Lucas until he pulled her to her feet. 'I'll fix us some drinks.'

'Yes, do,' replied Mrs Rathbone, waving her hand at the drinks cabinet. 'Bring the brandy back with you, dear. Your mother's glass needs refilling.'

'Henrietta Rathbone, that's not true,' scolded her friend, who promptly emptied the small glass and hiccoughed. 'Well, now it is, but don't try and pretend it's only for my sake.'

Lucas groaned and Clara shooed him away, pushing him back into his seat with a look that told him to behave himself. She was right, of course, but that didn't make him want to run and hide any less.

As she clinked glasses and bottles, making goodness knows what concoction with odds and ends of alcohol collected by his mother over the years, Lucas let the giggling and gossiping continue, avoiding drawing any attention to himself for as long as possible.

I'll start with a mundane topic, thought Lucas, pondering the problem of how to pry into Bunty's former life without appearing too eager to do so. *Wouldn't want to look like a gossipy old woman, after all.*

This, however, was not a concern for either his mother or Mrs Jenkins.

''Ere, what's been going on up at the hall?' asked Mrs R, readjusting her paper crown. It promptly slipped back to its former position 'I heard someone got *murdered* whilst you were there the other day.' She looked disapprovingly at her son with the eye not shrouded in yellow tissue paper. 'I hope you've not been getting involved with a rough crowd, my lad.'

Lucas closed his eyes in despair. 'No, mother,' he said patiently, ignoring the sniggering from Clara. 'And they weren't killed whilst we were there –'

'They might have been,' Clara said oh-so helpfully from near the drinks cabinet. 'Or at least poisoned while we were in the room.'

Lucas hoped she wasn't foreshadowing whatever dreadful experiment she was taking a worryingly long time mixing. A whiskey soda didn't take that long, and his hopes of getting something so delightfully simple waned by the second.

'Probably not killed whilst we were there,' amended Lucas, putting his own imminent poisoning to the back of his mind. 'And they're not rough people – again probably, before Clara says anything – and we've not been "getting involved" with them. Not really, anyway.'

He sighed, realising he'd managed to say

nothing at all of any use. He tried again.

'We were at Castlebury Manor to report on the ball and got dragged into another party whilst we were there, and one of them got murdered.'

'It wasn't that Lady Gaylesbury, was it?' said Mrs J, looking balefully at the remaining drips in the bottom of her glass. 'Always was a bad lot, that one.'

'Aye,' said Mrs R, nodding sagely. 'Wouldn't surprise me if she ended her days in a bad way.'

'What do you mean?' asked Clara, reappearing with two glasses in her hands and the brandy bottle tucked under her arm. She passed a glass to Lucas before taking her place back on the overcrowded sofa.

Lucas looked at the drink it in his hand.

It was... murky.

He pretended to take a sip of the pungent liquid, smiled encouragingly at his fiancée, and set it next to the fire irons on the hearth. There was no way it was going anywhere near his mouth, and he debated the effect of tossing it into the fire when no one was looking.

It was probably a bad idea.

Maybe not as bad as actually drinking the stuff, but still. Probably quite bad.

He moved the glass a little further away from the flames.

'Well,' Mrs Jenkins said, leaning towards

her daughter conspiratorially and dropping her voice for no reason whatsoever, seeing as the whole room heard it regardless. 'Rumour has it that when she was eighteen or nineteen, some bloke took her fancy and she found herself in the family way.'

'Oh dear,' said Clara, sipping her own equally unappealing-looking drink and pulling a face.

Whoops, he thought, grinning sheepishly in reply to her inquisitive look. *How was I to know she hadn't tried her own vile concoction?*

'Did the chap do the honourable thing?' asked Clara, looking into her glass as though wondering which ingredient caused the unpleasant taste. Lucas guessed the Worcestershire sauce he could smell on the gin-brandy-sherry fumes, but decided discretion was the better – and certainly safer - form of valour in this case.

'It *was* only a rumour, mind you,' said Mrs Rathbone, giving her friend a slightly squiffy look of disapproval. 'You really shouldn't go spreading gossip, Flora.'

'You told me in the first place,' retorted Mrs Jenkins.

'I was young and foolish then, wasn't I,' said Hettie, smoothing the skirt of her dress and sitting up slightly straighter.

'And you're old and foolish now,' replied Flora. 'So you may as well tell the children, now that they know there's something to be told,'

'I was going to,' she said, with a Cheshire cat grin. 'But I wanted to make them work for it.'

'I knew you wouldn't let us down, Mrs R,' said Clara, beaming at her. 'Now, tell us everything you know about Bunty – I mean, Lady Gaylesbury.'

'Bunty?' said her mother, surprise raising her eyebrows. 'Lucas, I thought you said you weren't getting involved with these people?'

'I wasn't,' he replied. 'I can't say the same for Clara, though.'

'I was just doing research,' said Clara, lobbing a piece of discarded Christmas cracker at him. It bounced off his foot, narrowly missing the abandoned and probably toxic drink nearby. 'And you were cosying up to Jonny Bourbon-Busset.'

'*He* was talking to *me*, not the other way around,' retorted Lucas, returning the scrap of cardboard with some velocity and zero accuracy. 'I haven't the foggiest why he was telling me all that stuff. He knew I was from the paper.'

'I shouldn't worry if I were you, dear,' said Mrs Rathbone, leaning across the small room and patting her son on the knee. 'If he wants to tell strangers all the family secrets, that's up to him. At least you'll have something to write about, won't that be nice?'

'Mum,' said Lucas reproachfully. 'I'm not a gossip rag you know.'

'Of course you're not, dear,' she said, sitting back and readjusting her crown, which slipped straight back down again. 'But everyone likes a bit of gossip, don't they, Flora?' Mrs Jenkins enthusiastically nodded her agreement - a little too enthusiastically, in Lucas' opinion. 'So you might as well give people what they want. You'll sell more papers, it's easier work, and you might actually move out of my house one of these days.'

Lucas felt his cheeks burn as Clara giggled. 'Yes mum,' he said with a resigned sigh. 'But it feels wrong to write gossip about the people we know.'

'Oh, nonsense,' replied his mother. 'Everyone likes to see their name in print. And you barely know them anyway, so what does it matter?'

'What were you going to tell us about Bu- Lady Gaylesbury, Mrs Jenkins?' said Lucas, deciding to just sidestep this portion of the evening.

'Well, *as* I said before I was so rudely interrupted,' said Flora, shooting Hettie a glare, which was met with total indifference. 'Lady Gaylesbury, being no better than she ought to be, took up with a chap – a married man, no less, and more'n twice her age – and got herself pregnant.'

'She hardly got *herself* pregnant, mum,' said Clara reproachfully. 'That wasn't *all* her own fault, was it?'

'Not the way she acted,' replied Flora. 'Practically threw herself at him. I heard she wouldn't leave him alone at any of the balls that season until he'd danced with her.

'Even so, it's not all her fault,' insisted Clara. 'This chap could have refused to dance, couldn't he?'

'Clara, darling,' replied her mother, taking her hands and looking at her with put-on patience. 'When a pretty young girl asks a man to dance, it's very rare they turn her down.'

'That goes for sex, too,' added Mrs Rathbone.

'Mother!' exclaimed Lucas in horror, as Clara collapsed into a fit of giggles. 'You can't say things like that!'

'Yes I can,' she said. 'I just did, remember?'

'Well you shouldn't,' said Lucas, standing up and going to the drinks cabinet.

I knew I'd die of embarrassment this evening, he thought, adding a healthy dose of whiskey to freshly poured soda water, telling himself it was medicinal. Good for the nerves, certainly. *I just didn't expect it to be like that.*

'Just you try and stop me, my lad,' said Mrs Rathbone, topping up her own glass for the umpteenth. Lucas opened his mouth to argue but his mother held up a hand. 'All right, if it makes you feel better, I won't say anything that'll make your delicate ears burn.'

'Thank you,' said Lucas, sitting back down and taking a sip of his new, palatable drink.

'Though don't you go pretending *you're* as pure as the driven snow,' added Hettie with a smirk. 'Because I know full well that you ain't.'

Lucas spluttered into his whiskey and soda, and started coughing violently.

'All right,' started Clara, possibly to save the love of her life from further embarrassment, but more likely because she'd thought of something she wanted answers to. 'So we've established that Lady G threw herself at some married chap -'

'Perhaps I was a little unfair,' said Mrs Jenkins guiltily. 'She was only a slip of a girl, when all's said and done, and girls get all sorts of fancies in their heads at that age, don't they? She may have started it, but he didn't have to carry it on. He really ought to have known better.'

Clara arched an eyebrow at her mother.

'Didn't I say that?' she queried with a haughty expression. 'Anyway, if it's only *rumours* you're dealing in, it's only fair to take it with a pinch of salt.'

'But the rumours also said that when he started chasing her,' said Hettie. 'She didn't try to outrun him for long,'

'That's not the point,' replied Clara

primly, not about to be put in her place by anyone, not even her future mother-in-law. 'The fault lies squarely, if not solely, at his door.'

'She has a point, Hettie,' said Flora. 'Her Ladyship was rather young, I'm sure she didn't quite realise what she was getting in to.'

'She was nineteen,' replied Hettie dismissively. 'I was married with this one on the way by that age,' she added, jerking her thumb at Lucas, who'd rather hoped he'd been forgotten and tried to hide in his glass. 'That was quite acceptable, and I seem to remember you walked much the same path as I did -'

'True enough,' agreed Mrs Jenkins.

'So don't give me any of that "rather young" nonsense, because you know full well that won't wash with me,' said Mrs Rathbone. 'We both had homes, husbands, and children at that age, and we were glad of it.'

'It was fine for *us*, of course,' said Flora. 'We lived in the real world, not in ivory towers. But for a girl of that status she was all but ruined. She was barely out in society before throwing away all her prospects for the sake of, of a *fling*, when all's said and done. Why do you think it took her so long to find a husband, and had to accept one so much older than she was?'

'She adored the late Sir Samuel,' said Clara. 'I don't think she was unhappy about marrying him at all.'

'I'm sure you're right, love,' said Flora,

patting Clara's hand in a way Lucas felt was patronising, but Clara held her tongue. 'But I can't imagine he'd have been her first choice had there been another, do you?'

Clara smirked, shooting Lucas a wicked glance with pretty, twinkling eyes. 'People fall in love with all sorts of people they don't mean to.' She jerked her head towards him and pulled a face at her mother, before smiling sweetly at her dearly beloved.

'Oi,' he said, with mock defence. 'It wasn't *all* my idea. Well, quite a lot of it might have been -'

'It really wasn't, dear,' interjected Clara.

'But I seem to remember you were quite in favour of it,' he finished.

'*Technically* you started it,' she said, freeing herself from the overcrowded sofa and stepping across the room. 'But I *had* been dropping hints for simply ages.' She took up a perch on his lap, wound her arms around his neck, and kissed his cheek before resting her head against his. He put one hand on her waist, the other on her thigh, and received a reproachful look from his mother.

He quickly returned both hands to the arms of the chair.

'Perhaps Her Ladyship really did love her late husband,' said Flora, although she didn't sound convinced. 'But it doesn't change the fact Sir Samuel was the only one who'd have her –

and even *that* was many years after the scandal.'

'Poor Bunty,' said Clara with a sadness that tugged Lucas' heartstrings. He hugged her, pretending he couldn't see his mother's disapproval. 'One mistake and her whole life got turned upside down. What happened to the child, do you know?'

'I heard it was packed off to some relative or other,' said Mrs Rathbone, eyeing her increasingly guilt-ridden son. 'Probably the best thing that could have happened to it, to be honest with you. Of course it's terribly unfair that a child born the wrong side of the sheets should have to live under that shadow, but that's how it is.'

'Was it a boy or a girl?' asked Lucas, struck by a sudden and rare flash of inspiration.

'One or the other,' replied his mother unhelpfully. 'Why would it matter?'

'Because,' said Lucas, hardly daring to breathe in case he dislodged the thought shimmering into being in the dark space behind his eyes. 'I wonder if Bunty's affection for her nephew might have less to do with him being her *sister's* son, and more to do with him being her own child.'

'That would make sense,' said Clara thoughtfully. 'If I had an illegitimate child, I'd ask Henry to take it in. Not only would it be loved and well cared for, and I could see it as often as I wanted - unlike if the poor little mite were given up for adoption.'

'An excellent idea,' agreed Mrs Rathbone, saluting Clara with her near-empty glass. 'Though if Lucas ever gets you into trouble, my dear, you let me know and I'll set him straight.'

'Mother!' he wailed, his face scalding hot once more, and not cooled by his fiancée's laughter. 'We're getting married. You don't think I'd desert her just because – well, for *any* reason, do you?'

'Just you mind you don't, and we'll all stay happy,' said his mother. 'Though as my mother always told me, if you can't be good, be careful.'

Lucas rubbed his forehead to hide his embarrassment as Clara howled with laughter. 'Yes mum,' he muttered, almost longing to be back outside in the ever-falling snow. At least that might help cool him down a little.

'Much good that did you, Hettie,' said Flora under her breath, with a significant look at her friend. Mrs Rathbone made frantic hushing noises whilst glancing anxiously at her son.

At this point Lucas gave up hiding his despair and sunk his head against Clara's back with a loud groan. She rubbed his hand sympathetically.

The continued giggling wasn't so comforting, but he supposed he couldn't have it all.

'Clara makes a very good point,' said Mrs

Rathbone loudly as she tried to steer the conversation back to its original course, despite cheeks warmed by drink and whatever else she was feeling – although in Lucas' experience the woman was immune to embarrassment, yet incredibly capable at doling it out, so it was probably just the drink.

'Though we have no proof that's what happened at all,' said Mrs J.

'I'm sure we could find some,' said Clara, subduing her laughter at last. 'Lucas, your friend Jonny seemed intent on pouring his heart out to you. I'm sure he'd tell you all the skeletons in the family closet.'

'What if he doesn't know?' said Lucas, glad of the change in subject but still unwilling to get involved in someone else's private affairs. 'I can't drop something like that on a chap, especially as we don't know if it's true or not.'

'Hmm,' said Clara, looking at Lucas with worrying thoughtfulness.

'No,' he said, suspecting any protest was useless but making it anyway. 'I don't know what you're thinking – actually, I probably do – but we're not doing it. At least, *I'm* certainly not,' he added. 'We're not married yet, you can do as you please.'

'Can you remember when all this happened, Mrs Rathbone?' asked Clara 'And us being married won't stop me doing whatever I want either,' she added, glancing back at Lucas.

'So you can get *that* idea out of your head if it's in there.'

'Of course not, dear,' said Lucas, though he hadn't expected anything different.

'Quite right too,' she replied, ruffling his hair playfully and pecking him on the cheek.

Oh yes, that's why he couldn't stay mad at her for long. She was just too adorable.

'Hmm,' said Mrs Rathbone. 'When was it, I wonder…'

'Don't tell her, mum,' begged Lucas, trying to delay the inevitable even if he couldn't stop it. 'I don't want to get any more involved in this than I already am.'

'Let's see,' said Mrs Rathbone, also ignoring Lucas in a way he was altogether too familiar with. 'I believe it was the year I met Jim, and we were married, hmm, five, maybe six months later in January – snowing harder than this it was, but we barely noticed – and then Lucas was born in… Lucas, how old are you, dear?'

'Can't you remember?' he said, aghast.

'He's twenty-four,' said Clara, shushing him.

'Twenty-four,' repeated Hettie as Lucas threw his hands up in despair. 'And we're in –' she turned to the calendar on the wall – '1928, and Lucas was born at the end of April in 1904, which would make it… 1903.' She beamed happily. 'The child would be twenty-five.'

'How old is Jonny?' said Clara, turning to Lucas.

'How should I know?' he replied, doing a calculation of his own and being less than thrilled at the result. 'That's hardly the kind of question you ask a fellow the first time you meet, is it?'

'Good point,' said Clara in a rare moment of agreement. 'We could ask one of the girls.'

'Under what pretence?' said Lucas, feeling the conversation slip further through his fingers.

'Well, I could ask whether there's much of an age gap between Sylvia and Jono, for example,' she said. 'Or I'll ask Glo if she thinks Jonny was such a rotter because he's a few years older and thought he could take advantage of her innocence.'

'I'm a few years older than you,' said Lucas, affronted. 'I never once thought about "taking advantage" of your innocence. And not just because Henry would quite literally murder me if I tried.'

'I could never accuse you of such a dreadful thing, darling,' she said, before whispering in his ear: 'Although if you'd have been quicker on the uptake, I'd have given you the advantage much sooner.'

Her scarlet-stained lips brushed his cheekbone, which he suspected was rapidly turning a similar shade. A glance at the sofa gave revealed this last sentence had, as intended, been heard by his ears only, and breathed a sigh of relief. Their mothers were gently bickering about some half-forgotten yet highly described detail of Lady Gaylesbury's life a quarter of a century earlier.

Horribly, salaciously, *embarrassingly* described detail, which at least could take the blame for his blushes should the question arise.

Small mercies, he thought, smiling wryly. *Very small. Positively microscopic. But a mercy, of sorts, if squinted at in the right light.*

At a particularly awful description of Bunty's youthful misconduct, Lucas groaned again and wondered if all women were as free and frank about such matters, or if he was just particularly unfortunate to have been landed with these three.

He suspected the latter.

'Anyway, that's how *I'd* find out Johnny's age,' said Clara, giving an amused look towards the happy squabble on the other side of the room and turning back to her own, rather cosier, chat. 'If you've got a better idea, my love, please do say.'

'No,' he admitted after a moment's thought. 'But let's wait until tomorrow, at least.'

'Fair enough,' she said, helping herself to Lucas' drink. 'I'm far too comfortable to go chasing after murderers just now anyway.'

'Excellent,' cried Mrs Rathbone, who had

presumably lost this particular discussion and was anxious to change the subject. 'Now, shall we talk about your wedding plans?'

Lucas took the suddenly half-empty glass from Clara and emptied it fully.

Perhaps digging around in the private lives of murderers was preferable after all…

***

The next morning found Lucas and Clara tramping up the slope to Castlebury Manor yet again, with Tommy in tow once more.

'We should just ask for a bed there at this rate,' grumbled Lucas, watching the interloper to their otherwise romantic walk romp around the hillside like a spring lamb. It was not helping his mood, particularly as Clara was watching her friend with an almost sisterly affection.

'Yes, Bunty would be delighted with that,' teased Clara, turning to Lucas with a barely concealed snigger. 'Come round to her way of thinking at last, have you?'

Despite the ice crystallising on his woollen muffler, Lucas felt his ears burn. 'I thought you said you'd warned her off,' he said.

Clara shrugged. 'I did, but whether she listens or not is another matter.' She nudged him playfully, mischief twinkling in her eyes. 'It's not just foolish old men who would have a hard time saying no to a young, lively person *begging* them to take them to bed...'

Lucas gaped at her, lost for words. 'But I wouldn't – I'd never – you know that, don't you darling?'

Clara linked her arm through his and kissed him on the cheek. 'Of course I do, dear,' she said, wiping the scarlet imprint from his face. 'I'm only teasing.'

'Well I wish you'd let up occasionally,' he said crossly. He wriggled his arm free and wrapped it around her shoulders, pulling her close to him.

'But where's the fun in that?' she said, grinning wickedly at him. 'Anyway, you should learn to flirt a little. It's a good way of getting information out of people.'

Lucas felt his jaw tighten and a familiar stab of jealousy strike his gut.

'Do I want to know how you know that?' he asked, knowing the answer was a resounding "no."

'Probably not,' said Clara cheerfully. 'But it's all in a good cause, and you know I only have eyes for you.'

'Hmm,' said Lucas with undisguised disapproval.

'Oh come on,' said Clara. 'You might even enjoy it, when you know what you're doing.'

'I'll leave the flirting to Tommy, if you don't mind,' said Lucas with a cool, proud air that he invented for the occasion. 'Anyway, I'm out of practice these days, now I'm engaged to your lovely self and don't need to flirt anymore.'

Clara laughed, the sound muffled by the white powder transforming a familiar landscape into a picturesquely strange land. 'Were you ever *in* practice, dear?' she teased, reaching up and playfully tugging the lapel of his coat. 'If you *were*, I'm afraid I never noticed.'

Lucas opened his mouth wordlessly, torn between the truth of how he'd carefully avoided anything *like* flirting with his best friend's little sister, for what he hoped was fairly obvious but likely to be scorned reasons, and a lie that might help him save face.

Thankfully no lie was needed on this occasion as Tommy created a magnificent diversion by losing his footing on the slope ahead and landing face down in the snow. He bounced back up like a rubber ball, unhurt and laughing fit to burst, then collapsed back on the ground to make snow angels.

The sticky question of Lucas' flirting capabilities - or more specifically, lack thereof – was forgotten for now.

Tommy waited for them, giggling and pelting them with handfuls of snow as they approached. After a short snowball fight followed by making themselves look presentable again, the trio continued their tramp up to Castlebury Manor in good spirits. By the time they rang the bell, their cheeks were rosy with cold and aching from laughter.

Even Lucas was cheerful, despite Tommy's persistent company.

As Lucas rang the doorbell, Tommy once again admired the magnificent building, and Clara imparted her knowledge of the manor's history to him in such an adorably sisterly manner that even Lucas couldn't help but smile.

Perhaps all Tommy needed was familial affection, thought Lucas as he rocked back and forth on his heels, an uncomfortable squirmy feeling of guilt starting in his chest. *Lord knows the poor chap didn't get enough of that as a nipper. And I haven't really been terribly nice to him, have I? Damn.*

The internal musings and Tommy's impromptu history lesson were cut short when the sour-faced butler opened and stared haughtily down his nose at them.

'Her Ladyship is not at home at present,' he said, looking rather pleased about this.

'That's all right,' said Clara brightly, peering around him. 'We actually have a word with Jono – that is, Lord Cassiobury, if you know where he is.' She stood straight again, grinning happily. 'I do believe that's his hat on the telephone table. Glo – Miss Gloria Hawkes, was telling me all about the rather smart bottle green hat she got him for his birthday, and how it's still his favourite even after, you know.' She leaned forward and whispered conspiratorially.

'After he broke their engagement. Terribly sad, isn't it?'

A small muscle twitched under the butler's eye. 'I shall see if the young master is in,' he said unhappily.

'I do hope he is,' said Clara, maintaining an air of cheerfulness, and turning to look down the hill. 'I should hate to think of him out on a day like today without his favourite hat. The hat he wears *everywhere.*'

'Nice work,' muttered Tommy. Clara kicked his ankle and grinned at the grumpy butler when he turned to see what the handsome young man was yelping for.

Lucas smirked and followed Clara into the hallway, with Tommy bringing up the rear as was quite right and proper in Lucas' eyes.

Oh yes, Tommy can be Clara's surrogate brother with my blessing, he thought smugly. *It might keep her occupied enough to stop managing me all the time. I doubt it, but one must live in hope in these dark times.*

As soon as they crossed the threshold, sounds of an argument could be heard spilling down the grand staircase. It sounded like Jonny and Shank having a dust-up, though what the affable young man and the equally laid-back herbalist had found to fight over was beyond Lucas.

Clara glanced at him quizzically, clearly wondering the same thing. Tommy, meanwhile, pretended to not hear the ruckus upstairs in favour of admiring the fine decor, whilst clearly hanging on every word.

The butler cleared his throat loudly.

'I shall enquire as to whether the young gentleman is receiving visitors,' he said.

'We can certainly hear he's in,' said Clara, cocking an eyebrow as the corner of her mouth twitched upwards. 'Although I'm sure we'll understand if he doesn't want any, er, *extra* company.'

The butler paused as he turned. 'Quite,' he said, before scurrying away, his soft-soled shoes barely making a sound on the marble tiled floor.

'I wonder what -' started Lucas

'Shh,' said Clara, waving him into silence.

Tommy gave him an infuriating look that said, "Come on, you shouldn't have to be told something so basic," which Lucas thought he ignored rather well as he obligingly shushed and straining his ears for snatches of the conversation.

'… frightful imposition on the poor woman,' cried Jonathon.

'Imposition!' replied Shank hotly. 'You'd know all about being one of those, my lad.'

'How dare you! And don't you "my lad" me, you silly old duffer. You might have fooled the aunt, chum, but you haven't pulled the wool over my eyes.'

'For the last time, you stupid boy, I'm not pulling the wool over anyone's eyes! I love Bunty with all my heart –'

'Love her house and title more like!'

'They might be the only reason *you're* hanging around her, but not me.'

The voices dropped, presumably having been interrupted by the lugubrious butler. A door slammed upstairs and Shank came tearing down the grand staircase, shrugging on a tweed jacket as he went.

'I will not be insulted like that,' he roared. 'Your aunt will hear about this, you impertinent pup, you see if she doesn't!'

Too late, he spotted Lucas, Clara, and Tommy, who hastily looked away and began a loud conversation about the weather.

Shank paused, adjusted his jacket with forced calmness, his hands shaking over the buttons, and trotted down the stairs with an affected spring in his step.

'Good day,' he said, a tense note twanging in his voice. 'I, uh, I suppose you heard some of that?'

The trio shared a glance.

'Hard not to, I'm afraid,' admitted Lucas.

'We weren't deliberately listening, of course,' added Clara.

'Speak for yourself,' said Tommy under his breath, earning him crushed toes courtesy of Clara's leather boot.

'Hmm,' said the doctor, unimpressed. 'I suppose I owe you an explanation.'

'Not at all,' said Lucas, cutting over Clara's eager acceptance of the gossip. She shot him a dirty look, and Lucas shuffled away slightly. After all, she had two feet in two hard-heeled little boots. He didn't fancy adding bruised toes to the list of mistreatments his feet had received recently.

Shank nodded at him. 'Thank you, young man,' he said. 'I don't like airing dirty laundry in public - but equally I don't like leaving my acquaintances, no matter how casual they may be, with the impression that I'm an unreasonable man.' He glanced anxiously up the stairs. 'I trust you won't tell anyone what you heard.'

'What we heard?' said Lucas, frowning. 'I didn't hear anything, did you, darling?'

'Nothing at all,' said Clara, shaking her head. 'Certainly not a figh- er, loud discussion, between you and Bunty's nephew.'

'Oh come on, are you really -' started Tommy, before fresh pain in his toes stopped the sentence before it could be completed.

Shank narrowed his eyes at them.

'It'll be all round the servants by now anyway, I should think,' he said with a sigh. 'But Bun is more likely to pay heed to someone like you.' He ran a hand over the back of his neck and looked up the stairs again. 'Look, before you hear it from *him*,' he said. 'Bourbon-Busset just accused me of young Chapman's murder - as though I'd be foolish enough to kill the boy with something that'd point to me.'

'Of course,' murmured Tommy, rolling his eyes at Lucas.

Lucas almost managed not to smile.

'No,' continued Shank, as though he hadn't heard. 'I rather fear someone is trying to put me in the frame by using mistletoe as the poison - but you must believe me when I say I'd never, *never* use the power of plants, the very thing that made my name and fortune, to harm rather than heal.'

He spoke with such earnest conviction that Lucas found himself nodding in agreement without a thought. His companions looked less convinced, but Shank saw what he wanted to see.

'I knew you were sensible young people,' he said with relief. 'Now my good fellow, you must look me up next time you're in London and in need of a tonic.' He pulled three business cards from an inner pocket with his address and profession written in elegant, professional, but most importantly, *expensively* restrained letters. Herbs twined around a Caduceus in place of the snakes, driving home the "healing with plants" message Shank was so keen to profess.

Neat, very neat – but not a cheap thing to have produced, thought Lucas, examining the card with interest. *I wonder if the doctor has more than just gambling debts to worry about...*

'Why would someone frame you for murder?' asked Clara, running her fingertips over the deep impressions left the by the letterpress with undisguised admiration.

Shank pulled a face. 'I'm sure you read in the papers that my treatments are, ah, somewhat effective?'

Tommy nodded enthusiastically, and shrugged when Lucas shot him a withering look.

'Well, some people don't like that,' continued Shank. 'Business rivals, of course, but also those who fell foul of the consequences' His thin lips twisted into a wry smile. 'Both those caught with their pants down and those doing the catching.'

Clara gave Lucas a "watch and learn" look, and moved a little closer to Shank.

'I can imagine that'd make life difficult for you at times,' said Clara sympathetically, brushing her fingers against the older man's forearm. He patted her hand gratefully and she snuck a sly, triumphant glance at Lucas.

He tried to pretend this blatant use of feminine wiles to get information from foolish old men didn't bother him at all.

It didn't work.

'At times, my dear, at times,' said Shank with a world-weary sigh. 'But it is a burden I am willing to bear if I can continue my life's purpose of helping people using the healing power of plants.'

Lucas and Tommy shared an unimpressed look.

'It makes me quite angry to think someone misused nature's gift like that,' continued Shank, the fire flashing in his eyes backing up his words.

'I'm not surprised,' said Clara in the same gentle, sympathetic tone. 'What a terrible way to use a beautiful plant.'

'Mistletoe is not only a beautiful to look at, my dear,' said Shank. 'It's a symbol of hope in the depths of winter, and frightfully useful for treating high blood pressure problems.'

He looked wistfully at a portrait of Bunty handing in the hallway.

'That's how Bun and I met, you know' he said, the lines on his face softening with affection. 'Her late husband called on me for assistance. Said he didn't trust doctors, and it was only after a lot persuasion by his wife that he didn't just pop off to the local healing woman. He'd been convinced in the end to contact a professional, but really, June Westerly taught me half of what I know. The rest was just developed using current scientific methods to refine the old processes, as is quite right and proper for this modern age.'

'You know Mrs Westerly?' said Lucas with a frown. 'I'd have thought such a connection would taint your reputation.'

'My dear boy, not in the slightest,' said Shank with a laugh that grated on Lucas' nerves. 'Indeed, without a strong tradition of healing by women like Mrs Westerly, there wouldn't be any medicine at all. I have a lot to thank her for – but of course, I studied natural healing methods of the ages and improved their efficiency, and made the natural healing arts a respectable and viable option again.'

I wonder if he can manage a whole sentence without dropping a sales pitch in there somewhere, mused Lucas. *Probably not, which is probably why he's so successful in his chosen profession. Perhaps I ought to try it?*

'But you must admit,' said Clara, her hand still resting on the arm of the herbalist. 'That if anyone was going to use a plant to commit murder, it'd be someone like yourself.'

'You might think that,' said Shank, turning his attention back to her, his eyes shining with righteous zeal. 'But I respect nature's gifts too much to abuse them in such a way. I have the highest possible respect for the healing arts, and I would never - *could* never – bring myself to commit a murder in such a fashion.'

The zeal turned to a malicious glint in an instant, causing Clara to withdraw her hand sharply and retreat to the safety of Lucas' side, slipping her chilly fingers into his.

'If I were to kill someone,' said Shank, his

gaze absent but thoughtful. 'I'd not use *poison*. No, no, not I. Not poison. I'd want to be up close and personal at the moment of death. I'd want to feel his pulse stop, see the life force ebb from his veins.' He paused a moment, before adding quite conversationally, 'I'd slit his throat, I expect. If I were to kill someone, of course, which I wouldn't - at least, not unless the circumstances particularly required it. Yes, or quite possibly stab him in the heart and feel the heat of the rotter's blood flow over my hands.'

He turned a bright smile towards the young couple and their friend, oblivious or, more likely, simply unconcerned by their frozen expressions. 'An interesting thought exercise. I thank you for it.'

A door slammed somewhere upstairs, followed by feet hurrying down the many flights stairs.

'That's my cue to leave,' said the doctor, retrieving his coat and hat from the stand beside the door. Knocking the Homburg onto his head, he tipped it at his acquaintances. 'Good day to you,' he said, before disappearing through the main door with his overcoat still draped over his arm.

'Thank God for that,' said Tommy loudly, wiping his brow. 'Right fruitcake, that one.'

'Shush,' said Clara. 'Someone's coming.'

As the words left her lips, Jonny appeared at the turn in the staircase, looking somewhat flustered and smoothing his dark hair into place as he passed a mirror.

'Sorry to keep you waiting,' he said, slightly breathlessly. 'Just, er, freshening up, you know how it is.'

Starting with a lie, thought Lucas, amused. *How many more will we hear, I wonder?*

Tommy was introduced, his effortless charm instantly putting Jonny at his ease.

However, Clara shattered it almost as quickly.

'We saw Dr Shank leaving just now,' said Clara with conscious sounding coolness. 'He's a fascinating chap, isn't he?'

And she says I lack subtlety, though Lucas, as Bourbon-Busset's face lost all colour except a rose-pink hue on his annoyingly perfect cheekbones.

'Ah,' he said, a wealth of discomfiture compressed into that one syllable. 'I was hoping he might have had the decorum, or at least the sense, to not – but it hardly matters.' He smiled, though it didn't quite reach his grey eyes, full of turbulent storm clouds. 'I suppose you heard our, er, little disagreement?'

'Not really,' said Clara. 'Though he did mention that you thought Chapper's blood was on his hands.'

'And so it is,' cried Johnny, all thoughts of saving face vanishing in righteous indignation. 'Who else would think to use such a poison, if not an herbalist?'

'But *everyone* knows mistletoe is poisonous,' said Clara, wide-eyed innocence radiating from her like the thought just dropped into her empty little head. 'Don't they?'

'*I* jolly well forgot,' retorted Johnny, his colour rising further, his face now unattractively blotchy.

Lucas thought this was interesting, and was almost glad Clara had chosen such a method of questioning. Not quite glad, but close enough to it to recognise its effectiveness.

'It's not the kind of thing most normal, sensible folks remember, is it?' continued Bourbon-Busset, looking queasier by the second. 'Is it?'

'Oh no, I shouldn't think so,' said Clara soothingly, linking her arm through his. 'Why don't you fix us all some cocktails and tell us what really happened?'

He gave her a sickly grin. 'All right,' he said. 'Let's go up to the parlour. The police have finished with it now, and the best drinks are kept in there.

He began leading her up the stairs, leaving Lucas and Tommy standing at the foot of the stairs.

'Not at all suspicious,' muttered Tommy, holding Lucas by his sleeve so he couldn't go racing after Bourbon-Busset and Clara. 'What do you make of that, then?'

'No idea,' replied Lucas, jealously watching his girl walk off with another chap. She shot Lucas a cross look over her shoulder that spurred him into life. 'But I think we'd better follow them.'

'Yes,' said Tommy, walking up the sweeping staircase beside Lucas. 'And keep your eyes on his hands whilst he's our mixing drinks, for God's sake.'

***

'Cocktails, yes - jolly good idea, old girl,' said - what was his name? Belgium-Basset, or some such double-barrelled nonsense these pretentious fools come up with – as Tommy and Lucas traipsed into a stuffy, old-fashioned parlour room behind Batwing-Brussel and Clara.

Bantam-Tussle seated Clara on a solid, well-worn Chesterfield sofa in oxblood leather, which Tommy enviously presumed had been bought by someone's great-great-granddaddy and would be handed down to a great-great-grandchild of the current owner at some point in the distant future.

However, Tommy noted with a wry smile, the reason Clara had been steered there was probably more to do with the proximity to the drinks' cabinet rather than the longevity of the furniture.

Lucas took a seat in the middle of the sofa

and placed a protective arm around her waist, which Tommy didn't blame him a jot for. If *he'd* got a girl like that, and they were near a shark like Blacksmith-Hussle, he'd not be letting go of her either.

Clara, however, did blame Lucas, and nudged his hand away irritably. She whispered something in his ear that sent black clouds scurrying across his average features. Tommy was quite used to seeing Lucas' face like that, although it was a pleasant novelty for it not to be directed at him.

Oddly, this put Tommy in rather a good mood, so he spent a few seconds admiring the room, absent-mindedly appraising the valuables as though he were going to fence them.

Which he wouldn't, of course. Not nowadays at least, but… well, old habits die hard, don't they? He was his father's son, after all, and daddy dearest would've had his guts for garters had he known Tommy was in a place like this and didn't case the joint. Less of a problem now the old devil was pushing up daisies, of course, but his shadow still hung over Tommy. And despite his newly turned leaf, he occasionally found himself doing things that would have pleased the old man. Or as near to pleasing him as was possible, anyway.

Tommy forced these thoughts away and focussed back on the room. He'd only let his mind wander for half a minute or so, and

Blackburn-Shuffle was still flirting outrageously with Clara under the guise of mixing her a drink.

'Now my dear, what would you like?' said Burnside-Huffer, flashing Clara a smile that, though undeniably handsome, made the hair on the back of Tommy's neck prickle.

Odd. Tommy thought he'd crushed his romantic hopes with Clara. Mostly, anyway, but he wouldn't act on them, even if he hadn't. Not now he and Lucas were pals.

Besides, he'd sworn off that sort of thing after... Well, the less thought about *her*, the better. Not Clara, she was an angel - but not all women were, were they?

Hadn't he learned that the hard way…

Yes, much better to focus on repairing his own shattered heart and bruised ego and all that, to take his mind off his recent romantic disappointments. He might even work on his career if he had nothing better to do, although he suspected things wouldn't be *that* desperate for a while.

No, Tommy Kilbourne was better off flying solo. Certainly for now, perhaps forever. Except for those fun little encounters whose recollections warmed a chap in the chill of the nights, about 3 am, usually. There was no point stripping his life of *all* its pleasures, after all. What would be the point of living without a little harmless fun every now and again?

So, if it wasn't simple jealousy giving Tommy the heebie-jeebies, perhaps something else made him mistrust this, uh, Turndown-Puffer fellow?

Tommy hoped so – after all, there was no point mending fences with Lucas only to burn them down again, to mix a metaphor. Despite their rocky history, Tommy was actually rather fond of the chap.

He went back to watching Burnt-Out-Lesser with mistrustful eyes.

'Now, let me guess,' said Burn-Toast-Leicester, putting his fingers to his temple and squeezing his eyes shut, as though reading her mind. 'A sweet girl like you would go for a Bee's Knees.' He pulled a bottle of gin and a lemon from the cupboard. 'I'll get Lewis to ring the kitchen to see if Cook has any honey, and I'll whip you one up, no problem.' He winked at Clara, who giggled coquettishly, raising Tommy's hackles further.

Whilst Blackout-Liar was explaining his need of honey to the butler, Lucas hissed 'What are you doing?' in Clara's ear.

'Flirting with him to get more information, of course,' she replied in hushed tones, though Tommy already knew this. A classic tactic, one he was personally extremely fond of.

Yes, there had been some delightful conclusions to that particular gambit.

'Take notes,' she added, nudging her fiancé. 'You might learn something.'

Before Lucas could protest, Blackguard-Friar was trying to take his order.

'Whiskey soda, thanks,' said Lucas stiffly, glowering at the man in a way that made Tommy's heart soar. At least he wasn't alone in objecting to this, whatever his damn name was.

'Come now,' said whatsisname - Background-Briar, perhaps? – in a gratingly ingratiating tone, playing the perfect host now his fluster from the hallway had subsided. 'Why don't you try something a little more interesting, eh? I could whip you up a Whiskey Sour, or pop some ginger ale in the stuff, that's jolly nice.'

Lucas grudgingly agreed to the second, declaring himself rather fond of ginger ale, whilst Tommy accepted a Whiskey Sour he had no intention of drinking. Buckingham-Crier mixed himself something called a Hanky Panky, a pretty drink somewhere between amber and ruby in colour, whose name made the impossibly prudish Lucas glow a similarly rosy shade.

Lucas, not being quite as dim as he looked, had sat in the middle of the sofa, so no matter the posh idiot's intentions there'd be no chance of him cosying up to Clara.

Which was a frightfully good idea, and Tommy was glad - almost glad, at least - that Clara had chosen someone with enough sense to know when to look out for her.

He'd taken a seat in chair opposite his friends, giving him a perfect view of his new foe, who was sitting next to Lucas and looking most put out about it.

Tommy faked a sip of drink before placing the heavy crystal tumbler on a side table, where he decided it would remain.

'How are you coping?' said Clara sympathetically, leaning around a rather peeved Lucas and batting her eyelids shamelessly at Birmingham-Buyer. 'What happened the other night was simply *dreadful*. And you and Chappers were like brothers... or so your aunt was telling me.'

'Yes, it is rather awful,' agreed the man with the ridiculous name, his staring vacantly into an unseen distance. 'We were neighbours growing up, you know. His people had the estate next to ours, and as there's only a few weeks difference in age, he and I have been pals from the start.'

He sighed dramatically, turning to Clara with a tragic look on his face. 'We played together from the very first days of our existence. Not always the best of pals, of course, but what boys don't have the occasional disagreement? I'm sure you both know what I mean,' he added, looking to Lucas and Tommy for support.

He didn't need any confirmation of his

point before continuing - which was fortunate, as Tommy certainly wasn't going to agree with anything this fool said, and Lucas was seething too much to reply.

Suddenly, Lucas winced and rubbed his eyes. Tommy watched him curiously for a moment, distracted from the main conversation. A glassy expression came over his friend's eyes and as Lucas started muttering out of the side of his mouth, Tommy twigged what was going on.

Allegedly going on, at least. The poor chap had one of his ghostly visitors to entertain, or so he'd likely claim. Tommy needed more convincing than a few party tricks and information that could have been sourced from anywhere – *but where?* said a treacherous voice at the back of his head, remembering the horribly accurate information Lucas presented Tommy with that time. He shivered and quickly silenced this thought, deciding to watch Lucas carefully instead.

He seemed to be having an argument with the voices in his head.

Poor fellow, terrible when a chap loses his mind. And so young, as well...

Tommy thought he'd perhaps be a little nicer to Lucas. Yes, that's what he needed, a little kindness. When there was no other, more entertaining option readily available, of course.

'Who do you think did it?' asked Lucas suddenly, smashing Clara's gentle investigation with his usual brick-like grace and subtlety.

Clara winced, though this went unnoticed by Blackjack-Bounder, who turned his attention to this interruption.

'I really couldn't say,' he said coldly. 'Everyone loved Chappers.'

'Clearly not,' said Lucas.

Tommy had to hide a snigger as Clara threw her hands up in despair, but Lucas clearly had a point to prove – presumably the foolish idea that it was possible to get all the information without any flirting.

Well, perhaps that *was* possible, but it wasn't nearly so effective, nor so fun. Best left to the cops, that approach, and Tommy was happy for them to take it.

'Perhaps it was an accident,' said Banjo-Counter in a tone that should have, by rights, frosted the near-empty glass in his manicured hand. 'Which I think is more and more likely,' he added, finishing the last drops of cocktail.

'How horrible,' exclaimed Clara loudly with an exaggerated shiver. 'If that's the case, any one of us could have drunk the poison by accident.'

'Indeed,' replied Brighouse-Saunter, turning back to her with a smile. 'Though of course, I'm glad neither of you were hurt.'

'Likewise,' replied Clara, leaning across and lightly touching the sleeve of his jacket, adding more dark clouds to Lucas' already stormy expression. 'But if the poison wasn't meant for *Chapman*, who could it have been for?'

Badhouse-Daughter looked into his empty glass. 'Do you know what the fateful drink was?' he asked. He held up the glass in his hand and jiggled it. 'My go-to tipple.'

Clara gasped, eyes like saucers in a way that would have convinced anyone except her friends. 'No!' she exclaimed with faked horror. 'You don't think…?'

Biglouse-Slaughter pulled a face. 'I'm afraid I do,' he said grimly. 'That's – that's what the argument with Shank was about.'

'But why on earth would Shank want to kill you?' said Lucas, who had been suspiciously quiet for some time. 'And how did Chapman get hold of your drink?'

'Well, the second part is easy enough,' said Woodmouse-Falter. 'Chappers was partial to a spot of Hanky Panky too – I'm sorry, my dear,' he said to an obligingly giggling Clara, leaning awkwardly across Lucas and patting her knee in an all too familiar manner. 'I don't mean to be uncouth, I meant the cocktail, naturally. Although – but that's not the kind of speech for a nice young lady to hear.

'Quite right too,' muttered Lucas, not quite under his breath. Tommy picked up his drink to hide his smile, absent-mindedly took a sip - then carefully returned the liquid to the glass under the guise of taking another drink.

Whilst it was unlikely this Titmouse-Fowler fellow would poison a man he'd only just met, Tommy knew better than to take chances.

'I was careless and knocked his over, so I insisted he took mine,' continued. His bottom lip wobbled. 'I'll never forgive myself for that.'

'Oh Jono, it wasn't your fault,' said Clara softly. He gave her a weak, brave little smile that made Lucas roll his eyes and Tommy fake another smirk-hiding drink.

'Perhaps not,' replied Figmouth-Tower sadly. 'But still, the cops say the drink that killed him was mine, and Shank has ample reason to want me dead.'

'Surely not,' gasped Clara in a show of girlish frailty that was rather repulsive, even though Tommy knew it was put on. It went against everything he lov- *admired* about the girl, and didn't suit her at all. 'A sweet chap like you couldn't *possibly* have made an *enemy*,' she concluded, batting her eyelashes at the scoundrel again.

'Not intentionally, I assure you,' replied said scoundrel earnestly, looking deep into her eyes with his own slate-grey sparklers. 'But one is the sole heir to a rather large estate, and when an underhand chap like Shank fixes his eyes on one's aunt, it's entirely possible to make the black list without having *done* anything, if you see what I mean.'

'Poor Jonny,' said Clara with a sigh. 'And

dear Gloria was telling me how frightfully *nice* you were, too. It hardly seems fair.'

Frogmouth-Lower blinked in surprise. 'She was?' he said, looking rather pleased. 'Well, it's been a while since she's said anything of the sort.' He toyed with his empty glass, not quite looking at any of his uninvited guests. 'I, uh, I suppose she told you what happened, did she? About how she and I were supposed to go riding off into the sunset together, until darling Sylvia stole my heart?'

He swallowed guiltily, as well he might. Though Tommy's own morals were somewhat flexible, he nonetheless despised such antics in other people - and welching on an engagement was beyond the pale.

No, Tommy would never allow a scheme to get so far as an *engagement*. Not if he didn't mean to go through with it, anyway, like with – ah, but no. Best not think about it, eh?

'Not my finest moment,' admitted the man, though no amount of humble admissions would stop his rapid decline in Tommy's opinion. 'But sometimes one does get rather carried away, especially when it comes to matters of the heart.'

Lucas was glaring at the cad with an uncharacteristic amount of venom. It was rather nice to see him take a strong opinion about something for a change, but it wouldn't help their sleuthing efforts.

Tommy coughed quietly to catch his attention, and nodded almost imperceptibly at Lucas to telegraph a silent vow to not leave "dear Jono" and Clara alone together, even for a moment. The small return nod and twitch at the side of Lucas' mouth showed the message had been received loud and clear.

Much to Tommy's surprise, Lucas relaxed his shoulders and sat back in his chair for the first time since they'd entered the room. It gave Tommy a warm glow in his chest – a little "boys together" project for the boy who had to fight against everyone to get anything.

If Clara hadn't been off limits before, she certainly was now. Tommy hadn't many friends, not the sort he'd trust with his life anyway, and he wasn't about to risk Lucas' good opinion by taking a shot at a girl he had no chance with.

Tommy settled back in his chair with watchful eyes on his charge, determined to do his best by his friends.

He knew Clara could handle herself perfectly well, of course, but it still wouldn't be the done thing to leave her with such a bounder.

'Yes, I'm sure,' said Clara sympathetically, having missed this silent exchange. 'Still, Gloria seems to have pulled herself together quite well.'

'With a little help from her friends,' said Backstab-Lover, a bitter note in his voice.

Curious – why should his ex-lover's

friends helping her recover from heartbreak cause such sourness?

A glance at Lucas' slightly flushed face told Tommy it was a friend of the *male* persuasion, which was an entirely different kind of situation.

Tommy's lips twitched. Interesting, very interesting. He wasn't good for much, but getting information from a lady was definitely in Tommy's skillset. He logged the information for future use, the germ of a very pleasant idea sprouting. Not that he'd be allowed to act on it, no doubt, but still, it was nice to hope he might be allowed to work his magic on this Gloria girl.

Especially if she was a looker.

'But of course,' continued Blaby-Liner, 'Gloria and I will always be jolly good chums.'

'Of course,' said Lucas with an impressively straight face. 'Why wouldn't you be?'

'Indeed,' was the reply, curt and rebuffing further comment.

A few moments of uncomfortable silence passed.

Well, it'd be uncomfortable if Tommy felt such things. He rather enjoyed the awkward little tableau before him, and took a sip of his drink, swallowing before he remembered he shouldn't. Chewing his bottom lip, he frowned into his glass. Oh well, a little probably wouldn't hurt…

'You don't think,' said Clara eventually, before covering her mouth with her hand. 'Oh no, of course not.'

'What?' said Bussell-Shoelace - damn, what *was* that fellow's name? Tommy couldn't recall, but he was fairly sure it couldn't be that. Oh well, whatever the devil's name was, he sighed as though his heart might break. 'I want poor old Chappers to see justice more than anyone else, and if you've had an idea about who might have done it, you should say without hesitation.'

'Well,' said Clara in a fragile voice designed to play on the masculine protectiveness of Whatsis-Thingamabob.

Tommy was proud; it was always pleasant to see a student perform so well on the field. Now, a little frightened wobble in the voice should finish the job nicely...

'Well, you don't think Gloria might have had a little bit of an axe to grind with you,' said Clara in a voice that made Tommy wonder if the future Mrs Rathbone had a touch of the supposed "psychic gift" as well as her fiancé. 'She could have slipped something nasty into your drink, and it was just bad luck that Chappers drank it instead?'

'No,' exclaimed, you know. Him, over there on the sofa. The posh one, not Lucas. 'Absolutely not. Not my Glo, she wouldn't – she'd never –'

'See, I told you it wasn't worth mentioning,' cried Clara, with more faked distress.

Tommy applauded her silently, and then himself for tutoring her so well.

'And now I've upset you.' she sniffed theatrically.

So very, *very* well.

'Oh no, no of course you haven't my dear,' said the posh boy in a rush, hoping to dam the flood of tears with a jumble of words. 'I'm sorry, it's a good suggestion, but Glo wouldn't hurt a fly, let alone *me*.'

'No,' said Clara tearfully 'I didn't think so, not really.'

'Now, don't go upsetting yourself, dear,' said – dammit, it was on the tip of Tommy's tongue… no, gone again – *that man*, pressing his handkerchief into her hand and watching as she delicately dabbed her eye.

Tommy eyed it curiously. Monogrammed hankies? There's a thing.

He wondered what J B-B stood for and began musing over the scoundrel's name again.

'No keep it, I insist,' said, uh – Jericho Blackbeard-Breadknife, perhaps? - as Clara tried to return the handkerchief. 'It's the least I can do, considering I've been such a rotter as to make a lady cry.'

'Thank you,' said Clara, hiccupping slightly as she tucked it into the front of her blouse. Lucas groaned, and even Tommy had to sympathise with him. There was flirting for information, and there was just being downright provocative.

He couldn't have been prouder.

'Well, thanks for the drink,' said Lucas, emptying his almost full glass in one and standing abruptly. Clara looked daggers at him, much to Tommy's amusement, but they bounced straight off. 'Come along, darling,' he said, offering Clara a hand up, which she reluctantly took without standing. 'Shouldn't we be off home now?'

'I don't think there's any rush, my love,' said Clara coolly, sending more bouncing daggers his way and remaining firmly seated.

'Well, I suppose not,' said Lucas, racking his brain for an excuse to get her out of there. 'But didn't we say we'd have lunch with your brother? Or, or was it your mum?'

Lucas shot a pleading glance at Tommy, who decided he probably owed Lucas a favour somewhere along the line.

'Isn't your mum putting on a spread to see off her guests this evening?' he said, acknowledging Lucas' grateful look with a tiny inclination of the head.

'Yes – yes, that's right,' said Lucas, too relieved to hide it. 'That's exactly it. And we can't be late, or we'll miss the fun.'

'Hmm,' said Clara, eyeing him

suspiciously as she finally rose to her feet. 'I suppose we couldn't miss something like that.' She glanced out of the window at the yellow-grey clouds skimming the hills in the distance. 'We should get moving before the next avalanche of snow comes down.'

'Exactly,' said Lucas, clearly kicking himself for not thinking of that much more plausible excuse. 'It'll be a much longer walk in a blizzard.'

'I'd get one of our chaps to run you back home,' said Judas Buttery-Blackbird apologetically. 'But the cars are dashed impossible to start in this beastly weather and Aunt Bun took the Roller for a pootle around the lanes, and it's the only reliable one in the snow.'

'We'll enjoy the walk,' said Lucas, all but pushing Clara towards the freezing hallway.

Tommy sauntered after them, debating slipping a silver candlestick into his pocket as a souvenir. Wouldn't want to get out of practice, after all.

No, probably not a good idea, not with Julius Bouncing-Bundle at his elbow.

Oh well, maybe some other time.

'Humph,' said Clara, which Tommy thought people only ever said in books.

Lucas handed her the red felt cloche, still damp from their walk up, and plonked his own misshapen hat on his head as he shrugged his faded black coat onto his shoulders.

Tommy smirked as he donned his own coat and the delightfully cosy hand-knitted hat Flora had given him on Christmas morning. *Ah Lucas, subtlety isn't your strong suit, my friend…*

'I quite agree,' said the man possibly known as Justin Braeburn-Bunny. 'There's something frightfully bracing about a winter's walk, isn't there?'

'Yes,' said Clara flatly, as Lucas helped her into her coat. 'Frightful indeed.'

'Come on, dear, before the snow starts,' sang Lucas, putting a hand to the small of her back and steering her towards the door.

The discontented butler appeared as though from thin air and opened it for them, and once more the trio stepped into the frozen countryside that looked like a painting Tommy once saw in the National Gallery.

Who knew places like this actually existed? And that people *lived* here?

He paused for a moment to look at the world painted white, and inhaled the wonder of the scene. The painting, beautiful as it is, hadn't prepared him for the scene to smell so fresh, or have snow that squeaked under his boots, or ice needles pricking his cheeks, and just generally make a body feel so alive! It really was a wonder, and he vowed that one day he should live permanently in such a place.

Once he'd made his fortune and could

retire comfortably as a country gent, of course. It wouldn't be half as much fun to live somewhere like that and *work* for a living, oh no.

He'd lingered too long, and after making hasty goodbyes to Jasper Barrington-Brown, Tommy jogged down the driveway just in time to hear Clara scolding Lucas.

He smirked.

Well, this should be fun…

***

'You, Lucas James Rathbone,' said Clara, after checking they were out of earshot from anyone at the hall. 'Are ridiculous and insufferable.'

'Me?' said Lucas guiltily, putting his arm around her shoulder. 'I haven't the faintest idea what you mean, darling.' He turned to glare at Tommy, who stopped jogging after them and became suddenly engrossed by a non-existent bird that hadn't swooped overhead.

Great, there'd be no hiding their spat. At least the dratted man had the courtesy to drop back a little and eavesdrop from a distance.

'Don't you "darling" me,' snapped Clara, crossly shrugging his arm away again. 'When will you learn that if I'm flirting with a chap, it's only for the greater good – in this case, catching a murderer!'

'I know,' said Lucas, skipping

occasionally to keep up with her furious pace. 'But have a heart, Clara. It's not easy watching your girl fawning over another man right in front of you, you know. How would you like it if it were the other way around?'

Clara stopped suddenly, causing Lucas to crash into the back of her. He looked at her face, and rather wished he hadn't. She had her eyes squeezed shut and was counting under her breath.

Lucas hoped those ten seconds might just save his life, or at least his relationship.

No, the other way around. Either way, he hoped it'd help.

When well over ten seconds had passed, he figured she was probably counting to an even higher number and it was probably best not to interrupt.

A glance over her shoulder showed Tommy still keeping a tactful distance and looking at goodness knows what in a hedgerow. Lucas wondered what had come over the man. He'd find out later - if Clara didn't murder him for messing up her scheme, anyway.

Lucas went back to watching her count.

Approximately a minute after first closing them, Clara opened her eyes.

'I suppose so,' she said, the angry tone in her voice subdued but not absent. 'But we may have missed vital clues because you don't trust me.'

'I do trust you,' insisted Lucas, reaching for her hand then hesitating. 'It's just – well, even in the pursuit of truth and justice and all that, it's still hard to watch you be like *that* with someone else.' He wondered if he sounded like he was whining, and decided to move to sullen instead. 'I wouldn't mind if you told me what you were planning beforehand.' Checking Tommy was out of earshot, he added, 'I talk to ghosts, I'm not a mind reader.'

She rolled her eyes, grabbed his still hovering hand, and all but threw herself into his arms.

'I know, darling,' she said, squeezing him tightly as he returned the gesture with surprise and relief. 'And if you like, from now on I'll tell you if I'm going to do something like that, all right? I'm sure I'd be as bad if it were the other way around.' She pushed herself backwards and fixed Lucas with a stern look. 'But it's still infuriating when you run my plans off the road like that. You know I've only ever had eyes for you.'

'I'm sorry,' he said, trying to mean it and pulling her in close again. 'But I'm sure we learned a lot anyway. For a start, don't you think it's interesting that Jonny thinks Shank was trying to kill *him*, not Chapman?'

'Is it safe to come over yet?' called Tommy, who definitely hadn't been listening at all from his self-imposed exile.

'Yes,' called Clara, before Lucas could tell the third wheel to roll off somewhere else.

'Hang on, I haven't told you what Chapman told me yet,' muttered Lucas. 'You know I don't like talking ghosts in front of Tommy, not after last time.'

'I'm sure it can wait, dear,' replied Clara, stealing a kiss in a blatant but successful attempt to shut him up. 'We should visit Henry anyway to find out if there's been any official developments and tell him what we've learned. Save it until then.'

Tommy bounded back over like a lost puppy and threw his arms around his friends' shoulders.

'All kissed and made up?' he asked. 'Excellent! I can't stand conflict.'

This was news to Lucas, but Tommy didn't leave time to comment.

'Let's go home for some cocoa,' he said, patting them both companionably on the back and taking the lead like he'd lived in Castlebury Magna his whole life. 'I'm frozen.'

'Is he always like that?' Lucas asked Clara, taking her hand as they followed Tommy, who continued his exuberant examination of the countryside.

'Like what?'

'I don't know,' said Lucas. 'Confident, at home wherever he is...'

Tommy started whistling at whatever

bird had caught his attention.

One of the feathered variety, for a change.

'Cheerful,' added Lucas disapprovingly. 'It's very off-putting.'

'Oh that,' said Clara, hooking her arm though his and snuggling up against him. 'Yes, generally he's fairly cheery. Quite remarkable, when you think about what he's had to deal with.'

'Hmm,' said Lucas thoughtfully, privately renewing his previous pledge to try being nicer to Tommy. 'And you're quite sure he's not in love with you anymore?' he added, looking for a loophole.

Clara crinkled her nose. 'Of course not,' she said. 'He never was, you know that. It was just a game to him, trying to win my loyalty for that silly scheme of his.'

She kissed Lucas on the cheek, leaving a warm imprint on his ice-stung skin. It faded all too quickly.

'Not that it ever mattered to me,' she added. 'I've loved you since – well, I've always loved you in one way or another, I suppose. I'm not quite sure when it changed from *friends* love to *romantic* love, but somewhere along the line it did, and I wouldn't change that even if I could. You drive me to distraction at times, it's true, but there's no one else in the entire world I want to spend my life with. Nothing and no one will ever change that. I promise.'

Lucas stopped and spun her around to face him, kissing her until the rest of the world faded away.

'What was that for?' she said breathlessly as they broke the kiss, her face happy and pink.

'Because I can, and because I wanted to,' he said, feeling his heart pound and, not for the first time, wishing very much that they had their own home to go back to. 'And because there was a very long time when I couldn't and I really, really wanted to, and I don't think I've quite made up for it yet.'

'Well in that case,' she whispered, eyes shining, lipstick slightly smudged. 'You should do it again.'

So he did.

***

'What do you mean, not enough poison in the glass?' demanded Clara.

The rest of the walk back to Castlebury had been curiously lacking in conversation but full of playful looks and plenty of flirting. They'd stopped briefly at Mrs Jenkins, partially to warm up with cocoa but mostly to leave Tommy there and avoid an unpleasant scene when they talked to Henry.

Tommy gladly stayed to be doted on by Mrs Jenkins, who had informally adopted the "poor orphan boy" and seemingly adored him, unlike her son.

But despite Tommy's absence, it seemed there'd be an unpleasant scene anyway.

Lucas sat by the fire sipping his tea and watched the show, glad to be a member of the audience for a change.

'I mean, the glass with the poison in didn't have *enough* poison in it to kill Chapman,' replied her brother. 'At least, not according to the coroner, and he ought to know.'

'But what killed him?' said Clara. 'Was the mistletoe a cover? Was it really rat poison or something?'

'No, it was definitely mistletoe,' said Henry, ruffling his hair distractedly. 'The dose in his system would have taken down an ox, or at least a fairly large sheep, so there's no doubt about it. But wherever it came from, it wasn't his glass.'

'Then where did it come from?'

'What am I, psychic?' snapped Henry.

Lucas narrowed his eyes at him. *Not funny,* he thought, though kept it to himself to avoid being dragged from comfortable observation and into uncomfortable argument. *And it wouldn't help anyway. The bloody ghosts never know a thing about their deaths - and if they do, they lie about it, the idiots.*

Clara coughed and jerked her head in Lucas' direction.

'Oh right, sorry,' said Henry, glancing

apologetically at his friend, who graciously decided to forgive this latest transgression. 'But the fact is, it got there somehow,' continued Henry. 'Can't you ask him, Lucas? It'd make my life a whole lot easier, I can tell you.'

'I will when I see him,' said Lucas with a careless shrug like it was nothing, although if he never saw another ghost in his life he'd be deliriously happy. 'I don't think he was eating or drinking anything different to the rest of us though, was he?' he asked Clara. 'At least, not as far as we saw.'

'No,' she confirmed. 'But I was rather preoccupied with Gloria sobbing all over the place and the scandalous gossip from Bunty, which was far more interesting than watching what anyone was eating, so I couldn't swear to it.'

'Me either,' said Lucas thoughtfully. 'Though I spent most of the evening watching everyone else –'

'Until you got drunk and let your hair down for the first time in centuries,' supplied Clara with her usual helpfulness.

'Yes, all right, until then,' said Lucas. 'But it must have been before that because I saw Chapman leave the room. We just thought he'd gone to sleep it off, didn't we?'

'How wrong we were,' said Clara, shaking her head sadly. 'If someone of us had thought to go check on the poor man...'

'It wouldn't have made any difference,' said Henry, taking his sister's hand and giving it a reassuring squeeze. 'Nothing anyone could have done.'

'Perhaps not, but it's pretty frightful no one thought to see if he was all right.'

'You have no reason to feel guilty,' insisted Henry, their argument forgotten as brotherly concern took over from brotherly annoyance. 'You were there to do a job - and besides, you didn't kill him. Whoever did is the only one who should feel guilty, though I doubt they do.'

'True, and truer,' said Clara, cheering up slightly. 'Rotten way to go, though.'

'There are less awful ways to shuffle off this mortal coil,' agreed Henry. 'But we still don't know how the fatal dose got into the chap's system.'

Henry and Clara looked expectantly at Lucas, who stared blankly at them.

'Oh, right,' he said as the penny dropped. 'When I see him, I'll ask what he ate or drank the day of the party.'

'Any idea where he's got to?' asked Henry.

'Probably still up at the hall,' said Lucas, putting his feet up on a low footstool to suggest he had no intention of checking. 'He was there earlier, though he was mostly just agreeing with Bourbon-Busset's claims that it was all a terrible accident, and Jonny was the real target.' He buried himself deeper into the sagging armchair and brought his teacup to his lips again. 'I shouldn't be surprised if he's chasing ghostly parlourmaids around the hall. He's that sort of chap.'

'Yes, I've heard about him,' said Henry disapprovingly. 'Think you can find another excuse to go back up to the hall today?'

'Absolutely not,' said Lucas, pulling a blanket across his knee.

'Of course,' said Clara, whipping it away again.

'Excellent,' said Henry, clapping Lucas on the shoulder and slopping tea into his saucer. 'Report back to me as soon as you can and I'll get one of my famous policeman's hunches about where to start looking for this mysterious poison.'

***

'… and I *really* think I might have lost it here,' said Clara in her best persuasive voice.

Lucas hated that voice. It always meant there'd be trouble sooner or later, and Clara had a knack for running headlong towards it, dragging him along with her.

Judging by the look on the butler's face, it wasn't cutting any ice with him.

So this time it's trouble sooner, thought

Lucas glumly, trying to stamp some feeling back into his once again frozen and aching feet. *At least Chapman isn't -*

'Rathbone!' cried a now familiar and unwelcome voice with a faintly hollow ring to it. 'Rathbone, my dear fellow, I'm so glad you've come back.'

Lucas suppressed a groan. Of course Chapman was around. As if this wasn't going to be difficult enough.

'One of the servants would have handed over any stray earrings they found, miss,' said the butler haughtily. 'In fact, several pieces of jewellery were turned over to me after the ball. We have been trying to match the items to their rightful owner as and when they call up for them.'

Clara beamed. 'Well in that case, I'm sure it's in your lost and found box.'

The butler winced, realising his mistake - but Lucas had other problems to deal with.

'Gosh, it's frightfully dull being dead, did you know?' said the late Chappers. Lucas tried to will the inconvenient ghost away, though it had never worked before, and was unlikely to now.

'What did you say this earring looked like, miss?' asked the butler, raising a suspicious eyebrow.

'Um… it was gold, I think, with a, uh, ruby – well, paste actually, but a jolly good fake I can tell you – and…'

'Oh, Lewis, stop being tiresome, do,' scolded Bunty, who chose that moment to appear at the top of the stairs, warmly clad in navy-blue lounging pyjamas in what Lucas assumed was a fashionable cut, a white fur stole flung around her shoulders for warmth. 'What did I tell you about these young people always being welcome in my house?'

'Oho, he's for it now,' said Chapman gleefully. He nudged Lucas in the ribs, which was a cold and slightly ticklish sensation. 'I never liked him, so this should be fun.'

'Yes, Your Ladyship,' said the butler sullenly, standing to one side and allowing Lucas and Clara into the entrance hall, which was still somehow colder inside then it was out.

'Oh, how disappointing,' said the ghost, following the new arrivals into the hall. 'Better luck next time, Bunty going ballistic is really quite the sight to behold.'

The disappointingly non-ballistic Bunty did the air-kissing thing with Clara, and stretched out her hands to Lucas, who took them and shook them awkwardly, not quite sure what the proper response was. Considering the amusement in her eyes and at the corner of her mouth, and the look of despair on Clara's face, he suspected it wasn't that.

'You mustn't mind Lewis, dear,' said Bunty after dismissing the cantankerous old gentleman and taking her guests' coats herself. 'He's been with the family simply *decades* and gets a little protective, particularly if there's any hint of scandal.'

'Protective my foot,' exclaimed Chapman. 'He thinks he runs the place. I mean, he does, that's what a butler does, but still…'

'He's particularly not keen on reporters,' said Bunty, dropping the coats and hats onto the coat stand and taking Clara's arm. 'Not after all that utter tosh in the papers about how I killed Sir Samuel – all poppycock, naturally.'

'Naturally,' interjected Chapman.

Was that a hint of sarcasm Lucas detected? He wasn't sure, but he couldn't very well ask now, not with Bunty ushering them up the stairs.

'We'd been married twelve happy years when his heart finally gave out, poor dear,' said Bunty with a sigh, leading them towards the parlour where the fateful party had been. 'But being over twenty years his junior, the papers instantly cast me in the role of gold-digging, murderous *harpy*, and when they get an idea like that into their silly little heads, it's very difficult to shake it.'

Lucas swallowed guiltily, thankful Her Ladyship couldn't see his face.

However Chapman *could* see Lucas' face, and ghostly laughter rang in his ears as he traipsed up the stairs behind the ladies.

'Come through, come through,' sang Bunty, beckoning them through to the cosy parlour room where the party had been. 'I do hope you don't mind being in here again,' she said anxiously. 'Only I know how these things can go. People get terribly superstitious about places where death has occurred – and though poor Bertie met his maker in a different room, it seems likely that the deed was done in here.' She sighed and looked around the room. 'This is one of my favourite rooms in the house,' she said sadly. 'It'd be a tragedy to let it moulder under dust sheets for the rest of my days.'

Lucas and Clara hastily gave their word that they weren't bothered at all, conveniently forgetting to mention their impromptu cocktail party with Jonny earlier in the day. Now she'd been reminded of the terrible facts, Clara looked less happy about being in the room. Lucas gave her hand a little squeeze as he took his place on the sofa next to her. This received a small but grateful smile that made Lucas' heart glow.

'So, old bean,' said Chapman cheerfully, perching himself approximately on the arm of Bunty's chair, facing Lucas. 'Any news for old Chappers? Found out who did the dirty deed yet?'

Lucas shook his head slightly, keeping his eye on Bunty and glad to see Clara was keeping her distracted with some feminine topic Lucas would've ignored even if he hadn't had a ghostly distraction. It sounded like flowers or dresses or something equally dull. It was almost a relief to have a spirit to talk to.

Almost.

'Pity,' said Chapman with a sigh. 'I've tried to find out what happened, really I have, but these ghosts didn't see *anything* – far too wrapped up in themselves to be worried about anyone else's problems.'

Oh, the irony, thought Lucas with a wry smile.

'How about you?' asked the ghost. 'Have you managed to find out anything about my, uh, you know, my death?'

Lucas glanced at the ladies, who were deep in conversation about – oh lordy, his and Clara's upcoming nuptials, good grief - and wondered if he could safely get away with having a conversation on the same room.

The chair was awfully comfortable, and all that tramping around the countryside in the freezing cold made his feet ache something rotten. The fire crackled merrily in the hearth, and all in all, Lucas really didn't want to move.

However, it was only a matter of time until he got dragged into the wedding talk, and past experience told him that conducting two conversations at once would only result in the most frightful headache.

Ignoring his aching joints, he cleared his throat and said, 'Excuse me, Lady Gaylesbury -'

'Bunty, please,' she insisted, turning to him and flashing her young guest an affectionate smile.

'Bunty,' he corrected himself, blushing slightly. 'I don't suppose I could use your facilities, could I? It was rather a long walk, and I'm afraid I had double helpings of tea before we came out.'

'Of course, dear boy,' she said, indicating the door to the adjoining room. 'Through the Ghastly Pink Drawing Room, down the corridor on the other side, and you'll find a water closet on the left. That's where they found poor Bertie, you know,' she added, bottom lip quivering. 'Slumped against the wall, quite dead.'

'Urgh, no need to remind me,' said the ghost, his face a picture of disgust. 'How very undignified.'

Lucas thanked Bunty and paused at the door to make sure Chapman was following. When it was obvious he wasn't, and had no intention of doing so, Lucas beckoned him with a small jerk of the head.

Then another.

Chapman looked over his shoulder, then back to Lucas.

'Me?' he asked.

Lucas wondered how this particular Bright Young Thing earned the accolade.

'Oh yes, I see. Bit of privacy, what?' said the ghost, leaping to his feet. He kissed Bunty's cheek, leaving her with a mildly puzzled look on her face, and followed Lucas.

'Look, we don't have much time,' said Lucas as he and his latest dead friend stepped into the Pink Drawing Room, which was indeed Ghastly.

'Speak for yourself, I have all the time in the world,' said Chapman gaily, though there was a hint of sadness in his voice as well.

'Er, quite,' said Lucas, heart aching for the fellow. 'What I mean is, I can't take too long or I'll be missed, so let's get on with it, shall we?'

He pushed open the door on the other side of the room, and stepped into a corridor carpeted with a wonderfully springy Turkey carpet that stretched the length of the walkway, and probably cost more than his mother's house, that of her neighbours, and probably the entire street. His lower-middle class carpet envy was interrupted by the fabulous view through the large windows flooding the corridor with light, the setting winter sun peeking golden rays through the clouds and making the scene glow like a Renaissance painting.

'Yes, of course,' said Chapman, bringing Lucas back to the present problem with a bump. 'What's the problem? Assuming there is one, and you're not here to tell me that the mystery is solved.'

The ghost looked so hopeful, it was tragic to tell him they were no closer to working it out than before.

So, Lucas didn't.

At least, not in so many words.

'Er, the police had your glass tested,' he said, tearing his eyes away from the shimmering landscape and sauntering down a corridor longer than the main street of his beloved Castlebury, trying to keep his green-eyed monster in check.

'Jolly good,' said Chapman. 'I expect it was that, was it? Where the poison was?'

'Sort of,' said Lucas. 'But also, not quite.' He settled on a window seat with unrivalled views along the corridor, in the hopes he'd spot any intruders before they heard him apparently talking to himself.

'Not quite?' said Chapman, looking crestfallen. 'If it wasn't in the cocktail, then how on earth did I get it into my system, eh?'

'There was mistletoe in the cocktail, but not enough to kill you,' said Lucas, trying to remember that this was far more difficult for the dead than it was for him.

At least, according to friend and mentor Mrs Bird, though as a ghost herself she was probably a little biased. She also used to tell him that spiders were more afraid of him than he was of them, which he didn't believe either.

'What!' cried the ghost. 'Then what was the filthy stuff doing in my cocktail?'

'They're still working that one out,' said

Lucas, who figured this was true enough. 'But it's possible the fatal dose was given somewhere else, and the glass was a bluff.'

'I say,' said Chapman, a note of admiration in this tone. 'If so, that's frightfully clever, wouldn't you say?'

'Probably,' said Lucas, who hadn't given it any thought and just said it because it for something to say. 'Anyway, I need to know if you ate or drank anything else that evening - outside the party I mean - that might have contained the poison.'

'I don't know,' said the ghost, frowning. 'I'm sure I'd have noticed white berries in my food, and there definitely wasn't anything. But I have been thinking - you know Johnny is claiming Shank was trying to do him in?'

'Ye-es,' said Lucas slowly, almost certain he wouldn't like where this was going.

'And Jonny knocked my hand and gave me his drink?'

'What are you driving at?'

Chapman paused, mouth open to form the next words, but he didn't seem to know what they should be, so shut it again.

'Well, it rather sounds like old Bourbon-Busset was trying to do his old pal in, doesn't it?' said Chapman eventually, looking downbeat. 'Then covering it up by throwing suspicion on someone else whilst making himself look like the victim.'

'When you put it like that...'

'But why?' cried Chappers. 'Why would he do a thing like that? True, we'd had our disagreements, but nothing that'd lead to this.' He gestured at his translucent body.

'You're sure he wasn't bent out of shape about you and Gloria?' said Lucas suspiciously. 'Because I'd be upset about a thing like that.'

'Oh that,' said Chapman dismissively. 'Yes, quite sure. Quite sure indeed. Bad form on my part, I admit, but he was no better than I in that respect. You know Syl and I were supposed to be married?'

'Yes, you told me already.'

'Oh. Well in that case, you know I'm just as much sinned against as sinning. More so, in fact. If anyone had a reason to kill *anyone*, it was me to kill him, not the other way around.'

'Uh, you didn't, did you?' said Lucas, as a suspicion snuck into his head. 'I mean, you didn't try to kill him, forgot and drank the poisoned cocktail when he handed it to you?'

Chapman gave him a disparaging look.

'No, of course not,' said Lucas hurriedly. 'It's just, I wondered if you'd mixed up the glasses or something…'

'How stupid do you think I am?'

'Uh…'

'No, I'd never do a thing like that,' continued the ghost firmly. 'Never ever, not in a million years.'

'Right,' said Lucas, wondering if he was protesting a little too much. It wouldn't be the first time someone did something stupid and ended up dead as a result.

'And anyway, if there wasn't enough poison in the glass to kill *me*, then it follows that there wasn't enough in there to kill *Jonny*,' said Chapman triumphantly. 'So there.'

'But that just means you must have been the intended target after all,' said Lucas, who should have realised this sooner. He wouldn't admit that, though.

It knocked the wind out of Chapman's sails all the same.

'I suppose so,' said the ghost with a heavy sigh. 'How rotten. How thoroughly, thoroughly rotten. It's rather unpleasant to think that someone really wanted to kill *me*. What did I do to deserve that?'

'If we knew that,' said Lucas, wondering which of the many motives he knew about was the one that actually caused the fellow's death. 'We'd be further along trying to figure out who did it,'

'But I don't know,' wailed the ghost. 'Oh my, does that mean I'll be stuck here *forever* if we don't work it out? I'll be left behind as all my old chums live their lives, get old, and die! I'll have to see them forget all about me.'

'Look, calm down, we'll figure it out,' said Lucas, looking around uneasily. Panicking ghosts were not easy to deal with at the best of times, and the last thing he needed was for someone to come along and interrupt the interview. 'But I need you to pull yourself together and help me.'

'Yes, yes of course,' said Chapman, taking a few deep breaths for no practical purpose whatsoever, no longer having a body in need of oxygen. Still, it seemed to help him gather his thoughts. 'Where do we start?'

'Logically, a murder method with plants points to Shank as the culprit,' said Lucas, glancing up and down the corridor just in case. Seeing the coast was clear, he added, 'If so, he might have distilled the berries earlier and added it to your coffee, or something like that.'

'Not coffee, that's for sure,' said the ghost. 'I know it's the in thing to drink, but the old heart need looking after.' Catching Lucas' disbelieving look, he added, 'Family history, old bean. The pater had a dicky ticker, and whilst the doc says I haven't yet, he gave me a long list of things I should and shouldn't eat if I want to live a long and healthy life.' He laughed bitterly. 'Didn't mention anything about mistletoe though. Probably thought I'd not be daft enough to eat that.'

'Uhuh,' said Lucas, growing increasingly anxious about how long they'd been talking. 'So, if it wasn't coffee, what *could* it have been? Tea, lemonade, what?'

The ghost leant against the window seat thoughtfully, oblivious to the fact he sat some inches into the sun-bleached wood. 'Let's see... there was lunch. Fairly light, seeing as it was Christmas Eve and the servants were buzzing around getting things ready for the evening shindig and Christmas Day itself, so that was... cold meat sandwiches, tea, and a slice of rather good seed cake. Had two helpings of the stuff, come to think of it. Dear Glo's eyes were bigger than her belly, so I had her slice. Rather partial to the stuff, always have been. Couldn't resist. But lunchtime couldn't have been when I was... you know.' His face twisted in disgust. '*Poisoned*. It was a help-yourself-from-the-sideboard affair.'

'Not the most reliable place to poison someone,' agreed Lucas. 'Go on.'

'After that,' said Chapman, thinking hard. 'Sylvia made me a cocktail – a Sidecar, I think. Does it matter? Jonny had one too, and she had a whiskey soda. We were all in the billiards room, yes that's right. Jonny and Shank played a game or two whilst I watched and smoked cigarettes with Gloria. Not sure what they were, you'd have to ask her. I'd left mine in my room somehow, though I could have sworn I remembered to put them in my jacket. Not that it matters, of course. Who ever heard of a poisoned cigarette?'

'Who, indeed,' murmured Lucas, glancing up and down the corridor again.

'Jonny came up to my room as we were changing into our evening kit,' continued Chapman. 'He gave me a rather fine fountain pen and a box of chocolates for Christmas. My favourites, as it happens. Mint creams, jolly good choice - although I think he must have cheaped out this year, as they tasted a bit funny. Then again, I'd had a cold, and everything tasted a bit hinky that day.' He laughed bitterly. 'What a way to end your life, eh? Not even being able to taste anything properly. Even smokes didn't taste right, though maybe that was just whatever Gloria had picked up. Frightful, really.'

Aha, something promising at last.

'Sounds like you were right about Johnny,' said Lucas, feeling happier than he had in a while. At this rate, they might even get this mess wrapped up before the new year, and it was probably nice to start a new year with no ghosts lingering around the place.

Chapman shook his head. 'No, I know what I said earlier, but Jonny ate one or two of them too,' he said. 'Would he have done such a thing if he'd have poisoned them?'

'Maybe,' said Lucas. 'If he was trying to divert suspicion away from himself by looking like a victim too.'

'Yes, but he didn't get sick, did he?' said Chappers. 'He'd hardly look like a victim by not taking enough poison to get even a little bit poorly, is he?'

Lucas supposed not, feeling an all too familiar sense of gloom settle on him again as the prospect of a ghost-free new year faded before his eyes.

'The vain old duffer was worried about fitting into his wedding suit,' said Chapman, chuckling at the recollection. 'I kept telling him Christmas wasn't a time for restraint, but he was adamant. Something about it wouldn't do for their future children to see their father a bloated mess in all his wedding photographs, or some such codswallop.' The ghost rolled his eyes. 'And us chaps have the nerve to say it's the ladies who are the vain ones.'

'I guess that answers that,' said Lucas, the briefly held hope dashed unceremoniously. 'If he ate them and wasn't ill, it can't have been Johnny with the chocolates. I don't suppose there are any left, in case the cops wanted to test them?'

'They're my favourites,' said Chapman. 'Of course there aren't any left.'

'Of course,' said Lucas, feeling glummer by the second. 'What did you eat at the party itself?' he said, trying to discover something, *anything* useful before someone came looking for him. 'Did anyone fetch your food or, or pass something on to you, maybe?'

'I helped myself, I think,' said Chapman, brow furrowed in concentration. 'I eat most things, you know how it goes, but I am partial to a devilled egg, so I know I had a few of them. Even had Shank's leftover one after he said he was stuffed, as well as his mushroom vol-au-vent.'

'Did he offer them to you?' said Lucas, hopes rising again.

'I did ask for the egg – but only if he wasn't going to eat it,' said Chapman. 'And he said I may as well finish up the whole thing, as he'd eaten his fill.'

'Did Shank know you liked devilled eggs so much?' asked Lucas.

'I really don't think Shank would do a thing like that,' said Chapman, clearly realising the direction of Lucas' thoughts. 'He's a brick, and he really does believe in the healing power of plants and all that rubbish. Not to mention, he's a frightfully good match for Bunty.'

'I heard he was only after the manor, and she wanted his cash.'

'Oh, they might say those things in public,' said Chapman with a dismissive wave of the hand. 'But she spilled the beans that night we got drunk. She told me all sorts of things that night, in fact.'

'I'm sure she did,' replied Lucas in a cool tone contrasting with his warming cheeks.

'Don't be such a stick in the mud, Rathbone,' said Chapman, shaking his head despairingly. 'Don't tell me you've never...? No, never mind, not my place.'

'No,' said Lucas icily. 'It's not.'

'Anyway,' said Chapman, quite unconcerned. 'If you *must* know, nothing actually happened between Bunty and me. That was just a story we concocted after she told me -' He broke off suddenly and bit his bottom lip.

'You can't leave it there!' cried Lucas. 'What could she have told you that both of you would rather claim you *slept* together rather than have the truth come out?'

'I can't possibly tell you, old sport,' said Chapman, examining his ghostly cufflinks as he regained his composure. 'I gave her my word, and a chap's word is his word, you know that.'

'What if this secret is the reason you were killed – or worse,' said Lucas, an idea occurring to him. 'What if *Bunty* was supposed to die instead. She could still be in danger.'

Chapman let out a small cry and looked away distractedly. 'No,' he whispered. 'No, anything but that.'

'And why would you fabricate a cover story anyway?' pressed Lucas, sensing a revelation was at hand. 'Why not just say you hadn't seen each other?'

'Because –' Chapman swallowed hard. 'Because Jonny asked me to do him a favour, you see, and, you know, get the old thing drunk and create a little scandal.'

'What! Why?'

'Well, to drive a wedge between her and

Shank, of course.' The ghost took a great and sudden interest in his fingernails. 'I might not think he's so bad, but Jonny positively loathes him. I don't know how much of this is to do with Shank himself and how much is down to Jono's fear of losing his inheritance to any new husband of Bunty's, but there you have it.'

Lucas was speechless. Aghast. Horrified. How anyone could concoct such a devious plan was utterly beyond him - and to treat one's own aunt like that was truly abominable.

'He didn't expect me to sleep with Bunty, of course,' insisted Chapman, catching the expression on Lucas' face. 'Just get her drunk enough that it *could* happen, then make a frightful fuss when she inevitably made a pass at yours truly.' He smoothed his perfectly slicked-back hair. 'She always took a bit of an interest in me, you see, though I realise now it wasn't *that* kind of interest.'

'What kind of "interest" was it, then?'

'Uh, just as the friend of her nephew, of course,' replied Chapman in a strangled voice, a frightened look flashing across his face. 'She lived with Jonny and his folks whilst we were growing up – nowhere else to go, poor thing. You're a local lad, I'm sure you heard the rumours about her? And with he and I being best pals, I was there a lot. She was a good aunt to Jono, and as good as an aunt to me as well.'

Lucas was about to make some comment

about this, but the long overdue interruption arrived.

'No, don't move Bunty, I'll find him,' said Clara's voice, carrying through the Ghastly Pink Drawing Room and down the corridor as the door of the parlour opened again. 'Probably took a wrong turn somewhere, he's got a terrible sense of direction.'

Clara appeared the door on the far end of the corridor a moment later, looking frightfully cross.

'Where the bloody hell have you been?' she hissed, scurrying towards him. 'You've been gone ages. There's only so many times I can go over the details of wedding dresses and invitations and the like before I want to poke my own eyes out, you know.'

'Getting the gossip from Cha-' Lucas looked around but the ghost had gone. 'Oh, he was here a second ago.'

'Yes, well I've been finding out some gossip myself,' said Clara, glancing back down the corridor. 'But Bunty is a tad on edge because you've been gone so long. I think she's worried we'll have a repeat performance of the other night and find you dead in a cupboard.'

Lucas groaned. 'She thinks I've got some dreadful illness or something, doesn't she?'

'No, I told her you'd got lost,' said Clara, grabbing Lucas' sleeve and dragging him back towards the Ghastly Pink Drawing Room. 'And she said you seemed the type to get fuddled by a big house with a rat's nest of corridors.'

'Clara,' moaned Lucas, trying not to despair too much. 'Haven't we been over this? About your excuses making me sound like an imbecile?'

'It's perfectly believable though, my love,' she said sweetly, pausing their speedy return journey just long enough to kiss him.

'Thanks,' said Lucas sarcastically.

'You're welcome,' she replied cheerfully, taking his hand and starting walking again. 'We should get back in there before she thinks I've got lost as well.'

'Can't have her thinking we're both idiots,' said Lucas.

Clara stuck her tongue out at him, but he didn't notice.

'I wonder where Chapman got to?' he mused.

'No idea, but he'll track you down when he's ready to talk again,' said Clara. 'They usually do, don't they?'

'Unfortunately,' said Lucas as they slowed to a more sensible pace through the aptly nicknamed drawing room. 'Although I don't mind Chapman as much as some of the others. He's not too demanding, which obviously is the main appeal, and he's fairly affable, which is a bonus. Most of them are annoyingly insistent and absolutely awful people all round. Although he's obviously hiding something, which is always a concern.'

'Aren't they all?' said Clara, giving Lucas a lingering kiss on the lips before they returned to join Bunty. Clara's violet perfume enveloped him with her favourite intoxicatingly sweet floral scent, and he wished for just a few more moments with her, alone like this.

'Now, let's make our excuses as swiftly as possible,' whispered Clara, smoothing Lucas' crumpled lapels as she placed her hand on the brass door handle polished by many generations of aristocratic hands.

'Great idea,' said Lucas, his hopes leaping along with his heartrate. 'Fantastic, the best. My place or the office? I think Mum's out today, so we'll have the place to ourselves…'

Clara prodded his chest playfully. 'No,' she said slowly. 'I meant, so we could compare notes on our gossip sessions.

'Oh,' he said, trying not to let his disappointment show too much. 'Yes, that's what I meant too, of course.'

She rolled her eyes at him, gave him one last kiss and, with a broad smirk on her face, stepped into the parlour.

***

'So,' said Lucas, turning his coat collar up against the icy chill as they walked away from the manor. 'What did Bunty have to say for herself?'

'The usual guff, mostly,' said Clara, huddling her muffler around her ears and pulling her hat down low. 'All about how "terribly sad" it was that "dear Bertie" died, such a "bright young talent" had been "snuffed out too young." That sort of thing.' Clara crinkled her nose in disgust. 'All a little too sickeningly sweet, if you ask me. Especially after their affair. Quite disgusting, really.'

'Ah,' said Lucas. 'But you see -'

'And as much as I don't want to think of her doing something awful,' continued Clara. 'I'm afraid all Bunty's eulogising makes me more and more suspicious of her. He was just her nephew's friend and her one-time fling. Not that she mentioned that, of course.'

'I know what you mean,' said Lucas, now Clara let him get a word in edgeways. 'But according to Chapman, Bunty lived with Jonny's family as he was growing up. The Bourbon-Busset and Chapman estates were adjacent, so she knew "dear Bertie" quite well. Treated him as though he were her own nephew, by the sounds of it.'

Clara gave Lucas a sceptical look, one that he was all too familiar with.

He persevered, nonetheless.

'I think she may well have had a perfectly innocent relationship with our ghostly pal,' said

Lucas, steading himself against Clara as his feet slipped on the snow.

'If you want to believe that, darling, I shan't disabuse you of the notion,' replied Clara, raising a sceptical eyebrow. 'However, I've met women like her before. Lonely, middle-aged, an eye for the younger chap…'

'Ah, that's as may be,' said Lucas, making his way gingerly down a particularly treacherous bit of slope, and watching Clara jump down after him. 'But according to Chapman, Jonny asked him to help him drive a wedge between Bunty and Shank, claiming Shank was only after his aunt's money. I rather suspect Johnny's merely had his eye on the money as well, but that's a different matter. The plot basically involved, er, taking advantage of Bunty's known fondness for male company.'

'Oh really, Lucas,' said Clara, tucking her arm under his. 'Why can't you just say Jonny asked Chapman to seduce Bunty?'

Despite the fresh snow on the ground, Lucas suddenly felt hot and uncomfortable. He undid the top button of his coat and welcomed the icy caress of the wind on his neck – for all of three seconds, before his flesh goose pimpled and he shivered violently.

'Oh, that's why not,' said Clara, pecking his cheek as amusement danced in her eyes.

'You did that on purpose,' he said accusingly, which just resulted in more smirking.

He wished he didn't embarrass so easily.

Actually, he wished everyone didn't find it so amusing that he embarrassed so easily, but that wasn't going to happen any time soon…

'Poor Bunty,' said Clara with a sigh, cosying up to Lucas a little more and melting his annoyance. 'How could they do such a thing to her?'

'In the event, she turned Chapman down,' said Lucas, hurrying past the subject before his ears started burning again. 'Gave him a good reason by the sounds of it – something they both wanted to cover up so much that they'd rather lie about an affair than reveal the truth.'

'Interesting,' said Clara, pity transformed into curiosity. 'What was it?'

'Haven't the foggiest,' said Lucas. 'You interrupted just as Chapman was going to spill the beans.'

'Curiouser and curiouser,' mused Clara, ignoring the mild reproof. 'Do you think it's because she's Jonny's real mum?'

'Why would that stop her sleeping with Chapman more than if Jonny were her nephew?'

'No idea,' said Clara. 'An attack of conscience, maybe?'

'Stranger things have happened,' said Lucas without enthusiasm. 'I don't try to work out why anyone does anything anymore. It's rarely the reason you'd expect anyway.'

'You're quite gloomy at times, you know,' said Clara cheerfully, tramping through the freshly fallen snow with a spring in her step. 'Isn't it fun finding all these things out?'

'You mean, "isn't it fun sticking your nose into someone else's business?"' replied Lucas. 'Because that's what it is, you know.'

'Why do you think I went into newspaper work in the first place?' said Clara. 'I like to know what's going on, and it gives me an excuse to snoop.'

'It wasn't because you fancied me, then?' teased Lucas, kissing the side of her head.

'Of course not!'

'No?' he continued, enjoying a little good-natured revenge for once. 'You didn't think following me to the Gazette was a great excuse to spend more time with me? The thought didn't cross your mind for even one second?'

'Don't be vain, Lucas Rathbone' she said crossly, although the attractive rose-pink hue on her cheeks belied the truth.

It was rather gratifying.

The happy, flirtatious squabble continued for the rest of the walk back into Castlebury Magna, and they were barely back in familiar streets muffled and muted by nature when a voice accosted them.

'Finally,' it said, making them jump. They looked around for the source and found June Westerly leaning precariously out of the sash window at the top of her house, waving enthusiastically at them.

'Come up to the gate,' she cried, before pulling her head inside and thudding the window shut, sending snow tumbling from the windowsill onto the thickly blanketed plants below.

Lucas and Clara shared a mystified look and obediently stood by the gate, stamping their feet for warmth as they waited.

Moments later, Mrs Westerly appeared at the door, huddled in an oversized greatcoat with the sleeves rolled up to free her hands. The hem of the coat skimmed her ankles, revealing striped socks knitted in scraps of yarn, creating an eye watering clash of colours, over her well-worn carpet slippers.

'You were at the manor the other night, weren't you?' she called, chafing her arms. 'The reporters?'

'Yes, Mrs Westerly,' replied Clara a touch cautiously. 'Why do you ask?'

'Come in my dears, do,' said Mrs Westerly, beckoning them up the unswept garden path. 'Before I catch my death out here. I have some information you might find interesting.'

Lucas and Clara cautiously made their way up the icy flagstone walkway, herbs and healing plants on either side bowed low underneath the weight of snow.

'What does she want with us?' whispered Lucas.

'I don't know,' replied Clara, clutching his arm a little tighter as her feet found a slippery patch. 'But I want to find out enough to risk an ankle on this path.'

'I have tea,' said Mrs Westerly encouragingly. 'Or cocoa, if you'd prefer.'

'That's why I'm risking my fragile body,' said Lucas, heroically catching Clara again.

'Fragile,' she scoffed, clinging to him. 'You won't be if you keep drinking cocoa three times a day. I saw you put four spoons of sugar in yours at my mother's house, don't pretend you didn't.'

Before Lucas could concoct a suitably witty reply, they found themselves in a surprisingly cosy, surprisingly well-kept little cottage, with not a thing out of place.

Mrs Westerly chuckled at their amazement. 'Yes, I know what you're thinking,' she said. 'Batty old Juney is a witch, so her cottage must be a cluttered hovel.' She took their coats and hats through to the kitchen at the back of the house and arranged them on the back of a chair in front of the stove. Herbs dripped from the ceiling in bunches, the smell of freshly baked cakes hung in the air, and a kettle was just coming to boil on the gleaming cast-iron range.

Three mismatched cups and saucers sat on the scrubbed pine table.

'Sit, do,' insisted their host, pulling a battered tin canister from a high shelf.

'Sorry Mrs Westerly, do you have company?' said Clara.

'I do now,' replied June with a smile, pouring steaming water into a teapot and swirling it around to warm the pot.

Clara slipped her hand into Lucas' and squeezed, giving him an anxious look.

He wasn't *that* kind of psychic, thank goodness, but on occasion Lucas could almost read her thoughts.

And, despite what Clara might think, he was sure Mrs Westerly hadn't foreseen their arrival in a crystal ball.

'How did you know we'd be passing?' asked Lucas, releasing Clara's hand and taking a seat. He pushed the seat next to him out with his foot, motioned to Clara to take it, and passed a cup and saucer to his fiancée.

Clara perched on the edge of the seat and jiggled a leg, glancing nervously around the room.

'Witchy senses,' she whispered dramatically, opening her eyes wide to make herself look wild, then continued heaping leaves into the teapot.

Clara took a sharp intake of breath and clutched the hem of Lucas' jumper, looking at him with alarm.

Lucas, however, gave the supposed witch

an unimpressed look.

'Or perhaps I saw you heading towards the manor earlier,' said Mrs Westerly, grinning as she poured boiling water into the teapot, releasing a cloud of steam into the room. 'And figured you'd be back sooner or later.'

'But you knew we'd been there the other night,' said Clara anxiously, slipping her hand into Lucas' again.

I'd never have thought she'd be frightened by the thought of magic, he thought, squeezing her fingers gently and smiling affectionately. *Especially when there's no such thing. Then again, people say the same about being able to talk to ghosts, so what do I know…?*

'More witchy senses, my girl,' said Mrs Westerly mystically, wobbling the teapot to distribute the leaves properly. 'By which I mean I asked my granddaughter who was at this party. You might remember Gloria from when she was little, she was always over here when she was a nipper - but even if you don't, you definitely met her at this "cursed" party she was telling me about.'

'Oh, Glo is your Gloria?' said Clara, relaxing a little at this perfectly natural explanation. 'I thought they moved away. She didn't say anything about having relatives in the village.'

'They did leave the village,' said Mrs Westerly, taking a seat at the head of the table, her back to the stove so she'd feel the full benefit on her old bones. 'But only by a mile or two. Hooten Hall, do you know it…?'

'The big red brick one?' asked Clara.

'That's right,' confirmed Mrs Westerly, nodding. 'Ghastly Gothic thing, all spikes and turrets. Her father doesn't like having a *witch* in the family, and didn't want his precious children exposed to such *wickedness*.' She sniffed and stirred the pot. 'Not that it's any of his business what his mother-in-law does, but I'm not a witch at all. Never claimed to be. I just know a thing or two about plants and let people think what they like.'

She poured the tea, serving her young guests first.

Lucas looked uncertainly at the greenish brown, grassy smelling liquid in his cup.

'Er,' he said, trying not to look too horrified. 'What's this?'

'Peppermint tea,' said June, saluting him with her own cup. 'Good for you, especially your stomach.'

'Oh,' he said.

He lifted the cup and sniffed it cautiously.

It smelled very… *green*, and put him in mind of a garden after a summer storm.

Very lovely, of course, but not necessarily something he wanted to drink.

Not unpleasant, he tried to convince himself. *It probably won't kill me, if I'm lucky.*

'But don't drink it yet,' said Mrs Westerly urgently, as he moved the cup towards his lips with more politeness than enthusiasm. 'You'll burn your tongue.'

'Thank God,' muttered Lucas, clinking the cup back into the saucer. 'Er, that you told me in time,' he added, forcing a grin and trying not to look too relieved.

'Uhuh,' said Mrs Westerly, a merry twinkle in her eye. 'Don't worry, my boy, I've got Indian tea as well if you'd rather. I just heard the party was a little, uh, raucous and figured your stomach might still need some soothing.'

'Very thoughtful,' said Clara before Lucas could comment. 'But how did Glo – I mean, Gloria know it was us at the party? She only met us that night, and I'm sure she wouldn't have remembered us from way back when.'

'Not many reporters in these parts, my dear,' replied June, blowing on her tea and taking a sip. 'And I figured "Caro" was probably Clara, and "Luke or Lucian, something like that" could well be Lucas. Doesn't take a genius to make the connection to our own little newspaper here in Castlebury.'

'Gosh, that's a terribly clever trick,' said Clara.

'Not especially,' said June, although the smile on her lips said she thought otherwise. 'But it's handy to be able to "read minds" when you've got someone who wants that kind of this.' She stood up and disappeared into the pantry. 'I'm not a witch, really I'm not,' she insisted, her voice slightly muffled.

'See?' whispered Lucas to Clara, who stuck her tongue out at him in reply.

'But some people like the illusion,' continued Mrs W, reappearing with an ancient biscuit tin and prising the lid off. 'The "magic" helps their belief in plants. If they don't believe, they won't try, and if they don't try, they won't get better. Sometimes a white lie does more good than a dozen scientific papers.' She held the biscuit tin out to her guests. 'Ginger snap?'

'So, why did you tell us?' asked Lucas, helping himself to three delicious golden-brown discs and popping one into his mouth whole.

'You're sensible young people,' continued June. 'As far as anyone young can be sensible, anyway. I reckon you'll be happier to help if you know I'm telling the truth than if I pulled the wool over your eyes. Besides, I'm sure you'd spot an old phoney like me anyway.'

'I'm sure we would,' said Clara with more confidence that the words deserved.

'Help?' said Lucas, choosing not to point out Clara's lie. 'What do you need help with?'

Mrs Westerly looked uncomfortable. She glanced over her shoulder as though someone could be listening. 'It's… awkward,' she said.

'If you want our help, you'll have to be straight with us, Mrs Westerly,' said Clara primly.

'Clara, we're guests in her home,' whispered Lucas, appalled. 'You can't talk to her like that!'

'No, she's quite right', said June, looking rather impressed at Clara's boldness. 'It's just – well, no one wants to think badly of their own family, do they?'

'You think Glo had something to do with what happened?' said Clara, frowning. 'I mean, I'm sure she had reason to…'

'That she did,' said Mrs Westerly. 'She told me all about what happened after Bourbon-Busset broke their engagement to chase money instead.' She shook her head sadly. 'It's a good thing I'm fairly open-minded. I tried to tell her that men like that simply aren't worth crying over, but when you're young and in love you just don't believe it.'

'No man is worth crying over,' declared Clara. 'Not that I wouldn't be heartbroken if things went badly between us, dear,' she said quickly as Lucas began to protest, patting his hand. 'Of course I would. But I'd be angry rather than sad.'

'I don't doubt it,' muttered Lucas.

She smiled sweetly at him.

She'd hide my body so well no one would ever know what happened to me, he thought, eyeing her suspiciously. *It's a good thing I love her desperately, because one way or another, I'm in this for life.*

'Angry was where Gloria started,' said Mrs Westerly, shaking her head. 'Silly girl, stooping to his level like that. But still, what's done is done. There's no use crying over it.'

'Absolutely,' said Clara heartily, toasting June with her teacup. 'And good on her for giving that rotter a taste of his own medicine, I say.'

'But I'm concerned she didn't just stick to revenge and crying,' said June. 'Of course, I should expect poor Mr Chapman drank the stuff by mistake, but…'

'You think she wanted to kill Jonny?' said Lucas, thinking this lined up nicely with a previous theory - albeit with a different killer, but that was just details, wasn't it?

'I don't blame her,' declared Clara. 'Not after how he treated her.'

There was a long pause.

'I don't *want* to think it, of course,' replied Mrs Westerly, running a finger around the rim of her teacup and looking anywhere but at her guests. 'But murderers have to be related to someone, after all.'

'True,' said Lucas.

The look on Clara's face told him this wasn't the time to agree.

'What, it is,' he muttered.

'And I can't help but feel guilty,' said Mrs Westerly. 'But years ago I taught her how plants are medicine - and of course, how they can be used for darker purposes too. Even showed her how to prepare a few things. And if I hadn't done that…'

'You're not responsible for anyone else's actions,' said Clara firmly. 'None of us are.'

'Oh, I know,' said Mrs Westerly, looking melancholier by the second. 'But perhaps Redmond Shank is right and it's time for a more controlled approach to herbal medicine - although it's not right to remove traditional healing knowhow from the general population. That's what I see happening with his approach.'

'He was your student, wasn't he?' said Lucas.

'A long time ago,' she replied. 'He was a willing and able student. It was a pleasure to teach someone with a natural affinity with plants and healing. But, without a stamp from the boy's club of medicine he'd never have been taken seriously, and that's all he ever wanted. Well, that and money. I told him a hundred times that if he wanted to chase that, he should go into surgery, but... well, Redmond wanted all the reward with none of the responsibility - though of course, without proper care our craft is just as deadly as chopping folks open.'

'Maybe it was Shank,' said Lucas, trying not to think about people being chopped open in case his head swam and he excused himself from consciousness. 'He was there that night, too.'

'It's possible,' said Mrs Westerly. 'But he's

not got the backbone for murder. He'd certainly not risk his reputation like that. Besides, what would his motive for killing that poor young man be?'

Clara opened her mouth to give the answer, but Lucas nudged her into silence. 'We spoke to him,' he said. 'And he said he had too much respect for plants to use them to kill.'

'That sounds like him,' said June with a chuckle. 'Always knew how to spin a good line.'

'Of course, that could all be bluff,' said Clara.

'It could well be,' agreed Mrs Westerly. 'And I can't deny that I'd rather it be him than Gloria, although I'd still feel as guilty. Yes, I know,' she added, holding up her hand to the impending objections. 'I'm not responsible for him either. 'But...'

'You taught him too,' finished Clara. 'However, we don't know where it came from. It might not have been either of them.'

'Who other than them could have known about it and had the skills to make the poison?' asked Mrs Westerly.

'Bunty, for example,' said Clara. 'She and Shank are very close – and he treated her first husband with a mistletoe concoction. Perhaps she had some left and decided to put it to a more deadly use.'

Mrs Westerly's mouth twitched up on one side. 'I told you he was ambitious. Yes, I heard

Redmond managed to get his slippers under Her Ladyship's bed after Sir Samuel died, and you're quite right of course. He could have told her how poisonous mistletoe is. She could even have looked it up in a book.'

'Exactly,' said Clara. 'Anyone could have looked it up. There's no reason it has to be either Gloria or Shank, just because you taught them.'

'In fact,' said Lucas, feeling cheered by Mrs Westerly's improving spirits. 'Aren't they less likely to use mistletoe as a poison, because you taught them to respect plants?'

'You're quite right,' said Mrs Westerly, looking like a weight had been lifted from her shoulders. 'Of course you are. I always made sure they knew nature's gifts were to be used to heal, not harm. I'm sure they both understood, and would never think of doing such a thing - certainly not to kill someone. Yes,' she said, relaxing back in her chair. 'I was silly to think it.'

'It's a perfectly reasonable worry,' said Clara, helping herself to another biscuit from the open tin on the table. 'I'd be worried about such a thing too, but I'm glad we've managed to put your mind at ease.'

'You have, my dears, you have,' said Mrs Westerly. 'And if either of you ever want a lesson yourselves, you only have to ask.'

Lucas was formulating his tactful decline to the offer, when Clara said, 'Ooh yes please, that sounds marvellous, Mrs W. Sign me up!'

Given the *other* interesting skills the girl had, Lucas didn't like the idea of her adding a knowledge of healing - and definitely not harmful - plants to her arsenal.

'Me too,' he said, much to everyone's surprise, especially his own.

'Really?' said June with a raised eyebrow. 'Of course, my offer included you and I'll be very happy to teach you, but I'm surprised you're interested.'

'I'm not,' he said without thinking. 'I mean, it's always good to broaden one's horizons,' he corrected himself.

Unoffended, June laughed. 'If you want to make sure your young lady doesn't get herself into any mischief, be my guest,' she said, correctly guessing his concerns. 'The more the merrier, I always say. Now,' she added, glancing out the window at the darkening sky. 'I expect you two will be wanting to get home before it starts snowing again, but you're more than welcome to drop in for a cup of tea any time you like.'

Lucas looked doubtfully at his untouched cup of oddly coloured, grassy-scented liquid.

'Indian, of course,' said Mrs Westerly, smiling. 'With milk and sugar, should you want it.'

***

'How can Jones *possibly* think it was an accident?'

They'd taken a detour home via Henry's house to tell him everything June Westerly had said, and now Clara sat in Lucas' lap in front of the living room fire, comfortably entangled in his arms as they compared notes with the official investigation.

Of course, they hadn't got as far as *their* information yet, as Henry had launched straight into ranting about how stupid, narrow-minded, short-sighted, and downright ridiculous his boss was.

'Because he's a bloody fool, that's why,' replied Henry bitterly, ramming the poker into the smouldering logs and bringing them sputtering back to life. 'He says because there wasn't enough of the poison in the glass for a fatal dose, it must have got there by accident. Therefore, Chapman *must* have accidentally eaten more berries during the evening to get the full amount into his body.' Henry's face darkened and the fire received a particularly fierce jab. 'Jones even suggested he *deliberately* ate the berries, either as a prank or dare - or to kill himself.'

'He most certainly didn't,' said Lucas indignantly. 'He'd have told me. Probably. Ghosts don't always like owning up to the truth, especially when it makes them look rather foolish.'

'I know,' said Henry, prodding the logs again and sending embers chasing up the chimney. 'But from what I heard, he hardly seemed the type to off himself.'

'Agreed,' replied Lucas.

'It can't have been an accident,' said Clara. 'How do you accidentally eat enough mistletoe berries to die?'

'Maybe it wasn't just in his drink,' suggested Lucas. 'Jonny Bourbon-Busset took Chappers some chocolates, perhaps it was in there?'

'Did he, now?' said Henry, pausing his cathartic fire-stoking for a moment. 'His Lordship didn't say anything about *that*, which in and of itself is suspicious in my book.' He looked impishly at Lucas, and added, 'I'd ask how you know, but I can probably guess.'

'Humph,' said Lucas sullenly. Clara stroked the back of his neck, easing some of the grumpiness, and glared at her brother.

'Thank you,' said Henry, putting the poker back in the rack at last. 'I'll ask him as soon as I can.' He stood up and brushed the dust from his knees. 'I knew I kept you around for a reason.'

'It's only because everyone else moved away,' said Clara, which brought both men out in useless protests. 'But we haven't told you that Gloria knew how poisonous mistletoe is as well.'

'Her and everyone else, darling,' said

Lucas condescendingly.

'I seem to remember *you* didn't know mistletoe was toxic.'

'I do now,' he argued. 'I learn fast.'

'First I've heard of it,' she said teasingly, dropping a kiss onto his forehead. 'But does everyone else know how to distil mistletoe juice so it's extra potent?'

Lucas opened his mouth to argue, but the good-natured bickering was interrupted by Henry.

'I think I'll jack in this policing lark and become a reporter instead,' he said, running a hand distractedly over his head. 'How on earth did you find that out?'

'We had tea with Gloria's granny,' said Lucas.

'June Westerly,' supplied Clara in answer to the questioning look from Henry. 'No, we didn't know they were related either. That's why we're here actually, to tell you what she told us. She collared us as we were coming back from the manor. She's feeling terribly guilty about having taught Gloria all this stuff ages ago.'

'Hardly her fault,' said Henry with a dismissive wave of the hand. 'Ancient knowledge, anyone could have found a book about it in virtually any library. But what motive would Gloria have for bumping off Chapman?'

'We think she'd have been aiming for Jonny,' said Lucas. 'And Chappers had the bad luck to drink it instead.'

'Lucky for Jono he spilled Chapman's drink,' said Clara. 'Dodged a bullet there, didn't he?'

'Very lucky indeed,' said Henry after a thoughtful pause. 'Yes, very, *very* lucky.'

'You've had an idea,' said Clara accusingly. 'Come on, Henry, spill the beans.'

He scratched his head. 'Well,' he said, looking as though he were working out the details as he went. 'Gloria and Bourbon-Busset were a couple before he took up with Sylvia, right?'

'Right,' confirmed Clara.

'And Gloria knows about poisons -'

'No,' corrected Clara. 'Gloria knows about plants for healing. Not poisons.'

'It goes hand in hand,' said Henry, waving away her objections. 'And you said Lord Cassiobury took Chapman some chocolates? And then he "accidentally" spilled the victim's drink, only to coincidentally replace it with his own poisoned cocktail?'

'You think it was Jono?' said Clara.

'But that doesn't make sense,' said Lucas. 'Jonny ate some of the chocolates -'

'As a decoy,' interrupted Henry.

'Jonny didn't get sick, did he?' said Lucas. 'So his decoy failed, if that's what he was aiming for.'

'It's only an idea,' said Henry. 'It needs

more investigation, although it's a shame Jones slammed the door on the whole affair.'

'I'm sure we could investigate,' said Clara. 'Jones hasn't told us not to snoop around.'

'Wait a minute,' protested Lucas. 'I'm not getting involved.'

'We're already involved, darling,' said Clara, kissing his cheek in a blatant attempt to get round him.

'I don't want to get *more* involved, then,' said Lucas. 'I'm done with the whole thing. It's Christmas, my feet have been frozen and thawed far too often over the past few days, and I am *not* putting myself in line for a mistletoe cocktail by sticking my nose where it doesn't belong.'

Henry opened his mouth to argue, but Clara silenced him with a look.

'Fair enough, darling,' she said soothingly, glaring at Henry again as he tried to interfere. 'But I'm going to-'

'You are not,' replied Lucas hotly.

'Yes I am,' she replied patiently. 'And there's not a deal you can do about it, as you well know. I'm rather fond of Bunty and Gloria, and it's terribly upsetting for them both. I hardly think it's fair to leave this mystery unsolved.'

'Poppycock,' declared Lucas. 'You just can't stand not knowing what happened.'

'That too,' she conceded. 'But just as you feel obligated to find out what happened to the ghosts -'

'I only feel "obligated" because they won't leave me alone if I don't!'

'Not because you feel sorry for them?' she suggested, arching an eyebrow at him.

'No,' he said, less confidently than before.

'Not because they'll be stuck here forever if you don't help them?'

'No,' he whispered.

'Not because they'll watch their friends and family get old and die, with no guarantee that they'll join them in the ghostly realm? Not because the spirits deserve to know what happened to them, and this will help them get wherever they're going afterwards and be at peace? Not because it's your duty and privilege to help them, and because you'd want someone to do the same for you if you ever found yourself as a ghost?'

'Oh all right, I feel *obligated* to help ghosts,' said Lucas irritably. 'Happy now?'

She gave a triumphant look to Henry, who looked rather impressed, then took her prize of a brief kiss from her beloved. This seemed to cheer him up a little, which was a nice bonus.

Henry cleared his throat and gave her a disapproving look, which she shrugged off as she did with all his brotherly disapprovals.

'Well, now you're helping, let's decide what we're going to do,' said Clara.

Lucas groaned, but this was also easily

ignored

'Do you want to try talking to Jonny,' Clara said to Henry. 'And I'll try talking to Gloria?'

'I have a better idea,' he said. 'How about –'

'Oh Henry,' said Clara, instantly exasperated. 'If you're going to be tiresome and tell us to stay out of it, don't bother. You know we'll do exactly as I please, and there's nothing you can do about it.'

'Don't you mean, "We'll do exactly as *we* please," darling?' said Lucas reproachfully.

'Isn't that what I said?' replied Clara, pecking him on the cheek.

'Well actually –'

'I'm not going to tell you anything of the sort,' said Henry, mercifully cutting short whatever Lucas was saying. 'I've got a suggestion that might make use of that stray you brought back from London…'

'Please no,' begged Lucas, looking pained. 'Tommy enjoys this kind of thing far too much.'

'You can't stand Tommy,' said Clara, looking at Henry suspiciously. 'Why would you ask for his help?'

Henry scratched the back of his neck. 'As much as he irritates me, Tommy has a few good qualities.'

'A few is about right,' muttered Lucas.

'He has many good qualities,' said Clara,

frowning at Lucas. 'Which one of them do you want to call on?'

'His affinity with ladies,' said Henry.

'You think Gloria had a hand in this too?' said Clara in disbelief. 'But isn't the evidence pointing at Jono?'

'It certainly is,' replied her brother. 'And at Lady Gaylesbury, Gloria, and Shank. They all had motive, and everyone at the party had the opportunity of slipping the poor chap something deadly.'

'I see,' said Clara, feeling a little subdued. 'I suppose if Sylvia is out of it, that's one less suspect to worry about, at least.'

'I wouldn't rule her out either,' said Henry. 'For all we know she has as much motive as anybody. And as you said, anyone could find out about how toxic mistletoe is.'

'You're right,' said Clara with a small sigh. 'We're not much further along than when we started, are we?'

'No,' said Lucas, which didn't help. 'In fact, I'd say we're further from finding out who actually did it than at the start, because we now know that there's some secret Chapman and Bunty were keeping, but the rotter won't tell me what it is.'

'But at least we know there is a secret,' said Henry optimistically. 'And we know Chapman was deliberately murdered, which we weren't sure of before.'

'Poor Chappers is devastated,' said Lucas.

'I'm sure,' said Henry. 'It can't be nice realising someone wanted you dead.'

'Even worse when they succeed,' said Lucas.

'And where does Tommy come into this?' said Clara suspiciously. 'You're not going to let him loose on Bunty, are you?'

'I hadn't thought of that,' said Henry, tapping his chin thoughtfully. 'Do you think he'd go for it?'

'No!' declared Clara, doing her best to sound offended on her friend's behalf, though privately thinking he'd be over there in a flash to work his magic, given half – no, a quarter of a chance.

'Of course he would,' said Lucas bitterly, who generally thought the worst of Tommy.

'Worth considering, then,' said Henry, clearly only hearing Lucas' answer. 'But what I planned for Tommy involved Gloria, although probably exactly what you expect.'

'He'll enjoy that assignment,' said Lucas darkly. 'I'm really not sure you should be encouraging him, you know.'

'You're welcome to take his place if you want,' said Henry, smirking. 'If you think you can do a better job at sweet-talking the ladies…'

Lucas turned a festive shade of scarlet.

'I'll take that as a no,' said Henry smugly.

'I could do it, if I wanted to,' said Lucas

belligerently. 'But I wouldn't, being a married man and all that. Nearly married, anyway. And to your sister, no less.'

'Clara wouldn't mind, would you dear?' said Henry, winking at her.

'Not in the slightest,' she said, playing along. 'If you think you have a better chance of sweet-talking Glo than Tommy, then be my guest.' She turned away in case he spotted her grinning. 'I'll even watch. It'd be highly amusing, I'm sure.'

Somehow, Lucas' colour deepened to a new and alarming shade of crimson. 'It wouldn't be fair on you, darling,' he announced, a noble, self-sacrificing tone to his voice. 'Besides, wouldn't I be more use talking to the ghost?'

Clara turned to Henry. 'It's a Christmas miracle,' she announced. 'Lucas is volunteering to talk to a spirit.'

'Wait, was this some sort of ploy?' cried Lucas.

'Nope,' said Henry, though his broad smile said otherwise. 'Just a happy outcome. So,' he said loudly before Lucas could protest again. 'Lucas is talking to ghosties, Tommy will be, er, mostly talking to Gloria, we hope. Clara, I assume you're happy to talk to Lady Gaylesbury again? Excellent. I'll poke around in the men's affairs while conveniently ignoring my superior officer's blindness to this nasty case of murder most fatal. Is everyone happy?'

'I wonder why Jones is refusing to see it?' said Lucas, presumably resigned to his fate. 'Perhaps it really was an accident and we're just looking too much into it.'

'You wish,' said Henry.

'Perhaps Bunty bribed him too,' suggested Clara. 'Though that would make Bunty look awfully guilty, of course.'

'Possible, but he's never been known to take a bribe before,' said Henry, taking up the poker again and jabbing the fire viciously, although it didn't really need it. 'I think Jones just wants this all to go away so he can get back to enjoying the festive period.'

'Yes, that sounds like Jones,' said Lucas. 'He might have the appearance of an ox, but he certainly doesn't enjoy working like one.'

'Indeed,' said Henry grimly. 'My point *is*, Chapman didn't die by accident. Whoever killed him, meant to kill *him* and no-one else. And it's up to us to find out who.'

For a few seconds, the only sound in the room was the hiss and pop of logs in the fire.

'That sounds rather serious, doesn't it?' said Clara quietly.

'It *is* rather serious, sister dear,' replied Henry, a little brusquely. 'We can't let a killer go free just because Jones doesn't want to do his job properly. What happens when there's someone else they don't like? We'll be up to our eyeballs in corpses. And then there's the matter of the ghost himself being a tad stuck in the afterlife, or whatever it is.'

'Don't remind me,' groaned Lucas. 'You know who will end up with him hanging around forever if we don't work it out? Me, that's who.'

'And who will have to listen to you complain about it forever if that happens?' said Clara, prodding his chest playfully. 'Us, so it's in all our interests to work out what happened.'

'It'd be a lot easier if you could ask Chapman who killed him,' said Henry.

'I tried that,' snapped Lucas, rising to the bait. 'It's hardly my fault if the silly old duffer hasn't a clue, is it?'

'Ask him again, then,' argued Henry. 'People don't always remember everything significant the first time you ask, you know.

'You know what,' said Lucas, wincing and starting to massage his temples. 'Chapman's just decided to put in an appearance. Of course he bloody well did. Why don't you ask him yourself? I'm sure he's here to help, after all.'

***

'Actually I'm here to find out if you've figured out whodunnit yet,' said Chapman, drifting into Lucas' line of sight. 'That and it's downright dull at the hall.'

'I know, you told me before,' said Lucas,

hushing Henry and Clara, who were watching the exchange with interest – at least, the half of it they could see.

Lucas decided a direct, forthright approach with the spirit might help wrap the conversation up quickly.

It'd never worked before, but there was a first time for everything.

'All right, Chappers, come clean,' he barked. 'Who'd want you dead. Bunty? Gloria? Shank?'

'Lord, I don't know,' said Chapman, losing some of his bluster. 'One doesn't like to think of one's friends wanting one dead, does one?'

'*We* can think of plenty of people who'd want you dead, and a few reasons why, so pick your favourite,' said Lucas. 'Starting with Bunty –'

'I told you, it's not her,' said Chapman.

'You know this terrible secret of hers,' continued Lucas, ignoring the interruption. 'Even if you swore you'd never tell, *she* might not believe that.'

'I don't want the world to know it either,' argued the ghost. 'You know that, don't you?'

'I don't know anything of the sort,' said Lucas. 'Because I haven't the foggiest idea what this "secret" is. So, unless you're going to tell me -' he looked expectantly at Chapman, who shook his head, '- then we're going to leave Bunty on the list. Especially as she'd taken up with the herbalist doctor, who could have told her what to do with - or even supplied - the poison. He just happens to be next on the list.'

'Shank wouldn't do me in either,' said Chapman wearily.

'So you say,' said Lucas, rather pleased that this approach seemed to be paying off – in a way, but it was better than nothing. 'But you've said that about everyone, and yet that can't be true, can it? On account of you being rather dead.'

'Urgh, don't remind me,' said Chappers, examining his fingernails. 'I've been trying not to dwell on it.'

'I can think of reasons Shank would want you dead,' continued Lucas. 'Starting with the large sum of money he owes you.'

'I told him not to worry about that,' said Chapman with a wave of the hand. 'It was only a few hundred pounds, he could pay me back whenever he could. I've got cash to spare, it was a pleasure to help a pal out of a tight spot. I most certainly wasn't chasing him for it. In fact, if he never paid me back I wouldn't have minded. He knew that.'

'In addition to that,' continued Lucas, rather envious that a few hundred pounds was nothing to this man. 'You spent the night with Bunty, who Shank has designs on. Even if nothing happened, as you claim, you're still saying it did in order to protect this secret.'

'There's more motive there, I admit,' said Chapman after a brief pause. 'But the chap hasn't got it in him to commit murder. He's a good egg.'

'I'm not so sure about that,' said Lucas darkly. 'But if you insist, we'll move on to Gloria.'

'Not Glo,' insisted Chapman. 'She'd never -'

'*Someone* did,' said Lucas. 'So you can't keep saying that. In fact, I'm going to just ignore you from now on, if it's all the same to you.'

'It's not,' replied the ghost sulkily. 'I don't like being ignored, and I've had rather a lot of it lately.'

'Tough,' replied Lucas, rather enjoying being in control of the situation. He'd have to try it more often. 'I'm the only one here who can see and hear you, so you'll have to start behaving yourself or you'll be stuck forever.'

'Oh, all right,' grumbled Chapman. 'Why do you think dear, sweet Gloria had a hand in my demise?'

'For a start, her granny thinks she might have done it.'

Technically not true, thought Lucas, a tad uneasily. *But it sounds rather convincing.*

'Her own granny?' said Chapman, aghast. 'How on earth do you know that? I thought she lived in Scotland. I must say, it's pretty rum calling her *granny* up to see if she thinks Gloria is capable of murder. Then again, Mrs Hawkes is very spiteful at times, just like her son. Thank goodness Glo takes after her mother's side of the family.'

'Not Mrs Hawkes,' said Lucas, hoping never to meet the lady, or her son for that matter. 'Gloria's maternal grandmother still lives in Castlebury Magna. She makes natural medicines and taught Gloria a few tricks in that department. She's rather worried her granddaughter used that knowledge in a way that wasn't intended.'

The ghost looked faintly puzzled.

'To kill you,' prompted Lucas. 'You know, with the mistletoe?' *There really is no helping some people,* he added silently. *What on earth did he think I meant?*

'Really?' said Chapman, fascinated. 'I didn't know darling Glo knew about that kind of thing. How terribly interesting. But,' he said, creasing his forehead. 'She told me her mother's parents both died in the Spanish 'flu outbreak of '18, which is why they never come to the big house for celebrations and the like.'

'If so, June Westerly is doing a worse job than you at moving on, seeing as Clara and I had tea with her earlier,' said Lucas. 'If you can call a handful of dry peppermint leaves in hot water "tea," anyway.'

'Golly,' said Chapman. 'The secrets

people keep.'

'Yes,' said Lucas sourly. 'Wouldn't it make life easier if people just told you them?'

Chapman mimed turning a key at his lips to indicate that Bunty's secret went with him to the grave, and apparently beyond.

'It'll come out eventually, you know,' said Lucas. 'So I'm not sure what you're so worried about.'

Sadly, this didn't work either, so Lucas moved back the question of Gloria's guilt.

'Mrs Westerly taught Gloria how to prepare all kind of things for medicines,' he said. 'Assuming you didn't notice any mistletoe berries bobbing around in your drink or hiding in the vol-au-vents, I'd say it's quite likely Gloria - *or whoever it was,*' added Lucas, cutting off the ghost's predictable objection. 'The murderer used some sort of pre-prepared poison. Far easier to pop a few drops of something nasty in your drink than it is to get a handful of berries into your dinner.'

'Or she - *they* could have dried the leaves and ground them up to look like herbs,' suggested Clara, who had been holding her tongue until this point. 'It needn't just be berries, pretty much all the mistletoe plant can kill you if you have enough of it.'

'Good point,' said Lucas. 'That would've made it easier to build up the dose over the course of the night. A few drops, a sprinkle of "herbs" there…'

'Whilst you make a good point,' said Chapman coolly. 'I can't think of a single reason why *Glo* of all people would want me dead.'

'Because you took advantage of her broken engagement for a weekend of illicit fun, perhaps?' said Lucas. 'I'm sure most women would be a little bent out of shape over a thing like that.'

'Hear, hear,' said Clara. She'd moved over to sit on the arm of Henry's seat when Lucas started talking to Chapman, and the siblings watched with quiet interest.

It was quite distracting.

'Not at all,' retorted Chapman in an offended tone that commanded Lucas' attention once more. 'She sought *me* out, if you must know, seeing as *my* fiancée had done a runner with hers. We decided we could cheer ourselves up a bit and get some revenge at the same time, that's all. We both knew what the deal was.'

Lucas ran a hand down his face in exasperation. That scuppered that theory…

'But what if she regrets her actions and was trying to keep you quiet?' he asked, seeking an angle that would give them a firmer motive to work with.

'She only had to ask,' said Chapman with a shrug. 'I'd never have said word about it without her permission. We never went into *details* when revealing our revenge to the world.

The code of the bedroom is sacred, after all.'

'Hmm,' said Lucas suspiciously. 'Perhaps she thought it was the start of a new relationship and when you didn't return her feelings…'

'Nonsense,' exclaimed the ghost. 'She's sworn off men for the foreseeable and told me it was a one-time thing, never to be repeated. Never.' He gave a sad smile. 'Which is a shame, really. It was jolly good fun for all concerned, even if I do say so myself, and I've always been fond of Glo. Personally I didn't see any reason why we couldn't make a go of it, when time had healed a few wounds - but there you go. I don't press my suit where it isn't wanted. That's never been my style, and frankly I never needed to.'

Lucas groaned. 'All right, I'll take your word on it for now, but only because we still have two other suspects to consider.'

Chapman looked between Lucas and Clara with some surprise. 'Oh, I don't suspect you two at all,' he said. 'Why would you want me dead? We'd only just met.'

'Not *us*, you idiot,' said Lucas, struggling to keep his patience. 'Jonathon Bourbon-Busset and Sylvia Pettigrew.'

'Jonny and Sylvia?' said Chappers, frowning. 'Impossible.'

Lord, give me strength, thought Lucas, without any expectation of his silent prayer being answered.

'Jonny because you took up with his very

recently ex-fiancée,' said Lucas, teeth gritted.

'And who could blame me?' said the ghost indignantly.

'Not to mention that you didn't follow through on the "favour' he asked you to do - yes, I know there's a good reason,' he added wearily as the ghost opened his mouth to argue. 'But consider that he might not have been best pleased, hmm? Besides, don't you think it's suspicious that he bought you a box of chocolates and didn't share them with you?'

'Not at all,' replied Chapman. 'I told you, he's worried about his wedding suit.'

'Right,' said Lucas, unconvinced. 'Then there's Sylvia.'

'If anything, I'd have killed *her*,' said Chapman. 'The way she treated me, running off with my chum like that. Dreadful.'

'Perhaps Sylvia had an inkling about this violent side of you and decided to strike first?'

'No!' cried Chapman, distraught. 'I'd never hurt her. I love her too much!'

'And yet she left you for Bourbon-Busset,' said Lucas. 'So I suppose that love was a little one-sided…'

'That wasn't permanent,' said Chapman scornfully. 'It was only until -'

'Until what?' cried Lucas. 'They're getting married, that's pretty permanent.'

Damn, he thought. *How many secrets is this chap keeping for other people? And how many on his own behalf?*

Chapman rubbed his forehead. 'Look, I promised not to say anything...'

'You do that a lot,' remarked Lucas, folding his arms. 'How's that working out for you?'

The ghost glared at him. 'Do you want to know or not?'

'Frankly, I couldn't care less,' said Lucas, shrugging to back up his words. 'It's you who'd stuck like this if we don't work out what happened.'

'I like that!' exclaimed Chapman. 'And there I was, thinking you helped unfortunate people like me.'

'Not if I can help it, said Lucas. 'So really, you're only hurting yourself by not coming clean.'

'Oh, all right,' grumbled Chapman. 'But only because I can't see any alternative.'

Lucas watched the ghost um and ah his way to confessing this latest secret.

'Jonny got himself into a bit of a sticky wicket with... a business associate,' said Chapman.

Lucas raised an eyebrow at him.

'Oh, fine,' said the spirit crossly. 'It was Sylvia's dad. He never liked me much, and he wasn't above a little blackmail. Syl's a good girl, but she's got no spine when it comes to dealing with daddy – except when it came to me, of course,' he added, preening slightly.

Lucas made hurry up motions.

'I told her it didn't matter if the old man cut her off,' continued Chapman. 'I'd enough dosh to keep us both happy for the rest of our days.'

'Where does Jonny come in to all this?'

'Well, a couple of months ago the silly boy came to me nearly blubbing and explained the situation to me. Why he didn't ask me sooner, I couldn't say, but the fact is, old Pettigrew – Petti by name, petty by nature, I always say – told Jonny to split me and Syl up and put a ring on her finger himself. Jonny protested, of course, but Petti had the poor chap over a barrel. I offered cash to pay the debt, and Jonny said he'd got the cash together but now the old man wouldn't hear of monetary payment, he'd waited long enough and now decided he only wanted his baby girl "rescued" from my clutches. Rescued! What an insult.'

'An odd arrangement, but go on.'

'Well, what could I do?' said Chapman, spreading his hands wide. 'I wanted to help the fellow out of a sticky patch, but for once throwing money at the problem wouldn't make it go away. So I had a word with Syl, explained it all, and she agreed to help Jonny out and break her engagement with me – at least, officially. We planned to come to an, uh, *arrangement*, at a later date.'

'But what about Gloria?' said Lucas. 'It sounds like she didn't take too kindly to it.'

'Of course she didn't,' scoffed Chapman. 'Would your girl?'

'No,' said Lucas. 'But I'd not be stupid enough to come up with such a ridiculous plan.'

'You say ridiculous, I say beautifully crafted,' countered Chapman. 'Anyway, Jonny told me to look after Gloria until he paid the debt owed to old Petti.'

'And "looking after" you took to mean "bedding enthusiastically and repeatedly", did you?' said Lucas, unimpressed.

'I didn't mean that to happen,' said Chapman, though he didn't look at all apologetic. 'I only meant to get her a bit tipsy, cheer her up kind of thing, and one thing kind of led to another. You know how it goes.'

'And yet it didn't go that way with Bunty,' said Lucas. 'Why was that? And none of that "you can't tell me" business either,' said Lucas, holding up a hand to stop the old argument before it sprang from Chapman's mouth. 'Because that's a lie. Whatever you know can't hurt you anymore.'

'But it could hurt *her*,' the ghost replied. 'And I don't want that. It could hurt other people, too.'

'Like who?'

'Like... well, if I tell you that, you'll probably guess the whole business.'

'If it's that easy to guess, someone will figure it out eventually,' argued Lucas. 'And if this big secret is the reason you were killed, Bunty could be in danger too.'

'Bunty is perfectly capable of looking after herself,' declared the ghost, although he didn't sound quite as sure as he might do.

'If you say so,' said Lucas with a shrug. 'We're going to do a little snooping around, if it's all the same to you -'

'It's not,' interjected Chapman, but seeing as Lucas was the only one who heard, it didn't make any difference.

'- So I dare say we'll figure it out even if you refuse to help us,' continued Lucas. 'In fact,' he added, brightening at the thought, 'My role was to talk to you, and seeing as I've done that, I'm done for the day.' He stretched, and settled back smugly in his seat.

'Oh no you're not,' said Clara, shattering his illusions. 'There's still a lot to find out, and I'm sure Henry will appreciate a hand looking at all the dull paperwork.'

'That I will,' confirmed Henry. 'Misery loves company, after all.'

'But, but I've spoken to the ghost,' whined Lucas. 'I did my bit. Can't you let a chap off the hook?'

'No,' said the Jenkins siblings in unison.

Chapman chuckled. 'Hard luck, old thing. Looks like you can't get out of it that easily.'

'Shut up,' he said, scowling. 'Not you,' he added quickly, for Clara and Henry's sakes.

'It had better not be,' said Clara, not quite under her breath.

***

'So,' said Tommy, after they'd explained the plan to him, 'You want me to flirt with two beautiful, wealthy, charming young women, possibly sleep with them –'

'*Do not* sleep with them,' said Lucas.

'Only if you have to,' corrected Clara, motioning him to be quiet.

'Clara!' protested Lucas.

Tommy smirked. '*Probably* sleep with them,' he said, delighting as Lucas quietly despaired. 'Just to get some information out of them about some posh boy's murder?'

'That's the long and short of it,' said Clara. She and Lucas had returned to her mother's house and torn a complaining Tommy away from card games with the doting relatives he'd never previously been blessed with.

He'd initially been rather miffed, but was forgiving them rapidly.

'Excellent,' he said, wondering just how much better this Christmas would get. 'Yes, I think I can do that.'

'Make sure you remember to get the information,' said Lucas disapprovingly. 'Don't forget when you're...' The chap blushed. 'Er, don't get distracted and forget,' he concluded.

He was such a prude at times. It was really rather wearing.

'Dear, dear Lucas,' said Tommy, patting him on the knee in a friendly, if deliberately patronising, manner. 'I'm perfectly capable of keeping my head in these sorts of situations.'

'Good,' said Lucas sullenly.

'And I'm even better at making women lose theirs,' he added, winking roguishly at Clara.

She rolled her eyes at him and swiped the gingerbread man he was conveying towards his mouth.

'Oi,' he complained.

'Serves you right for teasing Lucas,' she said, sticking her tongue out before snapping the unfortunate biscuit in half and passing the larger part to Lucas.

'I was looking forward to that,' complained Tommy.

She snapped a leg off her half of the gingerbread man and tossed it at Tommy.

'And that's more than you deserve,' she said.

It'd be more than he'd get from Lucas, who was crunching away noisily.

'I could *not* help,' said Tommy, examining the biscuit, now considerably than he'd intended on eating, before putting the whole thing in his mouth. 'You'll have to rely on Casanova here,' he added, waving a hand at Lucas, who turned an amusing shade of pink.

Clara glowered at Tommy. Nice to see her mixing it up, though she was still distractingly, confusingly pretty, even when cross.

In fact, Tommy thought he rather liked it. Damn.

'True,' she said, snapping another chuck off the unfortunate gingerbread man and lobbing it at him. 'But when else will you get the chance to work your magic on two ladies like that, hmm? It's not like you travel in the same circles.'

Tommy scratched the back of his ear. 'Never had any trouble before,' he said, smiling at happy recollections. 'It's amazing where being a reporter out will take you, and the opportunities it gives an enterprising, attractive young man such as myself. Not,' he added, 'that anyone would ever believe the tales of my brief liaisons, even if discretion didn't forbid me from kissing and telling all.'

'Convenient,' muttered Lucas, brushing gingerbread crumbs off his shirt.

'Believe what you like,' replied Tommy, shrugging this off. 'I do alright for myself, so I don't think I'll have any problems charming this pair.'

Clara clapped her hands together and beamed in a way that made Tommy's treacherous heart flutter again.

Urgh, he'd thought he'd dealt with that, but...

'Thank you, Tommy,' she cried, interrupting his thoughts. 'We know we could rely on you.'

'Did we?' said Lucas.

'Yes, we did,' she said firmly, scowling at him before turning back to Tommy with a broad grin. 'Tommy's a good egg, he wouldn't let us down.'

'Quite right,' he said, a warm glow spreading through his chest at such a recommendation.

Urgh, he could do without that. Perhaps it was just heartburn?

'So, what's this information you want?' he added, to distract himself as much as anything else.

'We need know how angry the girls were with the dead man,' said Lucas.

'You're far too straightforward at times, dear,' she said, ruffling Lucas' dull sandy waves playfully.

What she saw in the chap was quite beyond Tommy, but ignored the familiar stab of jealousy in the interests of keeping the peace.

Of course, he didn't want to risk this most entertaining assignment snatched away from him.

Yes, that might help him take his mind off

Clara, very nicely...

'Well, we do need to know that,' she continued, as Lucas scowled and smoothed his hair again. 'Of course we do, but we also need to know *why*, and whether they'd actually do anything about it. Things aren't always as they first appear, as you well know, and we've only heard some of the story from Cha - from what we've heard about Chapman. After all, there's a good chance he – it might not be telling us the whole truth.'

Oh lordy, not that psychic nonsense again, surely? Still, a chap's got to have a hobby, though how Clara could go along with it was a mystery.

'People rarely tell the truth,' said Tommy in his wisest-sounding voice, instead of scoffing like he really wanted to. 'That's where having good journalistic skills is vital, you've got to piece together the truth from everyone else's opinions.'

'Yes, indeed,' agreed Lucas.

Tommy managed not to laugh, though it was a hard-won battle. What journalistic skills were needed to write drivel on budgie club meets and church fundraisers?

'Which is why we need your help to get the truth out of Glo and Sylvia,' said Clara. 'So we can compare and see what lines up.'

'All right, but under what pretence?' said Tommy, sitting back in his chair and steepling his fingers thoughtfully. 'I can't just go up to them and try to seduce them, can I?'

'Pretend you're a reporter,' said Clara.

'I am a reporter!'

'So you won't have any trouble, will you?' she replied. 'Say you've heard about the recent tragedy and that you want to get the background on Gilbert Chapman from his nearest and dearest so you can give him the write-up he deserved. Or something of that sort, you'll work it out.'

'No, that'll do perfectly,' said Tommy. 'Especially the "what he deserves" part, that's a nice touch. If they hated him as much as you claim, they'll be sure to make sure he's remembered as the rogue that he was.'

Lucas winced slightly and rubbed his eyes.

'All right there, old chap?' Tommy asked, genuinely concerned. Friendly teasing was one thing, but in spite of everything – Tommy tried to pretend the "everything" had nothing at all to do with Clara –- he actually liked Lucas.

'Fine,' was the curt reply. 'Just a headache, that's all.'

'You should get your eyes checked, my friend,' suggested Tommy, thinking Lucas suffered with his head more than he ought to. 'Eye strain can do that, you know.'

'There's nothing wrong with my eyes,' said Lucas, massaging his temples. 'It's…

something else.'

'The weather, perhaps,' suggested Clara, rubbing Lucas' shoulders sympathetically. 'Auntie Vi gets terrible headaches when it's about to rain.' She gave Lucas a significant look. 'I expect that's it, isn't it darling?'

'Er, probably,' he said. He really was looking dreadfully pained and pale, poor chap. 'Do we really need to deceive the young ladies like that?'

'Yes,' said Clara.

'I can't think of a better idea,', said Tommy, who was very much in favour of the scheme. 'Can you?'

'It just seems... dishonest,' said Lucas, looking more miserable by the second. He winced – he really seemed to be suffering, poor fellow - and added, 'And it could hurt Bourbon-Busset.'

'Who cares about him?' cried Tommy. 'For all we know, he did it.'

'But think of the girls' reputations,' pleaded Lucas.

'Aren't they already spoiled?' asked Tommy, thoroughly confused by this sea change. 'I thought that was the crux of the plan, in fact.'

'Unless you *or anyone else*, can come up with a better suggestion,' said Clara to Lucas. 'I don't see what choice we have.'

Lucas cocked his head as though

thinking, and said, 'No, can't think of anything.' He winced again. 'More's the pity.'

'Well, that's settled then,' said Clara brightly. 'I'll call Bunty and get me and Lucas invited back up to the hall-'

Lucas groaned again.

'Oh come on, she's not that bad,' said Tommy.

'Can't you go on your own?' asked Lucas, almost begging Clara. 'I don't want to traipse all the way back up there again.' He shot a furtive glance at Tommy and dropped his voice. 'I'm sure there's *other* ways I could make myself useful.'

Clara considered him coldly for a moment, before relenting. 'Oh, fine,' she said irritably. 'You do whatever you want to do, while Tommy and I do the *actual* sleuthing.'

'Good idea,' said Tommy, enjoying the thought that he and Clara were working together a little more than he really ought to. 'If it works out, we should go into business together, what do you think? Kilbourne and Jenkins, Private Investigators.'

'Has a nice ring to it,' she replied, smiling in a way that made Tommy's pulse race. 'Though of course, it'll have be *Rathbone* and Kilbourne, once I'm married.'

Tommy struggled to keep the smile on his face. 'Of course,' he replied, ignoring the twist in his chest. 'Even better, in fact, because Lucas could join in the fun as well.'

'Uhuh,' said Lucas, still looking pained. 'Rathbone, Rathbone, and Kilbourne.'

'Bit of a mouthful,' said Tommy, a shade more frostily than he intended. 'We'd better think of a different name entirely.'

***

Clara hung the telephone receiver back on the hook and chewed her lip thoughtfully. Bunty was only too keen for Clara to go and visit in the morning. She even offered Clara the car, which was gratefully accepted. Walk a mile or two in the snow or be collected in a chauffeur-driven Rolls Royce? It was no competition, really.

It was a little pitiable, actually. Bunty hinted the other young people had been avoiding her since *the incident*, as she called it. Jonny hadn't been over all day, which wasn't like him, and Syl and Glo hadn't visited her at all since their rather strained Christmas Day celebrations. Even Shank was keeping his distance by the sounds of it, which really seemed to wound the lady.

Clara wondered if this general avoidance was thanks to suspicion of Bunty, or a general feeling that it was somehow inappropriate to go happily visiting after such a tragedy.

Perhaps guilt was causing them to keep away, but surely they couldn't *all* have had a hand in the murder? No, that'd be too dreadful…

Lucas rapped on the glass panel in the door of the public phone booth.

'Are you done yet?' he asked, hopping up and down. 'I know you have, you've stopped talking, so hurry up please. Some of us are freezing our ar- uh, our ears off out here.'

Clara opened the door, but instead of stepping into the chilly evening, she pulled Lucas into the tiny space.

'Oh, all right,' he said, clearly misreading her intentions and going to kiss her. 'Much cosier in here, I quite agree.'

She kissed him for a while - well, why not? - before backing off to say what was on her mind.

Other than Lucas, obviously.

'I'm worried about Bunty,' she said, slightly breathlessly.

'Why?' said Lucas, pushing her scarf down to caress her neck with his lips in a very distracting way. 'She can look after herself.'

'I'm not so sure,' said Clara, forcing her thoughts back on track. 'I think she's lonely.'

'Wouldn't you be?' replied Lucas, still being horribly, wonderfully distracting. 'Rattling around in that big house all on her own. Other than the fleet of servants, of course, but I don't suppose they count.'

'Hmm,' said Clara in as disapproving

tone as she could manage, which wasn't very. 'I think everyone is avoiding her.'

Lucas finally got the message that Clara wanted to talk and stopped taking her mind off the sticky subject of festive murder. He sighed and hugged her against his chest, which Clara was very grateful for. He was warm and comforting, and things never felt quite so bad when he was close by.

'All right,' he said. 'What are you thinking? That everyone thinks she did it?'

'I hope not,' said Clara, feeling hollow in her chest at the mere thought of the sweet, lonely lady as a cold-blooded murderess.

'Me too,' said Lucas softly. 'But they know her best. Don't you think they'd be able to tell if she'd done something like that?'

'Maybe,' said Clara. 'But maybe not. After all, how well do people really know each other?'

'I think I know you pretty well,' said Lucas, resting his chin on top of her head. 'I know how you'll react in certain situations. I know what makes you happy, what scares you, and I'm pretty sure I'd know if you'd killed a chap at your own Christmas party.'

'Yes,' said Clara. 'But you've known me my whole life. We grew up together, fell in love, and all that. You're my best friend, have been for years. I'd be worried if you *couldn't* tell if I'd murdered someone.'

'And all the other things.'

'That too,' said Clara, kissing him again. 'But people you don't know so well?' She avoided his eye. 'After all, I thought I knew Tommy, and look at what happened over summer.'

'But you've only known him a few years,' said Lucas, sweetly leaping to her defence. 'And he didn't do anything bad in the end.'

'Only because we stopped him,' cried Clara. 'How do we know he won't do the same thing again?'

'Circumstances have changed since then,' replied Lucas. 'And I think he just needed some good influences in his life.' Now it was Lucas' turn to avoid Clara's eye. 'He's quite a nice fellow now he's got some friends looking out for him.'

'Lucas Rathbone,' said Clara teasingly. 'Don't tell me you actually *like* Tommy?'

'"Like" is a bit of a strong word,' said Lucas, scowling. '"Tolerate" is more the sum of it. But I think somewhere underneath his, his...'

'Annoying ease and charm, good looks, and general cheerfulness?' suggested Clara.

'Humph,' said Lucas, unimpressed. 'Far underneath, you understand? But lately I've been thinking perhaps there's a decent man there after all.' He winced, and added, 'Just don't tell him I said that, all right? I couldn't stand him crowing about it.'

Clara kissed his cheek, delighted that

Lucas had finally come around to her way of thinking.

Well, almost.

It was progress, anyway, which was better than nothing.

It might stop a little of Lucas' griping, although Clara privately suspected Lucas rather enjoyed the fairly good-natured sparring with her friend.

Nonetheless, it was a relief to hear Lucas might not mind Tommy's tagging along with them after all.

'Your secret is safe with me,' she said. 'He might like to hear it from you sometime, though.'

Judging by the look on Lucas' face, that wouldn't happen any time soon.

'I don't think Bunty would kill someone though, was my point,' she said quickly, deciding a change of subject was in order. 'So it's terribly unfair if everyone else thinks she did it.'

'Well, probably,' said Lucas. 'And you must know I don't really think she'd do it. I'd never let you visit her alone if I thought there was any chance of her dropping mistletoe berries in you drink.'

This also cheered Clara up no end.

'Really?' she said happily. 'I thought you weren't ruling anyone out until we know for sure?'

Lucas shifted uncomfortably. 'I'm not,' he

said. 'But... of all the people it could be, I can't see Bunty as a cold-blooded killer. Not just because that'd give me permission to ask for that bribe money,' he added, just a little too quickly.

'You don't have permission to *ask* for it,' said Clara sternly. 'Only to take it if it's offered.'

'Hmm,' said Lucas, trying to think of a loophole. 'But if you must know, my money is on Jonny or Shank. Perhaps both - no reason why there couldn't have been a conspiracy to kill poor old Chappers.'

'Good point,' said Clara, rather impressed he'd thought of that, and disappointed she hadn't. 'Perhaps the argument we overheard was just an act? If they blamed each other, maybe it'd muddy the waters enough for them to get away with it. They probably thought the police would talk to the servants again at some point, and one of them would let slip that there'd been a set-to – or maybe even go directly to the cops and tell them what they heard.'

'Exactly,' said Lucas, sounding surprised. 'Yes, that's exactly what I was thinking.'

Clara raised an eyebrow at this obvious lie, but decided not to pursue it.

Instead, she wiggled an arm around his waist and squeezed. 'I'm glad you don't think it's Bunty either,' she said. 'She's a dear, really she is, and I'd hate if you thought badly of her.'

Lucas cuddled her for a few moments, then said, 'Come along, let's go home and warm up properly.'

'It's rather cosy in here,' murmured Clara, looking up at him coyly.

'Yes,' he said, kissing her again. 'But there's a draught going right up my coat, blummin' freezing it is, and your mother promised cocoa when we got back.'

Clara couldn't help but smile. 'All right, then,' she said, kissing him back, lingering over the pleasant task. 'But let's not hurry. I won't see you much tomorrow, with my quizzing Bunty and your - whatever it is you're doing.'

'Helping Henry interrogate Johnny,' he said, grimacing. 'And Shank. Urgh, what a bore. At least Tommy will be enjoying himself with Gloria.'

'I hope it's not her, either,' said Clara, untangling herself from Lucas and gently ushering him from the telephone box not designed for two adults to spend much time in, no matter how much they liked each other.

'She's jolly good fun,' continued Clara, noting that snow was drifting from the sky once more. 'And it'll scupper my lunch plans with her if she gets arrested.'

Lucas put his arm around her shoulder and hugged her tightly. 'You don't want it to be anyone,' he said. 'It's rather sweet. Naive, but sweet.'

Clara chose not to hear the naive part. It wasn't true, anyway. She just liked to give people the benefit of the doubt, that's all. Nothing wrong with that, was there?

Just to prove Lucas wrong, she thought about who it could be.

'I hope it's Shank,' she said eventually. 'I don't like him nearly as much as the others.'

'I hope so too, darling,' said Lucas, smiling affectionately at her. 'And not just because I bet your brother a shilling it was him after all. It's always the most obvious culprit, after all.'

'Since when?'

'Well, since I bet your brother a shilling, I hope.'

***

'... so you see, I want to find out what Mr Chapman was really like,' said Tommy, flashing his trademark dazzling smile at the rather attractive woman standing in front of him.

She was stunning, even with a scornful look on her face. The mid-morning sunlight illuminated her movie star looks wonderfully, and Tommy trusted his own attractive features were getting the same treatment.

What was he worried about, of course they were – and even if they weren't, his well-practiced charm could work wonders.

No, Tommy Kilbourne was supremely confident of success, despite this less than warm welcome.

He twinkled his eyes at her and pulled one side of his smile up a little further, dipping his head to look up at her. He suspected Miss Gloria Hawkes was a woman who liked a little deference in a man. The fact she stood in the doorway and he a step or two below made his happy task even easier.

He suspected correctly, as he always did.

There was a softening around the ice queen's eyes, and the shadow of a smile on her lips painted a stark scarlet.

Just a little more should do the trick...

'I know it's tradition not to speak ill of the dead,' murmured Tommy, dropping his eyes to her cherry red lips for a second, before darting them up to hers again and smiling apologetically, as though embarrassed by his supposed lapse in professionalism. 'But I always feel the public deserve the truth.'

Gloria worried her bottom lip with her teeth.

'Anything you say can remain anonymous,' added Tommy, sensing victory.

She glanced over her shoulder, stepped back from the door, and beckoned him in with a jerk of her head.

'Ten minutes, Mr Kilbourne', she said sternly. 'But not a minute more. The family are out and aren't expected back until evening, and the servants are preparing luncheon, so we'll be undisturbed, but... Come in. I'll ring for coffee.'

Servants, thought Tommy's green-eyed monster as he stepped into a dazzling hallway, resplendent with gleaming marble and glittering chandelier dripping crystals over the sweeping staircase. *One day, I'll ring the servants for coffee, and live in a house like this...*

He was lead through to a grand parlour room, decorated in the latest Art Deco fashion that came as a surprise after the High Gothic exterior of the house. The room was light, the dark wood panelling of the original Victorian decor was now painted white, and huge gold framed mirrors added to the sense of light and space. Shell-shaped chairs upholstered in a delicate pink were gathered around a glass coffee table with gleaming chromium plated legs.

Tommy was impressed, but knew better than to show it.

'Nice place,' he said to his hostess as she returned from ordering refreshments. He tried not to gawp at either the gorgeous room or the gorgeous lady clad in fashionable yet warm tweed skirt and cream jumper, which hugged her unfashionable hourglass figure. She set his heart racing and made it very difficult to focus on the task in hand.

As much fun as it was to tease Lucas, Tommy hadn't any real intention of seducing Gloria, glorious as she indeed was.

Well, not yet, anyway. Not whilst he had a job to do.

But once that job was completed...

'Thanks,' replied the Glorious Gloria, taking a seat on a sofa and patting the cushion next to her.

Tempting as it was, Tommy needed to keep a clear head if he was to succeed in his mission.

He smiled at her, raising a slight blush on her cheeks in response, and took a pew on the cream leather footstool in front of her instead. In addition to putting temptation a little further out of reach, it left Tommy once again looking up slightly at Gloria. He pulled a notepad and propelling pencil from his pocket and sat with an eager expression on his face.

She smiled approvingly and poured jet black coffee into delicate porcelain cup and handed it to a grateful Tommy.

'What,' he said, dropping a sugar cube or three into the steaming liquid. 'Can you tell me about the late Mr Chapman?'

Gloria pursed her lips and looked away sharply.

'I'm sorry,' said Tommy quietly. 'It must be terribly difficult for you to lose a friend like that. Were you close?'

Gloria gave a short bark of a laugh. 'Briefly,' she said, sipping her coffee.

'A recent acquaintance?' asked Tommy.

'A friend of a friend, perhaps? How did you meet?'

There was a pause as Gloria decided on a lie to tell.

'It's rather awkward, I'm afraid,' she said at last, taking another sip. 'I'd rather not talk about it, if you don't mind.'

'Of course not,' murmured Tommy, dipping his gaze again. 'We needn't talk about anything you don't want to. Although, anything you say can be attributed to an anonymous source...'

The cup clattered in her saucer. 'It won't be very anonymous to my friends, will it?' she said hissed. 'This was a bad idea.' She stood abruptly and smoothed down her skirt.

Tommy stood as well and reached a hand towards her, deliberately drawing back before his fingers made contact. 'I'm sorry,' he said, dropping his voice low and falsely apologetic. 'I didn't mean to make you feel uncomfortable.'

His eyes skated up and down her achingly perfect figure, and he allowed the corner of his mouth to twitch upward as his gaze returned to hers. 'Believe me, I'd like to make you as comfortable as possible.'

A delicate blush coloured Gloria's cheeks again, but she looked rather pleased, as Tommy knew she would.

'It's just,' she said, biting back the rest of the sentence. She fidgeted with the string of pearls around her neck.

'Yes?' murmured Tommy, taking a step closer to her, again not quite touching her but close enough to feel the warmth of her body.

The sharp intake of breath told him that he wasn't the only one aware of, and rather keen on, their increased proximity.

Their eyes locked, the gradually building electricity sizzling the air between them.

'I've been a terrible fool,' she whispered, biting her bottom lip again.

'Haven't we all?' whispered Tommy. He reached for her hand, pausing before taking it gently. 'I won't judge, I promise, and anything you ask me not to print will remain strictly between us.'

Her eyes darted across his face, clearly looking for the deception Tommy knew wouldn't - couldn't be there.

After all, he wouldn't be printing anything at all about this encounter.

'Sometimes,' he said gently, looking at her quite seriously. 'Sometimes it helps to talk your troubles over with a stranger. Someone who doesn't know any details already - who is a blank slate, if you will. Someone who won't judge you. You never have to see me again after today.' Tommy gave a small, sad smile, before adding in a voice perfectly pitched to flatter, 'Although that'd be a crying shame.'

She crushed his fingers in such a

desperately grateful way it made Tommy's heart ache.

Ha, perhaps he was even fooling himself with his act? Oh, it wouldn't be a *serious* entanglement, it never - well, rarely - was. But any flirtation should always be completely serious in the moment, and Miss Hawkes deserved his full attention...

Even it was just for the morning.

He steered her back to the sofa and took the seat next to her this time, keeping her graceful fingers in his and rubbing his thumb gently over the back of her hand.

She swallowed, eyes darting all over the place.

'The thing is,' she said, before hesitating. 'The thing is I, I did a rather silly thing. For entirely sensible reasons, I assure you, but I'm not terribly proud of myself.'

'Every woman should have a little scandal in her past,' said Tommy in a low voice, debating whether he should suggest adding to her score card. 'It makes them interesting,' he continued, seeing Glorious Gloria's resolve waver. 'I shouldn't dream of taking up with a girl who hadn't at least a few interesting tales to tell.'

Gloria gave him a sad, watery smile. 'I wish everyone was as open minded as you, Mr Kilbourne,' she said, shaking her head. 'But I'm afraid I've done something quite unforgivable.'

'I'm sure anyone could forgive you anything,' replied Tommy softly. 'I certainly would.'

'I'm not sure if I can forgive myself,' she said, a tearful wobble in the words. 'That's the problem.'

'Perhaps I can help you forget instead,' said Tommy, renouncing his previous good intentions and putting Lucas' parting request to not seduce the suspects out of his mind.

Who'd tell? Besides, a little pillow talk was the perfect way to get the information he'd been sent for.

There was barely a pause before Glorious Gloria pressed her lips against his.

He kissed her back, running his fingers through her bobbed curls, all thoughts of secret missions, Lucas' disapproval, and even Clara, vanishing as he allowed himself to sink into the moment.

'I'd like to forget,' she said breathlessly, taking his hand and standing up. 'I really would. Come on, let's go somewhere private.'

***

'Clara, my dear, this is such a trial,' said Bunty with a sigh, pouring a steaming stream of tea into a floral teacup. 'The police have been around three - no, *four* times already, and can you believe they think *I* had a hand in poor Bertie's death?'

'That's terrible,' said Clara, taking the proffered tea. They were back in the ill-fated parlour, which was rather cosy when Clara didn't think about the tragedy that had taken place there.

Bunty waved her hand irritably. 'I don't know how they could think such a thing, but they do. Then again, why should any of us want the poor boy dead?'

'Why indeed,' murmured Clara, wondering if Bunty knew P.C. Jenkins was her brother or not. She was sure she'd not mentioned her surname, but could Bunty have found out somehow?

'I suppose that really is at the heart of the matter,' added Clara, feeling rather guilty for being in Bunty's home under false pretences.

'Quite,' came the reply. 'It's true, he wasn't the most *sensible* of men, but he was good.' She gave a theatrical sniff, which Clara suspected was rather put on. 'He'd have done well in politics.'

'Did he have ambitions in that direction?'

'Oh no, not a bit of it,' said Bunty with a little half laugh that caught in the back of her throat. 'Quite a lazy little slug at times, but he'd have been an asset to the country had he worked harder and applied himself to a career.'

Clara couldn't help but chuckle. That sounded familiar. Not that Lucas wanted to go into politics either, but he could at least try and make the best of being a reporter.

'Perhaps all men are like that,' said Clara, raising a smile from her companion.

'I think so more and more,' replied Bunty, helping herself to a triangle of shortbread. 'The only truly hardworking, ambitious man I've ever met is Redmond – Dr Shank – and afraid he has a tendency to take thing a little too far.'

Clara suppressed a shiver, hoping that didn't mean what she feared it might.

'Oh?' she said, trying to make the strangled noise from her throat sound merely curious about a common acquaintance. 'What's he done?'

Bunty frowned at her, puzzled. 'Isn't it obvious?'

Oh dear, oh dear...

The fear must have shown on her face, because Bunty rolled her eyes and dunked her biscuit into her cup, in what was probably a most unladylike way.

'Don't be silly, there's a good girl,' she said. 'Redmond didn't kill Bertie. He hasn't the backbone for such a thing.'

That presented another, even worse suggestion to Clara's mind.

She put her tea down, just in case.

Which didn't go unnoticed.

'And neither do I, I hasten to add,' said Bunty coldly. 'And you may rest assured that if I had the merest inkling who did it, I'd be telling one of those policeman chappies straight away.' She shifted discontentedly in her seat. 'Accident, my foot,' she grumbled.

'Sorry,' said Clara, taking up her tea again and making a point of taking a sip. 'I suppose I'm a little on edge, with everything that's happened.'

Bunty smiled, though it seemed more forced than before.

'Yes, one does start jumping at shadows when faced with something like murder,' said Bunty, relaxing into her chair again. 'I too suspected Redmond for a time, especially after hearing which poison was used, but... a coincidence, my dear, pure coincidence.' She sighed heavily. 'I thought he was making a point, you see, by using the mistletoe distillation.'

'Why would he make a point with that?'

'Well, you see, Redmond and I first met while he was treating my husband for high blood pressure. He prescribed him a concoction using mistletoe.'

'So he wanted you to know he'd killed poor Chappers?'

'Or so I thought. They'd had some terrible quarrel or other, over money, of all things.'

'Chapman owed Shank money?' said Clara, deliberately guessing wrong.

'No, the other way around,' said Bunty. 'I told you Redmond was overly ambitious, and usually that means with business. This time, however, he was overly ambitious on a sure thing down at the races. Hah, a sure thing, indeed! The silly fool saw it as an easy way to get money and expand his practice – though why he didn't just ask me, I'll never know – and bet far more than he ought to have done. When the horse fell at the first, he hadn't the funds to pay...'

'So he asked the wealthy young man he knew for a loan, so he needn't admit to you that he'd make such a stupid mistake,' said Clara, nodding sagely. 'Yes, I expect Lucas would do the same in that situation. Are all men so silly?'

'I'm afraid so, my dear,' replied Bunty. 'But that's why we love them, isn't it?' Her cheeks flushed as she realised what she'd said, but Clara chose not to see.

'Of course,' said Bunty, moving swiftly on from her accidental admission, 'Dear Bertie had no concerns about money, his folks are simply rolling in the stuff, the lucky things, so he was in no rush to get it back. But Redmond, the old fool that he is, got more fretful each time Bertie told him not to worry about it, until he could barely look the poor boy in the eye and he was avoiding me altogether.' Bunty helped herself to another piece of shortbread and gave a short, bitter laugh. 'And I just thought his ardour had cooled towards this ageing widow.'

'But why would using the mistletoe

medicine be a message to *you*?' said Clara after a few moment's silent contemplation. 'And why would Shank want you to know he'd done the deed anyway? He wasn't threatening you, was he?' Clara frowned again. 'But even so, that doesn't make sense. He didn't owe *you* money, so it's not like he'd be warning you not to chase the debt. And why would killing Bertie be a message to you at all? Except -' Clara reddened. 'There were rumours about you and Bertie, weren't there?'

Bunty remained silent, pursing her lips anxiously, but Clara was so lost in her thoughts she barely noticed.

'But that doesn't make sense either - you wouldn't want to go back to a fellow that killed your lover. But I heard the rumours about your affair are false -'

Bunty flinched and looked at Clara, mildly panicked, but Clara was too distracted by problem solving to notice.

'- Even though everyone believed them,' continued Clara. 'But mistletoe as a message? That might make sense if Chapman and the late Sir Samuel were related, but -'

'More tea, my dear?' said Bunty suddenly, leaning across the small table.

Clara watched her cup refill, the light dancing on the stream of copper liquid as she tried to focus her thoughts.

She'd said something that made Bunty

react, but what?

Wait.

The affair was a lie, then…

Something about Sir Sam and Chapman being related.

Sir Sam was a lot older than Bunty, but even so, she loved him. Really, truly, not as a last resort but as a first choice.

Chapman must have been about the right age. Of course, she didn't know for sure - they hadn't found that out yet - but could it be...?

The more she thought about it, the more Clara could see there was no other option, until finally the words escaped her lips.

'Bertie's your son, not Johnny,' she blurted, then clapped a hand over her mouth.

Bunty pressed her lips together tightly. 'So you *have* heard the rumours about me?'

'I'm afraid so,' she admitted, wincing. 'But really, it was all so long ago, it hardly matters, does it?'

'Perhaps,' replied Bunty. 'Then again, perhaps not. People might have short memories, but it can still take them a long time to forgive. And it hardly seemed fair on the boy to uproot his life like that. It was only when –' a deeper shade of red coloured her face this time – 'it became unavoidable to admit the truth that I told him. In fact, it was rather a good thing I did. A trip to the doctor revealed dear Bertie inherited his father's heart problems.'

'So Sir Sam was Bertie's father?'

'Yes,' answered Bunty, a soft smile spreading across her face. 'It was love at first sight, despite the age difference. Unfortunately, Sam was married to the dreary Elinor, and as divorce is such an unpleasant, messy, and generally frowned upon business, we decided to wait for her to die before we could marry.'

'That must have been difficult,' said Clara sympathetically, thinking how awful it would have been had another woman snagged Lucas before her.

She wasn't sure she'd have been so patient.

'Very,' agreed Bunty. 'Especially as dreary Elinor took simply *decades* to shuffle off, which was disappointing considering how sickly she was. Well, maybe not decades, but I'm sure you know how long any separation feels when you're young and in love.'

'Yes,' said Clara sympathetically. 'It took Lucas an awfully long time to take the hint, and with me living in London and him here in Castlebury....'

Bunty gave a wry smile. 'Yes, they can be rather slow on the uptake at times.'

'Lucas more than most,' said Clara. 'Really, he's most infuriating at times.'

'You'll get used to that,' said Bunty.

'Oh, I am,' said Clara, sipping her tea. 'Don't worry about that. Didn't you and Sam ever want to take Bertie back?'

'Of course,' cried Bunty. 'But by the time Elinor had done the decent thing and popped her clogs - and we waited some time before marrying so it wouldn't look suspicious - Bertie was settled with the Chapmans - do you know Lord and Lazy Leazes? No, I don't suppose you would. They're lovely, I'll introduce you some time. They really loved the boy. It hardly seemed fair to upset the apple cart, so we left things as they were. It was better for Bertie that way, and that's all we really cared about.'

'I'm sorry,' said Clara with feeling. 'You'd have made a wonderful mother.'

'Yes, I rather think I would have,' said Bunty, smiling. 'Unfortunately, Sam and I weren't blessed with another child, so I had to settle for being a wonderful aunt instead. I like to think I fulfil the role well.'

'I'm sure you do,' said Clara, saluting her with a teacup. 'But that does rather leave the question of who killed Bertie wide open...'

***

'I assure you, this is just routine questioning,' said Henry, tapping his foot impatiently. 'There's nothing else to it.'

'I doubt that,' said Bourbon-Busset, seething with suppressed rage. 'But I suppose I don't have much of a choice in the matter.'

'I don't suppose you do,' said Henry placidly.

'Darling, I think it's better to work with the police, don't you?' said Sylvia, before shooting Lucas a filthy look. 'Though I don't see why that reporter is here.'

Lucas shuffled further behind Henry, doing little to conceal his presence at the old gatekeeper's cottage on the Castlebury Manor estate, where Jonny was staying whilst visiting his aunt. Seeing as Sylvia appeared to be sleeping there too - her canary yellow soft topped sports car was parked outside and blanketed in yesterday's snow - Lucas could quite understand why he'd rather slum it here rather than stay up at the manor itself.

Yes, a little privacy was wonderful at times...

'Always was a sharp one, our Syl,' said Chapman, who had tagged along with them in spite of Lucas' best efforts to get him to go somewhere - anywhere - else and leave him in peace.

'Mr Rathbone is here to act as stenographer,' said Henry smoothly. 'We're shorthanded over Christmas, and as he's adept at taking shorthand notes and has already been cleared from the investigation, he willingly offered his services.'

'News to me,' muttered Lucas, who didn't remember doing anything nearly so foolish.

'So we're stuck with him, I'm afraid,' concluded Henry, taking half a step back.

'Ow,' said Lucas, pulling his foot from underneath his friend's heavy leather boot. 'All right. Truth and justice and all that.'

'Plus I was a jolly fine fellow and you want to help find out who did old Chappers in,' supplied the ghost.

'Humph,' said Bourbon-Busset, glowering. 'That's as may be, but this had better not make it to the papers, understand?'

'You have his word none of this will be leaked to the press,' said Henry.

'I was just about to say that,' complained Lucas.

'And I just saved you the job,' said Henry, turning around to smile sweetly at him. 'Wasn't that kind?'

'All right, let's get this over with,' said Sylvia, placing a hand on her fiancée arm before he could make a comment, the emerald on her left hand dazzling in the morning sunlight filtering through ancient, uneven window panes. 'Sweetheart, the sooner you answer the questions, the sooner we can go back to what we were doing earlier.'

'Her lipstick on his collar should tell you everything you need to know about *that*,' said Chapman, nudging Lucas ineffectually. 'Given that their relationship is a sham, they're certainly dedicated to the part.' the ghost frowned.

'Rather an insult to my memory, if you ask me.'

'No one asked you,' muttered Lucas.

'Excuse me?' said Sylvia in her most offended voice.

'Uh, not you,' said Lucas hurriedly. 'Just a thought I had.'

'Just ignore Mr Rathbone,' said Henry cheerfully. 'I'm going to.'

'Good idea,' said Sylvia coldly. 'The best one I've heard all day.'

'Is she always like this?' said Lucas under his breath, thinking only the ghost would hear.

'Yes,' replied Chapman and Bourbon-Busset together.

'Humph,' said Sylvia, folding her arms indignantly.

'Would you care to step out of the room, Miss Pettigrew?' said Henry, gesturing to the door. 'Perhaps it's best if you didn't hear what I have to say to Lord Cassiobury.'

'Good ide -' started Jonny.

'Anything you have to say to him you can say to me,' she said, cutting off the relieved remark on her fiancé's lips. 'We are going to be married, you know.'

Lucas thought he saw Jonny blanch slightly, his already pale face growing deathlier in pallor.

'What's this about, officer?' asked Bourbon-Busset in a falsely helpful tone.

'I'm sure you can guess, sir,' replied

Henry cryptically, arching an eyebrow. 'But if you're happy for the young lady to stay and hear all about your -' he paused for effect to check his notes, '- *business dealings*, then I'm more than happy to continue...'

'See, darling, it's terribly dull,' said Jono quickly, pecking a fuming Sylvia on the cheek. 'Why don't you run along and get changed for luncheon, or something?'

'That isn't for ages.'

'But I'm taking you out, remember?' replied the unhappy man. 'We've got to drive into, uh, Oxford, and the roads are terrible, what with all this snow and ice and that.'

'When did we decide that?' said Sylvia suspiciously.

'Uh, it's a surprise,' said Bourbon-Busset, beads of sweat forming on his brow. 'Or it was going to be, but I suppose I've rather ruined it now, ha-ha.'

'Yes,' replied his fiancée sourly. 'I suppose you rather have.'

'So off you go and get changed, there's a good girl, because we've got reservations at noon.'

'Hmm,' she said suspiciously. 'Well, if you insist...'

'I do,' he said, a little too quickly. 'I mean, I wouldn't want us to be late.'

Sylvia muttered something that sounded like "We'll talk about this later," and stood to leave.

'Oho, he's for it now,' said Chapman gleefully. 'Syl can bear a grudge like no other, believe me.'

The door shut a little harder than strictly necessary behind her, making the unfortunate Lord wince. He was clearly having the same thoughts as his deceased friend.

Chapman vanished, before reappearing at Lucas' side moments later.

'Just as I thought,' said the ghost. 'She's listening at the keyhole. Can't say I blame her, I'd be simply *dying* to know what was happening if I were her - figuratively speaking, of course.'

Jono turned his worried eyes towards the police officer and licked his lips.

'I know why you're here,' he said. 'But it's not what you think.'

'It never is,' said Henry, indicating to Lucas to take notes. 'Why don't you help us set the record straight?'

'I... made a few bad investments,' said Bourbon-Busset, clenching and unclenching his long, elegant fingers repeatedly.

'On the horses,' added Chapman helpfully. 'I bet he doesn't tell you that part.'

'I see,' said Henry. 'And what has that got to do with our investigation, sir?'

'Nothing!' cried Bourbon-Busset, leaping from his chair and raking his fingers through his hair. 'I swear it, it has nothing at all to do with what happened to Chappers.'

'Told you,' said the ghost smugly. 'Write that down in your little notebook, why don't you.'

Lucas shook his head at him and scowled.

'Then why bring it up?' asked Henry.

Jono sank back into his seat. 'Isn't that why you're here?' he asked. 'You found out about my debts and the will, and -'

'What will?' asked Henry sharply.

'Aunt Bun's, of course,' said Johnny. His eyes went wide. 'You mean, you don't know? That she changed it? I didn't mind at all, of course – how could I? It was his birth right, and Chappers was like a brother to me anyway...'

'You were told that in confidence,' cried Chapman, striding across the room to wave an accusatory if unseen finger in his best friend's face. 'You swore you'd never tell.'

'She changed her will to favour Chapman?' said Henry, frowning. 'Why?'

Jonny leant back in his chair, chewing his knuckles distractedly. 'If you don't know,' he said at last. 'It's not my place to say.'

'I think it's exactly your place to say, sir,' said Henry archly. 'Particularly when you're our chief suspect in the murder of your so-called friend.'

'I am?'

'He is?' said Chapman and Lucas in

unison. The latter received a glare from the police office supposedly in charge.

'You are,' said Henry, turning back to Bourbon-Busset. 'So I suggest you tell me everything, and spare no detail.'

'Look, I told the old bird I'd not say anything unless it was strictly necessary,' said Bourbon-Busset.

'Pretty sure it's necessary, old chum,' said Chapman. 'I don't like it either, but – well, I'm sure she'll understand, given the circs.'

'Rich, coming from you,' whispered Lucas.

'It was never necessary for *me* to tell you what's what,' replied the ghost. 'But I was never looking at doing the hemp fandango, was I?'

Lucas narrowed his eyes at the ghost, who tried to shuffle out of the reluctant psychic's eyeline.

'I'm a police officer,' said Henry coldly. 'Asking you these questions because you're a suspect in the murder of your friend.'

'I say, steady on,' declared Chapman. 'I told you fellows already it wasn't him.'

'How much more necessary does it have to be?' finished Henry.

Bourbon-Busset paled further. He looked in worse shape than the spirit, which was quite remarkable, really.

He gulped, then took a sip of whatever he'd been drinking, his hand shaking violently.

Either Bourbon-Busset had been drinking his nerves away, or he was going to try.

Henry and Lucas waited in silence, either for an explanation or for the guilty man to make a bolt for it.

Eventually, Bourbon-Busset chose the former option.

'I know how this looks,' he started, taking another nerve-steadying gulp. 'And it's bad. Really, really bad. But I promise, it's not what it seems.'

'I'll decide that,' said Henry. 'It is my job, after all.'

'Yes, quite,' said Bourbon-Busset, with a sickly grin. 'Well, the thing is, I got in a bit of a sticky patch when it came to the old financials, you know. Made a few silly little investments, then a few bolder ones that should have paid off in a bigger way...'

'You bet the farm, in other words,' said Henry. He shot a look at Lucas, who suddenly remembered he was supposed to be jotting all this down.

'In a word, yes,' confirmed Bourbon-Busset, rubbing his forehead distractedly. 'I know, it's never the way to do things, but I was desperate.' He loosened his tie and ran a finger around his collar. 'Borrowed money from a couple of people it, er, wasn't wise to borrow from, if you see what I mean.'

'Like your future father-in-law,' said

Henry.

'How...?' exclaimed Johnny, before regaining his composure. 'No, I suppose you have your sources. Yes, I borrowed from old Pettigrew,' he said, clenching and unclenching his hands again. 'He agreed to terms he had no intention of keeping. What rotter does that? He changed his mind about how long I had to pay him back and... and of course, I didn't have the funds.'

'I see,' said Henry. 'And so you thought you'd hurry your inheritance along a bit, did you?'

There was a dreadful pause as Jono absorbed this statement.

'I presume,' began Bourbon-Busset hesitantly. 'You're suggesting I had designs on killing the aunt, inheriting her fortune, and,' - he glanced over his shoulder and dropped his voice. 'And buying my way out of this marriage? I assume you're aware of the, uh, nature of our betrothal?'

Henry moved his head in a non-committal fashion, evidently deciding to give the chap enough rope to hang himself.

Quite literally, if it came to trial.

'Not traditional, I know,' said Bourbon-Busset, fishing a silver cigarette case from his jacket pocket and lighting one with shaking hands. 'But necessary. Believe me, it was necessary. The alternative... And everyone involved knew the score. Yes, we knew what was going on, and happy enough to do it. The marriage only needed to last year or two, then we'd quietly divorce - at least, as quietly as possible with these things.' He sunk his head into his hands. 'I wasn't looking forward to the divorce trial, but me and Syl... She was better suited to Chappers, and Glo - I can't imagine my life with anyone else.'

'Which is why Sylvia's lipstick is on your collar,' muttered the ghost darkly.

'What about the financial side of that?' said Henry. 'Was your future, albeit temporary, father-in-law just going to write off your debts?'

'Part of the deal was that I'd get a little extra seed money from the father-in-law,' said Bourbon-Busset. 'With which to rebuild my fortunes and pay him back. Well, he didn't know that bit, he just doesn't want his baby girl living a life of poverty, but I fully intend to pay back every farthing I owed, with interest, in the hopes he might not actually kill me when it came time to, you know... give his daughter the old heave-ho.'

'Uhuh,' said Henry. 'Do go on, sir.

'Syl would be marrying into a genuine old family of the highest order,' continued Bourbon-Busset. 'Which is all daddy dearest really cares about. Can't seem to get himself knighted, so marrying his daughter off to a bona fide Lord is the next best thing. Awful lot, these nouveau riche - but then, riche is something I'm short on. And if the piper wants paying, he must play the right tunes.'

Henry pursed his lips. 'And if you couldn't repay your father-in-law? In financial terms, I mean.'

'The marriage would continue until I could.'

'And Mr Pettigrew was aware of your plans to divorce his daughter after the debt was paid?'

'Good Lord, no,' cried Bourbon-Busset, looking horrified. 'But Syl, the trooper that she is, was going to start sowing the seeds as soon as possible so when the inevitable happened it wouldn't come as too much of a surprise.' Bourbon-Busset gave a wry smile. 'Then again, the temptation to give the old goat a heart attack with the news is very strong. Very strong indeed. That'd do nicely, in fact, as Syl would get a nice chunk of change and we could go our separate ways without upsetting her father.'

Henry raised an eyebrow. 'The thought crossed your mind, did it?'

There was another awful silence as Bourbon-Busset processed this.

'For a second,' he admitted. 'But not a moment more, I assure you.'

Henry gave Lucas a look, presumably to make sure he wasn't slacking in his note-taking duties.

Perish the thought, thought Lucas, hastily summarising all the conversation he'd missed in the drama.

It was better than a radio play, and all too easy to get lost in. Even Chapman had fallen silent, something Lucas was immensely grateful for and prayed would continue for a long time yet.

'So, the thought of hastening an inheritance isn't new to you?' said Henry, always a stickler for dotting i's and crossing t's.

'I didn't kill Chapman,' cried Bourbon-Busset, thumping his fist on the arm of the sofa. 'I couldn't - how could I? He was my best friend since childhood. We've done everything together. Anything of mine was his -'

'Including your aunt's inheritance,' said Henry.

Bourbon-Busset closed his eyes and ran a trembling hand across his face.

'I told you it looked bad,' he said quietly. 'Is there anything I can do to convince you of my innocence, or have you made up your mind already?' he asked. 'If that's the case, you may as well just arrest me now and be done with it.'

He held his wrists out in front of him, turning his head away.

'Is that a confession, sir?' asked Henry.

'Sounds like it to me,' muttered Lucas, earning him a black look from his own childhood friend.

'No, it most certainly is not,' snapped Bourbon-Busset, dropping his hands back into his lap. 'But I know how you fellows work. You get an idea in your head and bam, that's it. Next thing a chap knows he's on the gallows with a rope tightening around his throat.'

'I hope you'll find me to be a fair judge of the facts, sir.'

Lucas noted that his friend didn't promise anything about finding Bourbon-Busset innocent, or in fact, believing him at all.

'I hope so too,' said Bourbon-Busset grimly.

'But what I don't understand,' said Henry. 'Is how on earth you persuaded the other three to help you out with getting Pettigrew off your back.'

Bourbon-Busset shrugged. 'Chapman and I would do anything for each other,' he said. 'So it was just a matter of convincing the girls to go along with the scheme. Once we explained the situation and told them the plan, they agreed easily enough.'

Lucas wondered at the likelihood of Clara ever agreeing to such an arrangement, and concluded it was more likely to snow ink.

He wondered why anyone would agree to such a ridiculous, degrading scheme, and decided Sylvia and Glo must have had the stuffing knocked out of them at some finishing school, or whatever dreadful thing these unfortunate girls get sent to. Someone who had suffered *that* was probably more likely to be more compliant than a girl who went to school with the boys, worked with the men, and didn't see any reason why her gender should mean she should be treated any differently at all.

Unless it suited her, of course, in which case she'd use it as an excuse for almost anything.

Lucas smiled, then focussed back on the task at hand.

'You persuaded them,' said Henry. 'How?'

'Oh, we came up with a plan, of course,' said Bourbon-Busset with a dismissive wave of the hand. 'Schemes and plots were our stock in trade since we were nippers, Chapman and I, and this was no different as far as we were concerned.'

'Details, if you don't mind,' said Henry tersely. 'Please focus on the details.'

'Oh yes, I see. You know I inherited the pater's draughty old manor house?' said Bourbon-Busset. 'No? Dear me, and there I was thinking you were the omniscient P.C. Jenkins. There we go. Well, after the old boy copped it, I took control of Wimberley Hall in Staffordshire. Horrible draughty place it is too, and so big I often felt lonely, even with all the family around - but there you go. Can't pick your family, can't pick your family pile.'

Lucas was suddenly thankful that he'd been raised in a terrace, even if it was tiny to the point of being claustrophobic. It was cosy and filled with love, which sounded far nicer than a grand house with no affection any day.

'If I had my way,' continued Jonny. 'I'd sell the thing and move to the South of France, but the lawyers say there's some frightful rule or other that means I'll give up a whole host of other things if I did tricks like that and... well, I learned to live with it, if not to like it. Anyway, Chapman's parents are hale and hearty folks, not likely to hop the twig any time soon, and it's terribly lonely rattling around Wimberley by oneself, so we came up with a rather cunning plan.'

'I'm sure you can see where this is going,' said Chapman to Lucas, who hadn't a clue. 'We'd have made quite the happy little troupe.'

'And what was this plan, sir?' asked Henry.

'Hmm? Oh, well once I'd married Sylvia, and Chapman had put a ring on Glo's finger – after a reasonable time, of course, it might look rather odd if we just switched girls on a whim - the freshly-minted Mr and Mrs Chapman were going to move into a cottage on the estate, and we'd go back to how things were before all this mess. We'd keep up appearances in public, and then after the divorces we'd get back to having the right spouse.'

'I see,' said Henry, in what Lucas recognised as his most disapproving tone of voice. He'd heard it a lot lately.

'I knew you would,' said Bourbon-Busset, relieved.

'Hmm,' said Henry. 'Well, it seems you had this all sorted out, but it still leaves the question of this will you mentioned, and how that would make you likely to kill your friend. How did Chapman convince your aunt to leave him part of her estate?'

'You mean you really don't know?'

'Humour me.'

'Oh, well you know the rumours about me not being Bunty's nephew but rather her son, don't you? They do the rounds on a regular basis.'

'Are you telling me that there's truth in the rumours?' said Henry, frowning as he was momentarily distracted by a noise outside.

It sounded like a car engine, and Lucas wondered who'd be foolish enough to venture out on a treacherously icy day like this. He decided it was probably some poor delivery driver going up to the hall.

'Don't tell him, Johnny,' urged Chapman pointlessly, cutting across these thoughts.

'Well, I always assumed so,' said Bourbon-Busset, with a careless shrug. 'One does hear these things, and no matter how much one's family *try* to convince one otherwise, once an idea gets into your head it's perfectly impossible to shift it sometimes - particularly when one is young. I just accepted it as truth and kept my trap shut to spare the feelings of my parents.'

'Keep it shut now, as well,' said the ghost.

'Or your aunt and uncle, if the rumours are indeed true,' said Henry.

Bourbon-Busset smiled wryly. '*If* the rumours were true, they would've been my aunt and uncle. However, as it stands, rumours of my illegitimacy have been greatly overestimated.'

'You promised,' cried Chapman, leaning close into his friend's face. 'You swore you wouldn't tell.'

'So, Bunty doesn't really have an illegitimate child?' asked Henry. 'Those rumours aren't true?'

Chapman tore at his hair and moaned, and it was all Lucas could do to focus on writing down the exchange between the living.

'I didn't say that,' said Bourbon-Busset, leaning back in his seat. 'But I'm not him. Come along, you're an intelligent fellow. If I'm not Bunty's son, but she changed her will in someone else's favour…'

Lucas stole a glance at his ghostly pal, who was staring blankly into the distance.

Well, it would explain a few things, wouldn't it?

'Come along, man,' cried Bourbon-Busset,

slapping his hand on arm of the sofa again. 'Who do you think is Bunty's lovechild, if it's not me?'

'Why don't you just tell me, sir?' answered Henry.

'Because I swore never to tell,' replied Bourbon-Busset. 'I made a promise, and now - now he's gone.'

Lucas glanced again at the ghost, who most certainly wasn't gone and stood next to Bourbon-Busset's shoulder.

'Even worse,' continued Bourbon-Busset, a slight catch in his voice. 'You think I killed him.'

Henry bit his bottom lip and glanced at Lucas, who knew the policeman shouldn't make guesses, even educated one. It's far better to have the suspect admit to things themselves - however sometimes they needed a helping hand.

Henry gave Lucas a look that suggested some pesky reporter should take a stab at the truth instead.

'Chapman,' said Lucas obligingly. 'Chapman was really Bunty's son.'

'Indeed I am,' said the ghost grandly, breaking out of his stupor at last. 'And a finer woman you'll be hard pressed to find in this land.'

Bourbon-Busset merely inclined his head.

'They chose to keep the truth of the matter from us,' he said quietly. 'Chappers was settled with his parents, and after all this time Bunty and Sir Sam couldn't very well claim the poor lad. So, they left me under the cloud of rumour instead.'

'Bitter about that, are you, sir?' inquired Henry.

'Perhaps a little,' admitted Bourbon-Busset. 'Wouldn't you be? But I'd never wish any harm on any of them, and that's the truth of it. They're my family, and Chappers was as good as my cousin even before I discovered the truth. I could hardly object to it.'

'And when exactly did you discover the truth?'

'A few months ago,' he said. 'Can't remember exactly when. It came as a bit of a surprise, as I'm sure you can imagine, but I was delighted.'

'Eventually,' said Chapman, though only Lucas heard. 'He spent quite a while declaring me a liar and a cad, but he's called me worse. Once his fit of temper was over, he was indeed delighted, as I was. I'd always been jealous of him and all his brothers. A cousin isn't quite the same, but it's better than I had before.'

'I'm sure,' said Henry, in a tone of voice that said the opposite. 'Nonetheless, it must have caused some issues when Bunty wanted to change the will in his favour, which I assume is what you were referring to.'

'Only partially change it,' said Bourbon-

Busset. 'She was very fair - very fair indeed, and split her estate evenly between myself and Chappers.'

'That was my doing,' said Chapman proudly. 'She wanted to leave the whole lot to me, as her and Sir Sam's natural child. That and she felt terribly guilty about the whole adoption thing - not that I cared. I didn't want for a thing growing up, couldn't have asked for a better life. My point is, I convinced her she shouldn't neglect Johnny. He's her family too, and he could use the cash more than me anyway.'

'But I assume,' said Henry. 'That now Mr Chapman is deceased, you're the sole heir again.'

There was a deathly pause from both sides of the veil.

'How could I have been so blind?' said Chapman weakly supporting himself against – and Lucas noted, slightly through - the sofa as his knees gave way. 'It all makes sense now.'

'You assume correctly,' said Bourbon-Busset decisively. 'However, I didn't kill him.'

'A likely story,' cried the ghost. 'Fiend! How could I have ever trusted you?'

'In that case,' said Henry. 'We have no reason to fear for the life of your aunt.'

'Bunty?' said Bourbon-Busset, frowning. 'Well no, she's as hale and hearty as they come.'

'That,' said Henry coldly. 'Is *not* what I meant.'

'Now see here,' exclaimed Johnny. 'It's one thing to accuse a chap of murdering his pal, but his own aunt?'

'You wouldn't be the first,' said Henry. 'And I doubt you'll be the last. If you are keen to get your hands on her money, how better than to hurry her journey to the grave?'

'Lord above,' moaned Bourbon-Busset, sinking his head into his hands. 'I see what you mean, but I'd never - I couldn't... She's the only family I have left. Having lost more people than I can count, I don't want to add to the list myself.'

'Hmm,' said Henry, clearly unconvinced. 'Have you a better solution, sir? Another suspect we could look at for the murder of your friend?'

'Well... no, not really.' Bourbon-Busset sighed heavily. 'What a mess,' he groaned. 'And at Christmas, too.'

He really was a pitiable sight, and Lucas wondered whether it was real, or a very clever act.

'What if,' started Jonny after another deathly pause. 'But no, surely not.'

'Out with it,' snapped Henry. 'It's your neck wrapped in rope if you don't, so you might as well air your thoughts.'

Bourbon-Busset swallowed hard.

'Well...' he said. 'Bunty was rather concerned Chappers might reveal who he was. As much as she wanted to own him as her son, she didn't want to rake up her past. She certainly didn't want to hurt his parents, who did her a real favour, as I'm sure you can imagine. She feels terribly indebted to them. Not that they care about that at all. As far as they're concerned, Chappers was their son and that's all there was to it.'

The pencil slipped from Lucas' fingers onto the floor, where it remained unnoticed.

He'd put Clara into Bunty's Rolls Royce only hours before and waved her off to tea with Her Ladyship.

'I wouldn't do anything of the sort,' protested Chapman. 'For exactly the same reasons. Bunty has already suffered enough - too much, actually - for her youthful indiscretion, and my Mother and Father are exactly that. There's more to family than flesh and blood, after all.'

'Are you saying Bunty would kill Chapman to keep her secret safe?' said Henry, putting Lucas' fears into words twanging with sudden anxiety.

'She's the only one I can think of who'd any motive to bump him off,' said Bourbon-Busset, which wasn't helpful. 'But even that's a stretch of the old imagination. Honestly, everyone thought he was wonderful.'

'Not Shank?' said Henry, unable to keep the fear and desperation out of his voice.

Lucas tried not to give in to the same dark

thoughts as his oldest friend.

Then again, perhaps Clara wouldn't accuse Bunty of murder whilst they were alone.

Who was he kidding, of course she would, and probably without a second thought.

Better hope it was Shank after all...

'I doubt it,' said Bourbon-Busset, shaking his head. 'Yes, he owed Chappers a few hundred quid, but he hasn't the guts for murder. Complete coward, though he'll talk the talk easily enough. Besides, if he was going to do something like that, he'd have used something that wouldn't lead you directly to him, surely?'

Henry swore under his breath. 'He told Lucas and Clara as much,' he said, forgetting that he shouldn't mention things like to with a suspect.

'Well, there you go, then,' said Bourbon-Busset. 'And Sylvia and Glo, though a little, uh, *upset* about things as you might expect, weren't so upset as to resort to *murder*. But Aunt Bun... Well, she's got more to lose, hasn't she? Her tattered reputation is barely repaired, after all...'

'And Clara's having tea with Bunty,' said Lucas hoarsely, feeling quite sick all of a sudden as his world dissolved around him. 'Good grief, she knows how to pick her friends, doesn't she?'

'That she does,' said Henry, snatching up their coats and tossing Lucas his jacket before sprinting out the door. 'Let's stop her getting murdered.'

'Again,' said Lucas, jogging after him.

***

Tommy, certain that the Glorious Gloria was in a more relaxed frame of mind, traced his fingers gently down her naked back, causing a sharp intake of breath and a small shiver of delight.

'So,' he whispered. 'Have you forgotten what was bothering you?'

She shuddered again, though it seemed far less pleasurable this time. Tommy felt a pang of guilt - he really hated to upset her, especially after they'd been having so much fun.

But needs must, and he did promise...

'I doubt I ever will,' she said in a small, sad voice that made Tommy's heart ache.

Having been given all the delightfully sordid details of Glo's brief affair with Chapman - which weren't *that* bad, really - Tommy thought she was rather overreacting. After all, a little naughtiness never did *him* any harm. Well, not much harm, anyway, and the trade-off was generally worth it, in his opinion.

'Miss Hawkes,' he started.

'Call me Glo,' she said, brushing her lips against his. 'All my friends do.'

He smiled as he kissed her back, wondering if he could perhaps upgrade from merely being a friend someday. After all, they got along tremendously well, and if he couldn't have Clara the Glorious Gloria might make a very nice replacement indeed.

'Glo,' he said, a warm, happy feeling spreading through his chest as he said her name, his heart fluttering and an unfamiliar somersault turning in his stomach at the thought of a beautiful wife and home. Something he'd never felt within his grasp and yet here she was, lying in his arms...

'Everyone makes mistakes,' he continued, reining in his romantic daydreams for now. 'Some of us make them repeatedly.' He kissed her neck, eliciting another delighted, and quite delightful, little gasp. 'But I always say, as long as you haven't killed anyone, there's no real harm done, is there?'

Glo tensed and moved away.

No, he thought, his briefly buoyed heart plummeting down the elevator shaft of despair. *Not the Glorious Gloria, surely not...*

'Ah,' she said, as Tommy's hopes crashed and burned. 'Then I think I have a problem...'

***

'Have you really no idea who might have done it?' asked Clara, helping herself to another biscuit.

'One can't help but speculate,' replied Bunty after a pause. 'Particularly when murder was committed under one's own roof.'

'Quite,' said Clara, guiltily thinking about how much time they'd spent on Bunty's all too personal tragedy.

Not that we knew, she tried to console herself. *Bunty would have saved herself a lot of suspicion if she'd only told us the truth. And she could have spent more time with Bertie if only she'd had the courage to own up to it. Poor Bunty...*

'It seems I've been associating with a murderer,' continued Bunty, apparently oblivious to Clara's discomfort. 'Of course, at one time in my life this would have been rather thrilling, but considering the circumstances...'

'Indeed,' murmured Clara, for want of anything better to say.

'At least, I *hope* it was murder,' said Bunty, looking thoroughly depressed. 'As hideous as it is. The alternative - the alternative, my dear, is simply too much to bear.'

Clara's heart ached for her. 'Bunty,' she said, reaching out to her. 'Whatever you think Bertie did, he didn't. I'm absolutely, completely sure.'

Bunty took her hand with a grateful smile. 'Thank you, my dear,' she whispered. 'But I can't help but think - poor Bertie was devastated when he found out. He seemed quite all right later on, but I still wonder... What if he couldn't cope with discovering his whole life had been a lie?' She took a deep breath. 'What if he chose my Christmas Eve party to let me know why he -'

'I can,' interrupted Clara, squeezing Bunty's hand. 'With complete confidence, assure you that your son did not kill himself.'

Bunty whimpered, but gave her young guest a feeble smile of thanks.

'For instance,' added Clara. 'Why wouldn't he take the full fatal dose in one go?'

'You're quite right,' replied Bunty, her voice thick. 'But that leaves the question of who hated my son so much that they'd kill him.'

Clara bit her lip, watching the agonies on her new friend's face.

When put like that, it really did make the tragedy all the more, well, tragic, didn't it?

'Who,' continued Bunty. 'Who of my happy little group must I think of as killing my only child? Redmond?' She shook her head. 'A foolish man, I cannot deny that, but a murderer? All he did was owe Bertie a little money, surely that's not worth killing a man over?'

She sighed and looked across the magnificent view of the countryside with unseeing eyes.

'But of course,' she continued. 'Money is a motive as old as time. It could well be the motive for my nephew, as well - but how could I not change my will to include Bertie, once he knew the truth? It's only right. And as much as I adore Johnny, he's not very sensible when it comes to managing money. Not very sensible in a lot of ways, if I'm honest.'

'Yes, I know a few chaps like that,' said Clara with a smile.

'There's plenty of them out there, my dear,' said Bunty, with a soft chuckle that lightened Clara's spirits a little. 'It doesn't mean they're bad people, of course. The opposite in a lot of cases, but some of them are quite unpredictable. Quite unpredictable indeed.' She bit her lip thoughtfully. 'Perhaps I don't know my friends as well as I thought I did after all.'

'I'm sure you do,' cried Clara. 'Certainly your nephew - surely your nephew...'

Bunty shook her head. 'I thought I knew him perfectly well, but what about all that business with him and Gloria? Poor girl, she was heartbroken, as I'm sure you can imagine. They were so much in love, absolutely suited for each other one week, then the next week...'

'Yes,' said Clara. 'I heard about that. Do you know what happened?'

'Haven't the faintest idea,' said Bunty. 'He just claimed the radiant and saintly Sylvia had stolen his heart, and there was simply nothing he could do about it. How he could be desperately in love with one girl and suddenly switch his affections like that - but the heart wants what the heart wants, doesn't it? I'm living proof of that - and so was darling Bertie, until...'

She broke off to compose herself again before continuing.

'I wasn't terribly pleased with Jonathon, as I'm sure you can imagine,' said Bunty, a shade frostily. 'I'm terribly fond of Glo, and I'd have hoped he'd have treated her better, regardless of the circumstances. I thought I'd instilled a little respect into him, but… It was quite a shock for all of us, shall we say, and words were had.'

'I'm sure they were,' said Clara with a smile.

'But of course,' continued Bunty. 'Sylvia is a dear as well, and were circumstances different, I'd have been delighted Jonathon had found such a girl. She's a very nice girl indeed, and as far as we were all aware, she was utterly devoted to poor Bertie. He was quite upset by it all, as I'm sure you can imagine.'

'So I heard,' murmured Clara.

Bunty gave a tight little smile. 'Yes,' she said. 'I hoped he and Gloria might… but no. Apparently she wouldn't have him, if you can believe that. But nonetheless, the little quartet decided to put all that nastiness behind them and be firm friends again, and much credit to them.'

'Indeed it is,' exclaimed Clara, indignation rising. 'I'd not be half so forgiving if Lucas went off with one of my pals like that.'

'No,' said Bunty, amusement dancing in

her eyes. 'I don't doubt that for a second. I'd have been the same at your age. To be perfectly honest, I'm not sure what any of them were thinking - but who am I to judge, or even enquire? They're adults and perfectly capable of making their own decisions, no matter how foolish they are.'

'Hmm,' said Clara, who had been putting herself in Gloria's shoes and coming up with quite a nasty little plan. 'You don't think that perhaps Glo wasn't as all right with the whole thing as she made out?'

'She was perhaps the most wronged in the group,' said Bunty thoughtfully. 'Oh, I know poor Bertie was equally jilted, but that boy is made of rubber. Nothing bothered him for long, even as a child. He and Jonny would fall out terribly, but they'd always be friends again by nightfall. But,' added Bunty with a frown. 'I can't imagine why on earth she'd poison my poor Bertie. He never did anything to hurt her - quite the opposite, from what I hear.'

'Well, yes,' said Clara. 'But perhaps she didn't mean to hurt *Bertie*.'

Clara closed her eyes, imagining the scene playing out.

Yes, it was all so obvious, wasn't it?

'If I were Glo,' said Clara, looking at Bunty once more. 'I'd want revenge - but not on Bertie. On Johnny, or perhaps Sylvia. Yes, I'd definitely have a grudge against the woman who stole my man, and if I knew a way... But my point is, what if Glo tried to kill one of them, and somehow Bertie picked up the poisoned drink by mistake? Or whatever it was,' she corrected herself, remembering that there wasn't actually enough poison in the glass to kill a man.

That really was a puzzler, wasn't it?

But that could wait.

It would have to wait.

'Tommy,' cried Clara, her hand flying to her mouth. 'Oh no...'

Bunty raised her eyebrows. 'What about him?'

'He's –' Clara suddenly felt lightheaded. 'He's gone to have a little, uh, chat with Gloria about what happened. I don't think he's worked it out - at least, I hope he hasn't...'

Bunty drained her teacup and put it back in the saucer with a clatter. 'Come along, my girl,' she said, rising abruptly and holding her hand out to Clara. 'We'll take the Rolls. Let's stop that nice young man meeting a tragic end.'

***

Lucas didn't enjoy cycling at the best of times.

Uphill in the snow on a borrowed cycle that hadn't seen use for half a decade whilst wearing heavy woollen trousers certainly didn't make his list of best times.

'Hurry up,' called Henry over his shoulder, from about a quarter of a mile ahead. 'Clara could be dead by now.'

Lucas ignored the burning in his thighs and pushed forward. There was no-one else he'd suffer such torture for, not even Henry, but he'd do anything for her.

The hall within his sights, and Lucas redoubled his efforts.

Which meant when he hit the patch of ice, it just went all the worse for him.

He landed heavily in the ditch, getting a face full of prickly hedge at the same time. Pain shot through his knee and an ominous crunch told him something bad had happened to the bicycle.

Henry appeared just as Lucas was struggling out of the ditch.

'Are you all right?' he asked.

Lucas pulled a twig from his hair before ramming his hat back onto his head.

'Fine,' he said. 'Better than the bicycle, at any rate.' He dragged it out by its handlebars, a task made more difficult by the new and unnatural angle in the front wheel.

Henry swore. 'Right, I'll meet you up there,' he said, turning his own cycle around.

'You can't leave me here,' cried Lucas, grabbing his friend's arm.

'Clara is in danger,' snapped Henry, shaking himself free. 'I haven't time to wait for you to run along behind me.

'We can both fit on your bicycle,' argued Lucas. 'We used to do it all the time when we were children.'

'We're not children anymore,' replied Henry curtly. 'You'll slow me down.'

They were so busy arguing at the side of the road that they only noticed the Rolls Royce once it had passed them.

'Was that...?' started Lucas.

'Yes,' said Henry, turning his bicycle around again. 'And Clara's in the back seat. Well, what are you waiting for?' he asked after a moment. 'Are you getting on this bicycle or not?'

'I thought I'd slow you down?' said Lucas, swinging his leg over the frame and plonking his backside on the hard leather seat.

'We're going downhill,' said Henry, huffing slightly as he put his feet on the pedals and started getting them moving. 'The extra weight will make us go faster, so long as I can keep us steady.'

'Extra weight, indeed,' groused Lucas.

'Oh, shut up,' said Henry, pedalling furiously and picking up speed at an alarming rate. 'We haven't time to squabble over nonsense. And besides, you'd never let me hear the end of it if I left you there with that knackered cycle.'

They followed the Roller along the twisty lanes, or tyre tracks in the snow when the silver car was out of sight, and eventually ended up in front of a Victorian Gothic mansion a couple of miles outside of Castlebury Magna.

After a lot of complaining from both parties, Lucas and Henry pulled up in front of a large house a couple of miles out of Castlebury Magna.

'Hooton Hall?' said Lucas, as they zipped past the sign at the gate. 'Isn't that Gloria's house? Why on earth have they come here?'

A gunshot rang out from the house, the sharp crack muffled by the heavy snowfall but still all too plain to hear at the end of the quarter mile long drive.

Henry pedalled harder, puffing again as they started going uphill.

A second gunshot broke a window, which made the woman's scream sound all the louder.

'Clara,' cried Lucas, a million awful possibilities flashing through his head, all of them involving the love of his life meeting some dreadful end.

'That wasn't her,' gasped Henry. 'I don't know who it is, but it's not her, thank God.'

An angry woman's voice came tumbling out of the room, mingling with a cacophony of other voices.

'*That's* Clara,' said Lucas, relief washing in waves over him, removing all his previous fears. 'And I'm glad I'm not on the receiving end of that, she sounds furious.'

'Shut up, there's a good chap,' said Henry, panting heavily. 'Why must these things always be up a hill?'

After an age, they reached the stone steps outside the imposing red brick building. Henry skidded the bicycle to a gravel-spraying halt and leapt off, catching Lucas a painful blow to the inner thigh. Henry bounded up the steps, hammered on the door, before throwing his weight against it. Lucas hobbled up the stairs behind him and added his weight to the endeavour.

'That's Sylvia's isn't it?' he said, looking at the pale-yellow sports car as his shoulder thudded into the all too solid woodwork. 'Why's she here?'

'Who cares?' said Henry, landing against the door again. 'She can be here if she wants. We, however, need to get inside.'

'Window,' suggested Lucas. 'This door isn't going anywhere.'

Henry moved to the nearest sash window, tugged the truncheon from his waistband and used it to smash the panes. He ducked down, cupping his hands to boost Lucas into the room.

'Pull me up,' he said, when Lucas was safely inside. Once both men were in the living room, they sprinted through the hallway and up the stairs, dashing towards unknown horrors.

The voices were still loud, someone

sobbed uncontrollably, and someone groaned in pain.

Henry pressed his finger to his lips and held his truncheon aloft. Lucas looked around for something to arm himself with and settled on a brass candlestick.

Not ideal, but better than nothing.

'Stop, police!' yelled Henry as he burst through the unlocked door.

Lucas followed, and was astounded at the scene.

Clara was comforting a bare-shouldered Gloria, who sat on the bed wrapped in a white sheet and weeping like her heart would break.

Tommy, a bedsheet held around his otherwise naked waist, was cornered by a furious Sylvia - who had an old army gun pointed at his face.

She swung it round to face the interlopers and squeezed the trigger.

The bullet grazed Lucas' earlobe and embedded itself in the door frame with a sickening splintering of wood.

Tommy leapt forward and rugby tackled Sylvia to the floor, sending the gun flying onto the hearthrug and, unfortunately for Lucas' mental wellbeing, sending the sheet wrapped around the hero's waist flying as well, exposing his all too naked backside to the room.

The gun landed next to Bunty, who leant against the wall next to the mantelpiece clutching her shoulder. Blood oozed between her fingers, but with a whimper of pain she removed her hand from the wound and took the pistol in bloodied fingers. She pointed it at Sylvia, who was battling uselessly against the horrifically naked Tommy. He'd pinned her hands to the floor and sat across her stomach whilst she kicked and writhed, screaming bloody murder to no avail.

'My son,' whispered Bunty, the gun trembling in her outstretched hand. 'My only son, and you killed him.'

'It was an accident,' shrieked Sylvia, struggling fruitlessly to free herself. 'We never meant to kill him.'

'We?' said Henry, as Gloria let out an anguished howl. 'You mean, you were in it together?'

'He treated them both abominably,' said Clara crossly, as Glo sobbed on her shoulder. 'Do you really blame them?'

'Yes,' said the men and Bunty in unison.

'Yes,' said another voice only Lucas heard.

Oh good, Chapman's here, he thought bitterly, wondering how long he could ignore the ghost for. *As if I didn't have enough to deal with.*

'I don't,' said Clara, which Lucas found very worrying indeed.

Fortunately for him he planned on

treating her like the wonder of the natural world that she was for the rest of his life.

Which, if he played his cards right, might even be a long and healthy one.

'He deserved it,' said Sylvia, before sending a spray of saliva towards Tommy's face.

He grimaced, transferred both her hands to one of his, and wiped the spittle from his cheek.

'That,' he said, running his now damp finger down the side of her face. 'Wasn't very ladylike,'

'And that wasn't very gentlemanly,' she wailed, redoubling her efforts to free herself. 'How dare you -'

'Gentlemanly?' said Tommy, chuckling. 'Never claimed to be anything of the sort. I'm not a gentleman.' He smirked at Gloria, who turned a marvellously rosy shade. 'Although as I'm sure your friend will testify, I can be very gentle indeed when the occasion calls for it.'

'You're *not* a gentleman?' said Sylvia, pausing her struggle in surprise. 'Glo, who is this chap? What were you doing with him if he's not a gentleman?'

'Use your imagination,' murmured Tommy, casting a sly look towards Gloria and deepening her colour further.

'Given his state of attire,' said Bunty, before Gloria could make her own defence. 'You should be able to tell he's no gentleman.

However, he is from the papers, so I expect he'll have some interesting things to say about this little episode.'

The gun still pointed at Sylvia's head, although Lucas noticed with relief that Her Ladyship's finger was nowhere near the trigger.

'A reporter?' shrieked Sylvia, beginning her useless struggle for freedom again. 'Daddy will go off at the deep end if he reads about this.'

'That's the least of your worries,' said Henry gravely, moving forwards with his handcuffs at the ready. 'Miss Sylvia Pettigrew, I'm placing you under arrest for the murder of Mr Gilbert Chapman.'

'I knew it!' cried the ghost in question, though as Lucas was the only one who heard, he decided it was easier to ignore this than respond in any way. Especially as Chappers hadn't said anything of the sort.

'No,' screamed Sylvia, as Henry clamped the bracelets onto her wrists, still firmly held by the ungentlemanly reporter. 'It wasn't my fault. Gloria made the mistletoe solution too strong.'

'I didn't,' sobbed Gloria, who was making no attempt at leaving the room despite her crime being uncovered. 'You used too much. I told you, only a few drops in each piece of food or drink, and they'd get a bit sick, but nothing serious.'

'They?' said Clara, keeping hold of Glo's hand. 'You mean it wasn't just Chappers you were trying to make sick?'

Glo shook her head, sending tears flying. 'No,' she sobbed. 'We decided that the boys treated us so badly, we should teach them a little lesson. I know it's childish, but they were playing with our futures for, for the sake of a silly boy's game, essentially. Oh, we weren't bothered about the scandal, not now or in the future, but the fact they thought we'd just happily play at being the other one's girlfriend or wife whilst they sorted out Johnny's stupid mistakes was offensive.'

'So we wanted revenge,' said Sylvia, who had been hauled upright by this point.

Lucas noted with considerable displeasure that Tommy was now stood as well, still wearing little more than a smile, and with his hands on his hips quite proudly.

Some people were beyond the pale.

'But we didn't want to actually kill them,' insisted Gloria, turning to Clara. 'You do believe me, don't you?'

'Of course,' said Clara gently, patting Glo's hands sympathetically. 'Why don't you tell us what happened?'

'I don't know,' whispered Gloria, tears pouring down her cheeks again. 'I simply haven't a clue why Bertie died. He shouldn't have, not at all. We laced a few cigarettes with dried mistletoe and made sure they smoked them.'

'I knew they didn't taste right,' cried Chapman, quite unnoticed by most of the room, and ignored by the only one who could hear him. He turned to Lucas. 'Didn't I tell you everything tasted hinky?'

'A few drops of mistletoe here and there should have given him an upset stomach and a few flu-like symptoms, not -' Gloria broke off, pressing the back of her hand to her mouth as her face crumpled and tears leaked from the corners of her eyes. 'He was such a sweet fellow,' she said in a barely audible whisper. 'How could we do such a thing?'

'But mistletoe?' asked Tommy, unwisely drawing attention to himself. Clara snatched up a throw pillow and hurled it across the room, landing it squarely in his chest. 'Bit of an odd choice,' continued Tommy, picking the pillow up and swinging it back and forth thoughtfully. 'Seasonally appropriate, of course, but not what you'd first think of.'

'Never mind that,' said Clara, frowning at him. 'Cover yourself up, man.'

'Why?' he said, obligingly using the pillow to cover his modesty. 'I'm not ashamed of what God gave me, should he exist - and if you've never seen a naked man before, Clara Jenkins, young Lucas here has some explaining to do.'

Lucas wished he would spontaneously combust, as his flaming cheeks threatened to do.

Henry cleared his throat loudly and scowled at Tommy, who smirked in reply.

'That's no way to speak to a young lady,' he said disapprovingly. 'Especially when that young lady happens to be my sister.'

'Oops,' said Tommy, grin widening. 'I quite forgot. Sorry, old chap.'

'Mr Kilbourne makes a very valid point, despite his lack of trousers,' said Henry, switching back into his official role of police officer. 'Why mistletoe?'

'It amused us to think that something so festive would spoil their fun,' said Sylvia. 'And it should have just made them sick. I really haven't any idea how he managed to eat enough of it to die.'

'You know,' said Chapman, sounding rather pensive. 'I did eat most of those chocolates. And I drank Jono's cocktail. And finished off his vol-au-vents, now I come to think of it. And smoked a few of his cigarettes whilst he wasn't looking, as well as my own. And Gloria's of course. I suppose it's possible I got both of our doses of this mistletoe muck...'

Damn, thought Lucas, who'd planned on lurking in the corner fairly unnoticed. *That's what happened, isn't it? Oh well, here goes nothing...*

'Er,' said Lucas aloud, blushing again as six pairs of eyes turned towards him. 'What if Chapman accidentally ate Johnny's doctored food as well? Would that have been enough to finish him off?'

The accidental murderesses looked at each other in horror.

'That's what happened, isn't it?' moaned Sylvia, turning a sickly pale colour. 'Gilbert always was a pig when it came to food. I should have thought...'

'Oh Syl,' said Gloria, tears welling in her eyes again. 'What have we done?'

'I told you it was an accident,' said Chapman triumphantly. 'I knew no one could really want old Chappers dead.'

***

'Well, that was miserable,' said Clara glumly as they traipsed out of the police station.

Not that there was anything she could do, of course. The law was the law, as Henry said. It didn't make any difference whether you like the person or not. If they killed a man, they needed to be punished.

'It wasn't going to be jolly, was it?' said Lucas, putting an arm around her shoulder. She pretended not to see Tommy looking slightly hurt.

If only he could find a nice girl of his own - preferably one who hadn't just killed a man, albeit accidentally.

Clara would have liked Tommy pair off with Gloria, though little chance of that now.

'No, I suppose not,' she said aloud, putting those matters to the back of her mind for the time being. 'I just think it's rotten.'

'Well yes,' said Tommy. 'That's what happens when you murder someone.'

'But it's not fair,' wailed Clara, the injustice of it all making her miserable again. 'Those men were absolutely beastly to those girls, but it's Glo and Sylvia who will be punished for it.'

'I mean, Chapman's dead,' said Lucas, a little too glibly for Clara's liking. 'It's not like he got away scot-free, is it?'

'Jonny didn't even get sick,' argued Clara.

'True,' said Lucas, squeezing her tightly, which was comforting even when she was angry at the world. 'But I can't imagine Bunty letting him get away with treating the girls like that, can you?'

'No,' said Clara, leaning her head against his shoulder. 'She'll make sure he gets some repercussions, even if she has to dole them out herself.' She paused and bit her lip. 'I hope they don't hang Glo and Sylvia. It was an accident, after all.'

'Oh, I shouldn't think so,' said Tommy, shoving his hands into his pockets and looking at the clear night's sky. 'Two pretty young things like that? Get the right judge and lawyers - not to mention a few sympathetic newspaper reports, and I know there'll be at least one of those - and they'll barely see the inside of a cell. A couple of years at most. Do you normally have so many stars out here?'

'See,' said Lucas, hugging her again. 'They'll be fine. Probably. And I'm pretty sure the stars are the same everywhere, you just can't see them because of the streetlamps and filthy smog,' he added, turning to Tommy.

'Ah,' he said, nodding sagely. 'Another bonus of living in the sticks. I suppose you've got to have more than just pretty snow going for you country bumpkins.'

'Now look here,' started Lucas, at which point Clara decided to intervene.

'Perhaps they won't hang,' she said, adding a little tremor to her voice to tug on the boy's heartstrings and stop the squabble before it started. 'But they'll be locked up for a long time. Their families will probably disown them, they won't be able to find jobs, and probably not husbands either. All because a silly prank went wrong.'

'It might have been silly,' said Tommy, tearing his gaze away from the glittering sky. 'But it was dangerous. You can't go putting poison in a chap's drink, even if you don't want to kill him.'

'I suppose you're right,' sighed Clara. 'It just seems terribly unfair, that's all.'

'A lot of things are, when you think about it,' said Lucas.

'Best not to think about it, then,' advised Tommy.

'I don't think that's quite the idea,' said Lucas.

'Perhaps not,' replied Tommy with a shrug. 'But if you can't change something, what's the point in worrying about it?'

'Why can't you change it?' said Clara.

'Now see what you've started?' muttered Lucas over her head, which she chose to ignore, on account of not wanting to end up in a cell next to Glo and Sylvia.

'What's stopping *you* from changing it either?' asked Tommy defensively.

'Good question,' she said thoughtfully. 'I suppose that, as a weak and feeble woman -'

Lucas scoffed, earning him a prod to the ribs.

'*Or so our society seems to think,*' said Clara. 'Which was what I was going to say, if you hadn't been so rude.'

Tommy sniggered and Clara glared at him until he nearly stopped.

'If our society remembered how hardy women were during the War,' said Clara. 'And let us do all the things we're capable of, then perhaps I *could* change things. But unfortunately, we women must wait around on your fellows to do things, which really isn't going to get us very far very fast, is it?'

'Isn't it?' said Lucas.

'Oh Lucas, you really are an innocent, aren't you?' said Tommy, teasingly. 'The thing is, the people in power want to *stay* in power, and the best way to do that is stop anyone else from taking it.'

'Exactly,' said Clara. 'Just look at them banning women's professional football.'

'Oh yes,' said Lucas. 'Dad took me to a game when I was a kid. Jolly good fun, and those girls could knock a ball about just as well as any man.'

'Better, in some cases,' said Tommy, in a rare moment of agreement with Lucas. 'And they like to play dirty. Much more fun all round. Shame they can't play anymore, I'd much rather see a bunch of birds run around a muddy field in shorts than a bunch of blokes.'

'Exactly,' said Clara. 'I expect the men were losing money to the women, so, them having the power, they banned the women from playing.'

'Ah,' said Lucas. 'I think I see.'

'Yes,' said Clara. 'And until some *man* says they can start a league again, women won't be allowed to play again for *years*. It could be... five or ten more years before a man lets us girls play again.'

'Now that I'd like to see,' murmured Tommy, looking at Clara's legs, even though they were safely encased in practical, warm tweed trousers.

'So you see,' said Clara, ignoring him. 'It's not just that we need to stick up for *ourselves*, we need you chaps to stick up for us too.'

'And you'd stick up for us too, I suppose?' said Lucas, too sceptically for Clara's liking.

'Of course,' she said. 'If you deserved it and it wouldn't hurt anyone else. The more people who have a say about things, the more people can try and make life better for everyone.'

'I don't know,' said Tommy, taking his usual role of Devil's Advocate. 'Have you met people? Most of them aren't very bright.'

'Or nice,' added Lucas.

Clara knew she wanted them to get along better, but not at the cost of them ganging up on her.

'Look, things will be fairer if we all looked out for each other's interests instead of everyone only looking out for themselves,' she said crossly.

'Some of us haven't got any choice,' said Tommy mournfully. 'Some of us don't have anyone to look out for them.'

'You've got us,' said Clara, linking her free arm though his.

'I never signed up to that,' protested Lucas, though Clara suspected this was just for show.

'I signed us up for that,' she replied.

'What if I said no?'

'Then I'd overrule you,' she said cheekily, stretching up to kiss his cheek. 'Obviously.'

'Obviously,' came the sullen answer.

'Thanks,' said Tommy brightly, patting her hand. 'I appreciate it.'

'And you've got my mum,' added Clara.

'And my mum too, I suspect,' interjected Lucas. 'You've done a sterling job of charming half the village.'

'I have rather, haven't I?' said Tommy cheerfully. 'It's nice to be appreciated.'

Clara rolled her eyes. 'And people at work like you too,' she said, doubting the wisdom of petting his ego further but doing it anyway. 'You're not exactly friendless and alone in the world, Tommy.'

'I know,' he said, a spring entering his step. 'It's just nice to be reminded occasionally.'

'Look, never mind that now,' said Lucas, looking over his shoulder as the door to the police station banged shut again. 'We should see how Bunty is holding up.'

'Oh, poor Bunty,' said Clara, pivoting on the spot and turning the boys around with her. 'I forgot they took her there to get patched up.'

Bunty look tired as she leant against the wall next to the police station door. The sleeve of her coat hung empty, the abnormal bulge diagonally across her chest telling a tale involving a sling, bandages, and rather a lot of pain.

Nonetheless, she smiled warmly when the trio of young people approached, and held her good hand out to them. Tommy took it and kissed her gloved fingers reverently, which brought a happy glow to the older lady's face.

'How are you feeling?' asked Clara sympathetically, detaching herself from the boys and kissing the air next to Bunty's cheek.

'Broken,' said Bunty. 'Physically, mentally, spiritually fractured. But I'll survive.' She smiled, though it didn't quite reach her eyes. 'I always survive.'

'That's because you're a fighter,' said Clara, taking Bunty's hand.

'That I am,' agreed Bunty. 'It'd be nice to win occasionally, though.'

'I know the feeling,' said Tommy sympathetically. 'What will you do now?'

'I don't know,' sighed Bunty. 'Everyone I've ever known and loved has been taken away from me, and he who is left,' here her face clouded, 'behaved so abominably I doubt I'll ever want to welcome him to my house again. I thought I'd taught him better, that I'd ensured he'd treat the woman he loved with the respect she deserved but… apparently he needs a stronger lesson.'

'But you still have Dr Shank, don't you?' said Clara, trying to think of anything to cheer Bunty up.

'I do,' she replied, though she didn't seem overly pleased about it. 'He's a dear man, of course, but something like this rather makes one reassess one's life. I had a lot of time to think in that police station and –' she held her hands wide, '– I don't see him waiting for me, do you? It's a sad state of affairs, but I rather think I'm alone and friendless in the world right now.'

'Oh Bunty, that's not true,' cried Clara, and Tommy and Lucas gave their agreement. 'You've got us, for a start.'

Bunty smiled at them gratefully. 'You're very kind, my dears, but it's not as simple as that. A woman at my time of life can't fool herself into thinking she's younger than she is by merely keeping youthful company. She needs friends her own age to keep her grounded.'

'I think we can help there,' said Lucas, looking at Clara. 'What do you think?'

'Oh, excellent plan,' she said, grinning broadly when she caught his meaning. He really was terribly thoughtful at times, it was very sweet. 'Why don't you run home and get the kettle on, and we'll follow?'

***

'Well I never,' said Hettie Rathbone, holding her teacup out towards Bunty. 'Tea with a real Lady of the Manor. In my own front room, no less.'

'It's very good of you to welcome me into your home like this,' said Bunty with complete sincerity, adding another jot of brandy into Hettie's cup before topping her own up with the same.

'Bunty,' gasped Clara. 'Aren't you on pain medication?'

'Of course,' she replied, sipping her tea. 'Brandy makes it work better.'

'I don't think...' started Clara, but was cut off by the raucous laughter of her mother and Mrs Rathbone.

'If I'd have known you were such fun,' said Flora Jenkins, wiping tears from her eyes. 'I'd have worked a little harder to raise my station in life.'

'Likewise,' replied Bunty, toasting her new friends with brandy-laced tea. 'It's so nice to meet people who aren't concerned with competition or money or reputation, or any of those other tiresome things.'

'Well, I wouldn't say that,' said Mrs Jenkins, helping herself to a ginger biscuit. 'We've all got our concerns, but Hettie and I take folks as we find them. It doesn't matter to us that you've got a scandalous past -'

'Mother!' cried Clara, aghast.

'Well, it doesn't,' replied Flora, before turning back to Bunty. 'Or that you have more money and status than us. None of it really matters, does it?'

'Not at all,' said Bunty. 'In fact, I might sell the hall and go travelling. I have no one to leave it to anymore.'

An uncomfortable silence followed this statement, thankfully broken by the good-natured bickering of Tommy, and the plain standard bickering of Lucas, who arrived back from their errand at that moment.

'Look, all I'm saying is that you need to loosen up a little,' Tommy could be heard saying from the hallway. 'It doesn't do a body any good to be as tense as you are.'

'It's you making me tense, Kilbourne,' replied Lucas. 'Why are you still here, anyway? Don't you need to get back to work or something?'

'Terribly ill, old chap,' said Tommy cheerfully, coughing a couple of times. 'See? Can't go into the office with my bad chest.'

'I'll go check on the boys,' said Clara, hauling herself off the sofa. 'Before they kill each other.'

'Good idea,' said Mrs R cheerfully. 'More tea, Bunty?'

'Did you get everything?' said Clara, stepping into the hallway and between the grinning Tommy and fuming Lucas. The latter was easily remedied with a kiss, which also dampened Tommy's teasing spirits. Useful to know.

Tommy held the wicker basket out for

inspection. A quick peek under the cloth covering the goods showed they'd gone above and beyond the call of duty.

'You are good,' she said, beaming at them. 'Both of you. Come along, let's go show Bunty.'

They stepped back into the small, cosy, and increasingly brandy-scented living room, where the three women were giggling like schoolgirls.

'Oh, here they are,' said Mrs Rathbone, stifling her laughter. 'Where have you boys been?'

'Just picking up a few things,' said Lucas, dropping a kiss on top of her head. He sniffed the air. 'Have you been drinking?'

Clara stepped in before an argument could start. 'Bunty, we thought that since Christmas has been thoroughly awful for you, you deserved another try at it. Amongst people who really care about you.'

Bunty blushed happily and looked about the room at the smiling faces. 'Really?' she said.

'Yes, really,' said Tommy, sitting on the arm of her chair. 'And frankly I'm owed a few happy Christmases as well, so I was all for the scheme.'

She prodded him playfully. He caught hold of her hand and squeezed gently.

'It seems none of us are as happy as we might appear,' he murmured in her ear. Her smile barely wavered, but she looked at the young man with concern mixed with understanding and gratitude.

He nodded seriously in response, then turned to Lucas, who was helping Clara explain proceedings.

'We went and got the last cake from the bakers,' said Lucas. 'It's not a Christmas cake unfortunately, but Guthrie cut us a sprig of holly from his garden for the top and found us some rock cakes, which he sends with his compliments.'

'Roast ham from the butchers,' said Clara, displaying the contents of the basket to their guest. 'Tangerines from the greengrocers, and sugarplums from the newsagents. And,' she added, dipping her hand in to the bottom of the basket, 'We wanted to get you a gift. It's perhaps not as extravagant as you're used to, but it's the best we could do at short notice.'

She handed the parcel over with a slight frown. Wrapped in brown paper and string, it was clearly a book - but it wasn't quite the shape Clara expected it to be.

It was much larger, for a start, and really rather thick.

She glanced at Lucas as Bunty undid the twine.

He pulled a face that, without words, explained how despite Clara's crystal-clear instructions to buy a particular book she thought

Bunty would enjoy, he'd actually bought something entirely different.

That couldn't be good.

Bunty peeled back the paper and let out a laugh.

'A Girl's Own Annual,' she cried with delight. 'I haven't had one of these since I was a nipper, but it was never Christmas without one.' She beamed at Lucas, Tommy and Clara. 'You clever things, you.'

Lucas waited until Bunty looked away again and stuck his tongue out at Clara, who rolled her eyes in return. She doubted his success was as intentional as he'd clearly claim, but she'd deal with that later.

'Thank you, all of you,' said Bunty, a slight emotional wobble in her voice. 'For trying to cheer up an old lady who has made more mistakes in her life than she'd care to admit to.'

'Haven't we all,' said Mrs Jenkins. 'No one deserves to be judged their entire life for one or two mistakes.'

'Or three or four dozen,' muttered Tommy, giving Clara a cheeky wink, which she pretended not to see.

'Still, onwards and upwards,' said Bunty cheerfully. 'Can't sit around moping, just because one's entire life came tumbling down and one's only living relative is a stinker - and one's own son wasn't much better when it came down to it. Besides, it'll soon be the start of a whole new year. 1929 must be better than this year.'

'It can't be any worse,' said Lucas with feeling.

'Now, let's go and get the dinner table set up,' said Clara, taking Lucas by the hand.

'Why us?'

'We're hosting,' she said, dragging him out of the room. 'At least, we are now.'

He groaned. 'You have to stop signing me up for things, at least without warning me first,' he complained.

As they reached the hallway, she took his hand, placed it on her waist, and stretched up to press her lips against his.

'And,' she said, fitting words around kisses. 'I couldn't do this in front of everyone. Merry Christmas, Lucas.'

The End

Thank you so much for reading! I hope you loved *Festively Fatal* and had fun solving the puzzle.

As I'm sure you know, reviews are an important way for authors to spread the word about their books, so if you have a moment please use it to let other people know what you thought of this book on the Kindle store you bought it from, or on Goodreads. Or both (both would be awesome. Just saying...)

Thank you :)

Acknowledgements

Many thanks to my friends and family (you know who you are!) for all your love, support, and encouragement – not to mention, for humouring me when I talk about imaginary people like they're real, and for reading my dodgy first drafts. I love you all.

Special mention goes to my fantastic team of beta readers, who helped squash a load of bugs that otherwise would have made this book look rather shabby. So thank you, Alix Ward, Robin Castle, and D.P. Haka. You're all far better at spotting typos than I am!

Thanks also to the writing community on Instagram (who are too numerous to name individually) for being a constant source of friendship, amusement, and generosity with knowledge and resources. Without you, this writing lark wouldn't be nearly so much fun.

About The Author

Saffron Amatti lives behind a keyboard in Nottinghamshire, where she can normally be found drinking oversized mugs of tea, burning an unhealthy amount of incense, and thinking up inventive ways for fictional people to murder each other and (almost) get away with it.

This last point apparently concerns her family somewhat, who are all being exceptionally nice to her at the moment. This really isn't the way to discourage such behaviour, but let's not mention that…

Saffron spends far too long on Instagram and would love you to join her there, where she's **@saffron.amatti**.

Also by Saffron Amatti

Novellas

The Seeds of Love
(A Lucas Rathbone Mysteries Prequel)
The Ghost of a Story
(Lucas Rathbone Mysteries #1)
The Ghost of Jazz
(Lucas Rathbone Mysteries #2)
The Ghost of Revenge
(Lucas Rathbone Mysteries #3)
The Ghost of a Con
(Lucas Rathbone Mysteries #4)
The Ghost of Mercy
(Lucas Rathbone Mysteries #5)

Novels

The Ghost of Betrayal
(Lucas Rathbone Mysteries #6)
Festively Fatal
(A Lucas Rathbone Mysteries Christmas Special)

Collections

Lucas Rathbone Mysteries #1-5

All books* available on **Amazon**

*Except The Seeds of Love. Read on to find out how to claim your free copy.

The Seeds of Love

A Prequel to The Lucas Rathbone Mysteries

***

It's Clara's 21st birthday and there's a 'flu outbreak in Castlebury Magna - which has decimated her guest list and claimed the life of one of the villagers.

And now, Clara is ill.

Then Lucas receives some information from a ghostly "friend" which makes him realise something more sinister is going on.

Concerned for the health of the girl he's secretly been in love with for years (if only she wasn't his best friend's little sister…) Lucas investigates and learns the truth is more complicated than he could have imagined...

***

The Seeds of Love is a novella exclusively for my newsletter subscribers. If you'd like to get your free copy, please visit **saffron-amatti.co.uk/free-book** and let me know where to send it :)

Printed in Great Britain
by Amazon